Tor Books by Andre Norton

The Crystal Gryphon
Dare to Go A-Hunting
Flight in Yiktor
Forerunner
Forerunner: The Second Venture
Here Abide Monsters
Moon Called
Moon Mirror
The Prince Commands
Ralestone Luck
Stand and Deliver
Wheel of Stars
Wizards' Worlds
Wraiths of Time
Grandmasters' Choice (Editor)
The Jekyll Legacy
  (with Robert Bloch)
Gryphon's Eyrie (with A. C. Crispin)
Songsmith (with A. C. Crispin)
Caroline (with Enid Cushing)
Firehand (with P. M. Griffin)
Redline the Stars
  (with P. M. Griffin)
Sneeze on Sunday
  (with Grace Allen Hogarth)
House of Shadows
  (with Phyllis Miller)
Empire of the Eagle
  (with Susan Shwartz)
Imperial Lady
  (with Susan Shwartz)
To the King a Daughter
  (with Sasha Miller)

THE SOLAR QUEEN
(with Sherwood Smith)
  Derelict for Trade
  A Mind for Trade

THE TIME TRADERS
(with Sherwood Smith)
  Echoes in Time

THE WITCH WORLD
(Editor)
  Four from the Witch World
  Tales from the Witch World 1
  Tales from the Witch World 2
  Tales from the Witch World 3

WITCH WORLD:
THE TURNING
  I   Storms of Victory
         (with P. M. Griffin)
  II   Flight of Vengeance
         (with P. M. Griffin &
         Mary Schaub)
  III On Wings of Magic
         (with Patricia Mathews &
         Sasha Miller)

MAGIC IN ITHKAR
(Editor, with Robert Adams)
  Magic in Ithkar 1
  Magic in Ithkar 2
  Magic in Ithkar 3
  Magic in Ithkar 4

THE HALFBLOOD
CHRONICLES
(with Mercedes Lackey)
  The Elvenbane
  Elvenblood
  Elvenborn

CAROLUS REX
(with Rosemary Edghill)
  The Shadow of Albion

Tor Books by Sasha Miller

Ladylord
On Wings of Magic
  (with Andre Norton & Patricia
  Mathews)

THE OAK, YEW, ASH, AND
ROWAN CYCLE
  (with Andre Norton)
  To the King a Daughter
  Knight or Knave
  A Crown Disowned

A Crown Disowned

VOLUME THREE OF

THE CYCLE OF OAK, YEW, ASH, AND ROWAN

Andre Norton & Sasha Miller

TOR®
fantasy

A TOM DOHERTY ASSOCIATES BOOK
NEW YORK

A CROWN DISOWNED

Copyright © 2002 by Andre Norton, Ltd., & Sasha Miller

Maps by Miguel Roces

A Tor Book
Published by Tom Doherty Associates, LLC
175 Fifth Avenue
New York, NY 10010

www.tor.com

Tor® is a registered trademark of Tom Doherty Associates, LLC.

ISBN: 0-812-57760-4
Library of Congress Catalog Card Number: 200200605

First edition: October 2002
First mass market edition: November 2003

Printed in the United States of America

0 9 8 7 6 5 4 3 2 1

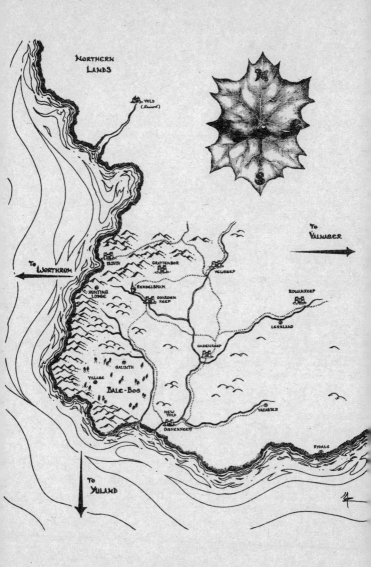

A Crown
Disowned

Prologue

In the Cave of the Weavers, the Youngest of the Three sat a little apart from her sisters, struggling with a section of the Web Everlasting that seemed to resist her every effort to create harmony and order. The pattern beneath her fingers had not, as yet, unfolded or revealed itself to her. She knew only that every time she tried to work on this particular design and make clear what could only be glimpsed in what resembled a heavy snowstorm, very few threads she added sank into and became a part of the Web. The rest crumbled into dust.

"It is not yet time, sister," the middle one of the Three had told her when that part of their eternal work kept drawing her attention. The Middle Sister was an imperturbable sort, neither as sentimental as the Youngest nor as crusty as the Eldest. "But soon. Yes, very soon."

The Youngest glanced back at the Web where work was complete, or nearly so. All had become white, as if heavy snow fell most of the time, and yet the pattern was not obscured elsewhere as it was here. "You told me that the spot just past, where the joining of the ill-omened brought with it a shift in the pattern, would also make clear this one."

The Youngest indicated a particular snarl of white, where the Web of Time accepted no thread of color except for the occasional strand of red—the color of blood—and where fell shapes moved obscurely on hidden business of their own. Once she had recoiled from them. Later, searching that portion of the Web already woven, she had discovered their dreadful origins. Now she could not let them be. "We know there is horror here, but the Web has yet to tell us what it is."

"Come and work with us. Leave the past alone and do not inquire into the future. Work for *today*. When tomorrow is ready, it will tell us. You know that."

"Aye, you have always known that," said the Eldest. She looked up from her work and frowned. "But then, you were always ready to rush ahead, to find out what lay in store for those whose lives weave in and out of the Web of Time."

"Is it really forbidden to care about them? They are so frail, so short-lived. . . ."

"Again I will tell you, and this time I hope you listen, for you have not heeded me before. The affairs of mortals, frail and fleeting as they are, must not concern us."

"The Web is fighting you because you are trying to change it," said the Middle Sister.

"Let it form as it will," the Eldest said sternly, "for we cannot take pity on the ones whose lives are interwoven in it. To do so would be to create a tangle that could never be put straight again. Please do not speak of it again."

The Youngest looked away, unable to bear either the opprobation of her sisters or the hideous segment of the Web of Time over which she toiled. She had to accept the truth of their words. She could not remove all traces of compassion for the mortals who bravely arose to face the horrors in the snow and the many who perished here, trampled under the feet of the monstrous beasts that appeared from out of the past where they had once been locked away. Gently, she touched one of the life-threads entangled in the struggle. It was strong and vigorous, but she knew it would snap ere long. "This is one of the great ones," she observed, trying to keep her tone neutral. "Or, he could have been great had he been wise. And had he not been cut down untimely."

Interested in spite of herself, the Middle Sister came and peered over her shoulder. "And you wonder if his death is in vain?" she said.

"There must be those who mourn. He leaves confusion in his passing."

"And so has it ever been with great ones of the mortal kind," said the Eldest, more than a little crossly. "Very well, if that portion of the Web draws you so irresistibly, then by all means, work on it."

"I agree," said the Middle Sister with a sigh. "But let it direct you, and do not meddle."

"Thank you, Sisters."

Grateful for the permission given, the Youngest straightened the kinks from her shoulders as she glanced back along what had been completed in Time's Web. There all was order, in recorded lives and death, and even Kingdoms' rise and passing. There the Three had worked generally in harmony until this latest coil had arisen. With some measure of tranquility restored among the Weavers, she knew that she was now strong enough to suppress the pity she could not help feeling. She would offer no mercy to those who were doomed, and above all not meddle with the design, for it would be folly—and worse, it would ruin the work.

At peace once more, the Youngest addressed herself to the area where the white tangle was deepest and most confused. Under her patient fingers, it began at last to take form and shape, though what it showed would have daunted any but one of the Three.

And as always, the living continued to believe that they were free to make decisions, to act as they believed fit, even as their threads passed through the fingers of the Weavers.

One

*R*ohan tightened his grip on the hilt of his sword, though he did not unsheathe the weapon. Much depended on this meeting between himself, as leader of the Sea-Rovers, and Tusser, leader of the Bog-people.

Instead of returning to Rendelsham as Granddam Zazar had instructed him, or even to the Oakenkeep, he had gone south to New Vold, wanting the companionship of blood kindred. There he had learned that the Bog-people had resumed their raids on farms and small holdings.

"Hunger drives them," Snolli said, "but that doesn't put bread on our table. These raids must cease."

"I agree, but not for the reasons you think."

"Then give me the benefit of your wisdom, young Rohan."

Rohan did his best to ignore the heavy irony of his grandfather's tone. "We should make a treaty with, them," he said.

"And I suppose that means we feed them as well," Snolli replied more than a little sourly.

"Yes. It is certain," he told Snolli, "that we will need the help of the Bog-men when the Great Foulness from the North comes, and a little grain now and then is a small price to pay. Hard times are upon us all."

Snolli shook his head. "I have almost come to believe that what we fled is no longer interested in us. If Kasai wasn't always stroking that drum of his—"

The Spirit Drummer looked up from where he sat near the fireplace. "Be glad I do it, Chieftain," he said. "You'd have been in more than one pretty pickle before now, if it wasn't for me."

"But what have your foretellings come to?" the aging leader of the Sea-Rovers demanded. "Nothing!"

"Not yet," Kasai muttered, as if to himself. "Not yet. But soon, yes, very soon. . . ."

"Rubbish," Snolli declared stubbornly. "Nothing but rubbish."

And so, despite his grandfather's dismissive words but with the warning of the Spirit Drummer still in his ears, Rohan had decided to seek out the Bog-men on his own and make alliance. Surely Snolli wouldn't do it of his own accord, Rohan thought, and much as he admired and respected Gaurin, leader of the Nordors, husband of his stepmother Ashen, he doubted that Gaurin would have thought of such a move, either.

Bog-men were of no consequence to the Nordors, nor to the people of Rendel, whence the Nordors had come for refuge, as had the Sea-Rovers. Yet, Rohan knew in his heart that all those who were able would be needed when the fighting came.

With that in mind, he had sought Granddam Zazar's help in setting up this meeting with Tusser. Though word had come that Tusser's father, Joal, had gone to the deep pools alive, Rohan knew that it was just a story told to frighten those who heard it. Even Zazar had been taken in until she realized the ruse to give Tusser's claim to be headman legitimacy. Joal had not died; he had merely been hidden away until Tusser was accepted by all in his village. Rohan's grandfather Snolli lived also, though both men had long ago retired from such pleasant pastimes as making war on each other.

Rohan hoped to make of that a common bond, through which he and Tusser might come to an agreement. Also, though this was something he was reluctant to admit even to himself, it was in the direction of the Bog that he had last heard tell of his sweetheart, Anamara, traveling. Still under the effects of a spell the wicked Sorceress had put on her in Rendelsham, she could well be expected to return to the place where, convinced she was a bird in human form, she imagined she belonged. Or—he hardly dared hope—where she might think to find him again, as he had found her on the verge of perishing in the cold and dangerous Bog.

At first, Zazar had been inclined to be cross with him for going against her instructions. But then, as Rohan explained how matters were with both the Bog-people and the Sea-Rovers whose crops the Bog-men raided more and more often, she relented.

"I can't guarantee that Tusser will meet with you," the Wysen-wyf said. "I can't guarantee, should he meet with you, that he'll go along with such a scheme. I can't even guarantee that you'll come out of a meeting with him with your skin in one piece."

"Yet I'll risk it," Rohan had said.

"And also, I will keep an eye out for that silly Lady Lackwit of yours, in case she decided to come back here instead of staying where she was warm and safe."

Rohan's ears had burned, but he made no retort. And so, now he waited in a place of Zazar's choosing, at a time Tusser selected, and the Wysen-wyf stood across the little clearing hard by what had once been a far outpost of Galinth, the ruined city, watching for Tusser's arrival. Behind her, inside a shelter hastily thrown together from stones and brush, a wisp of smoke arose in the cold, dank air.

"I think he's coming," Zazar said.

A boat emerged from a concealing fringe of vegetation that had scarcely a trace of leaf on it, for the chill that continued to grip Rendel discouraged any plant growth. Nevertheless, the twigs formed such an effective barrier that Rohan had not seen the little Bog-craft until it was almost in plain view.

True to his agreement, Tusser—if that were truly him—was alone. Rohan had no doubt, however, that he was heavily armed with additional weapons stowed in the bottom of the boat, and that he had companions stationed within close hailing distance. He glanced across the clearing at Granddam Zazar. She nodded and took a step forward.

"Hail, Headman," she said, though there was scarcely a trace of deference in her manner. "I have prepared a talk-fire so that you and my grandson can confer properly." She indicated the conical twig-walled hut prepared behind her, and ducked through the curtain covering the doorway ahead of the two men.

Neither seemed willing to let the other precede him. Rohan held out both of his hands, showing Tusser that he held no weapon. When Tusser did the same, Rohan ducked through the opening. When both were inside and seated by the small fire, Zazar dropped the makeshift curtain over the door again and snugged it against a random wind with a few well-placed stones.

"It's a poor meeting place at best, but the only one even partially acceptable to both parties," she explained. "Here. I have some broth to warm you."

"Waste of time," Tusser said gruffly. Though comparatively young to be a headman of a Bog-village, nonetheless he appeared to be capable as well as strong. He accepted a mug of the steaming broth with an air of indifference, but Rohan noted that he cradled it in his hands as if grateful for the warmth.

"Thank you," Rohan said, accepting his own mug. He sipped appreciatively. "Let's hope we can find, if not a warm friendship, then at least a way to lessen animosity between us."

"Too much silly talk," Tusser said with a scowl. "I have time only for good talk, not silly. Why you want meet with me? You just Outlander. Maybe I send to deep pools instead."

Rohan set his mug aside and put his hand on the hilt of his sword again. "I'd dispute you over that ambition," he said mildly.

Tusser continued to scowl at him. Then he looked away, indifferent again. "No matter," he said. "Maybe another time."

In the shadows, Zazar made a muffled sound that Rohan recognized as a stifled laugh. She scooted forward until she had a place at the talk-fire as well. "It's plain to me that I'm going to have to serve as go-between here." She turned to Rohan. "Oh, I'm sure you have come here in a reasonable manner, but despite the fact that I've explained the situation to this lout several times, he thinks he has to impress you and show you how strong he is before he's willing to make treaty." She turned her head and fixed Tusser with a gaze that Rohan was all too familiar with. He had been on the receiving end himself when he had been acting particularly thickheaded. For all of Tusser's many years on Rohan, the look seemed to be affecting him in very much the same way. "Very well, then, say it and have done. Get your stupid pride out of your system all at once, or you can believe that I'll kick out every last spark of the talk-fire and the Bog-people can starve or freeze or die when the invaders come. And you can be sure that your gabble of the deep pools won't mean a thing to them. Now. What's it to be?"

Tusser shifted a little, trying to avoid Zazar's implacable stare. "I ready to treat. If terms good enough."

Rohan spoke up. "There are terrible times coming. Our land—" He spread his arms, indicating not only where they sat, but the entirety of the Bog and beyond it. "—all of our land, both yours and mine, is in danger. I have heard rumors, tales, of people from the north who long to take it from us. And so my message here is a simple one. We must make pact with each other and stop our warring, or these invaders will find us easy picking indeed. If, however, we stand together—"

For the first time, Tusser appeared interested. "You think we like one village makes war on another?"

"Something like that."

"And then, when big birds come, or Outlanders come, even villages that not like each other all fight together?"

Rohan took a deep breath of relief. "That's right. We must all fight together, when the—the other Outlanders come."

"Tusser agree. But until then, we fight. Now I go."

"No," Rohan said hastily. "We must stop our fighting—I thought I had made that clear." He turned imploringly to Zazar.

"You did," she said, "and so did I. But trying to get something through Tusser's thick skull when he doesn't want to understand, is well nigh a hopeless chore."

"Look," he said to Tusser. "What's to be gained if we continue to make war on each other and when the other Outlanders come upon us, we are so weak we can't fight them, even all together?"

Tusser frowned again, trying to work out what Rohan had said. "Yes," he said at last, "but what we do between times?"

"There is much the Sea-Rovers can learn from you, and much that we can teach in return," Rohan said. "Later we will go to the rest of Rendel. I'm sure that—"

Whatever prediction he had been on the point of making was lost as a small, furry creature nudged its way under the door curtain. With a high-pitched squeal, it made a straight line for Zazar. Tusser recoiled, reaching for his shell dagger, but Rohan grasped his wrist before he could draw it.

"Weyse!" Zazar said, taking the little one on her lap. Weyse stood up, her clever little paws on Zazar's shoulders, and trilled and squeaked at her in what could only be interpreted as an urgent manner. Her fur-covered face held a definitely anxious expression; and her entire manner radiated fear.

"This is a friend," Rohan explained to Tusser. "I know her well. What is Weyse saying, Granddam Zazar? It must be important, to bring her here."

"Danger," the Wysen-wyf said. "Much danger. Men from the Outside, and they are burning as they go. That's hard to believe." She held Weyse out a little distance from her, so she could look into her eyes. "Are you certain?"

Again the little creature chittered and trilled in a highly agitated manner.

"Smoke," Tusser said, his already wide nostrils flaring as he sniffed the air. "Not from talk-fire, not from hearth." He leapt to his feet, drawing the dagger whose hilt he was still clutching. He appeared on the verge of attacking Rohan where he sat. "You! Betray Bog-people!"

"Don't be a fool, Tusser," Zazar said, getting to her feet in turn. "Do you really think Rohan, an honorable knight of Rendel, is going to set fire to everything while he's apt to get caught in it himself?"

"Granddam Zaz is right," Rohan said. He was last on his feet only because he paused to pick up Weyse and cradle her in the crook of his arm. "I know nothing of these men, except that whatever it is they think they are doing, setting fire to the Bog, they must be stopped!"

"Well, now's your chance," Zazar said to the two. "If ever you had any plans or hopes of working together, you couldn't find a better place to start."

"I'm for it," Rohan declared. He handed Weyse to her and loosened his sword in its scabbard. Then he turned to

Tusser. "I'll face them alone if I have to, but it would go better with an ally."

Tusser stared at him for a long moment. Then he nodded. "We two not alone. I have men also."

"I thought you had. Better call them."

With Tusser and a half dozen of his warriors close behind, Rohan approached the scene that Weyse had described to Granddam Zaz. He could immediately see that it was even worse than he had thought.

They were on the outskirts of the ruined city of Galinth, a place Rohan had visited before in the company of Zazar, Ashen, and Gaurin. Now four men clad in nondescript clothing seemed bent on burning what was left of it. No wonder Weyse, whose home this was, had come running to Zazar for aid.

Tusser gave a hand signal, and his followers crouched down, eyeing the scene as warily as did he and Rohan. "Make fire on water," Tusser observed. "I hear about this once before."

"When?"

"When still just spear man for Joal. Father," he explained as Rohan looked at him quizzically. "They go after Outlander girl once one of us, find more Outlanders. Take away. They burn water."

Rohan thought a moment. "Ashen," he said.

"Yes, Ashen." Then Tusser turned to stare at Rohan. "You know Ashen?"

"She married my father," Rohan said, wondering how to

explain the tangled circumstances to somebody as untutored as the Bog-man. "She is my foster-mother."

Tusser nodded. Apparently the notion of fostering was not an unfamiliar one to the Bog-people. "She Outlander demon spawn, Joal say. She lives?"

Rohan decided not to give any more details than necessary. "Yes."

"Not want kill Ashen. Once maybe, when she make me want woman. Forbidden. Not kill now, though. Maybe later. We attack now?" He indicated the four men out in the open.

"I think this is just a small part of them. Look there."

To the west, a plume of black, oily smoke was rising. Another began to boil upward just a little way east. The crackle of dry, cold trees and underbrush filled the air. Tusser made another signal and one of his warriors silently fell back and vanished the way they had come.

Going for aid, Rohan thought. It seemed a good idea under the circumstances.

The ones Rohan and Tusser were observing had finished opening bags and spreading what these bags contained over both land and water. One of the men held a container Rohan recognized as the kind used to carry live coals, and he was now trying to light a twig from it.

"Better be ready to pole for our lives once I get it going," one of them said. "This stuff goes quicker than the old powder. Burns on land as well as water, too. Don't get any on you."

A quick, disciplined rush, Rohan thought, and we'll have a good ground from which to fight the rest, when they come. Before the soldier could get his flame going, Tusser erupted from his place of concealment and, followed by his warriors, began a wild attack. His and his followers' war-cries filled the air.

"No, wait—" But there was no turning back. Rohan jumped to his feet and leapt forward.

The Outlanders' surprise was complete. They stopped dead in their tracks, staring at the ones who seemed to have dropped out of nowhere. With swift, brutal efficiency the Bog-warriors cut down the Outlanders. It was all over in an instant, and Rohan looked at Tusser with new respect.

"You are a worthy fighter," he said. "It will be good to have you as my ally, when the real fighting comes."

Tusser nodded his thanks, but didn't loosen his grip on his shell-tipped spear. "More Outlanders come, I think. This place cursed, but maybe good for fight. Can hide until more of my people get here."

"Then let's get to a high ground, where we can see what is happening."

The two men, with three of Tusser's warriors behind them, picked their way over the rubble. Behind them, Rohan heard splashing and chose not to look at how the Bog-men were disposing of the bodies of their enemies.

He would remember the way to the chamber where he and Granddam Zazar had held their meeting and she had discovered the true identity of the one known variously as the Magician and the Sorceress, depending on which guise she had decided to assume, but was reluctant to take them there. Instead, he chose a spot where a portion of the city wall was still more or less intact. From that sheltered vantage point, they had a good view of the surrounding territory.

They didn't have long to wait. Tusser pointed in the direction of the big plume of smoke rising in the west. "They come," he said.

"I hope your fellows make it in time, or it will be an even shorter fight than the last one," Rohan observed.

Tusser grinned. "They make it in time. I hear both."

By straining his ears, Rohan could just discern the quiet sounds of poles pushing the Bog boats in their direction. These were almost drowned out by the noise the Outlanders were making as they headed for the ruins. Also, the interlopers were talking, obviously not thinking there was anyone to hear them.

"What's got into Morrice and his men?" one of them was saying. "We should have been seeing their smoke a long time ago."

"Maybe they found a Bog-woman to take their minds off their jobs," another voice said, laughing.

"The Dowager won't be pleased to hear it," the first voice rejoined, and Rohan jumped a little despite himself.

Was she the one behind this attempt to burn the Bog? He could scarcely believe that even Ysa could be so blind as to commit such a foolhardy act, and yet the men had used her title. What could be her reason? He didn't have time to ask more questions before the men were upon them.

He took a tighter grip on his sword, the Rinbell weapon that was his father's legacy, and, with Tusser, swarmed over the low wall, taking the battle to the enemy.

In a moment the air was full of yells and the clash of weapon against weapon, punctuated with an occasional cry of pain.

The man Rohan found himself facing had pulled a sack out of his belt, and had it open.

"Throw the powder!" another man, obviously the leader, yelled above the din.

Obediently, the soldier flung the contents of the sack into the air, aiming it at Rohan. He leaped back, and most of it missed him. But some clung to his left sleeve. The smell was reminiscent of oil sometimes used in lamps when the candle supply grew low. He didn't have time to brush away the substance. He made short work of the man in front of him and then sought the one who had given the command.

As he fought, he could see out of the corner of his eye that these new attackers had managed, by accident or by design, to set light to the powder, and the flames were beginning to leap skyward. Intent on his opponent, it wasn't until he had dispatched his enemy that he realized his peril. The powder, which clung to his mail, was ablaze. He managed to strip off the metal shirt only to find that the sleeve beneath it was also on fire. Hastily, he began to beat out the flames, trying to keep himself from panicking. The conflagration did not yield at once to his attempts to extinguish it.

A woman's scream. "Rohan!"

Beyond all belief, Anamara was running toward him from the direction of the center of the city. She barreled straight into him, pushed him down and rolled him onto his side, smothering the flames. Despite her efforts, they blazed up anew and without hesitation she ripped off a piece of her skirt, wrapping it around his arm until the fire was well and truly extinguished. "Oh, Rohan! You're hurt!" she cried.

"Not so bad," he managed to say. He looked up at her,

fearful of what he would find, but her eyes were clear and her own.

"Where have you been?" she said. "Where have I been? I remember only a little. There was an old woman—"

"Later, my darling girl," Rohan said. "Later. Right now—" His arm was beginning to throb horribly. He was afraid to remove the covering and see the injury he had sustained. "The old woman—that is Granddam Zazar. Tusser—"

"Tusser here." The warrior knelt beside Rohan. Dimly he was aware that the Bog-warrior was tucking some items into the lupperskin shirt he wore. "You hurt."

"Yes."

Tusser started to shove Anamara aside roughly, and Rohan grasped his arm with his uninjured hand.

"Please. This lady—she is my lady. You understand? Please. Get us—both of us—to Zazar. I beg you."

Tusser frowned, staring first at Rohan and then at Anamara. Dirty and disheveled, her clothing in tatters, she looked anything but a suitable person for Rohan to claim as his own. She could have been mistaken for a wild creature of the Bog herself, had it not been for her skin, pale beneath the grime, and her light-colored hair. Rohan gritted his teeth, his world spinning around him. He wondered at the strength of the newly made alliance between him and the Bog-man leader, and whether it would stand this strain.

"Zazar have much power," Tusser said finally. "I take. Let her deal with you and Outlander woman."

"Thank you," Rohan said. Finally he was relieved enough to feel the pain of his burned arm, and he fainted dead away.

When Rohan returned to his senses, he found himself in the familiar surroundings of Zazar's hut. He was surprised by how little his injury pained him. He smelled one of Zazar's concoctions and, examining his arm, he discovered that the pungent earthy odor was coming from under the clean cloth that wrapped it. His burned clothing had been removed and he wore a shirt of lupper skin, similar to the ones that the Bog-men wore. The lacings holding the left sleeve to the rest of the garment had been removed, to make tending to his arm easier. He did not see his armor or his sword, but knew that Zazar would have seen to it that they had been cleaned and laid aside for safekeeping.

He didn't think he had stirred much, but Zazar noticed his waking anyway. "Oh, so you're back with us, are you?" she said. "It's a wonder you didn't get yourself burned to a crisp, and your precious Anamara with you."

He noticed that she had not referred to Anamara as "Lady Lackwit" and reasoned that Zazar had noticed her return to reality as well. Therefore, it was not a dream engendered by his need to have it so.

"Tusser and his fellows brought you in on a litter, with Anamara trailing behind," Zazar continued. "You must have impressed him quite a bit during the battle. They don't do that for their own, but make them walk if they're able."

Zazar's words triggered a memory. "They're burning the Bog," Rohan said urgently. "Ysa's men—"

"Don't worry. I'm taking care of things." Zazar indicated a pile of smoldering ashes on a flat stone.

A tiny flame sprang up and she turned away from Rohan instantly. Crooning a song that had no real words, she made curious gestures over the bit of fire and then spat on it. At that moment, Rohan became aware that the sound of light rain on the roof intensified. The little flame died at once.

"There," the Wysen-wyf said, satisfied. "That should be the last of it. We'd have had a warm time of it if they'd been able to complete their task. That powder was very hard to deal with. It won't come off, but burns itself out where it sticks."

"I know. I had gotten some on my sleeve. I take it that our defense was successful."

"Apparently, the Outlanders didn't expect any resistance. There are a few Bog-men in the deep pools, but more Outlanders. The rest ran away as fast as they could, with no stomach to carry on someone else's fight. Tusser is so proud of himself with what he's calling his trophies of war that he's called for a general talk-fire with the headmen of all the other villages. I think he fancies setting himself up as headman over all of them and he gives you most of the credit. You stand in very high regard with him. Joal is in a black fit of rage, but he's toothless by now." Zazar's face split in an unexpected smile. "Really toothless. Not a fang left in his mouth. A headman or one who once was a headman gets first shares of the harvesting. His wives have to chop his food very, very fine or he would go as hungry as the rest of us."

Rohan had to smile.

"I said it was someone else's fight. You muttered the Dowager Ysa's name while I was working on you, and then when you awoke you said it again," Zazar continued. Her light tone vanished, and her expression grew serious. "Do you think she was responsible for this?"

"I believe so. They wore no livery or uniforms, but I

heard the men talking before the fighting began. Can I sit up now?"

"You might as well. But don't try to stand, not yet. You'll be all right. It's deep blisters mainly, and those are the most painful. But you'll come out of it with only a few scars as souvenirs. The powder hadn't touched your skin, or you'd be dead by now. You were lucky."

"My lady saved me. Where is she?"

"Here," Anamara said. She entered his field of vision, balancing a bowl of noodles in broth and a chunk of bread on one of Zazar's platters. She, too, wore lupperskin garments— tunic and breeches. "Here. You need something to eat after your ordeal."

"Are you all right?" he said.

"I am now."

"But how?" He looked from Anamara to Zazar, who shrugged and began stirring the ashes to uncover any sign of a new flame. "You were—confused for so long."

"I don't know how it happened. I think Madame Zazar worked over me, in a place where I had my own bed, and a warm little creature called Weyse stayed close by."

"That was the Oakenkeep. I was there, too, at times."

"Weyse was with me when I was hiding in the Bog. In fact, she found me and took me to a room—"

"Yes, I know that place."

"She fed me and showed me where fresh water came from a pipe. She gave me mats to sleep on, and to keep me warm. She saved my life."

Rohan set his bowl aside. "She saved us all, for she was the one who alerted us to the danger. Where is she? Did she escape from the fire?"

"Of course she did," Zazar said, a little crossly. "She is no fool. Until you began to stir, she was curled up beside you."

"I'm glad she's safe," Rohan said, relieved. He dipped the bread into the last of the broth, to soak up every drop.

"Perhaps it was seeing you in danger that took the last of the veil from my sight," Anamara said. She was now sitting beside him, and as she spoke she clasped her hands and looked down at them with her old shy manner. Rohan's heart turned over.

"I want to marry you," he blurted suddenly and felt himself go warm in a way that no flames could have done. "I mean—"

"I know," she said. "Yes."

"Y-yes?"

"Of course she said 'yes,' you ninny," Granddam Zaz said, her voice sharp. "As soon as you're fit to travel, you'll go back to the Oakenkeep, tell Ashen and Gaurin what you've accomplished in the Bog, marry the girl, and then off you'll go to war, riding in a Sea-Rover ship. That is what I have seen, and I'm never wrong."

"Oh, no, not to war," Anamara said. Her eyes began to fill with tears.

"If Granddam Zaz is correct—and she always is," he added quickly, to forestall Zazar's retort, "we will have fighting, one way or another. The only question is, whether it is between the Dowager's men and the people of the Bog, or if she comes to her senses and we unite against the common foe from the north."

"We will have to rely on Gaurin's good sense in that regard," Zazar said. Her tone had softened a little. "And, I must suppose, yours as well."

"There has obviously been much happening at Rendelsham while I was at New Vold with Grandfather Snolli, or making alliance with Tusser, or searching for my lady."

"Well, the world wagged on without your guidance," Zazar said. But the corners of her mouth softened just a little, and Rohan knew she was not seriously annoyed with him. "I am of half a mind to go with you to the Oakenkeep. With Weyse. The Bog has become an inhospitable spot, with the Dowager being stupid enough to try to burn it down."

"I know Ashen will be glad for your company," Rohan said. "She has always worried about you. But will the Bog itself be safe, with you gone?"

"I'll set wards," Zazar said. "And, if what Tusser told me is true, the survivors of the battle will take a tale back to Ysa that will make her disinclined to repeat her folly. Also, I will ask Gaurin to post sentries at the river."

"Then we are safe," Rohan said. His eyelids drooped. He was growing very sleepy.

"For the time being."

Two

ess than a week later, Rohan, with Anamara and Zazar, set out on foot for the Oakenkeep, home to his step-mother Ashen and her husband, Count Gaurin of the Nordors. Rohan and Anamara had double-layered capes over their lupperskin clothing, and Zazar wore the warm fur-lined cloak that Gaurin had given her. Rohan, his injured arm in a sling, had his sword slung on his back, and Anamara and Zazar took turns with the burden of his armor. All three carried pouches filled with trail food.

Rohan was still a little unsteady—the effects of the shock of his injury, Zazar said—but determined that he would make it on his own. Now and then, when she was unencumbered, Anamara walked close beside him, and occasionally put his good arm over her shoulder in an effort to spare his carefully hoarded strength. He was grateful for the assistance, but unwilling to lean on her too heavily. Her own strength had not yet fully returned after the ordeal of madness inflicted on her.

"Do you have any idea where the Sorceress has gone?" he asked Zazar the first evening of their journey.

They had stopped close by a little copse of trees, where a small measure of shelter could be found. Zazar built a small fire and they warmed their dinner over it.

"My guess is that she fled north, to where her true allegiance lies. Her last bit of evil had to be the enchantment on Anamara to make her think she was a bird. Flavielle wouldn't have had time for more."

"Well, it was effective, if it was something she rushed through," Anamara said. "It's a wonder I didn't leap off a cliff, trying to fly."

"You undoubtedly would have, if there had been such in the Bog where she left you," Zazar said. "You were quite a mess when Weyse and I began to work on you. You didn't speak, but merely whistled."

As if she had been called, Weyse popped up from behind a bush and squeaked at them. Then she bounded ahead beyond the firelight and stopped, looking back over her shoulder.

"I think she wants us to hurry," Rohan said.

"With good reason," Zazar commented. "We're going as fast as we can," she told the furred one. "In fact, we're almost there. But we won't travel in the dark, so you might as well come back and be patient here with us."

Despite Rohan's best intentions, they were another night on the way. But the next morning, shielding his eyes with his good hand, he could just make out the pennons flying from the topmost towers of the Oakenkeep, and their design, in the distance. "Good," he said. "That spring green one means that Gaurin is in residence, and not off on some errand, or hunting, or away at Rendelsham. Come on. We can pick up our pace a little, now that we're all but inside the gate."

Nevertheless, it was more than an hour before Rohan and the two women reached the Oakenkeep. He was swaying on his feet, and gratefully accepted the assistance of the servants who came hurrying to show the guests up the stairs and into the Great Hall and notify the lord and lady that they had guests. The three newcomers went into the small area that had been screened off for warmth and privacy. Even more gratefully, Rohan sank into the big chair beside the hearth, not caring if it was the one Gaurin customarily occupied. Weyse hopped up onto his lap.

Footsteps on the stairs, echoing in the vastness of the Hall, and then Gaurin and Ashen were greeting them. "Oh, you've been hurt!" Ashen exclaimed. She knelt beside Rohan, and cautiously examined the bandage on his arm. Then she looked up at Zazar. "How did this happen? And what is *she* doing here?"

Anamara's cheeks, already reddened with the cold, turned scarlet. Rohan shook off Ashen's hands. He gently set Weyse down and, despite his fatigue, pushed himself to his feet.

"She is here because, by some miracle, she is alive and I found her in the Bog." He turned to Gaurin. "Greetings, sir. I apologize for our intrusion."

"It is no intrusion. Please get up, Ashen," he said. "We

must greet our guests properly. Will you be staying with us for long?"

"Yes," Ashen said, obviously struggling for civility. "Your apartment, as always, is ready for you, Zazar. And there are rooms available for all. I'll have Ayfare start warming them at once."

"I'm staying for a good, long visit," Zazar announced. "At least until I think it's time to go back to the Bog. The Dowager Ysa tried to burn it down."

"What!" Gaurin said, startled out of his usual composure.

"That's what I said. Now, send for some heated wine or ale or juice or whatever you drink these days and let us all sit down so we can rest—we have been traveling on foot to get here, you know. Then, if Ashen can stop fussing and fretting and generally acting like somebody had just put sour-thistle berries in her soup, we'll tell you what's been happening."

Gaurin laughed then, and kissed the Wysen-wyf's hand. "Madame Zazar, we can always count on you to get to the heart of matters. By all means, something hot to drink now. Later, Ayfare and her staff will have hot baths and warm woolen clothing for you. In the meantime, we will provide a respectful audience for your remarkable tale." He gestured to the stewards to begin carrying out his wishes. "Nalren, please ask the Dowager Rannore and Captain Lathrom to join us. I have a feeling this is something they need to hear as well."

Nalren, who had been elevated to the rank of chief steward at the Oakenkeep, nodded and left immediately, taking the other servants with him. In a few moments, the Dowager Rannore, who now seemed to be a permanent resident, and

Lathrom, captain of the soldiers under Gaurin's command, entered the little private place. Stewards had already set up the trestle table. With Gaurin and Ashen, they sat down and waited, silently, while the three newcomers related their almost incredible tales.

*

"Well," Gaurin said in mild astonishment when they had finished. "You have, indeed, had some interesting adventures. What happens next?"

"We must get to Rendelsham and confront the Dowager," Rohan said. "If these are the games she wants to play, we must make sure that she understands the cost. But before that, I want to marry my lady Anamara."

"No—" Ashen said automatically. Gaurin looked at her, quirking one eyebrow, and her cheeks turned hot, but she persisted. "No. Absolutely not. She is not the right one for you."

"She saved my life," Rohan said, "at the risk of her own. She loves me, and I love her. How else do you suppose that she could cling to life in the Bog, unless she was hoping that I would find her?"

Ashen had no answer, but nevertheless she folded her lips firmly. The girl had made an unfavorable impression on her the first time she'd seen her, and her recent—well, *enchantment* was not too strong a word, when she thought she was a bird and had acted just as empty-headed—had not enhanced her in Ashen's sight.

Rannore reached out and took one of her hands. "It is like a story out of a book," she said gently. "And it is very obvious that they do love each other. Surely you remember how it was, with you and Gaurin."

The young Dowager, widow to the late King, mother of the present King, looked not at either Gaurin or Ashen, but at Lathrom, and her smile was answered by an upturning of his lips.

Ashen glanced at Zazar for guidance, but the Wysen-wyf seemed entirely engrossed in taking a tangle out of Weyse's fur. Ashen knew her Protector was deliberately going to be of no help.

Anamara sat silent, head bowed and hands clasped, but she peered up at Rohan through her eyelashes with such a look of adoration that Ashen felt she was intruding on a private moment. She also knew there was no gracious way to maintain her opposition. Rohan was a man grown, without need to beg.

"Very well," she said reluctantly. "The girl has proved her mettle. If you want her, and she wants you, I will raise no further objection."

Rohan got to his feet and lifted Anamara up also. Then they went and knelt before Ashen. "Thank you," Rohan said. "Though we could have wed without consulting you, nevertheless, I am glad that you accept our union."

"If we could, I would like to be married here, at the Oakenkeep," Anamara said shyly. "It is where I first began to come back to myself after, after—"

"That is over and done with," Ashen said. "We will not look backward, but forward from this moment on. We will have the wedding here."

Gaurin got up in his turn and pulled Ashen to her feet

and into his embrace. "That's the wonderful, level-headed Ashen I know," he said. He kissed her hair. "But we have no priest."

"We can send for the good priest Esander," Ashen said. "Rohan needs a little time for further healing before embarking on marriage."

"Esander? The one who married you two?" Rohan said. "That would be perfect. Make it soon, though, for I am nearly well already thanks to Granddam Zaz's medicines."

"There'll be a messenger on the road within the hour," Gaurin said.

Rannore and Lathrom glanced at each other. When she nodded, Lathrom spoke. "For that matter, sir, he might as well perform two ceremonies," he said.

For the second time in as many hours, Gaurin was startled out of his composure. "Two?"

"Aye. My lady here and I—well, we've decided that we'd marry at our first opportunity. We thought we'd have to wait until you returned to the capital city. It would be much better if we could do it somewhere else besides Rendelsham." He turned to Rohan. "We'd make it a different day, of course, so you wouldn't have to spare your special time."

Rohan grinned and clasped the older man's hand with his good one. "We'll make it a double ceremony, and the sooner the better." Then his grin widened. "This whole thing will just about give old Ysa a seizure, won't it!"

Gaurin frowned. "Perhaps that isn't a good idea," he said.

"She always had a strong sense of propriety," Rannore said. Her eyes twinkled in turn. "I think she would be entirely outraged if I married someone she considered below my station." She turned toward her prospective husband and added softly, "No matter how I might feel about it."

Ashen was no less startled than Gaurin. She had thought that if Lathrom married anyone, it would have been her former maid, Ayfare, now the Oakenkeep's head housekeeper. Yes, Rannore had remarked on Lathrom's attractive manliness, but Ashen had never imagined—

From the entrance to the screened-off area, Nalren cleared his throat discreetly. "Your chambers are prepared," he said, "and tubs of steaming water await. I will see to your bath myself, Sir Rohan, so that you do not do any further damage to your wound."

"No, I will," Lathrom said. "I practically raised the boy, you know."

"Help me," Rohan said, looking pleadingly at Zazar.

"Fend for yourself," she retorted. "This is one of the things I've been looking forward to, soaking my old bones in hot water and getting really warm for once. The Bog is too chilly and damp for me these days and I've no mind to let my tub get cold, cosseting you."

Gaurin laughed out loud. "Resign yourself, Rohan," he said, his good nature entirely restored. "We'll have an early supper, some more talk about what's to be done about this new pastime of burning out the Bog the Dowager has embarked upon, and then tomorrow we'll start making wedding plans."

❧

The morning brought, however, yet another visitor to the Oakenkeep. Just as the residents were sitting down to their meal of rusks of fresh-baked bread and hot oaten porridge laced with honey, Nalren announced the newcomer.

"The gentleman said to tell you it was Hynnel, sir," the steward said. "He says he knows you well, and you him."

"And so I do!" Gaurin exclaimed. "Bring him in, bring him in. No, even better, I'll go and greet him."

Suiting action to words, he arose from the table and, pausing only to fling a light mantle over his shoulders, rushed out of the vast Hall. There, in the frozen slush and snow at the foot of the stairs leading to the inner ward, a rather road-weary man and a troop of soldiers were dismounting. Ashen followed hastily, hugging her own mantle around her for warmth. More snow was falling. Nalren trailed behind.

The two Nordorn men embraced heartily and, after the manner of their custom, kissed each other on the lips. "Oh, it has been so long," Hynnel said. "We've both grown up now. And just look at you—master of this great stronghold and a beautiful lady to wife!" He turned to Ashen, bowed, and took her hand to kiss it, but she forestalled him.

"Gaurin has spoken to me often of you, his childhood companion, and his close kinsman," she said. She kissed him on the lips, as well. "Welcome, Prince Hynnel, son of Cyornas NordornKing, and a thousand times welcome."

"Yes, close kinsmen indeed. Gaurin is my cousin, for his mother was my father's sister. If I hadn't been born, he would have been the heir—" A cloud went over Hynnel's face. "The truth is, I am no longer Prince, but King, of sorts. My country lies in ruins, the palace destroyed. And my father is no more."

"That is sad news, though not unexpected," Gaurin said. "All knew that the first attack would come against King Cyornas, and that he would not refuse the challenge."

"He made a good end, I am told," Hynnel said. "He had already sent me away for safekeeping, over my objections."

"Well, you're here now, and that's what matters." Gaurin turned to Nalren. "All of Prince—King Hynnel's men are to be found lodgings in the barracks, and their horses stabled. Let all be fed well, for they are our honored guests. And you will come with me, Hynnel, for there are others inside that I want you to meet. Your voice will be valuable as we decide on what course to take when we go to Rendelsham, our capital city."

"I passed close by," Hynnel said, "but I did not tarry except long enough to learn where you were living."

"We are in a precarious situation," Gaurin said. "But that talk will come later. Now, come and eat. Our fare is plain, but hearty."

"That suits me well," the exiled King said. Then all three climbed the stairs to return to the Oakenkeep Hall and the warmth of the screened-off little room near the fireplace.

As they went, Ashen examined the newcomer, her royal kinsman by marriage, hoping that she was not being too obvious in her scrutiny. There was a definite resemblance between them, with the honey-colored hair and skin, and it was plain that they were blood cousins. And yet there were differences. Hynnel had been born to be a king, but in a council, it would be to Gaurin that men would turn when they sought a strong voice.

All the ones at the table, even the Dowager Rannore, would have risen from their seats when King Hynnel was introduced to them, but he stopped them with an uplifted hand. "My title is meaningless," he said. "When I am in Rendel—or, let the Great Ones allow—while I am fighting against our common enemies, I am just Hynnel, a man of the Nordors, and one of you. Time enough later, when we prevail—if we prevail—for the ceremonies and trappings of kingship."

"As I recall, your father wasn't much for the trappings of kingship either," Gaurin said. He seated Hynnel on his right. Rohan hastily shifted farther down on the bench to accommodate the newcomer. Hynnel looked askance at his rustic appearance, but made no comment.

"We escaped from a fire in the Bog that destroyed our belongings. Granddam Zaz gave us these." Rohan indicated the lupperskin clothing, which now looked out of place in their surroundings.

"Ah. I see. Very practical. Well, as for my father, Cyornas NordornKing thought ceremony was a waste of time and never bothered except when the occasion demanded," Hynnel said. He accepted a big bowl of steaming porridge and poured hot milk over it. "This looks delicious. We've been up well before dawn, wanting to get on the road and not risk freezing as we slept."

"But the Nordorn regions are known for their cold climes," Ashen said as she picked up her spoon. Her porridge had chilled, and had a thin skin over the top. Nalren unobtrusively replaced her bowl and Gaurin's with fresh ones that steamed even in the warm air of the little screened-off dining room. "Surely you had little to fear, in more hospitable lands."

"Yes," Hynnel said around a mouthful of bread lavishly spread with honey and butter. "But this kind of cold is different. It is, well, malignant if I am explaining it right. It seeks you out, even here in the south." He glanced around at his surroundings. "It disguises itself so it can find you in an ordinary winter—which this is not. In fact, it is springtime, isn't it?"

"Almost summer."

"Yes. Well, in an ordinary winter, this little room that you have created would be almost too warm, with the great fireplace and all. Now it barely keeps the edge off the chill."

"I can imagine how much worse it is in the north, closer to the source," Ashen said.

"I don't have to imagine," Zazar said around a mouthful of porridge. "I've been there. In a way."

"Indeed?" Hynnel said politely.

"When I introduced you, there was no time to tell you the specifics and pedigree of the ones who honor me by sharing my table," Gaurin said. "In addition to Madame Zazar being my wife's foster mother she is also the famed Wysenwyf of the Bog."

Hynnel inclined his head in respect. "Even in the faraway land of the Nordors, your fame has reached us. It is good to know that we have such a powerful ally as you. I take it you have visited us by magical means?"

"I needed to see what—and who—we were up against. And so, while Rohan here was unconscious at my hut after being burned, I took myself there. Your people are very brave."

"Thank you, Madame Zazar. We only did what we could, and were defeated at the end."

"Pushed back, maybe. But defeated? Never." Gaurin's voice was strong, but Ashen heard the words that were not spoken—defeated, *not yet*.

"There really is to be war, then," she said in a faint voice.

"Yes, my lady, I fear there will be," Hynnel said. "But how it will affect you and your charges—" He looked from her around the table quizzically, his gaze lingering on Rohan.

"My hurt is only a minor one and even now heals," he said. "Lady Anamara and I are to be married as soon as the priest from Rendelsham arrives. And this lady and this gentleman as well." He indicated Rannore and Lathrom.

Hynnel got to his feet and bowed to both couples. "Then congratulations are in order. I have come at a happy time, and a sad one as well. My greatest regret is that I will be tearing bridegrooms from their ladies' arms too quickly, but need waits not upon desire."

"The boons of your knowledge and skill are very welcome," Lathrom said.

"I will do what I can to advise you to the best of my ability." Then Hynnel seated himself again and picked up his spoon. "Once you are fully healed, are you prepared for a journey to the NordornLand, young Rohan? You will need special clothing, and your weapons must undergo some modification—"

"What sort of modification?" Rohan asked. He did not go armed inside the Oakenkeep, of course, and so did not have his sword at his belt. Nevertheless his hand went to his side as if he missed its weight.

"Well, for one thing if you use your sword the hilt must be wrapped to keep it from freezing to your hand. Most of the time you will wear mittens, of course, and you can't fight with a sword that way. Instead, you'll be using a mace, or perhaps an axe. Sometimes a spear."

"I am passable with mace and spear. I have never mastered the axe," Rohan said, "though my grandfather's people favor that weapon above all."

"All the better for them, and it will be wise of you to practice. I have seen it cold enough that the metal of a sword blade will not hold an edge, for it is so brittle that it will snap. A mace is far superior. And your clothing—do you think you can march off with nothing but a light shirt under your mail, and a jupon and cloak over it? Oh, take your mail if you like, but be prepared for it to be as useless as your sword—all weight, and no protection when it shatters at a light blow. Leave your warhorse, if you have one, behind and let your lady worry and fret over him. There is no place for chargers in a land of deep snow. If there are no sleds and trained dogs to pull them, you will walk. And how do you plan to keep your feet from freezing in thin boots? No, my young friend, there is a knack to surviving the bitter cold we will be facing and that is where my knowledge is even better than Gaurin's, for he has lived long in the south."

"We will learn well from you, sir," Lathrom said. He turned to Anamara. "Fear not," he told her. "I will look after young Rohan." He smiled at Rannore. "Which means that I will be much too busy to think of putting myself in any great danger."

The Young Dowager returned the smile, but her eyes were shadowed. "I fear there will be danger in every direction."

"And so there is, and will be, until the Great Foulness is vanquished. And the Ice Dragons with their riders." Hynnel accepted another bowl of porridge. "I was hungry!"

Ashen pushed her bowl away. "And now I have no appetite," she said. "Please, let there be no more talk of war, or of weapons, or of preparations for war. At least not just now."

"Of course, my dear," Gaurin said. He kissed her fingers.

❧

If she had not had to begin making new cold-weather garments for Rohan, Ashen would have been able to set aside the specter of war in all the preparations for Anamara's and Rannore's weddings. Rohan's lack of clothing was easy to remedy; he was enough of a size with Gaurin to wear his garments. Anamara presented a much greater problem. She had only the lupperskin tunic and breeches she stood up in, and was so thin that both Rannore's and Ashen's dresses hung on her. Nor could she be expected to wear servants' garb. Therefore, some time had to be spared to put together a dress for her. Though Ashen had sent for the clothing she had prepared for the girl what seemed to be years ago, it might not have time enough to arrive before the wedding. She had thought to move Anamara to safety in Rydale. There dwelt her daughter and Gaurin's, young Hegrin.

Her heart cramped. Oh how she missed Hegrin! She wondered what the child was doing. Did she ever miss the young woman who chirped and whistled at her, instead of speaking? Was she studying her lessons? Was she happy? Did she miss her parents as well?

But she had little time to dwell on this loss. She had to be content with the reports the tutors sent back from time to time. Already a messenger was on the road toward the seacoast, away to the south and east, and he would bring back fresh reports as well as Anamara's clothing. And so, because it was unlikely to arrive in time, Ashen's thoughts came full circle as to how the girl could be decently clothed until she was wed.

The shoemaker had already come, and gone. Charged with the responsibility of seeing to it that everyone in the Oakenkeep was shod, men and horses alike, he made a fresh cast of everyone's feet and began making slippers for Anamara. He also began making boots for Rohan, in much consultation with Hynnel, who had notions contrary to what fashion dictated.

Wulvine skin was the choice both for the footwear, with the fur side in, and for the hoods of outer garments. Wulvine fur did not gather frost, even from a person's breath, and the people at the Oakenkeep had begun to seek out wulvines when they went out hunting, and to prize the pelts highly. Ashen had used one for lining the hood of her cloak. Also lined with a different fur, it fastened down the front, with slits through which she could put her hands, if need be.

The chore of actually constructing Rohan's warm outer garment—his a kind of tunic with a hood that could be tied close to his face—went to the armor-maker. To Ashen it was given to make the many layers of undertunics, and Anamara insisted on taking over most of that chore. Though these layers made a man look nearly twice as bulky as he actually was, Gaurin assured her that they kept him safe from the elements. His own Nordorn garments had once been packed away in trunks with sprigs of rosemary in the folds, and he had not thought to need them in the milder climes of Rendel. Of late, however, he had unpacked and begun wearing them when he ventured out into the snowy grasp the unseasonable weather had on the land. Ashen could not get used to the sight of his lithe, athletic figure so muffled that he was nearly shapeless, but he fared well in the frigid outdoors.

Those who went with him copied this mode of dress as best they could, and Lathrom declared it to be superior to a single heavy layer of wool, or even a fur-lined cloak. Ashen could not duplicate the delicate materials; they looked frail as silk or the reed-fluff she used to gather in the Bog but much more durable, and so she had to make do with the finest grade of wool, as whisper light as a lady's finest gown.

Every woman in the keep, even Zazar and Head Housekeeper Ayfare, was similarly occupied. Rannore and Anamara stitched steadily, both somewhat faster and more efficient than Ashen, who was constantly distracted by other matters. Rannore's maid, Dayna, and Nacynth, the maid newly assigned to Anamara, worked with them. Gaurin could not be positive that other Nordors, refugees from the beleaguered lands, could convince their neighbors to borrow from many years' experience in how to survive and even thrive in extremely cold weather.

"We can't outfit the entire nation," Ashen complained one evening. She and Gaurin were in their apartment, and she was putting the final stitching on another of the winter tunics before bedtime. She sucked one finger that she had pricked with a needle so badly it bled.

"No, but we can set the example for others to follow," he told her. He laid aside the hunting spears he was sharpening; it was upon his shoulders and Hynnel's that the brunt of providing meat for the castle fell, for Rohan was still not fit. "And if your efforts keep one man on his feet when the fighting comes, it will be worth it."

"Yes, I suppose it will," she said. She drew the candle a little closer, and returned to her task.

The entire castle buzzed with activity. Even the occasional shaking as another fire-mountain erupted or coughed molten rock into the air went almost unnoticed. The Dragons and their riders, Hynnel said, were speaking to the land. Even in the Bog, new fire-mountains appeared—enough that Zazar remarked that despite the danger the Bog-people must be warmed by them.

When at last the good priest, Esander, arrived at the Oakenkeep, an astonishingly big part of the preparations had been accomplished. Both Anamara and Rannore had splendid new woolen gowns, Anamara's white trimmed in blue, the color of the House of Ash of which she was a distant member, and Rannore's of the Rowan color, deep gold trimmed in black as befitted her status as a widow. The messenger from Rydale was due back at any time, and the piles of winter garments for the men of the Oakenkeep were stacked high in the sewing rooms and the solar, waiting to be packed into trunks and boxes. The chapel had been prepared for the wedding ceremonies, decorated as best as they could provide, given that no flowers bloomed in the snow. But the place had been made gay with ribbons and many candles. It would do.

Even Rohan had laid aside his sling, for he claimed that Granddam Zaz's ointments had cured his hurt all except for a little soreness.

Esander, somewhat to his dismay, had been given a room to himself despite his protestations that he was accustomed to sleeping in a dormitory, and bunking down in the soldiers' quarters would do nicely for him. Ashen let him have time to unpack the small bundle of belongings he had brought with him—a sharp contrast to the many trunks and boxes of goods the lowest noble could not seem to do without—and was waiting at the foot of the stairs when he came down for dinner. There was one good thing about having all these people living in the keep, she reflected as she waited; it was much warmer now with so many bodies inside it. The spare figure of the priest came into view from the shadows on the stairway.

"Greetings, Esander," Ashen said.

"And greetings in return, Lady," said Esander. "You look well."

"As well as might be, when I am consumed with worry. You have heard that there may be war."

"There will surely be war. There is talk of little else in the city."

"And here also. The men speak in low voices and think I do not know, but how can I ignore the fact that all of the women have been kept busy night and day, preparing winter clothing for them to go and fight in?" Tears trembled on Ashen's lashes, and impatiently she brushed them aside. "Perhaps it is not as bad as everyone supposes."

"Perhaps. Now, might I meet the happy couples before I say the words over them?"

"Of course. They will be with us at the supper table."

Even Esander could not repress a rising of his eyebrows when he learned that the Dowager Rannore was one of the ladies he would be marrying the next day. "Do you then have the approval of Our Gracious Dowager Queen Ysa?" he inquired.

"It is not required, good Esander," Rannore replied. "I have the permission and blessing of King Peres, who wishes nothing for me but my heart's own desire. And I have found it."

Ashen could not remember seeing her more happy as she exchanged glances with Lathrom, their hands clasped.

Esander bowed. "Then I could wish for nothing better," he said.

Privately, Ashen thought that having the Dowager's permission might have been more prudent. She hoped she could stay out of any trouble between Rannore and Ysa that was sure to arise from this union.

"And this young man and woman?" Esander continued.

"This is my foster son, Rohan, and his lady, Anamara, who is shortly to become as my daughter to me." To her surprise, Ashen discovered that the polite words she uttered were the truth. She had initially thought that acceptance would be the best she could muster where Anamara was concerned. However, in all the hard work in close company that she and Rannore and Anamara had engaged in, with the accompanying talk of women who were friends and women who were edging cautiously toward friendship, she had come to like the girl.

Gaurin moved to her side, in the loving support she had come to rely on from him. "Both couples are following where their hearts lead," he said. He put his arm around Ashen's waist. "Do for them what you did for us, and I assure you that nothing but good will come of it."

Esander bowed his head in acknowledgement. If he had any objections, he did not voice them.

The next morning, on a clear day when the sun sparkled on the snow and even gave off a frail warmth, King Hynnel, at Gaurin's request, knighted Lathrom. Gaurin would have done it himself, but he thought to do Lathrom as much honor as possible. Then the two couples were wed. There was much rejoicing in the Oakenkeep, for the inhabitants had little enough diversion these days. Hynnel danced with both brides, as did Gaurin, and the feasting went on for a day and a night.

*

"Now I must go to Rendelsham," Gaurin told Ashen in the privacy of their apartment, "and Rohan must go with me. Also Hynnel and our new Sir Lathrom. We have tarried as long as I dare. There is much we must do there, and not the least of our tasks will be to confront the Dowager Ysa with this incident in the Bog. Rohan knows this and Hynnel, who has his own errands, knows it as well. We cannot have a country divided because of the whims of one woman who fancies that she rules because she wears four mysterious Rings."

If Ashen had not realized long ago that he was correct, she might have protested. None of the men had made any pretense that they would not be going to the capital city as soon as they could. If it weren't an affront to his bravery and valor, she would have wept. Instead, she kept back her tears and merely nodded. "I am going with you," she said. "And Rannore and Anamara with us with their maids as well. I think Ayfare will be glad to have her duties lightened with only me to take care of, and Dayna and Nacynth both look forward to being in Rendelsham to see the great nobles in person. Zazar will return to the Bog."

Gaurin quirked one eyebrow, but if he was surprised, he did not show it. "It will make for slower going, with the women in the company."

"Don't blame that on us," she said. "You'll have dozens

of carts just to carry your gear lumbering along in your wake. Put the other women with the carts and let them go at their own pace with a guard to look after them and I will keep up with you. Just you try to outride me."

He began to smile. "What a fierce woman I have married! In your careful planning, have you considered how the Oak-enkeep is to be defended in our absence?"

"I have. Nalren will be in charge of the residence, and Lathrom will leave a few men for the actual defense of the castle, if such is required. He can pick his own leader."

"Well, my dear. You seem to have it all worked out." Then he chuckled aloud. "And you should know that your plans are very much like mine, if you had allowed me to voice them."

"Gaurin."

"Do you think that I could bear to leave you behind, when we have so little time left together? Of course I will have you with me in Rendelsham. But when I ride away, you must return here. Promise me."

Carefully, she avoided saying the words. "You will have to set a guard to prevent me from running after you."

He opened her jewel chest and picked up an iridescent stone circlet. "Remember the bracelet that was my father's, an heirloom of my house. Remember also what I said to you the first time we met, and I recognized it for what it was even as I recognized you as the one woman whom I will love until I die and beyond. If ever you are in need of anything, put this on, think of me, and I will know, and whatever separates us, even if it is half the world or I face an entire army alone, I will overcome it to be at your side."

She took the bracelet and slipped it onto her arm. Now

she allowed the tears to reach her eyelashes. "How I love you. Yes, until I die and beyond. You are more to me than anything or anyone else in this world, even our daughter. How can I bear being apart from you."

"Ashen."

They embraced, clinging to each other so tightly it seemed that both were trying not to let anything, any danger, any peril to them or to others, to come between them.

Three

The Countess Marcala of Cragden studied the amulet she had finally managed to filch from the little chest where her husband kept certain items hidden from view. It depicted a winged creature, furred rather than feathered, and it had tiny, glittering yellow gems for eyes. The whole artifact possessed a gray sheen, as though well rubbed. It did not look new.

I can't imagine why the Dowager insisted so much on my stealing this insignificant thing, she thought. Nevertheless, she had been successful, had followed orders. At her earliest opportunity, she would give it to Ysa. So thinking, she slipped it into a small pouch and tucked that into her bodice.

There were more important matters to think about than a silly amulet. Count Gaurin of the Nordors, and a man rumored to be not only the new NordornKing but also Gaurin's cousin, were supposed to arrive in Rendelsham this day. With them would be the Young Dowager, King Peres's mother, and a large retinue of fighting men.

And Ashen of Ash, of course.

Marcala had never entirely gotten over her suspicion and jealousy of Ashen. The King's by-blow daughter had married Gaurin and Marcala herself was safely the wedded wife of Harous, Count and Lord High Marshal of Rendel. However, Marcala had not forgotten that Harous had once had designs on Ashen, possibly even thinking that, through her, he might obtain a grasp on Rendel's throne. She knew her husband; nothing in the reach of his ambition could surprise her.

No, I am being silly, she reminded herself firmly. I am his wife, and the Dowager Queen Ysa is my friend. Together we are more than a match for Harous's ambitions—yes, and Ashen's, too, if she has any hidden away under that innocent guise of hers.

Marcala turned her attention toward selecting the gown she would wear when she journeyed from Cragden Castle to Rendelsham. It was so difficult, these days, to find something fashionable and at the same time warm.

Two hours later, clad in peach velvet, she was being ushered into the Dowager Queen Ysa's chamber dedicated to the reception of honored guests. Ysa's face and figure, Marcala noted, were still as youthful in appearance as they had been shortly after the Four Rings had come into her possession. But the Rings themselves adorned hands that were showing signs of age. Perhaps, Marcala thought, there was a limit to how much the Dowager could enhance her looks. Or perhaps Ysa hadn't noticed that her hands were bony and heavy with veins, the backs showing many brownish blotches. The Dowager was even now holding these hands out to Marcala in greeting.

"Welcome, Countess!" Ysa exclaimed. "What a bright spot of color you always bring to the Court."

Marcala took the outstretched hands in her own, and dipped a graceful curtsey. "Thank you, Your Highness," she said. "I wish you sun and warmth for the day, and for many days to come."

"Come and sit with me for a few minutes, before I have to attend the Council. Many of my nobles, including your husband, are gathering and wish to speak with me."

"And also with the King?" Marcala murmured. She held an innocent expression as best she could when Ysa glanced at her sharply.

"Later. First they wish to consult with me. They have not told me why."

"They recognize both your wisdom and your experience," Marcala answered. "In the meantime, I have brought you a present. Just a tiny thing, a trinket, but something you once said that you wanted."

Ysa raised one elegant eyebrow. "Then I am sure that I will like it, whatever you have for me." She gestured and her ladies retired, drawing the door to but not latching it. It was well known among them that the Dowager and the Countess liked private conversation.

"What is it?" Ysa asked, when she was certain they were alone.

"Just this." Marcala opened her peach-colored velvet handbag which matched her gown, and drew out a smaller, dark gray velvet pouch, tied with a silver cord. The Dowager opened it at once.

"Ah," Ysa breathed, looking at the little amulet. "You found it at last."

"Yes, but I fear that my lord Harous shall miss it sooner or later."

"Has he used it, to your knowledge?"

"No, but that is only as far as *I* am aware."

"Where was it?"

"There is a secret room at Cragden, off the apartment we share. Harous thought I didn't know about it. However, in my, um, former life, it was my business to discover such things."

Ysa nodded. Marcala's former occupation, earning her the title of "Queen of Spies," had brought her to the Dowager's attention in the beginning. "I am glad to know that you have lost none of your skill," Ysa said.

"It was necessary to wait until I was certain I would not be discovered. The hiding place is small, and contains only a chest and a large book, on which the chest rested. In it I found a metal headband like a diadem, set with an oval adornment, and a few other odds and ends including the amulet you now hold. The chest had been locked, and I relocked it. I did not disturb the book."

Ysa laughed, the sound like the cackle of a vorsehen. "Maybe he will think his little trinket flew away on its own," she suggested with a sly smile.

"Perhaps. I hope so." Marcala closed her velvet handbag. "I would rather that the disappearance never be discovered."

"What of the headband?"

"I recognized it for what it was, though the oval gem was something new to me. It is a Diadem of Concealment. It makes a fog appear around the wearer, so that he may go unrecognized when he wishes."

There was a discreet tap at the door. Ysa tucked the amulet back into the little pouch and put it in her bodice. "That will be Lady Grisella, to tell me that the nobles are assembled. Thank you, Marcala. I will hide this gift in a safe place."

She arose from her chair; Marcala stood as well, dipping another curtsey as the Dowager swept from the chamber in a cloud of spicy perfume. Thus alone, Marcala decided to wander the corridors, hoping to discover what the great matter was that had brought the nobles of Rendel to meet with their one-time queen, rather than petition an audience with King Peres, Ysa's grandson.

The Dowager Ysa knew full well what the meeting with her nobles was about. Those men who had survived the ill-fated foray into the Bog had brought her the news of its failure, and so it was only a matter of time before questions would be asked by the ranking nobles. Her only surprise was in the numbers assembled before her. The last time so many of the high ones of the land had gathered had been at the Grand Tourney, when all the nobles, young and old alike, had met in friendly combat or—in a certain few instances Ysa preferred not to think about—not so friendly combat.

Looking at the men around the Council table, Ysa was sure she could see glimmers of the same kind of animosity so much in evidence on that occasion. Only this time she knew it must be directed at her. Well, she could deflect it. She had done this, and more, in the past.

"How now, gentlemen?" she said, seating herself at the head of the table. "What brings you here with such gloomy countenances? Come now, be frank with me, I pray you."

Rohan of the Sea-Rovers was the first to speak. "Men who said they were under your orders tried to burn the Bog." He held up his left arm and stripped back the sleeve to show the newly healed burns. "It was only by accident that I myself survived."

Rohan, again, Ysa thought with distaste. At the tourney, it had been Rohan's doing that the man Flavian, the Magician, had been revealed as Flavielle, the Sorceress. It was well known that this person had been in Ysa's employ, and she had avoided censure only by claiming innocence of all knowledge of what Flavielle had been doing. Well, as then, so now.

"I assure you I know nothing of such orders. Anyway, what profit would one gain by setting fire to the Bog?" Ysa said. "And how could such be accomplished? The place is mainly water, from the accounts I've heard, frozen these days, and what isn't water is worthless."

"They had a powder that burned when spread upon the water and anything else it touched," Rohan said. "As to what good it would do to burn it, only the one who ordered it done would know."

Clearing a house of rats with fire did good also, Ysa thought, even though the rats might not agree. "To repeat, I know nothing of any such orders," she said. "I assume that all is now well in that strange place?"

Royance, Head of the Council, seated at the far end of the table opposite to her, nodded. "The fire has been put out," he said. "Since then, there has been no word. I can only hope that there are no unfortunate aftereffects."

Harous, sitting at Ysa's right hand, spoke up. "Then it is of no importance now who, pretending to speak for our gracious lady, made use of fire. No great harm has been done, excepting the injury suffered by our young friend." He nodded to Rohan, and Rohan returned the gesture. "And I see that even that was a minor matter, and he has healed rapidly."

Gaurin then spoke. "Allow me to introduce my cousin, once Prince Hynnel, son of Cyornas NordornKing, and now King in exile himself. He has brought news from the north."

Hynnel arose and looked around the table. Almost all of the Council were in attendance, and a few others of the nobility as well. Ysa followed his glance. Gattor of Bilth examined his fingernails, his expression typically sleepy and bored. Wittern of Rowan, attended by his deputy Edgard, sat near his old friend Royance. Valk of Mimon was also present, as well as Jakar of Vacaster. Who was missing? Liffen of Lerkland. But another was in attendance—Ysa searched her memory. It was the one-time sergeant who had been implicated in the late King Florian's abduction of Ashen, for what purpose Ysa preferred not to consider. What was his name? Oh, yes—Lathrom. But why was he here? He was in no wise of the nobility. However, she had heard he had been elevated to the position of Gaurin's second in command. Perhaps he was here as Edgard attended Wittern. But Gaurin was in no wise in need of a deputy. It was disturbing.

"Madame," Hynnel said, "let me speak plainly. As one sovereign whose throne is no more to another royal lady whose successor occupies the chair she once held, I say to you that regardless of who issued what orders and what was the outcome, we must all cease pleasant Court pastimes of pitting one faction against another."

Ysa started to speak, and Hynnel silenced her with a gesture. "I make no accusations," he said. "It is simply a part of the kind of life you lead, and that I once was a part of. I know these games well. Fortunately, there has been, as Lord Marshal Harous so astutely notes, no great or lasting damage done and few lives lost. The fire is out, and what was in the past is gone. Let us now address ourselves to much greater matters."

"I think you speak of the question of Rendel's safety, King Hynnel," Ysa said. She held up her hands so that all could see what adorned her thumbs and forefingers. She told the litany of the Four Great Rings. "Oak, Yew, Ash, and Rowan. These symbolize the Four Great Families of our country. It is through these Rings that I have found the strength to do what had to be done, to protect Rendel. Tirelessly have I worked, as all here can attest to you."

"There is no need," Hynnel replied. "It is known far and wide how great have been your efforts. Pray you, however, please do not name me king. I am but a Nordor, perhaps better born than some, but not king until my homeland is free of what has destroyed it and what now advances to do the same to Rendel."

"The Ice Dragons, and their riders," she said, and was rewarded by looks of surprise on many faces. This was surely a piece of knowledge that would make all forget any lingering questions concerning that unfortunate incident in the Bog.

"Madame?" One man—Lord Royance—was not surprised, but wary, and Ysa suddenly recognized that she had blundered. Only then did she remember that she had never mentioned the glimpse of Ice Dragons she had had through the eyes of her flying servant, Visp, nor that she had held this secret for some time.

Hynnel sat down again and looked from her to Royance, puzzled and wary in his turn.

"I did not think you commanded so much Power," Lord Royance said. His silver brows were drawn together. "How did you know of these creatures, of which I have only recently been informed?"

"I saw them in a dream last night," she added hastily, "as well as the armies that follow them. I was frightened, and then I awoke. However, I thought it only a grim fancy born of overwork, but with King—I mean, Lord Hynnel's presence, he obviously being a refugee from just what I saw when my mind was roaming, set free in sleep, I now must think it a true sending."

"Indeed," Royance said.

Ysa breathed a little easier. He seemed accepting of her explanation and not inclined to pursue the matter. She reminded herself again not to underestimate Royance, or, for that matter, any of them. Complacency was her worst enemy, especially in these perilous times. "What then do you make of all this?" she asked Royance. "As Head of the Council, surely you must have a recommendation."

"I do. The time I have dreaded for so long is upon us. We must now form our armies, to march out and fight these Ice Dragons and their riders and any other followers, before they can do the same here as they have done elsewhere."

Ysa had long since come to that conclusion, since the day she had seen the destruction of the NordornKing's palace by the great pale beasts that breathed crystals of ice. If she closed her eyes the sight of the aged NordornKing being cut down with his nobles and stretched cold upon the ground came back much too vividly for any comfort. She rubbed the Rings on her hands, but they brought her little comfort.

Why else, she thought, did these great nobles think she had ordered the destruction of the Bog, if not to clear out that which would only be a detriment to the effort of war. Who could say what those mud-rooted less-than-humans might do, once all the army had marched north and they would be free to roam through the countryside at will, no longer confined behind the Barrier River?

But that question was, as Hynnel had noted, of the past.

"Let it be as my good lords advise," she said graciously. "Assemble your forces, and if you require an order from my grandson, King Peres, you have only to ask."

"Much of what this assembly is responsible for is already accomplished, Your Highness," Gaurin said. "We will have four great armies—"

"Four? Your Nordors, yes, and the army of Rendel, but then who?"

Rohan cleared his throat to speak again. Always Rohan, Ysa thought with some bitterness. Why was he forever meddling?

"The Sea-Rovers, Your Highness. You made pact with my grandfather, Snolli. Under the terms of that pact I dare speak for him, though he is not yet aware that his ships will be called into service."

"That makes three. And where does the fourth come from?"

"It comes from the Bog," Rohan said.

Ysa gasped and others in the room scowled at the idea. "The Bog? No—" she said.

"Why not? Do they have less to lose from the terrors advancing on our land than we do? Can they not fight, at need? There are plenty to tell the tale of how fiercely they defend themselves. Therefore, as the Sea-Rovers made pact with Rendel, so did we make pact with the Bog-people. They may not be as we are, Your Highness, but when the fighting begins, we need every man we can muster."

Around the table, most of the ones who had frowned had now begun to nod reluctant agreement. Wittern of Rowan, King Peres's maternal grandfather and arguably the ranking noble in the room, spoke up. "The youngster makes sense," he said. "If only I were twenty years younger—even ten years younger—I would be marching out myself."

"And I," Royance said. "I could get together winter gear in a matter of days. In fact, I'm of a good mind—"

Gaurin bowed to the elderly noble. "Sir, your valor does you nothing but credit. But as it has always been, sometimes the situation requires that a few of the wisest must stay behind to manage the affairs of state while those others of us go and fight. Thus it is now. Let your young relative, Nikolos, lead your muster of troops in your stead. If you will take my advice, engage Steuart as well. He is an excellent young man, one who has conducted himself well both during his training for knighthood and after."

"Please, Royance," Ysa said. "Your presence is needed here in Rendelsham. Stay here with King Peres, and with me."

Royance bowed. "As you command, Your Highness." But he looked wistful.

"If the important business of our meeting is past, then I ask leave to return to New Vold," Rohan said. "My grandfather Snolli will want to know that his ships must be made ready for war. Also, he will be interested to know about the men of the Bog, and other matters we have discussed today."

"Of course you have our leave to depart," Ysa said. "I have one question, though. I see that Lathrom is with us. He is, if I remember correctly, your captain of soldiers, is he not, Gaurin?"

Before Gaurin could reply, Lathrom got to his feet and answered. "That I am, Your Highness, and more besides. I dare to sit with the nobles of Rendel because King Hynnel has made me knight. Also, I have married one of the noblest of them. My wife is the former Young Dowager, Rannore of the House of Rowan."

Every nerve in Ysa's body quivered so violently she thought it would make an audible sound. With an enormous effort she maintained her composure. Despite her shock and dismay, she noted that the rest of the men in the Council chamber greeted this news with no surprise. Therefore, they knew it beforehand.

She forced herself to smile. "How very—very clever of you," she said. "And what good use you made of her visit at the Oakenkeep. Is your—your wife here in Rendelsham with you?"

"Of course, Madame. We are but newly wed. I would not leave her behind, nor would she be left."

"Then send her to me within an hour, so that I may give her my congratulations in person."

With that, she arose from her chair and, ignoring the bows of the men who leapt to their feet in courtesy, she swept from the room. She was glad that her pace held steady; she did not sway or stumble.

"How could you!" Ysa raged at the young woman standing before her. "How dared you couple with a—a commoner!"

"I love him," Rannore said.

"Love," Ysa returned with a sneer. "Dishonor! You spit on the memory of my son, your late husband, the King—"

"He dishonored his own memory," Rannore said. Her cheeks were beginning to redden and she clasped her hands low in front of her. Suddenly Ysa realized, with that gesture, that Rannore was pregnant.

"Not as much as you have," the Dowager said in a dangerously quiet voice. "I see that you must have anticipated your wedding by at least several months, just as you did before with my son. And who else have you bedded with, like the whore you are?"

At this, Rannore's reticence vanished. "You dare accuse me of whoring? With Florian, I was forced. With Lathrom, I went to him out of love, not for gain." Her expression hardened and her anger paled as well, making her cold and dangerous. "No, Madame, be careful whom you label. It is not I, but you! Oh, your sins are not ones of the flesh, to be sure, but you have whored after power ever since King Boroth placed the consort's crown upon your brow."

"You could be executed for the treason you are spitting now, and your paramour with you."

"And who will order it so? Not you, for Rendel's king, my son, favors my union, even though the tiny world of the Court might think it unworthy of my station. He cares more for my happiness than you or anyone else, except Lathrom."

"If what you wanted was a bed companion, I could have found you one of a suitable rank."

"So that you could still dictate to me where I should go, whom I should see, how I should behave? How often I should be intimate with this 'bed companion' you so graciously deigned to give me?" Rannore laughed harshly, a strange sound to come from one usually so meek and retiring. "No, Madame. Thank you, but I have arranged my life to suit myself."

"There is no place for you and your disgrace at Rendelsham Castle. How do you propose to live with your commoner?"

"I will return to the Oakenkeep, where you do not rule," Rannore replied proudly. "And he is a commoner no more. Even now, my son, King Peres—" She put a faint but unmistakable emphasis on the words. "—is granting him lands and properties as befitting one of his loyal knights."

Ysa recognized defeat when she saw it, but she wasn't about to let Rannore know. "Then go your ways, and be certain that if you ever come back here, it will be without my prior knowledge and certainly without my welcome."

"When was it never thus?" Rannore said, a little sourly. "You barely tolerated me while Florian was alive, except that I had borne the heir to the throne of Rendel."

"And perhaps not even that—" Ysa tried to bite back the words, but they had already been spoken.

"Do not make idle threats," Rannore said. "I know your tricks. You might try to cast my son's heritage in doubt, but too many witnessed the marriage with his father. Peres is the rightful king."

Ysa's manner changed abruptly. Rannore had, unwittingly perhaps, presented her with a weapon she might use at some future time. It had been common knowledge that this conniving slut had been pregnant when she married the young King of Rendel, aye, and farther along than she was now. Fainting and sick she had been as well, not blooming with health. Who was to say that Florian had truly been responsible for Peres's getting? With Rannore's subsequent behavior in taking up with someone who had once been a common soldier, who was to say how many more she had accepted into her bed, perhaps even while Florian lived? Some women did that—accepted lovers only while pregnant, so as not to have any untoward consequences from their dalliance.

Lore had it that physical characteristics for males skipped a generation. Florian had been on the reedy side, but Boroth had been a spectacular specimen of a man in his prime. Peres did not take after the man presumed to be his grandfather.

Therefore, all Ysa would have to do would be to cast doubts on his paternity. Given public doubts, she could set him aside at will, should a better prospect come along.

She smiled at Rannore. "Perhaps I was too hasty," she said, making her voice gentle. "I should be congratulating you instead on your newfound happiness. It was just that I was surprised. I thought you might have consulted me before you acted, not that I would have stood in your way. Come, let us be friends again."

She held out one hand to Rannore, who took it warily and kissed it. "Thank you, Your Highness. I will be glad if there is no enmity between us."

"Of course not." The Dowager took back her hand and indicated that Rannore should sit. Then she sent for hot fruit juice and cakes. "I would give you wine, but that is not the best thing in your condition. Come, speak with me for a while. Have you begun thinking of a name for your new son, or daughter? Do you need any baby clothes? I have Peres's clothing packed away in silver paper and all we need to do is air it out and it will be perfectly usable."

Slowly, Rannore began to relax. Ysa continued to chatter about matters concerning new babies, providing no outward sign that her mind was churning with the possibilities of this new scheme of hers.

Who, she wondered, would she select if she decided that Peres should be declared the illegitimate child of some commoner such as the one Rannore had chosen this time, and be deposed?

Four

*R*ohan made the journey to New Vold in record time, reluctantly leaving Anamara behind in Rendelsham. But he was obligated to confer with Snolli.

"Married, eh?" his grandfather said sourly. "The prospect of some good fighting pleases me but I don't want to have my backshield a puling bridegroom lonesome for his lady when he gets to lead my marines."

"Well, you won't have to put up with anything even near that," Rohan retorted. He had long ago learned that when Snolli barked, he should bark back. "Anamara understands what we're up against, as much as I do. Incidentally, I actually made that alliance with the Bog-people you've only talked about so long, and there'll be a small army of them with the Rendelians."

"Now that I would pay good coin to see!" Snolli exclaimed, his good humor restored. "How did it happen?"

Rohan proceeded to tell him of his adventures in the Bog, and how he had found Anamara when he had feared her dead, and how brave she was. When he had finished, Snolli looked at him with a trace of respect.

"Maybe you'll do after all. And you say you want to have the marines bundled up and they're to leave off their ordinary gear?"

"I've tried both ways and have found this to be the more effective. We probably won't be quite as cold out on the water as the men who will be fighting on land, but we'll be among them sooner or later. I see no reason not to try their ways."

"They're nothing new," Snolli said. "You forget, because you were still in swaddles at the time, that we came from the north. On land, we make sure to dress so we won't stick out like bandaged thumbs among our neighbors. But at sea, we do as we please."

"I'm sure that nobody will object if you continue to do so," Rohan said. "Now. This battle will be very difficult. Are you sure you're up to the effort—"

At this implication that he was too old to fight, Snolli came straight up out of his chair. Around him, his men tried unsuccessfully to hide their smiles and Kasai, the Spirit Drummer, sniggered openly. "How much effort do you think it takes to give orders from the deck of a sailing ship?" the Chieftain demanded in a roar that shook dust from the rafters. "If you think I'm staying out of a good fight, then think again!"

"Sorry, Grandfather," Rohan said hastily. "I was only thinking of you—"

"Such thought is the last thing to occupy your empty head."

Rohan knew that he had to change the subject, quickly. "Grandfather, if you would, please tell me about how our homeland was destroyed."

"You've heard it before."

"Yes, but now I need to hear it again. Please, sir."

Snolli subsided with only a few additional rumbles, and Rohan breathed a little easier. His head was safe for the moment. Then, once more, the Sea-Rover Chieftain began to recite the terrible tale of the invasion led by sinister riders mounted on beasts out of nightmares, armed with rods blasting a mist which seemed to burn out a man's lungs. None of Snolli's spies had learned what had dragged these horrors out of the ice regions to stamp a way into the fair land that the Sea-Rovers had held for time out of mind.

Yes, the enemy could be killed, those stunted, twisted creatures who followed the riders, but any captured seemed to die by will alone before any information could be extracted from them. They themselves took no prisoners; man, woman, and child coughed under the cloud of poison mist and quickly died.

"Thank you, Grandfather," Rohan said into the silence when Snolli had finished the story that was too grimly familiar to all of the Sea-Rover kin. "It's definite. I can now tell you what your spies could not. I know what these beasts are, and whence they came."

Now it was his turn to tell his kindred of the Ice Dragons that had awakened when the Palace of Fire and Ice, long guarded by Cyornas, had suffered great harm when a thunder-star fell to earth.

"From the reports of those who survived, one of the walls adjacent to the tomb cracked. This held the sleeping body of the entity who was only whispered about as the Great Foulness. Our Nordorn kinsmen now know it was at that moment the Foulness began to stir and then to wake. The Ice Dragons demolished the palace of Cyornas NordornKing, killed him—" gasps around the fireplace, for Cyornas had always been a good friend to the Sea-Rovers—"and then turned south."

"We are all in grave danger," Snolli said.

"How many ships will you command?" Rohan asked.

Snolli began to tick them off on his fingers. "Well, there's my flagship, the old *Gorgull*," he said. "She's showing her age a little but she's still sound. And then we have *Stormbracer* and *Wave-Ruler*. *Wind-Singer* needs some refitting. Two ships are no longer seaworthy, and another ship was lost at sea last sailing season."

Rohan nodded. It was a Sea-Rover custom never to mention the name of a ship that had sunk.

"Since then, though, we've built *Spume-Maiden*," Snolli continued. "She's small, but swift. Harvas is her captain, and we have a couple more ships close to completion. We can put five in the fight now, with the two new ones still to come."

Rohan nodded. "That is better than I dared hope. There is a harbor, close by Castle Bilth."

"I remember the place. Poor anchorage, but as good as is to be found along the coast."

"There is the best place to gather, while the armies prepare. I will go and tell them to expect you."

"We will be there, with a full complement of marines for

you to command." Snolli's eyes gleamed, and Rohan knew he was in for at least one more sharp verbal jab from his grandfather. "Never fear. I'll have men stationed to save you from making a fool of yourself in front of your friends."

The laughter of the Sea-Rovers still rang in Rohan's ears as he started the long, cold trip back to Rendelsham. If only, he thought, he could persuade Snolli that he was a capable fighter in his own right! But that, like so many things, would have to be proven in combat. Never would Snolli accept Rohan's claim otherwise.

He wondered if his father Obern had had to endure the same sort of half-amused, half-contemptuous treatment from Snolli and then decided that yes, probably, he had.

🌺

The city of Rendelsham could not hold the muster of fighting men who were rapidly assembling. Thus, a great camp was erected on the plain between the city walls and Cragden Keep. Only a few of the mustered men visited the city occasionally. Those whose wives were nearby wanted to be with them, but all knew that it was better for morale if they remained with the rest of the soldiers.

Rohan felt that he suffered more than the others did, from being separated from his bride, but reason told him he was not alone in this. Upon his return to the city he discovered he had been given a small apartment in one of the buildings near Rendelsham Castle, and there Anamara waited for his infrequent visits. He dared not tell her they would grow even fewer and farther between when Snolli had brought his ships up to the harbor at Bilth. Then he would join his marines and they would be based on the vessels until the combined armies would begin to march and the ships move out to support them from the sea.

His daily routine and their preparations were not things she wanted to hear about, which meant they had less and less to say other than how much they loved each other and how greatly they would miss each other once Rohan was gone.

In his eyes, however, the goings-on in the camp were fascinating. Many if not most of the soldiers had adopted the Nordorn way of dress, setting aside their regular armor for the many layers of clothing, which were almost as good as chain mail for protection. Every woman in the city was kept busy sewing the many tunics and breeches now required, while all the armorers and leather workers toiled to create hooded outer garments and warm boots. Wulvine fur became more valuable than gold, and those men of the city who weren't going to war were kept busy hunting the animals.

Rohan had never been able to get the marks from the fire off the left sleeve of his chain mail, no matter how hard or how often he polished it. He now considered the burn mark a badge of honor, and had a pang of regret when he packed away the armor in a chest entrusted to Anamara's safekeeping.

Gaurin and Hynnel, along with others of the Nordors, had to be everywhere at once—supervising the construction of sleds, choosing likely dogs to harness for the pulling of such transport. There were arguments with those who tried to insist on taking their familiar weapons. The Nordors organized daily drills with mace, axe, their own type of spear, and a particularly nasty weapon that was just two metal rods joined with a short chain. When used as a club, however, it was deadly indeed.

From the area between Grattenbor Keep and Yewkeep came trainers with prized war-kats, now unfortunately so scarce that only the highest ranked nobles rated a pair. If Rohan had not been assigned to a ship where war-kats would have been useless, he, too, would have found himself in possession of a pair of the coveted, intelligent animals.

Once these sleek and beautiful creatures had roamed free and deadly in the winter wastes to the north. As their numbers grew they made a pact with men. Taller than most dogs and much fiercer, these elegant felines with their long legs and heads small in comparison to their lithe bodies had golden fur marked with dark rosettes in the summer. In winter, that fur faded to almost pure white. They stalked through the camp with the kind of careless arrogance that bespoke their superiority as fighters alongside the nobles to whom they had been assigned.

The dogs gathered for the sleds had to have some protection from the weather, and so they, too, were provided woolen garments and well-lined mittens for their feet. Not so the war-kats, who actually seemed amused by this, judging from how often they gathered to watch the dogs at training. War-kats had triple-thick fur coats—the outer sleek and waterproof, the middle dense and all but impenetrable, the one nearest the skin the texture of warmest down—while their paws were covered so with fur that if they even felt the snow and ice over which they trod they gave no notice.

Yet, for all their fierceness when they went into battle, they seemed to develop a genuine fondness for the men to whom their care had been entrusted. If they were not roaming through the camp, investigating everything with that curiosity any cat displays, they could be found lying at ease in their human companions' company, being stroked and fed with scraps of the soldiers' rations.

Gaurin, naturally, had a pair of war-kats, as did Hynnel and the other ranking nobles except for Harous, who refused his.

"My duties are such that I cannot spare the time to see to them properly," he said. "Nor do I wish to burden any of my staff with the task. Chevin, my lieutenant, is almost as busy as I am."

"Would that they could be persuaded to pull a sled," Gaurin said. He smiled. "But they are obviously too smart to agree to such a menial task, if they are anything like Rajesh and Finola, my two. Only dogs will allow themselves to be put in harness. I fear that any hopes our soldiers had of riding north to meet the enemy are for naught. The sleds will have to be reserved for carrying food and other supplies, and furthermore, many of them will have to be pulled by men. Our dog power is limited."

"Have someone draw up a schedule, so that all bear such duty equally," Harous said. Then he was gone on another errand demanded by the multitudinous details occupying all the leaders. However, the High Marshal bore the greatest responsibility in the preparations for war.

❧

As usual, Ashen and Gaurin occupied the suite that had been permanently assigned to them in Rendelsham Castle. Ayfare had been left behind to unpack and store their belongings while Ashen joined Gaurin in the Great Hall for the midday meal. To her relief, the Dowager was not among those gathered. Instead, young King Peres occupied the royal chair on the dais.

"Greetings, cousin," he said to Ashen with a pleasant nod. "Your fair face is ever welcome at our table."

She smiled. Peres was quite a nice, polite young man—a far cry from his father, her half-brother Florian. "Greetings, sir," she said, and dropped a curtsey.

"Oh, don't stand on ceremony," the King said, waving away such fripperies with a gesture. "I grow weary of it, especially from people I like. Do tell me, how does our fair cousin, your beautiful daughter?"

"Hegrin?" Ashen said. "She does well. We sent her to Rydale, for safety. But we get regular reports on her progress with her lessons."

"I could wish for her presence in Rendelsham," Peres said, a little wistfully. "I like her, too, very much."

"Perhaps when the war is over, sir, a court visit could be arranged."

"Yes. We will send for her then. We are eager to see her once more."

The resumption of the formal tone told her that she was now free to find her place at the table while Gaurin and others made their own greetings.

To her pleasure, she located her assigned seat near Lord Royance. His hair had grown, if possible, even whiter since she had last seen him, though his blade-thin figure was still as erect and elegant as ever.

"Lady Ashen!" he exclaimed. He took her hands in his and kissed her fingertips. "How well you look. The exile you have chosen agrees with you."

She smiled. "Indeed, being out of the moil of Rendelsham is all that I have ever desired."

"And your handsome husband."

Her cheeks grew warm. "Yes."

"He is as fine a fighting man as I have ever seen. I fancy that I was very like him, once, when I was younger. Not that I have lost my edge, you understand."

"Of course not, my lord. How well I remember your prowess in the Grand Tourney of not too distant memory."

By this time Gaurin had joined them. The meal was beginning and the trenchers of bread were being placed on their platters, preparatory to the diners being served. He took the bowl of warm, scented water from a page, and handed it to Ashen and then to Royance before dipping his own fingers in it and wiping them on his napkin. "You acquitted yourself well in the Tourney, sir," he told Royance.

"Pity I was matched against poor old Wittern. At first, anyway." Royance smiled with more than a touch of mischief.

"You nearly killed Jakar, before that wicked Magician's spell was shattered."

"Would have, too. Those of Vacaster would have been absent a lord."

Ashen had a sudden suspicion that Royance, in spite of his years, had decided to join the fighting men, as one of them. Hoping she was wrong, she asked, "And how many men have you added to the roster of the Army of Rendel?"

"Five hundred, not including my staff."

Gaurin glanced at her and she knew that this was not a new concern. "Edgard has charge of Lord Wittern's levy. Your young kinsman, Nikolos, leads your men, of course."

"That honor I have reserved for myself."

"Then what shall I do for companionship here in Rendel?" Ashen said. "I had counted on many long and pleasant talks with you, for I shall be very lonely."

"Such are the times, my dear," the elderly noble told her.

"Such are the requirements of war that sometimes our best must stay behind," Gaurin said. His tone was gentle, but Royance's snowy eyebrows drew together in a frown.

"I like not the sound of those words, Gaurin," he said. "Are you implying that I am not fit for battle?"

"Sir, we discussed this before, and I thought the matter settled. Please. Give me your word."

"I think that my husband is right," Ashen said hastily. "It is the wisdom and experience of such as you that we require most in these perilous times. We who must needs stay behind will rely on you the most. Also, where would there be a substitute for someone to help guide King Peres? He needs you now, more than ever."

The truculent expression on Royance's face eased somewhat. "It is true that none of his other councilors—" His glance went, perhaps involuntarily, to the chair the Dowager Ysa customarily occupied. "—are fit to advise him in time of war."

"Then give the matter consideration," Ashen said, "as to where you are needed the most."

Royance looked at her and a smile began to curve the corners of his mouth. "You've learned more tact since last I saw you," he said. "Once you would have innocently told me that I would be a hindrance, someone to be looked after and protected."

"Never, sir!"

"Well, maybe not in so many words." The white-haired

noble drew a long sigh. "Perhaps you are right. Perhaps my best fighting days are behind me." Then the old burhawk which he had taken as his symbol peered out at her between his eyelids. "But only my best days. I still have a battle or two left in me."

"None could doubt it, sir," Gaurin said.

"Very well," Royance said. "Barring unforeseen circumstances, I will not ride out to war."

"Thank you, sir," Gaurin said.

"I thank you as well," Ashen said, in some relief.

Then, with the arrival of the meat, the meal began. Ashen relaxed a little, now that a small crisis, one among many, had been averted. Much as Royance hated to be left behind, he had agreed. It was widely accepted that his word had always been better than another's signed pact. She knew that Gaurin planned to be off ahead of the Rendelian contingent to ready the proposed campsite. It was over the Rendel border, where he was well familiar with the land. Also, he commanded fewer men in the Army of the Nordors than marched under the Rendel banners. Consequently Rendel's muster would take more time, being a far more complicated affair. Even Ashen thought it not wise to wait.

She turned her full attention to enjoying every moment she could of her husband's company, while he was still in the city.

❦

Harous was not kept so busy that he did not find time to return to Cragden Keep now and then. Marcala, he noted with some measure of pride, did not hang on him or beg him to remain behind the way some wives did. Still, he knew she was sorry to see him depart.

"When you go, I will not weep," she said. "I will not send you off with sad memories. But I will wait impatiently for you to return."

He nodded approvingly. "You are a true soldier's wife," he said, caressing her cheek. "You must know that I appreciate that."

Freed of that particular worry, he turned to considering the selection of those items he would take with him. Because of Gaurin's and Hynnel's greater experience in the field, he would be leaving most of his favorite weapons behind. Also, he needed to test the multilayered clothing the two Nordors favored, to make sure the garments didn't hamper his movements. Marcala, unaccustomed to anything but decorative needlework, had commissioned their making and, obscurely, Harous had a secret wish that they were the work of her own hands.

Ah, another thing—magical protection. Harous went into the bedchamber he and his Countess shared and found the key in its hiding place under his chain of office as Lord High Marshal. It bore the images of the Four Trees and was ever kept in a chest with other jewels for court occasions. Touching a certain spot on the fireplace mantle, he heard the almost inaudible sound of a panel sliding open. Harous lifted the arras and entered the secret room.

Out of habit, he checked with quick glances. Nothing appeared disturbed since his last visit—how long ago? For a long time he had had no need of the items he kept carefully hidden. Because of its seclusion, the chamber was practically dust-proof. He couldn't even see any evidence of his own footsteps—how long ago *had* it been? When he had last entered the Bog, swathed in mist, to encounter, among others, Ashen.

The room was very small, with only a small chest to furnish the space remaining. It rested on a book of arcane knowledge that Harous deemed powerful enough to keep a very close secret. The key slid easily into the chest lock. He lifted out the metal headband. Designed to center above the brow of the wearer was the oval talisman that would increase the spell of concealment, as well as grant immunity from certain weapons. This, definitely, must go with him. He gave the other contents a cursory glance. They would not be helpful. Let them remain for now at Cragden. He closed the chest, preparatory to locking it again.

Suddenly he stopped, pricked by a feeling of subtle wrongness. Something was missing. Harous snapped the chest open again and searched with more purpose. So that was it. The amulet to summon a flyer, similar to the one those in office knew by now the Dowager kept in her tower room, though hers was not completely twin to this one. He remembered well the day he had shown it to Ysa, telling her it came from Zazar—a blatant lie, for what reason could Zazar ever have to grant him such a boon? Nevertheless, though he had never used it, it had served his purpose if only to reveal to him the Dowager's possession of the magical creature.

Harous stirred the contents of the chest with thumb and finger. He was positive that it had been here, locked into safety. Now, he leaned against the wall with an ever deepening frown twisting his brow. Someone skilled in locating secret rooms, picking locks, and searching out hidden matters had been a-hunt here.

Who was the intruder? No one knew about this safe place except himself.

Harous's frown became a scowl. Who? One name kept presenting itself. Marcala, his countess.

As his wife, she had access to most of his secrets, could even have discovered this room by accident. She was a woman, and so bound by her nature to be curious. She was Ysa's friend and confidante. Therefore, Ysa could have sent her to rummage, perhaps, indeed, to seek the amulet. Why?

He could answer that easily—because Ysa could not bear to believe anybody save herself possessed such a tool. Harous remembered the look on Ysa's face when he had shown the amulet to her—an instant flash of recognition followed by an almost palpable desire to take it out of his hand.

Well, now she had it. For all the good it would do her. He alone retained the secret of its animation, and without that spell, the amulet was useless. But then, perhaps Ysa's motives never extended beyond depriving him of a power that she felt was hers alone. He was reasonably certain that, by now, Ysa must have destroyed it.

Just as she had destroyed his faith and trust in the now stranger who was his wife.

As he considered it, Harous realized that his regard for her had bloomed very suddenly, as had hers for him. He could make a good guess at the compulsion put on him and shuddered, as if he had discovered a tissue of spiderwebs enveloping his skin.

Harous lifted the plundered chest off the book. Then he squatted on his heels and opened the book.

Eventually he found what he was looking for. Rapidly reciting a counterspell, he felt his "love" for Marcala dissolve.

He could hope the spell had not been as loose for Marcala. It would be greatly to his advantage to have her still in thrall to him. If not, well, that scarcely mattered. Very soon he would be gone to the northern wars, and he could deal with her later—if need be.

The war. And how Ysa's stupid, selfish meddling had very nearly riven the country in twain, just as the enemy was on the march. His lips shaped a soundless snarl at recent memories. She had thwarted him at every turn, even to marrying him to her favorite, just to control him.

Now that the scales of being bespelled had fallen from his eyes, Harous realized that not only had he ceased to love Marcala but now he detested Ysa as well. He could barely tolerate the idea of risking himself for a couple of women who had used him so cynically. Was even the safety of Rendel worth it? Perhaps, rotten as the country was from the top down, it would be better destroyed, allowing a new realm to rise from the ashes.

Making sure that the secret room was once more in order, he left, taking the headband with him. He thumbed the spot on the fireplace once more until the door slid shut behind the arras.

It was good that Marcala had promised him no tearful farewell. He would have had difficulty in restraining himself from denouncing both her and the Dowager Ysa, if she had put on a show of deceitful grief at his departure.

Five

Despite his best resolve, however, Harous was unable to conceal his change of heart and mind. Marcala knew him too well. Perhaps she, too, had experienced the breaking of the bonding spell which had held them both in thrall. In any event, her manner toward him changed sharply, even as his toward her.

Tension stretched almost palpably taut between them and the evening before he was to depart at dawn, it broke. They faced each other, full of accusations and recriminations. The best either of them was left with at the bitter end of that encounter was that they were honest with each other at long last. Outside their chamber, servants scuttled past on soft feet, having no desire to be caught listening and so turn such wrath toward them.

"Yes," Marcala said recklessly, drawing out the word so

that it became the hiss of a striking snake. "I stole your precious amulet and yes, I gave it to Ysa. I was bound, for she commanded me to do it."

"I suppose she didn't tell you why."

"No. Why should she? It was enough for her to give the order."

Harous scowled. "Then why didn't you steal my headband while you were at it?"

"The one you used to wear when you journeyed into the Bog?" she said, too sweetly.

He drew in a breath, surprised, and Marcala laughed. "A hit! I was only making a guess, but the look on your face tells me I am correct. Whatever was your errand in the Bog that you had to go wrapped in mist? The capture of the Ash heiress? It certainly wasn't to visit Zazar."

"Woman, you are treading on dangerous ground," Harous said, grating the words between his teeth. His fingers flexed as if he would clutch at her.

"Again, a hit, and in the gold, too. Well, let me tell you a few things. I have ways of gathering information that you do not know of."

"Enough. Say no more."

"Not nearly enough, now that we are being frank with one another. I know of many more of your crimes. I know, for example, of a certain cairn of stones erected over the body of a Bog-woman, killed by a man clothed in mist. I know also of what was taken from her, and what became of it."

"I could snap your neck like a twig."

"You wouldn't dare." Marcala laughed again. "I am beyond your threats, for I hold the title of Countess of Cragden and I have made full use of the privileges such a title brings with it. If you attempt to murder me, if you take one step in anger toward me, all I have to do is cry out and servants loyal to me will rush to my rescue. Then you would be the one to have to explain what cannot be explained. Right at the brink of war, at that."

Harous had to concede that much, at least for the moment. Any revenge he might take against Marcala would have to wait. Still, he strove for some semblance of a victory in this battle between them. "When the war is over, I will divorce you."

"And marry Ashen, as you always schemed, or so you think." Marcala's laughter turned to an open sneer. "She was never yours, not for a moment, even when she married the Sea-Rover Obern. There was I, close to hand, willingly your leman and only later—" She stopped abruptly.

"Only later, when Ysa worked a love spell, did I ask you to become my wife, is that it?" Harous supplied for her.

She shrugged. "I know of no spell. Royance was the one who gave you the push you needed to make you do the sensible thing."

"I am going off to battle, and in battle men die. But whichever side triumphs, I promise you that I will do what I must to survive. I *will* divorce you for your treason."

"You might live through the war," she said, her eyes glittering, "but after you come home?"

Every nerve in Harous's body tingled. He knew that what had begun as a quarrel had suddenly become a threat to his own life. He would have to be careful indeed, in the hours he had left before he departed from Cragden Keep and this very dangerous countess of his.

"Let us leave it at that," he said carefully. "I spoke in haste and anger. We both did. When the war is finished, then perhaps we will all be sufficiently changed that we can put this unfortunate episode behind us, and perhaps make a fresh beginning. After all, we have discovered, at the very least, that we are equally matched. What say you, lady?"

She seemed mollified by his words. "Let us consider that when the war is over. After you fulfill your promise and return to me."

Not even if they had made up their quarrel completely would Harous have shared a bed with his wife. Claiming that his duties as marshal dictated that he should be with the soldiers, he stayed in the barracks with those of his men who ranked highly enough to be given quarters inside the keep. The foot-soldiers, comprising the largest number of the men, camped outside.

At dawn, while he was conferring with his officers and sergeants about the best marching order, Marcala appeared from the doorway behind him, bearing a tray on which two goblets of warmed wine steamed. Behind her came servants also bearing trays and others bringing a cask on rollers. The tap was already driven in, ready to decant the contents.

She picked up one of the goblets. "A stirrup-cup, husband," she said clearly, her voice carrying to the assembled soldiers. "To wish you luck on your way. And also for your brave warriors. It is meet for the Countess of Cragden to give you this farewell."

From behind him, Harous could hear the approving murmur of his officers. She made, indeed, a brilliant spot of color with her deep rose velvet dress embroidered with pink vaux lilies. "Thank you, wife," he said with a certain irony. "I can always trust you to do the appropriate thing."

She smiled for the benefit of the waiting men and offered him the tray. They were standing at the top of a short flight of stairs leading to the ward where they were assembled. Outside, on the plain where the rest of the army waited the order to march, nobody had brought wine, heated or otherwise. "Let all here be served, the lucky ones with your own hand," he said, "and then we will drink a toast together."

She raised an eyebrow, but moved to comply. Carefully, he marked which goblet she had offered him. Then, as he set the tray aside, he turned it so that the positions of the goblets were reversed, making sure that Marcala did not see him do it. There was nothing amiss in Marcala's gesture; it was, in fact, both expected and the proper thing to do. Nevertheless, there was no sense in taking chances and Harous had always been a prudent man.

When all in the waiting company had been served, the Marshal did not touch the tray, allowing Marcala to pick it up. He took the nearest goblet, not the vessel she had intended for him to drink from.

"Let us link arms, to symbolize our resolve," he said. "And our lasting union."

This time her smile, for him alone, was one that he recognized as false. She twined her arm with his, so that their faces were so close their eyelashes almost brushed and they warmed each other's cheeks with their breath. "To victory," she said. "You must drink it all."

Harous drained the goblet, as did she, and he wiped his lips with the back of his hand. In the ward, everyone followed suit.

Then he took his place as leader, giving the signal to begin that action which would take the assembled to the camp of the Four Armies. There, very soon, they would face the perils from the Country of Ever Snow that lay beyond even the NordornLand.

*

Because the Nordors had preceded them, the Army of Rendel was not the first of the four to arrive at the rendezvous point, but it was not the last. That dubious honor went to Rohan. The winds were against the Sea-Rovers, seas running high. Nevertheless, two days late and a few sails tattered, the little fleet pulled into the indifferent harbor serving the stronghold of Bilth and the marines disembarked.

Rohan entered the gate in the stockade wall that earlier arrivals had erected and was escorted immediately to the tent erected for the use of the generals of the Four Armies and their staffs. A russet flag, bearing the device of a tower, floated above it, indicating that this was the headquarters of the Lord High Marshal of Rendel. Snow was piled high on all sides, leaving only a narrow path to the entrance guarded by two Rendelian soldiers. "My apologies," he said as he went inside. Once in, he realized there was another room behind this one, set aside for Harous's living quarters. A burning brazier made the conference space cozy. The remnants of a meal lay on a tray on a small table, waiting to be removed. Chairs were set here and there, and between two of them, a game board.

Gaurin glanced up from the map he had been studying. The medallion proclaiming him General of the Army of the Nordors swung from a chain around his neck. "No need," he said. "You are not very late. We are currently working out strategy, and trying to decide from which direction these invaders will come." He made room for Rohan at the table. "There are two possible routes—this one to the west between the upthrust of mountains and the sea, and the other in a narrow gap between these same mountains and another range of them, stretching to the east." He pointed to map lines.

Rohan pulled off his mittens, massaging his cold fingers, as he peered at the map. "Either way has its advantages. And its disadvantages."

"That's the conclusion we have reached," Harous said.

In a far corner of the tent, Tusser looked up. He had been sitting on a blanket, hunched over, his head propped on his arms that were wrapped around his knees. Over his customary garments of lupperskin, he wore a knee-length tunic of heavy wool, and his feet were wrapped in dirty cloth. "Maps silly," he said. "We go fight."

"Greetings, Tusser," Rohan said. "I didn't see you there."

"He arrived an hour or so before you did," Harous said. "We've been having difficulty making him understand that we can't just go out all at once, without plans or direction, and no amount of shouting gets through to him." Harous made a dismissive gesture toward the General of the Army of the Bog and turned away.

"Ah," Rohan said. "I believe that I recognize the problem." He recognized also that Tusser's sitting apart from the generals of the Army of Rendel and the Army of the Nordors was not entirely accidental. There must still be a great deal of distrust, particularly between Rendel and the Bog. Gaurin could be counted on to be much more tolerant and accepting, but he was not the High Marshal, who outranked even the generals, as Harous's badge of office, surmounted by a coronet, proclaimed. Rohan wondered where Tusser's badge was. Or, for that matter, if he had been given one.

Rohan went over and squatted down beside Tusser. "Yes, we will go and fight, this I promise," he said. "Tusser is my friend. Do you remember our pact?"

"Tusser remember."

"Then Tusser knows that I tell the truth. Come with me, and I will explain the map."

"Not hurt ears?"

"No, I won't shout at you. I promise."

Tusser got to his feet and followed Rohan to the table. There, on top of the map spread out on its surface, he set a piece from the game board atop the symbol for the nearby keep.

"This stands for Castle Bilth. You passed by it on your way to the camp."

Tusser nodded, interested. "Big stone place."

"Yes. The big stone place will be our fallback point if it should come to that. Here are mountains—" He tore up some scraps of bread from the discards on the tray, piled them in the appropriate place, and scraped the opening to the east that Gaurin had noted. "—and here is the second way they can come at us. Out here is the water, where I will be most of the time."

A dull light began to dawn in Tusser's eyes and he nodded again. "Tusser see. Map is flat pictures of country, you show me which is mountains, which is big stone place. Can't make map wet for show water. Spoil pretty drawing."

"Yes. That's it. We will fight, but we do need to go to the right place to do it. If we don't, then the enemy will slip past us and the war will be lost before it starts."

"Now Tusser understand," he said. "Land between mountains like two rivers in Bog. Why we not put armies both places?"

"There aren't enough of us for that," said Hynnel, who had moved to watch Rohan's efforts in making the Bog-man comprehend what they were about. Hynnel's badge indicated that, king in exile or not, he was Gaurin's second in command.

"Huh," Tusser said. "Then do like Bog-men do. Put men to watch both places of land river. Then all go where enemy goes."

"Post scouts, to avoid ambush. That is a very good plan," Gaurin said seriously. "And we will take your advice. Thank you. The snow is deep, though, and our armies cannot move fast enough from one—er, river, to the other. So I would rather put most of our troops in place beforehand."

Tusser nodded. "Yes," he said. "All have good plans."

Satisfied, he went back to his corner and Harous stared at him, a sour expression on his face. "That," he said, turning to Rohan, "is the first time since he arrived that anybody has been able to get through to him."

"All it takes is—" Rohan bit back the words he was going to say, that all it took was explaining and showing rather than shouting, and substituted "—patience."

"Well, you obviously have more of it than I do. So I'll turn General Tusser over to you in future when it comes to discussions of strategy."

"Tusser glad," the Bog-leader said from his corner. But he picked up a medallion on a chain from nearby from where he had been sitting, and slipped it over his head. Rohan recognized it as identical to the one Gaurin wore, symbolic of his rank, except that the emblem it bore was of a Bog lupper.

"Where can my men set up their tents?" Rohan said hastily. "We'll be spending much of our time at sea, of course, but being marines, we'll have our land duties as well. Most of my fellows have already awarded themselves a place in the front lines, when the fighting comes."

"And so they shall have it, if circumstances allow," Gaurin said. "Come and see the area set aside for the Sea-Rovers. It grows late and I want to stretch my legs anyway."

He exchanged glances with Hynnel, and Rohan noted that Hynnel nodded slightly. Gaurin, Rohan realized, was making sure that Tusser would be treated with respect in his absence.

They ducked through the tent flap and began making their way through the lanes cut into the snow in what Rohan recognized as a kind of city-camp. Row upon row of tents lined each lane, all with their sides covered with loose snow to insulate the inhabitants from the northern winds.

"We live in luxury now," Gaurin said, "in good shelter and with hot meals at least once a day."

"Harous seems stretched a little thin," Rohan said. "Or is that just my imagination?"

"No, it is my observation as well, young Rohan. I do not know what is eating at him, but something obviously is. Perhaps he is just on edge, waiting for the fighting to begin."

"Perhaps," Rohan agreed. "We all are." But privately he thought it was more than that. Furthermore, he thought that Gaurin shared that opinion but didn't care to discuss it for he changed the subject.

"How was Ashen when you left, and your lady wife?"

"Both well, and both missing us. But brave, as we might hope for them to be. Before I left, Ashen moved Anamara into her quarters, for company. Anamara has begun calling her 'Madame Mother.' "

"That is charming. Let us hope our absence is brief. It already seems like years, though it has been only a few days." They came to a cross-lane in the camp. "Just one moment," Gaurin said. "I want to see how Rajesh and Finola are faring. Also, I have been keeping Keltin and Bitta for you."

"Who?"

"Your war-kats, of course," Gaurin said with a smile. "You have the ones that would have gone to Harous. Also, you need to pick up your badge of office." He tapped the medallion he wore. It bore his personal badge, the image of a snowcat with a silver collar around its neck. "Yours is of second rank, like Hynnel's. I had the symbol on that amulet put on it—the one with the crashing waves. Snolli's has a ship under full sail. We awarded your grandfather the title of Admiral-General. We thought he'd like that, and I knew you wouldn't mind."

"Of course I don't mind. Snolli will love it. Shall I take it to him?"

"No need. I sent an envoy the moment I heard the ships had arrived."

"Thank you. Gaurin, I'm not sure I can get used to the notion of being responsible for a pair of war-kats."

Gaurin's smile widened. "They are quite agreeable company," he said. "Once you get used to them, that is. And they to you."

"I'll do my best," Rohan said dubiously.

Rohan picked out Gaurin's headquarters by the spring green flag, with his emblem of a silver-collared snowcat. The war-kats, very different animals, lounged inside. To his amazement, Gaurin introduced the creatures as seriously as if they had been courtiers newly arrived from another land. "Keltin, Bitta," he said, "this is Rohan. He will be your new friend. You are to look after him when he is on land. When he is away, you will stay with me or with Hynnel or Cebastian."

They stared at him out of eyes bright with intelligence, and swallowed, licking their lips. Cautiously, Rohan, under Gaurin's supervision, tickled them under their chins. They accepted this familiarity and, listening to their rumbling purr, he began to see that it would, indeed, be pleasant to have their company so far away from home. They weren't Anamara, of course, or even Weyse. But neither his wife nor the strange little creature from the Bog were nearby, and he would not have them here on this exposed plain beyond Bilth keep.

"Are they really such fierce beasts?" he said, as Bitta rubbed against him and then gave him a head-butt, almost knocking him over with the force of the affectionate gesture.

"When they are in combat, yes. They seem to enjoy it."

"It is hard to imagine."

"They eat food we give them, though they can catch their own. I'll give you a stiff-bristled brush to groom them with. They like that, too. These are young, as you are. Well, come along. You still have to set up your portion of the camp."

The two war-kats followed the men as they made their way to the spot that had been set aside for the Sea-Rovers.

They did not tamely trail at their heels, however, being given to dashing to one side or another or chasing each other and plowing into a pile of snow apparently for the sheer, kittenish joy of scattering it high into the air. Once Keltin caught a rodent hiding under one of these snow piles and gulped it down before Bitta could rob him of his prize. Rohan began to understand that these independent creatures considered themselves the equals of the men who supposedly looked after them. That they would condescend to fight by the side of these men was, he decided, almost unbelievable.

"What's to keep the other side from having war-kats?" he asked Gaurin. "Don't the invaders come from where it used to be war-kat range?"

"The war-kats always choose with whom they will ally," Gaurin replied. "Though they are very efficient predators, they are not aggressors, nor do they appear to approve of man's aggression against his fellow man. Or, in the case of many of the invaders from the north, demi-man. The bulk of the enemy foot soldiers are Frydians, nomads who have always lived in the most appalling conditions for they will not trust anyone they deem better than themselves. Until now, that is. They follow the Dragon-riders without question."

"Perhaps these Frydians think they will be rewarded."

"Most likely. War-kats hate them. You will notice that Tusser has no war-kats both from his preference, or, I imagine, theirs. They have yet to put themselves on the side of any but the defenders in a dispute."

"Remarkable," Rohan said.

"Yes, very. Ah, we're here."

"Here" proved to be an open space, far enough to the

northern side of the camp to satisfy the Sea-Rover marines' craving for danger, and yet well within the stockade. Nearby, a number of shelters made from the fragrant, dark green branches of trees were being constructed under Hynnel's supervision. He caught sight of Rohan and Gaurin and waved to them. Then he checked to see that the building was proceeding correctly and made his way over to them.

"The Bog-men did not bring any tents," he said, "and so we have to make do with hunting shelters."

"They will be as well off that way as they were in the Bog. I notice that Harous has placed the Army of the Bog-men near Rohan's encampment."

To keep even this small a group—perhaps a hundred men in all—segregated from the Rendelians, Rohan thought. Aloud, he said, "Well, the pact was between us and them."

"You can rest assured that your allies will be treated fairly," Gaurin said, "with my kinsman in charge of their welfare."

Giving Gaurin a casual salute, Hynnel returned to his task. In the area set aside for the Sea-Rovers, some of the marines had already set up Rohan's shelter and supplies along with his battle flag, and were now busy erecting their own tents. Good smells were wafting from the cook tent. Rohan recognized fish stew, a Sea-Rover staple while out on raids.

Rohan ushered Keltin and Bitta inside, and, under Gaurin's instructions, fed them some of the stew. They lapped at it enthusiastically.

"I think they'll be all right here for a while," he told Gaurin. "I'm going back to the fleet. At first light, I want to take *Spume-Maiden* up the coast a few leagues, and see what

I can discover. She's our fastest ship, and her captain used to dandle me on his knee."

"That is a sound notion," Gaurin said. "I will be eager for your report."

❦

After Gaurin left with Rohan, Harous indicated to Hynnel and Tusser that their session for the day was over. "We've done enough," he said to Hynnel. "I suggest that you go with the Bog general to see to the disposition of his men and make sure that they are snug and well situated. We should get as much rest as possible now, for we do not know when we will be called to arms."

Hynnel saluted and left at once. To Harous's mild surprise, Tusser put up no argument, though he had been quite vocal ever since the moment the Bog-man had arrived with his tiny, ridiculous rag-tag "army" at his heels. Instead, he obediently followed Hynnel through the tent opening though he did not offer the courtesy of a salute. No better than Frydians. They were the same, really, except that the Bog-men lived their lives wet and the Frydians slogged through their days in deep and heavy snow. Their only difference lay in the fact that Bog-men were on the side of Rendel, and Frydians weren't.

Amused by his own thoughts, Harous decided not to make an issue of it. Then he gave orders that the brazier be moved to his private quarters, at the back of the tent, accessible through a double flap in the wall between the rooms.

He could have had two braziers; his rank entitled him to that and more. But he felt it best, as a matter of morale, to forego such minor luxuries. Actually, it was no great hardship. Within a matter of only a few minutes, the smaller room was comfortable. Even the flooring was not exceptionally cold throughout the structure, being a double layer of wood planks with space between them.

Harous took off his outer garments and lay down on the camp bed, stretching out with his hands behind his head. This bed, at least, was a luxury he allowed himself. Common soldiers rolled up in blankets, or fur robes, or slept in their clothing on whatever ground cover they had been able to find to line the floor of their shelters.

He counted the days since he had left Cragden Keep. More than enough time for any effects of the stirrup-cup to have made themselves known if she had somehow switched the goblets again. Or—the thought suddenly struck him—if she had foreseen that he would switch them and had drugged her own goblet in anticipation of such a move. Would that subtlety be beyond her? He thought about it, and then decided that it would not. It would not even have been beyond her to drug both goblets with a mixture to which she had carefully rendered herself immune.

Now that, he thought, was indulging in sheer fantasy— more than a little sick fantasy at that. He wished he could dismiss the notion that she had put something in the wine. But that nagging suspicion would not go away.

He seemed healthy enough. He felt well. Perhaps the whole matter was just his overwrought imagination at work. In the morning, he decided, he would go out reconnoitering and have a look for himself at those notches in the mountains, and perhaps find a suitable ground for battle, when it finally came. And he would go alone. He was tired of the company of men. Indeed, he was tired of the company of Rendel.

Harous made sure the candle on the little table beside his bed was properly trimmed before he pulled up a fur-lined robe, turned over, and fell asleep.

Six

The Lady Marcala, Countess of Cragden, awakened
with a dull, persistent pain in her midsection. It was
still dark, the middle of the night, and the candle at her bedside was close to guttering out. She dragged herself out of
bed, wondering if she had eaten something that disagreed
with her at supper. Perhaps she had made a mistake to allow
herself a degree of festivity after Harous's departure, eating
heartily of meat, which she usually avoided. She found another candle, lit it, and carried it to her dressing table.

She looked awful—awful! She had dark circles under her
eyes and her complexion had turned to paste. Then, as she
continued to gaze into the mirror, realization came to her.

In a burst of sheer fury mingled with terror, Marcala
snatched up a silver-gilt box of face powder and hurled it at

the glass. The mirror shattered; the box broke and powder fogged the air, to dust the table.

"No," she whispered. And then, louder, almost a cry of panic, *"No!"*

Heavy-eyed with sleep, Reuta, her maid, hurried into the room. "Lady?"

"It's nothing," Marcala assured her. "I just had a little accident, that's all. You can go back to sleep and clean up the mess in the morning."

"Yes, Lady."

The last thing Marcala wanted at the moment was to have someone hanging over her, offering to help. Knowing that she was probably already beyond help, nevertheless she carried the candle over to a chest where she kept certain medicines and hurriedly mixed an emetic. With an effort, she forced herself to drink it down. Purging her stomach would surely draw the trouble out of her system.

That treacherous beast, Harous. And it was she herself who had been stupid! If only she had not drunk the stirrup-cup. She had planned not to swallow a drop, just in case he managed to switch the vessels. Too confident, she had been so sure all was in perfect order! He had not touched the tray from the moment he set it down to wait until all in the ward had been served. How had he done it?

A wave of nausea gripped Marcala. She stumbled to snatch at a basin, just in time. When she was finally able to lift her head she did, indeed, feel a little better. The next few days would tell the tale. If she had been quick enough, she would be very ill for a time, but she would live. If not . . .

Marcala climbed back in bed, but not to sleep.

I am not poisoned, she told herself. It is too soon. It must be that the joint had gone off a little and I am not used to meat. Better in the morning, I know. If I had drunk the poison, it would have taken longer for me to feel the effects.

Yet, she had mixed that dose for a strong, active man, not a slight woman. He would have ailed slightly for a few days, and then—well past the time for anyone to make a connection between the ceremony of departure and his current illness—he would sicken rapidly, linger for a while, and then, most regrettably, die.

I think I was in time if it was the stirrup-cup, Marcala told herself. Why didn't I put it in his food, in the bowl of breakfast gruel? Why did I have to be so reckless and hasty to give it to him before all his men?

Maybe—just maybe—he had drunk the poisoned wine after all and even now could be feeling the effects.

No, it was the meat that sickened me, she told herself. It is only that.

After all, it had been a long time since she had poisoned someone personally. Her last victim had been the real Lady Marcala, and that had been accomplished at a great distance, away back east in Valvager.

Now she recalled the Dowager's words, describing the lady when Ysa was proposing that Marfey—the name she was using at the time—take the woman's place. Ysa had been queen then, wed to King Boroth, who was still clinging to life.

"She has black hair. By the left corner of her mouth there is a small dark mole which is said to enhance her charms rather than detract from them. Graceful, she dances well, and ever has an eye for a well-built man. Her favorite colors are violet, deep rose, gold and the peach-pink shade of vaux lilies for which she has a great liking and wears in her hair whenever there is a chance to do so. Also she wears perfume made from these flowers."

Marcala knew the woman well, but nonetheless asked for a likeness. Appearances might have altered over the years. As she had gazed at the miniature, she knew that their close resemblance to each other, even to the beauty mark Marcala habitually covered with cosmetics, had not diminished at all. Even Ysa had remarked upon it.

Not surprising, considering that the real Marcala had been her half-sister. They shared the same father. Marfey, or Darya, or Vira, or whatever other name the woman who had become known as the Queen of Spies chose to use, had been sent away as a small child from Valvager and reared elsewhere. An embarrassment to the earl, she thought bitterly. Hated by the earl's wife.

Thanks to Queen Ysa, she had come into the estate that her noble blood entitled her to. Harous —She remembered how, at first, her association with him had been only Ysa's wish. Marcala had always been too prudent to allow herself the luxury of falling in love. Still, she had come to love Harous, had been jealous of him and his transparent ambition to gain the Rendel throne through the Ash heiress, that simpering little twit, Ashen.

The irony struck Marcala anew and, in spite of the fear she had managed to push aside for the moment, she chuckled. Two women, engaged in making their way in the world, both the bastard daughters of noblemen. But in Ashen's case, her father had been Boroth, King of Rendel, and Marcala's only the Earl of Valvager. Nevertheless, the similarity of their situations had always amused her, in a bitter sort of way. She, the daughter of a minor earl, had managed to snare the leading nobleman of Rendel. Ashen had not fared so well. At Marcala's suggestion, Ysa had married Ashen first to the Sea-Rover heir, and then to a near stranger from the North. That the fellow was rumored to be a kind of prince in his homeland meant nothing in Rendel. Here he was just one more noble among many, his rank inferior to Harous's. This had always been pleasant to contemplate.

Until recently.

When had things changed between Harous and herself? And, for that matter, how had it happened that she had forgotten her own rule sufficiently to fall in love with him?

Marcala forced herself to think, to remember. Such was better than dwelling on what might just be happening within her body. Harous had said something, during that quarrel on their last night before he left, about a spell. . . .

A hazy memory swam into her mind, an occasion when Ysa had invited her up to the very private chamber at the top of the highest tower in Rendelsham Castle. Marcala concentrated, and the recollection sharpened.

Without surprise, she had noted that Ysa was indulging in spell-casting. When a rustling noise as of something shifting in its sleep attracted her attention she noted the presence of something near, hidden in a satin-lined basket. It must be what she had only heard rumored—a flying creature, not natural, that the Queen sent out from time to time when she was gathering information. Spying on whomever she chose.

No wonder, Marcala thought now, Ysa was so interested in that amulet she had stolen for the Dowager Queen. That must have been the means for summoning a similar creature.

She herself had not been exactly honest with Ysa. She had told the Dowager she didn't know how to use the amulet. In fact, she had read the spell in the book on which the chest had rested, there in Harous's secret room. Now she wished she had not been so quick to turn the amulet over to the Dowager. She would have liked to have known how Harous fared.

She clung to her memory, reconstructing how it had been when she stopped being entirely her own woman and became in thrall to Harous. Ysa had instructed her to put her hands on the royal shoulders during the spelling, to lend strength. Just as well, for Ysa had collapsed. Without Marcala, the Queen might have died. Could it have been from the effort of casting the spell to affect both Harous and her? It had been very shortly after that moment that she had begun to think of him as more than someone she could use—a very distant relative who had been kind enough to open his house to her.

It could only have been the effects of Ysa's spell that caused Marcala to open her bed to Harous, to divert his attention from Ashen. It had been not merely for her own pleasure, though that was certainly a part of it. She had burned for him and he was not indifferent. Also, she yearned then to save him from himself. His ambitious pursuit of the Ash heiress, with her measure of royal blood, would have netted him nothing but the headsman's axe, when his schemes became so blatant that they could not be politely overlooked.

Just as she in turn could not overlook the threats he had made against her. Nobody—not even Count Harous of Cragden, Lord High Marshal of Rendel—could threaten to kill or divorce the Queen of Spies, and go unpunished. For that alone he had to die. A momentary pang of pity touched her. Once, there had been a time when they had been happy with each other. . . .

Ysa, contrary woman that she was, at first tried to block Marcala's plan for marrying Harous. Marcala smiled to herself, remembering. How frightened Ysa had been, when she let the Dowager know that the real Valvager heiress had died. Marcala made certain, without saying anything outright, that Ysa was quite aware of who had been responsible for that very convenient death, even if she didn't know the particulars. The Countess was confident that Ysa had since investigated, and was equally confident that her agent who had handled the matter had left no traces. In fact, he had used the same poison as the one she had put into the stirrup-cup meant for Harous.

Which brought her full circle. Fresh fear gripped her.

I am not poisoned, she told herself. I am not.

The Lord High Marshal of Rendel would normally have gone nowhere without a squad of soldiers at his back. However, now he gave orders that he was to go out of the camp alone.

"Chevin," he told his lieutenant, now holding the office of aide-de-camp, "being penned in here has begun to irk me. I want to see what I can discover on my own. You know that I am a skilled man of the out-of-doors, and so I can avoid the enemy if I should come upon them. A company of heavy-footed soldiers would be my doom."

"As you command, sir," Chevin replied, but Harous could

see that he did not approve. "Please, for all our sakes, do not be gone long."

"That I promise. Now, get about your duties. You will be in charge in my absence."

Glad to escape the confinement of the camp and his responsibilities as leader of the Four Armies for a little while, Harous donned a white cloak over his winter garments and slipped out. In a short time, he had left the stockade behind to make his way toward that narrow gap in the range of mountains where his chances of seeing without being seen were better than on the sea road.

Chevin, he thought, was completely loyal, but nowhere near the caliber of Hynnel. How had Gaurin managed to get an exiled king for his second in command? Also, Cebastian and Lathrom were excellent members of Gaurin's staff, not to mention Rohan. He envied Gaurin his ability to attract able men to him. And women. Ashen—

He put that thought aside firmly, resolving to study the Nordor closely to learn what his secret might be. Until Gaurin had come to Rendel, it had been Harous who was considered the rising noble, to whom all drew nigh in hopes of having his luck rub off on them. But now it was all Gaurin, Gaurin, Gaurin. The man moved like a war-kat, with never any wasted motion but always purposeful and, above all, confident. In any other man it would have been arrogance. Harous felt awkward by comparison.

Gloomy thoughts, also to be put aside firmly. His discontent deepened until it was almost palpable.

It was a gray day, promising more snow, and clouds veiled the thin winter sun. The cold air seemed to burn in his lungs.

Something—or someone—was coming, and only the faintest squeak of snow being trodden underfoot betrayed that person's approach. Quickly, Harous took refuge behind some rocks in the snow-filled glade, knowing that any sound he made would carry as clearly in the unnatural stillness of the air.

"Harous?" a woman's voice said.

Startled, he drew in a sharp breath.

"I can hear you, you know. The throbbing of your heart is as clear to me as my own. If I can detect your heartbeat, what makes you think I couldn't hear you breathe just now?"

There was, he thought, nothing to be gained by trying to carry on the pretense that this person, whoever she was, did not know he was there. He moved out of his hiding place.

The woman stood there as if she had been waiting for him to arrive. She moved her head so that the hood of her light cloak fell back, to reveal a face so beautiful he caught his breath again. Her fingers moved also, and a few glittering flakes of snow drifted from them.

"Don't you know me, Harous?" she said. Her voice was low and vibrant. "Don't you remember me?"

"I—I don't know."

"You saw me last at the Grand Tourney, when that meddling youngster, Rohan, interfered with my plans."

"You are the Magician—"

"The Sorceress. I am Flavielle."

"Why are you here?"

"For you, Harous. Only for you."

Without conscious volition, he walked forward and took her in his arms. She melted against him, warm and willing.

The scent of her perfume filled his nostrils, at once earthy and sophisticated.

"I can scarcely believe this," he murmured in wonder.

"Believe that I am yours," she said. Her lips parted. They were very red.

"But why? How?"

"So many questions. Let us say that I sensed your anger at the Dowager, and at the betrayal of the unworthy wife you were tricked into marrying. It drew me here, even as it drew you to where I waited."

He cradled her head in his hands and kissed her then, hard enough to break the skin of those red, red lips. She laughed, deep in her throat, and returned his passion in full measure. Then she pulled back far enough to look into his eyes.

"Shall you in turn be mine? Are you the one I have long awaited, come to me at last? Shall I offer you what I have offered but once before, only to be spurned? You are a man with some Power, though raw and untrained. This I have sensed in you. Shall I increase your talents a hundredfold? I can do this. All you would have to do in return is to join me."

"Join you," he echoed. It was as if he was losing himself in the depths of her eyes. He still held her head, feeling her fine, delicate skull between his hands. Harous was strong enough that he could have crushed it like an egg. She smiled at him, unafraid.

"Shall I show you?"

"Please."

She turned her head in the cradle of his hands, brushing

her lips across his palms. Then she slipped out of the circle of his arms and, holding him by the hand, led him to where, in the shelter of an outcropping of rock, an enormous white beast waited. It had a long neck, and sharp spines decorated its back. It raised its head and stared at him out of black, bottomless eyes. Instinctively, he recoiled and reached for his sword.

"Do not be alarmed," she said with a laugh. "He will not harm you, as long as I am with you. You will need to drink this, however, so that you will not freeze where I am taking you."

She drew out a small vial, unstoppered it, and handed it to him. Without question or hesitation, he drank down the contents. It had almost no taste but immediately warmed him to his core. She showed him where and how to mount, in a spot just behind the great head. Then in a graceful bound she was seated behind him, wrapping her arms around his waist. "Up!" she commanded.

Huge wings that he had not noticed before now unfurled from where they had been folded tightly against the creature's body.

"This is an Ice Dragon, isn't it," Harous said.

"Yes."

She nudged the Dragon by digging her heels into its neck. Then in a sound like a clap of thunder they were airborne. Snow scattered in their wake. Harous sensed that the Dragon flew reluctantly, and asked about it.

"They are not fond of flight for in milder climes the effort can warm them too much. Here, though, we are cold enough for them. It will be even colder, the higher we go."

Harous did not feel the chill. A magical warmth enveloped him. The philter she had given him must be responsible. Even his breath did not puff out white and frosty now and he threw back the wulvine-lined hood of his cloak.

They soared high over the mountaintops. He could see that they were so sharp-edged that he fancied he could cut his fingers on them if he touched. As they cleared the cloud cover into bright sunlight all became brilliant and glittering—the scales of the Ice Dragon he rode, his own garments full of ice crystals, and, behind him, Flavielle. Her hair blew in the wind.

"I wanted to show you this," she said. Her grasp around his waist tightened, and she put her head against his shoulder.

"I have no words for it," he said. He was beginning to feel more at ease on the Dragon's neck. The seat was not that much different from riding a thick-chested warhorse. He grasped the scaly protuberances on its head the way he would have held reins, to keep his balance.

Flavielle nudged the Dragon again and it banked, gliding majestically on widespread wings. Then it descended once more.

He recognized that they were near the point at which they had first broken through the clouds.

"Look," Flavielle said. "To your right."

He saw that she was referring to a shiny thread of ice high atop one of the mountains guarding the narrow pass. From this distance it looked narrow, though it filled the space it had cut for itself.

"What is it?" Harous asked.

"An ice river. Usually such crawl along the ground until they reach the sea. There they splinter off great blocks of ice dangerous enough that ships avoid them."

Harous nodded. He had heard tales of such things. "I never knew they formed high on mountains, though."

"Not often. Here, they will drop ice on anything unlucky enough to be under them at the time." She loosed her hold with one arm and pointed in the direction of the flow of ice. "Watch. Observe my power."

As she gestured, the thread of ice became larger, both in width and thickness. It trembled on the precipice. Even as high as they were, Harous could hear it begin to creak and snap. He was reminded of the crackling of ice when liquid was poured on it. A few glittering shards fell from the lip. Then the noise stopped. The frozen river was, for the moment at least, at rest.

"It is ready," Flavielle said, pleased. "Now, you must lead the Rendelians into the pass. At the proper time, I will see to it that the river cascades huge blocks of ice onto the vanguard, where all the leaders but you will be. Then the war will be over." She turned him so that he could look at her. "And you will be mine and I will be yours, completely. It is difficult to wait until then."

"Must we?"

"No."

Harous felt that he was drowning in her eyes. He scarcely noticed the Ice Dragon returning to the ground until they had dismounted. A shelter constructed of tree boughs waited nearby. The fragrance of the deep green needles filled his nostrils. Within, such formed a smooth, slippery floor. A small fire burned in a rock-lined pit in the center, and an almost invisible thread of smoke escaped through the place where the sloping walls came close to meeting. On either side of the fire was an open space. In one of these, fur robes had been laid, making a bed. He didn't know if he took her in his arms, or she clasped him in hers.

"I love you," he said, much later. He brushed the hair back from her forehead. It still sparkled as if filled with crystals of ice, though the interior of the little shelter had grown quite warm.

"You will never regret this," she said. "I will give you Power such as no human has ever known."

He thought of Ysa, and of Zazar. As if she had read his mind, the Sorceress laughed.

"No human," she repeated. "Those back in Rendel only think they know what Power is. They only sip it. With me, you will drink it deeply, in full measure."

Again, he found himself lost in her as he had not been with any woman before. Outside, the Ice Dragon's teeth gnashed once, as if it snapped at an insect, and at the sound Flavielle laughed.

Eventually, he let her go with a sigh and reached for his discarded clothing. "I must return to the camp. They will come looking for me."

"Then I will not hinder you."

"But how can I leave? Why can't we fly away on your Ice Dragon, and then I will lead your hosts against those who are now my enemy?"

"No, my Harous. Not yet. You must pretend to be loyal to Rendel until the time is right. Then we will be together, I promise, and Harous the Conqueror will lead us in triumph into our new lands—even into Rendelsham Castle."

With that pledge lingering in his ears and the taste of her mouth on his lips, he reluctantly left her and began to retrace his steps back toward the camp. He wondered, belatedly, at the ease with which he had accepted the philter. A long time ago, it seemed, someone—his wife—had offered a stirrup-cup, possibly poisoned. It should have taught him caution. That long-ago wife was a treacherous bitch to be sure, and not to be considered in the same breath as his radiant, scintillating Flavielle. Far from suffering the effects of any poison, Harous had never felt so well, so strong, so much in command of himself as at this moment. Indeed, he would trust Flavielle with more than his life.

He had been correct in his surmise about being missed. As he crested a rise, he caught sight of Chevin, leading half a dozen men. There would have been no adequate explanation had they found him in Flavielle's embrace.

He waved to show that he was unharmed.

"We had begun to worry about you, sir," his lieutenant said when they had caught up with each other. "I know you are both wary and cautious, but still, this is enemy country."

"As you can see, your concern was for naught, though I do thank you for it."

Chevin looked at him curiously. "You do seem better for your outing," he said. "Something about you has changed."

"I found no battleground, but I have discovered what I feel is the best route for us to take when we carry our quarrel to our foes," Harous replied, smiling. And, he added to himself silently, I have rid myself of a wife I never loved, who wed me falsely. No wife at all. I discard her.

Then Chevin gave him information in return, including the intelligence mission Rohan had undertaken on *Spume-Maiden*. Harous nodded.

"That was a good idea on his part." He glanced up. The cloud cover was lower and a dark, slate blue. "It will begin to snow soon and heavily, I think," he said. "We will be immobilized for a while, as will the enemy. However, this is a boon for we can use the time wisely. Young Rohan should be back soon, with what information he has gathered. While the enemy have not troubled themselves to learn about us, to the best of anybody's knowledge, that has to work to our advantage. We shall have a meeting of our generals and their staff this afternoon so that we can lay out our order of attack."

Three days passed, and Marcala did not leave her bed. Her condition deteriorated steadily though she kept it from Reuta and the rest of the servants. It was a temporary indisposition, she told them, and longing for her absent lord. Reuta cleaned away the mess on the dressing table, and tended Marcala to such degree as her lady would allow.

In the privacy she craved, Marcala could be honest. Must be honest. By this time she could no longer convince herself that she had merely eaten something that disagreed with her. Not only had she failed to kill Harous from a safe distance, but also it seemed she had destroyed herself in the attempt.

Yet, all was not lost. There was still one way she could get a measure of revenge against him. If she hurried.

She got out of bed and dressed herself in her finest, astonished at how weak and thin she had become. It was as if her body was being eaten from within. Calling for a carriage, she had herself conveyed to Rendelsham, and thence to the castle. Ysa would see her unannounced; the Dowager had always done so in the past.

Ysa turned pale when Marcala, leaning heavily on a staff for support, staggered into her private chamber.

"Madame," Marcala said. "Pray let me not stand upon ceremony. In fact, let me not stand at all."

"Marcala! You should be home, in bed. You are ill."

"No, Madame, I am dead."

The Dowager waved her ladies out of the room and with her own hands drew up a chair for Marcala. She dropped into it gratefully and, with equal gratitude, accepted a cup of spiced wine, once heated but now cooled to tepid. The beverage had the effect of restoring her, if only a little.

"Thank you."

"What has happened?"

"Much. Pray, send for Lady Ashen. She is still here in Rendelsham, is she not? There are matters that concern her and I will not speak until she is with us."

Ysa arose, touched a bell-pull, and Lady Gertrude entered the room. "Go and fetch the Lady Ashen," Ysa ordered. "Her presence is required here."

"Tell her to hurry."

Marcala's voice had become a croak. She patted a few drops of cold perspiration from her forehead with a scented kerchief. She held out her goblet for more wine but the small pitcher was empty except for a few drops.

"And Gertrude," Ysa said, "bring more heated wine."

"A large pitcher," Marcala added.

The Dowager added some other instructions to Lady Gertrude so softly that Marcala could not hear what was being said. She didn't care; she was beginning to float in and out of reality anyway. The lady-in-waiting hurried off to do Ysa's bidding.

"Ashen will be here presently," Ysa said. "Would you like to lie down?"

Marcala smiled wanly. "I fear that if I do I shall never rise again."

"You should have come here earlier, the moment you began to feel ill. Well, better late than never. Master Lorgan surely has something to cure you. I've sent for him—"

"He can do nothing," Marcala said. "Pray remember my— my former occupation, Madame. I know my symptoms. There is no help for me. But if we hurry, I can give you and Ashen such information as is needed to bring a traitor to justice."

"Rest yourself until Ashen gets here."

The hot spiced wine arrived first. With a fresh goblet in her hand, and not having wasted her strength by speaking, Marcala felt a little better by the time Ashen was shown into the chamber. Lady Gertrude would have lingered, but the Dowager dismissed her.

"Lady," Ashen said, a shocked look on her face, "they told me you were indisposed, but they did not reveal the half of it."

"Marcala is very ill," Ysa said. "And she says there is something to tell you."

Marcala sipped at the strengthening wine. The process of heating it had eliminated most of that which caused a person to get tipsy; she wondered why she hadn't thought of this herself, then understood that her mind was not functioning as well as it should. The poison, no doubt. She could have slept where she sat, and never awakened. Instead she forced herself to temporary alertness. There was the story she must tell.

"Harous and I had a terrible quarrel. Things were said on both sides, and things were done—" Deliberately, Marcala decided to tell the truth but twist what had happened to put it in its worst possible light. "I am poisoned, Madame Dowager and Lady Ashen. And Harous did it."

"Surely not. Why would he?"

"He has done even more dreadful things, Madame. Dreadful. He is a traitor."

"I cannot believe this."

"You must." In a low, steady voice, saving her strength as much as possible, Marcala told the two shocked women what had come out during the great quarrel with Harous. "I see that you wear the necklace he gave you," she said to Ashen. "The one made from the old brooch pin."

Ashen's hand went to her throat. "Yes. I wear it often, as an heirloom of my house."

"The brooch is something he stole from a Bog-woman, when he killed her."

Marcala's words rocked Ashen back in her chair and she stared at Marcala unbelievingly. "No."

"Yes."

Ashen turned away numbly, staring at nothing. Then she began to speak in a monotone, as one who has been stunned by a blow to the head. "Kazi. It was Kazi. She was a—a woman in Zazar's house while I was growing up. Zazar protected her. But she couldn't protect her when Joal, the headman, brought her to the ruined city. She was bait, you see, to get me to come out of hiding. But I wouldn't, and then Joal went away and Kazi went away and I knew I had to go after her because if I didn't she might get eaten by Gulpers and then I saw her with a man who was covered in mist. I had a power stone and made mist appear around myself and then I could see him all but his head and he killed her with his fist. I saw it all, I saw it—"

"You're babbling nonsense, girl," Ysa said. "Pull yourself together at once. There is no evidence that this man was Harous or even that there was a man at all."

"I never knew who it was. I never saw the misty man again."

"Harous has a diadem that creates such a mist," Marcala said. "I saw it. There is a talisman in the band that strengthens the spell against magic, and most weapons."

Ashen went on speaking as if unable to stop. "I saw the man take a bright thing from Kazi's body. Kazi never let me look at what she wore around her neck on a thong."

Ysa exhaled sharply through her nose. "There is no reason to suspect that the 'bright thing' you claim you saw and the old Ash brooch were one and the same."

Ashen turned to the Dowager. "To the contrary, Madame, I think there is. Once, just before Marcala and Harous's wedding, Gaurin asked me where Harous had found the brooch. I said he had never told me. It set me to wondering, but the matter was dropped and I didn't pursue it. There was never anything to tie Harous directly to Kazi's death. Until now, that is."

"You must have been mistaken in what you thought you saw," the Dowager said. "Even if someone did put her out of her misery—you said she was crippled—this Kazi creature was only a Bog-woman after all."

Ashen drew herself up. "She was a woman, Madame, and she had done Harous no harm. If you do not consider her murder a crime, I do!"

"Of course," Ysa said smoothly. "I only meant—"

"Perhaps my murder is sufficient?" Marcala said, an edge to her voice. She sat up straight in her chair, but the effort cost her too much strength and she sank back again. "Do not forget that he schemed to marry Ashen and, through her, gain the throne. Now, I think he intends even greater treason. His parting words led me to believe this. He promised he would do anything—*anything*—necessary for his own survival so that he could come back to divorce me, and in his eyes was a look that told me he would even go over to the enemy, should they prevail. With my dying breath I swear my words are true."

Ashen was fingering her necklace, the one that bore the badge of her house, a flame rising from a vessel set with a large sapphire, that hung from sapphire beads. Marcala knew the item well, for Harous had ordered her to find and hire the goldsmith to have it repaired from its nearly ruined state, and turned into the handsome ornament he intended to give Ashen. Around the edge of the former brooch ran words, what was called a canting pun. "Without flame, there can be no Ash."

Marcala had nearly had it melted for the gold, planning to claim later that it had been stolen, but then had thought better of it. She had known all along, if Harous did not, that he would never marry Ashen. So let him give the wench presents. It did no harm, and Harous was rich enough to afford it ten times over.

"I must go back to my apartment," Ashen said, her voice shaky. "If there is more, Lady Marcala, pray leave it for another occasion. I cannot bear any more."

"For my part," Ysa said, "I must be frank, even though it

pains me to say this. I believe that your illness, Lady Marcala, has caused your imagination to carry you away into a kind of madness. I cannot give countenance to these wild tales of yours."

Ashen turned to her, disbelief plain on her face. "Then you do not believe what Lady Marcala has told us?"

"No, I do not. Not a word."

"Shouldn't someone be notified?"

"No. There will be no messenger sent to disturb the Four Armies. Harous has enough on his mind as it is." Ysa turned to Marcala. "Master Lorgan should be here at any moment and he will give you medicine to make you more comfortable at once. Poor child. Poor, dear, sick friend. You needn't even walk to the rooms next to my own. You will be carried on a litter. You must be tended carefully, and I will see to your well-being personally."

"For whatever small amount of time I have left," Marcala said with wry bitterness.

"You are wrong, my dear. Master Lorgan is very skilled. You will yet recover your health, in both mind and body, and live for many, many years to come."

"And I add my hopes for your recovery to the Dowager's," Ashen said. "We have had our differences, you and I, but please believe me when I tell you that I have never wished you harm."

Which, Marcala thought, is more than I could ever say about you. She hadn't even the strength to protest at the way Ysa thought she was lying. Or mad.

Now all Marcala wanted was to lie down quietly and sleep forever. She couldn't even summon up resentment for Ysa's betrayal of rejecting her story. After all, the Dowager was notorious for believing only what was comfortable or convenient. One more defeat. Then a spark of hope flared, faint and almost imperceptible, from an unexpected direction. The Ash wench had believed her. Maybe she could do something, where Ysa refused. Ashen had taken the question for unraveling, and sooner or later someone was bound to find the truth. Actually, Marcala was too tired to care. It didn't matter. Nothing did anymore. And by the time all was known, she would be beyond caring about anything whatsoever, for she would be well and truly dead.

Seven

shen could not get back to her own apartment swiftly enough. Anamara was sitting in the main room, mending a shirt of Rohan's that had been left behind. Without pausing to greet Anamara with more than a nod she found Ayfare where the maid was busy putting a chest of clothing into order.

"Good," she said. "Please find for me some garments suitable for travel over what is bound to be a rough trail, and some that will keep me warm. Lay out my cloak with the wulvine lined hood. Is there any of the winter gear left from outfitting those soldiers who would accept it?"

"Yes, Lady," Ayfare said, startled. "But—"

"No questions, please. I have just learned some dreadful news. The Dowager dismissed it as the ravings of a woman who is very ill—and she is. The Lady Marcala truly looks as if her hand is on death's door. However, at least one thing she told me has the ring of utter truth. I cannot put the rest aside. Therefore, I am going to warn Gaurin that there may be a traitor in their midst."

Anamara spoke from the doorway. "Rohan has enemies who might lie about him."

"No," Ashen told her daughter-in-law. "It is not Rohan. I would rather that the man's identity remain a mystery for now, but the gossip will be all over Rendelsham Castle within an hour. It is Count Harous."

Both ladies gasped, hands to their mouths. Then Anamara spoke up. "I will go with you."

"And I," Ayfare said.

"No," Ashen repeated. "I must do this alone."

"It is madness, Madame Mother! You cannot possibly undertake such a dangerous journey all by yourself!"

Ashen had to smile, if a trifle wanly. "And I suppose my safety will be assured by having two other women with me? It is impossible. But this I will do. I will ask someone to accompany me, someone we can all trust. Will that calm your fears?"

"It will help," Anamara said. "Who?"

Ashen's smile grew wider. "Someone who has expressed a wish to be with the fighting men, someone whose reputation for honor—as well as for his fighting prowess in years past—has no stain upon it. Someone who promised he would not go, unless, of course, an honorable excuse could be found."

"Lord Royance?" Anamara said, her eyes wide.

"The same. I can think of no better. Now, Ayfare, please get clothing together both for Lord Royance and for me. I must go and ask him now, and I think he will not refuse me. Have the winter garments ready by the time I return, if you can. There is no time to waste."

Ayfare nodded. "It will be done, Lady," she said, already beginning to rummage through the chest for whatever might be appropriate. That this completely undid all her previous work didn't seem to matter to her.

A few minutes later, a steward ushered Ashen into the room Lord Royance used for meetings. There was someone with him now, a gray-haired man Ashen had seen once or twice. She started to leave again, to wait outside in the corridor, but Royance motioned for her to stay.

"Sir Brean and I are finished with our business, Lady Ashen. We were merely exchanging pleasantries."

Brean arose from his chair across the table from where Royance held a kind of court. He bowed to both. "Then, sir, you will take this matter before the Council?" he said.

"I will, as I told you, put it under advisement," Royance replied. "I must think about it first."

"Thank you." Sir Brean bowed himself out and closed the door behind him.

Royance arose in turn and came to greet Ashen. "You are a welcome sight, my dear—I hope you don't mind an old man's affectionate familiarity."

"I welcome it. I have come asking for your help."

"If it is mine to give, then it is yours."

"It is a very private matter."

"Then we shall discuss it in private." Royance led her into the small chamber opening off the formal one, where they both sat down beside the fire.

Leaning forward and mincing no words, Ashen told the

old gentleman what had taken place in the Dowager's apartment. She took off the necklace Harous had given her, and held it out to him. "This is the proof that, to me at least, what Lady Marcala said was true. I witnessed that murder, sir. I saw a misty man—and now I am certain it was Harous—kill Kazi and take this from her body. At least, the Ash badge. The rest was added later, when it was reworked into its present form."

"But why would Harous do such a thing? Steal a ruined brooch from a dead Bog-woman."

"I cannot fathom a reason. Perhaps he saw some possible use for the trinket later. Perhaps Kazi had annoyed him. Perhaps he did it for sport." Ashen's lips twisted bitterly. "There are those who hunt Bog-people as if they were beasts."

Royance shook his snowy head. He closed his eyes and Ashen could tell that he was thinking deeply. Eventually he spoke.

"Harous comes from an ancient family. I have known him since he could toddle. He was always too ambitious for his own good, but I never thought—No, I will not judge him prematurely on the word of a sick woman, even though your evidence is strong. Men have been convicted and even executed for less. Still, there might have been a misunderstanding. Harous could always have found the old brooch after you were brought out of the Bog, and had it made into the necklace out of sheer generosity. Another man might have been responsible for Kazi's death."

"I know. I am trying to keep all that in mind." She picked up the necklace and ran the sapphire beads through her fingers. "Once, a long time ago, Zazar pulled some cords out of a tangle she kept as one of her ways of seeing into the future.

She called these cords 'trimmings from the Loom of the Weavers.' On this occasion she pulled out six and laid them on the floor between us. Three were gold, one brighter than the others. Another was such an intense blue it hurt my eyes to look at it. The fifth was spring green, and the last was black with a few flecks of gray. It lay apart from the others."

"What does this mean?" Lord Royance asked. "I don't understand."

"If you had been brought up by Zazar, you would. The golden threads were the King, the Queen, and Prince Florian. His thread was thin and weak; the Queen's the strongest. The blue, Zazar said, was me. The green one I thought was Obern but I was mistaken. Gaurin's color is spring green and I knew he was the man I loved from the first moment I saw him." She swallowed. The next words would come hard. "I never guessed who the last was, until now. The black thread, I fear, was Harous."

"This is no evidence."

"I know. And yet—" She picked up the necklace and studied it. "Part of me wants to throw this away. Another part of me feels that my—my mother must have been wearing this brooch when she came to Zazar, the night I was born."

Royance frowned. "Now I will tell you something, though I don't know if it will help or not. I often saw the Lady Alditha wearing a brooch very similar to the one in question except the vessel holding the flame was a lapis lazuli. But what became of it, I do not know nor can I attest that you have it now." He spoke slowly.

Ashen's eyes filled with tears. "Harous gave me the fragments of the blue stone that had been originally set in the brooch. I still keep them in my jewel box. They are lapis. Lord Royance, thank you. In my heart I believe that you have solved this one mystery at least. The brooch was my mother's. I will keep it for it is all that I will ever have of her." She fastened the ornament around her neck once more. "But as you say, more questions remain. Is Harous guilty, or innocent? Whatever the truth may be in this moil, I feel that Gaurin is in grave danger. I must go to him," she stated. "I must."

"Why not let a messenger from the Dowager, or the King, or even the Council carry this news?"

"Because Ysa has forbidden it."

"I see. Well, it is no disloyalty to think that the Dowager wrong. I agree with you." Lord Royance spoke firmly. "I think the threat of treason was something spoken hastily, in the heat of a quarrel between two headstrong people, and there is nothing in it. Nevertheless, Harous must be informed. If he is innocent, he should be given the chance to clear himself. If he is guilty—" He left the rest of the thought unspoken. "Also, he should know about his wife's illness." He got to his feet, his movements brisk. "Knowing you, I suspect that preparations are already underway for our journey."

Ashen's cheeks grew warm. "Yes, sir. I hoped you would go with me. But if not, I was determined to go alone."

"I wonder if Gaurin knows what a treasure he has in you. Well, I told him at dinner the other night that I still might have a battle or two left in me. It seems that boast is about to be put to the test. I will not have broken my word, now there is need." He returned to more practical matters. "What preparations are you making?"

"So far, warm clothing, enough for both of us. We will need food, of course—"

"I have a little carriage on runners that will take us to a rendezvous point near a certain hunting lodge of infamous memory. We can go that far without escort."

Ashen grimaced to think of it, but the old gentleman was right. The lodge where she had been taken, years ago when she had been abducted and Obern had come to her rescue, was close by the road north and a convenient meeting spot.

"I will send a messenger to Grattenbor. I am seldom there these days, but I daresay they have not yet forgotten their lord. There must still be a sled or two left there, or at Yew-keep. Jervin, my chief steward, will find them for us, and dogs to pull them. I know my kennels were not entirely emptied. My guards will bring the sleds and dog teams and join us at the lodge, and thence to the road north. I will personally handle the one that carries you."

"Can you drive a sled?" Ashen asked in some disbelief. She had envisioned a march along the road the soldiers had taken, and had never hoped for anything swifter.

"I did, in my youth," Royance answered. Unexpectedly, he grinned and a ghost of the high-spirited boy he had once been shone through his customary dignity. "Grattenbor is very close to the mountains, and sledding and snow traveling out in the high country is something we all do. I loved it and practically had to be dragged back home. I can give your Gaurin competition crossing snow fields unless he too knows how to make woven frames for your feet that will keep you from falling through the crust."

Now that the adventure was taking shape, he seemed downright jaunty about it. A dozen years seemed to drop from his shoulders, and once again Ashen was reminded of the way he had welcomed the opportunity to participate in the Grand Tourney with the other senior nobles.

"Your various talents never cease to amaze me," she said, smiling in return.

"Put your worries to rest, my dear," he said. He patted her hand. "As soon as we are able, we will be at the war-camp, where these terrible questions will find answers."

It was late afternoon and the first heavy flakes of snow had begun to fall by the time Rohan and Snolli arrived back in camp.

Rohan touched the hilt of his sword with his gloved hand, grateful that the Nordor leaders had relented and allowed edged weapons after all. He hoped the weather would not grow too cold to use them. The approaching snowstorm added to his apprehension. He was warm enough, but he missed the comfort of armor. The brush of dried herbs and grasses Granddam Zazar had given him to wear was useless without a helm to wear it in. However, he had tied it to a thong and now kept it close to his skin. Another item she had given him—a silver amulet with the design of crashing waves—he wore more openly. "I'm late again," he stated with some degree of guilt.

"Never mind, boy," Snolli told him. "They need what we bring. They'll wait for us." He fingered the elaborate badge of office he wore. Rohan hid a smile, remembering how delighted his grandfather had been at the title Admiral-General, and how he had tried to hide it.

"That's more than just a general, isn't it," he had said, scowling.

"Indeed it is, sir," Rohan had said.

"Do I keep the badge, once this war is over?"

"I see no reason why you can't, sir. In fact, I see no reason why yours shouldn't be a permanent office, in Rendel."

His grandfather had grunted dismissively, but Rohan knew better than to believe his gruff act. The Council of Rendel would be wise to have just such a scheme in mind, he thought, or I'm in trouble again for speaking when I didn't know all the facts.

"Well, judging from the number of guards and the flag there, I'd say we've arrived." Snolli tramped straight to the men stationed at the entrance to the command tent. "You there. Make way for the Admiral-General of all of Rendel and his second in command. We bring information."

"High Marshal Harous and all the other leaders of the Four Armies are waiting for you eagerly," one of the guards replied. He saluted and ushered them inside.

As before, the interior was warm, not only from the brazier, but also from the presence of many more men than had been there the previous day. Rohan recognized his friend Cebastian, seated beside Gaurin, and remembered that there was kinship between them. Hynnel was on Gaurin's other side, and next to him was Lathrom. He looked up at Rohan and nodded a welcome. Steuart, the champion of the Grand Tourney, sat next to Chevin, Harous's lieutenant, and Rohan realized that he was a part of Harous's staff. Elsewhere around the table he recognized Jabez of Mimon, Vinod of Vacaster, and Reges of Lerkland, all young nobles of his acquaintance, who had found positions as junior officers. Nikolos of Grattenbor, Royance's deputy, had the seat that would have been his lord's. Gidon of Bilth acted as his second in command. Harous himself occupied the seat at the head of the table, and Tusser was relegated to a spot as far down from him as possible. Rohan deliberately chose a chair close by the Bog-man. "I know these men. Let me do the talking," he whispered to Snolli.

Harous spoke first. "Welcome, Admiral-General, and Rohan," he said. "As you can see, we have been studying the map of the area and making conjectures as to where our enemy has gathered, but without firm information our guesses are only useless exercises. I hope that you have brought us something we can use."

"I have," Snolli retorted. His chest puffed up a little. "The Sea-Rovers have made themselves more than useful today. Rohan, you tell them."

Relieved that his grandfather was taking his advice, Rohan began, though he left out certain private observations.

The grizzled old Admiral-General insisted on leading the mission in person. "You may be young and hot for battle," he told Rohan, "but it is too soon to engage the enemy. Not until we know what we're facing. Takes somebody seasoned to get in and out in one piece when we go to take a look. They are bound to object, if they catch us."

Without reminding his grandfather that the reconnaissance mission had been his idea, Rohan surrendered command of the *Spume-Maiden*, chosen because she was faster than any other ship in the fleet. Snolli promptly took his place beside Captain Harvas. Rohan's battle flag floated in the breeze, sea-blue with the device of crashing waves, and the old Chieftain ordered his run up above it. In moments, Snolli's ensign floated free, crimson with an attacking sea eagle.

Skillfully, Harvas took advantage of the slight breeze to take the little ship north, far enough from the shore for safety, but still close enough so that, with the use of Snolli's far-see glass, they could note what was to be seen. The stubby little vessel pitched and rolled in the dark waves.

They rounded a promontory. "Huh," his grandfather grunted. "There they are." He passed the glass to Rohan, who gazed through it eagerly.

If it had been a brighter day, he could have observed more, but it was enough.

*

"We counted five great beasts, all in stalls made of stone. The Frydian invaders must have gathered the stones and built them," Rohan told the generals. "I think there was a sixth stall, but it was empty."

Harous raised one eyebrow. "Six Ice Dragons," he said.

"Add to that a host of armsmen," Rohan continued. "They are camped not in good order the way we are, but huddled in clusters here and there. This made it difficult to count, but I think we may be outnumbered roughly three to one."

"Interesting odds," Gaurin commented. "However, the important news is that the Frydians must be planning to take the sea road and make a direct assault on us."

"Of course they are," Snolli said impatiently.

"And how, Rohan, did you manage to find out all this without being spotted from the shore?"

The Admiral-General took this question himself. "It's an old Sea-Rover trick. We sailed on past, innocent as you please, as if we were out on an errand that had nothing to do with the people from the North. And then, when we were out of sight of them, we headed out to sea until we couldn't see the shore and turned back south once again. Harvas used to be a wave-reader until his ship was destroyed, when first we came to Rendel. He can smell his way across the water both coming and going."

"That name is familiar," Harous said. "He was in Rendel-sham briefly, was he not? When the late King Florian was flirting with an alliance between our two peoples?"

"Your spies are competent. Yes, I sent Harvas as surety for the hostage the cata—I mean, King Florian had left with us while we were discussing terms. He was just a Prince then. All came to naught, though. Wasn't until my son Obern married that skinny, pale girl that we could treat with your Queen."

"Ashen," Gaurin said mildly.

"Oh, yes," Snolli said. "You married her later, didn't you."

Rohan wanted to put his elbow in Snolli's ribs or his fist in his mouth if there were room, what with Snolli's large foot occupying it already. He might wreck the whole alliance among the several peoples of Rendel with his rough tongue. Also, there was more important information to relay. He had to speak up, and break into his grandfather's pleasant game.

"We killed one of the Dragons," he said, "and its rider."

Every man in the room, except for Snolli who just sat complacently in his chair, leapt to his feet. Even Tusser was impressed. The air was full of their questions. How, where, what had they used against it—Rohan also had to stand, and gesture for silence.

"Admiral Snolli went back to his own ship. Something told me there was more to be seen. Before Snolli could stop me, I sent *Spume-Maiden* sailing north again. The Dragon was in the air by the time we turned back," he said. "So their suspicions must have been aroused despite our pretense."

"We've seen these things before," Snolli observed judiciously, "though mostly on the ground. They came after us, when Vold was destroyed. That's our old stronghold," he added for the benefit of those who didn't know the Sea-Rovers' story. "But we outran them with a favoring wind, and their being weary from destruction. This time luck was all that saved this young fool."

The generals and their aides sat down again and Rohan took up the terrible, necessary tale once more.

🌹

Snolli, of course, was in hot pursuit but the much slower *Gorgull* couldn't catch up before the battle was over. The Dragon seemed as large as the ship they sailed in, but that could have just been their imaginations. It swooped down for a closer look at them. Even without the far-see glass Rohan could see a man seated just behind the enormous head.

He turned to Dordan, one of the steadiest of the marines. "Archers," he ordered.

"Have our bows warmed, greased, and drawn already," Dordan said, grinning. "A giant crossbow or a catapult would be useful, but we don't have any."

"Stay hidden until it comes close enough."

"Count on me, even as your father did." Dordan gave a signal and the bowmen under his command took what shelter they could find on the deck of the little ship.

When the Dragon came within range, Dordan leapt up with a loud cry. He and his archers took deadly aim, and fired. The Dragon veered off as its rider, startled, tried to dodge the hail of arrows. Some missed, but many more found a mark. The rider clutched at his shoulder but kept his seat.

An arrow had lodged in the beast's eye and it began raking at the injury with its great claws. It tossed its head, and its rider lost his perch. The force with which the caped figure hit the water must have killed him. If he could have held his seat just a few moments longer, he would have lived, at least for a little while, because the Dragon drifted down and settled onto the surface. It spread out its great wings for buoyancy.

"Quick, before it can take flight again!" Rohan shouted.

A boat was already being lowered. He scrambled into it as it cleared the deck.

"Let us keep on putting arrows into the beast, from a distance," Dordan said. "No use in getting too close, too soon."

Rohan gripped the hilt of his Rinbell sword, grateful to have it in his hand. Grandfather had called him hot for battle. That was an understatement. He was feverish for real action, wanted to grapple the creature and subdue it with only his own strength as a weapon, but he recognized the archer's wisdom. He nodded. Dordan gave a signal and another flight of arrows arched over their heads. As before, most found their mark but a few had been aimed at the rider whose body floated nearby.

"These things can be killed," Rohan said. "They are not invincible, as we had thought."

"We haven't bagged this one yet," Dordan warned. "And we brought it down only because its rider wasn't expecting us to attack. I think he just came out to give us a looking-over."

"Well, then, let's finish it off."

By this time, more boats had left the ship, all filled with armed men. They circled the downed Dragon, approaching cautiously; the creature was very dangerous. It lashed out with its wings, threatening to swamp any boat that came too close.

"We've just been scratching at it. Those arrows aren't any more to it than a speck of sand would be to us. If we're to have a chance, we have to blind it completely," Dordan reported. He stood up in the boat, keeping his feet with difficulty as the Dragon's continued flailing created a heavy chop. Nevertheless, his next arrow lodged in the beast's other eye. Its struggles grew more intense. It could not claw the arrows out without losing the buoyancy of its outstretched wings. Immediately the other archers began aiming for the same target and, in spite of the threshing of the creature's long neck, many found their mark.

"Bring us in closer, toward the head," Rohan said.

"Dangerous move, Rohan, but probably necessary," Kather said. He didn't have Dordan's skill with the bow, and hefted a spear instead. An axe, the weapon the Sea-Rovers liked best, hung at his belt. "Those arrows are just annoyances, if I guess right." He hefted his spear. "It'll take a few of these in just the right place—"

Kather launched the spear and found his target. Within

a matter of moments, the Dragon's head bristled with spears and its movements—Rohan hoped—grew feebler.

"We can't throw hard enough to make the spear points go deep," Rohan said. "The skull is too strong. We can't hope to reach the heart, not with its body half under water. That means someone will have to go up close, try for the brain. I mean, I can try for it."

"That is *too* close," Dordan said dubiously.

"I have to try. Take me in."

The men began working the boat as close as they dared, but it was useless. The Dragon was still flailing its head back and forth and there was no hope of Rohan's being able to leap up and catch it, even if he could have been able to avoid the huge mouth filled with sharp, white teeth. Snolli would be furious if he failed, and take credit if he succeeded. Well, so be it.

"The wing," he said. "I'll try for the wing, and then climb up the neck."

"You're mad."

"I'm a *Sea-Rover*," Rohan said, grinning. "If I fail, then tell my grandfather I died well."

Eight

🌿

*T*he Dragon made no extra effort to fling Rohan off into the sea, perhaps because it simply didn't notice his presence. Nevertheless, a spasm of its wing flipped him high into the air and it was only by luck that he was hurled in the direction of the body and not into the water. Rohan grabbed one of the sharp spines that ran down the Dragon's back and, having a handhold at last, pulled himself slowly along these protuberances toward the beast's head. He was careful not to let go of one before he had a secure grasp on the next. Still, it seemed that days must have passed before he reached the saddlelike spot just behind the enormous skull where its late rider had sat. Here there were two depressions on either side that seemed perfectly designed for human legs. He scrambled up and into the natural saddle and gripped the beast's neck with thighs and feet. Then, as if sensing a stranger on its neck, the Dragon began to thrash in earnest in an attempt to fling him off. If Rohan had tried to mount the biggest, meanest, wildest horse in all of Rendel, he would not have had as rough a ride as the Ice Dragon was giving him now.

He had to trust in the strength of his thigh muscles to keep from joining the Dragon's late rider, who was floating out past the spot where this desperate battle was going on. Out of the corner of his eye, Rohan spotted one of the boats, making for the body. But he didn't have time to think about it.

He drew the Rinbell sword and held it high, point down, waiting for the right moment to strike. There had to be a vulnerable point somewhere, and Rohan was betting his life that it was very close to the natural saddle.

"They say Rinbell blades, if they choose, fight for those who wield them," he cried out, his words lost in the din of battle. "Let it be so!"

Closing his eyes, he struck. The blade hit solid bone and Rohan knew that he had failed, and would forfeit his life. "Anamara—"

Then, as if of its own volition, the point of the sword slid past the bone and went in, up to the hilt. Rohan moved it back and forth, trying to do the maximum damage. He felt something give deep in the Dragon's skull and it spasmed violently. All its limbs flailed out once more, and then its head drooped and it went limp.

"Here, Rohan. Jump for the boat. We'll catch you."

Rohan looked up. Dordan waited in the little vessel. He had brought it in perilously close. His men had hard work to keep the craft steady while lending what aid they could. The waters were still violently agitated from the Dragon's struggles.

"In a moment." Rohan set his foot on the back of the Dragon's skull and pulled. At first the sword refused to budge and his heart sank. Then the blade came out, reluctantly. It would have to be cleaned with care, he thought, lest the Dragon's ichor damage it. For the moment, he returned it to its sheath for safekeeping.

Suddenly weary in every bone, he summoned a last bit of strength and jumped. At that moment the boat was tossed and he missed, landing heavily in the icy cold water. The men hauled him out before he could sink and drown.

A few thick, heavy flakes of snow were just beginning to fall.

🌿

"What a tale!" Cebastian said. "Comrade, I almost envy you your adventure!" Around him, the other young nobles nodded their agreement.

Rohan shrugged. "There'll be fighting enough for all of you on land, and perhaps even harder than my skirmish. We were lucky because we took the rider unprepared for us."

"I've heard they are monsters who ride the Dragons," Chevin said.

"This one looked rough and cruel, to be sure," Rohan said, "but he also looked human enough. At least on the outside. We were lucky with him but it will not be thus with the others. They will be ever on their guard from today. Anyway, we sailed on south, as my grandfather said, to Bilth harbor. I changed into dry clothes, and we came here at once."

He did not mention the tongue-lashing Snolli had given him. Then he remembered something.

He took a hollow rod about half the length of a man's forearm out of his sleeve. It was the color of silver, or perhaps of steel. There was a thong handle at one end but otherwise the rod was unremarkable, perfectly plain except for a protuberance on one side. "When the men retrieved the Dragon rider's body they found this."

"Be careful!" Snolli shouted. "You didn't tell me you were dragging that thing with us. It is a terrible weapon!"

Rohan examined the rod curiously, peering into it. "Really? It seems empty to me—"

"You fool. Do you see the stud, just where your forefinger could reach if you had the thong over your wrist, holding the thing? That makes a mist shoot out of the rod. It'll burn the lungs out of anyone unlucky enough to be in the way."

Rohan put the rod down hastily. "I'm sorry, I—"

"You didn't know," Snolli said sarcastically. "There's a lot you don't know."

"Let me put it away for now," Harous said. "It is good to have one of the enemies' great weapons, so that we can study it."

"Nothing to study," Snolli said. Nevertheless, he passed it down the table, where each man who had to handle the thing did so gingerly, and with great caution.

"Let us hope that we can have half your success with the Dragons," Harous said soberly. He unlocked a chest and put the deadly rod into it with a clink of metal. All the assembled began to breathe easier.

"Now," the Lord High Marshal continued, "let us consider two facts I have been pondering while Rohan related his terrible story. One, the enemy's camp is on the sea road."

"Yes," Rohan said. "There is a gap between the mountains, where there is a small plain, much like the one our camp occupies."

Harous nodded acknowledgment. "Two, it is very possible that they are not even aware of the narrow pass that, according to the map, would lead us to a spot almost behind them. Surely to their flank."

There was a silence. Then Gaurin spoke. "You are proposing a surprise attack."

"I am. We will split our forces. A small number will go along the sea road, exposing themselves to the most danger—"

"My marines," Rohan said.

Harous nodded. "The assignment is yours. The main body of our forces will make our way through the pass and fall upon them while Rohan has them occupied. The fighting will be fierce, I promise you, but if we have luck on our side, it will all be over with one great battle."

"Tusser like fight," the Bog general said. "We go with Rohan."

"No," Harous said. "I want you to follow the Rendel troops. You will be our reinforcements, if they should be needed."

Tusser started to protest, but Rohan laid a hand on his arm. "Do as he says," he urged quietly. "Harous is a good general and he knows—" Rohan started to say "human" but stopped in time. "He knows this kind of fighting, under these conditions."

"Snow," Tusser said. He thought for a moment, scowling. "Rohan is right. I do."

"Thank you."

"It is a good plan," Gaurin said thoughtfully, "but aren't you risking all on a single line of attack?"

"I am," Harous returned. "But great danger warrants great risks. Can you think of a better course?"

"I think we should learn more, if we can, about what faces us before we commit ourselves to a battle against the kind of odds Rohan spoke of. And I think we should have an alternate plan, perhaps two, in case our original goes awry."

"We will send out scouts," Harous promised. He went to the flap of the tent and peered out. A bolt of lightning flashed and thunder reverberated through the mountains. Snow blew through the opening, and the sentries posted outside were already covered with it. "Go and get warm," he told them. "Nobody is going to stir while this storm is going on." Gratefully, they saluted and left.

"I suggest that we all find our quarters now, for evening is drawing on. Think of your best men for the unpleasant but important assignment of spying out the enemy. Tomorrow, we will send out the first ones."

Harous could hardly get the generals and their staffs out of the command tent fast enough. His head throbbed and had done so ever since Rohan had told of the killing of a Dragon rider. *It could easily have been Flavielle!* His heart had nearly stopped, and he breathed again only when Rohan had been quite specific that the one they encountered had been male.

One of the soldiers assigned to him brought him his supper, and he ate without tasting. He left the tray; someone would pick it up in the morning. Candles placed here and there in the main area of the tent had lighted the recent deliberations. He pinched out all but one and carried it into his private quarters.

Flavielle waited for him there.

He almost dropped the candle but caught it in time. "How did you get here?" he said.

"I told you. I have powers that others only dream of."

"Are you real? Or am I dreaming you?"

She took the candle from him and put it on the table beside his camp bed. "Find out for yourself," she said. Then she came into his arms. The scent of her perfume enveloped him. Her thin, filmy garment fluttered to the floor.

Later, she propped herself up on one elbow and brushed the hair back from his eyes. "We saw a ship," she said, "and sent out a Dragon. It did not come back."

He told her of Rohan's adventure. Her eyes darkened. "That must have happened while I was occupied with other matters. If I had been there, Shrang would still be alive, and Rohan would be dead." She lay down beside him once more, resting her head on his shoulder. The narrowness of the bed encouraged closeness. "I know this Rohan," she said, an unmistakable edge to her voice. "He is a meddlesome, stupid boy."

"He is the one to whom you offered Power once, isn't he?"

"Yes. Forget him. He does not concern us. Now, tell me of what you and your generals talked about later."

He related the plan for the flanking attack. She listened intently.

"It is a splendid opportunity to turn the ambush against them," she said.

"That's what I was thinking, only I didn't know how I was going to find you to tell you about it."

She smiled then. "You should have trusted me more. Anyway, there will be no battle, no ambush, until the snow stops. And that will last for at least three days. I shall be here with you whenever you want me, during that time."

"I want you."

"But I must go, before you begin your march. There is much to do. Remember, the men must go beneath the frozen river I showed you. I will drop the ice upon them."

"I know. But how shall I escape it?"

"I will wait until you are safely past. And I will shield you when my troops fall upon what is left of your men. You are mine, now, and I will look after you."

"And later, when you have won and Rendel lies open to you?"

"Ah, later. Later I will bestow wonders upon you such as you cannot even begin to imagine."

Harous could not imagine why or how he had ever found the pale, anemic Ashen attractive, or even the warmer-blooded Marcala. Both receded far, far into his distant memory, not to be thought of again except with contempt. Here in his arms was his mate, his counterpart, his equal—the one for whom he had been created. The woman in whose delicate hands he had placed his life and his future.

"You are wonder enough, all by yourself," he told her.

She kissed him.

❧

Ashen twisted the iridescent bracelet tighter on her arm. All her other adornments she had left behind, when she started on this journey except for the Ash badge. She packed the badge away, for proof if necessary. The bracelet she insisted on wearing. It had once been an artifact of Gaurin's house. She had discovered it by accident, in the ruined city of Galinth deep in the heart of the Bog, on the arm of the skeleton of a murdered man. He had been Gaurin's father, though neither of them knew of those terrible circumstances when, instead of claiming the bracelet, he had given it to her, on the occasion of their first meeting.

"Let this be a pledge between us," he had told her. "If ever you are in need of anything, put this on, think of me, and I will know, and whatever separates us, even if it is half the world or I face an entire army alone, I will overcome all barriers to be at your side."

Ashen dared not issue such a silent plea now, for she knew he would heed it. Nevertheless, because the bracelet made her feel closer to him, she wore it.

"I think we should make an early stop for the night," Lord Royance said. "The sky is darker than the day suggests, and so I believe there will be snow."

"Can we keep going?" Ashen asked anxiously.

"We may have to wait out a storm, but then we will be back on the way as swiftly as possible."

Already Royance's men were hacking boughs from trees and beginning to construct double lean-tos from them. Interested, she observed how they were made. The flooring was thick and springy and the sloping sides nearly met at the top. They finished hers first, and established her in it. There was plenty of room both for her and her few belongings, and a good quantity of the supplies they had brought with them. Calling on the trail-craft she had learned as a child, she kindled a little fire where the smoke could escape easily through the roof of her makeshift dwelling. The interior warmed quickly. The boughs were fresh and green—she inhaled their fragrance with pleasure. They would not burn but she ringed the fire with stones anyway, as a precaution.

A few flakes of snow managed to make their way through the opening at the top of her shelter, to fall sizzling into the fire, but where she now lay on a bed of boughs covered with a fur robe, she was snug and warm. She wondered if Gaurin knew the secret of constructing such a convenient thing, and then decided that as a Nordor he did.

They were two days in their temporary camp, and Ashen fretted at the delay.

"We were caught just on the edges of the snowfall," Royance assured her. "It was much worse farther north as you know from the echoes of thunder. But that is a boon," he said before she could cry out in dismay. "With such a storm to contend with, nobody on either side could venture out. Never fear, dear Ashen, I predict that we will arrive in plenty of time before the real hostilities begin."

And you hope to be in the midst of those, she thought, but kept it to herself.

Royance's chief steward, Jervin, had charge of the camp. He was a taciturn man, almost as old as his master and even leaner. Like Royance, he had refused to be left behind though his presence meant that there were only five soldiers to guard them and not the six that Royance had ordered. "I will take care of you," Jervin said. And no argument could budge him.

The morning of the third day dawned bright and clear, and both Jervin and Royance judged that it was safe to take up their journey.

Ashen had never seen working dogs pulling sleds before. Contrary to what she imagined, they did not have to be forced to their task. Rather, they seemed to be laughing, with open mouths and lolling tongues as they leaped eagerly into their harness, ready to go. Indeed, they had to be restrained lest they run away before the men could put the dogs' coats and mittens on, dragging the empty sleds behind them. Once the conveyances were loaded, Ashen rode on the one where the food and other supplies had been arranged to allow her to be as comfortable as possible. Most of the time Royance stood just behind her, guiding the sled by putting out his foot from time to time and nudging it in one direction or the other. Jervin had charge of the other, and the rest of the men took turns riding or trotting behind. Now and then, they halted to rest the dogs, who didn't seem to need it, and to let the guards catch up. To Ashen's relief—and she had to admit, her hidden amusement—Jervin bullied his master into riding now and then on the other sled, taking his turn resting like the others. None of the men would allow him to run along behind though he insisted that he was fully able, despite his years.

"It is not seemly," Jervin said, and that was that.

If they had not been on a serious errand, Ashen would have greatly enjoyed the adventure, particularly the spectacle of the dignified Head of the Council of Rendel reliving his youth. She settled for taking each moment as it came.

Sooner than she had dared hope, the stockade fence surrounding the camp came into view. "Oh, faster, faster!" she cried to Royance. "We must get there *now*!"

"In good time," the old nobleman said, but he whistled to the dogs and they redoubled their efforts.

As they approached the gate of the stockade, however, Ashen sensed at once that something was badly amiss inside. The place was too quiet. Perhaps the enemy had fallen upon them, killed them all—

"Oh, no," she whispered. She put the back of her hand to her mouth. The gesture reminded her of the bracelet and she pressed her lips against it. "Gaurin, Gaurin," she murmured. "If you are still—"

She couldn't finish the thought.

Then, as if by a miracle, he was there, coming through the gate. She threw back the fur robe and scrambled free of the sled, slipping and sliding in the snow as she ran to him. He hurried to her no less quickly and caught her in his arms just as she fell.

"You live, you live," she said brokenly, her face buried in his shoulder.

"Yes, my Ashen. I am unharmed." He kissed her hair where her hood had fallen back on her shoulders. "My Lord Royance. What brings you and my wife to this dangerous place? I thought you remained safe in Rendelsham, with the King."

"Ashen has news you must hear. And she would not be stopped from coming to tell you herself, so I escorted her."

Ashen pulled herself free enough so that she could look up at him. "You must be careful," she said tensely, her words pitched so that only he could hear. "I fear there is a traitor in your midst."

His eyebrows drew together and a single deep line etched itself between them. "A traitor."

"Yes. Please, if you have not yet fought, do not go out against them, not until the traitor has been uncovered."

"We still need to prove the charges," Royance cautioned.

"I need no further proof than what I have already. Oh, Gaurin, please. Do not face the enemy, not yet."

"You are too late, my Ashen. The battle was yesterday. We gave good account of ourselves and it is too soon yet to tell, but I fear that we have lost."

Nine

"*An excellent day for* a battle." Harous's breath puffed white as he surveyed the assembled troops. The worst of the blizzard had eased during the night, the thunder and lightning ceased, and now the sun shone bright and clear, sparkling on the scattered flakes of snow that continued to fall.

"I am ready to start up the sea-road," Rohan announced. Behind him, his Sea-Rovers grinned behind their shields and each took fresh grip on axe and sword. All had wrapped the hilts and handles of their weapons with rawhide, for a better grip. One man, a little ahead of the rest, held Rohan's battle ensign. Without a stiff breeze to make it flutter bravely, it hung limp.

"At my command," Harous reminded him. "You must give the rest of us time enough to beat through any deep snow in the mountain pass. Then you will engage the enemy long enough for us to fall upon them unexpectedly from the flank."

"Count on me, sir." Rohan put his hand on Keltin's head and the war-kat began a noisy purr. On his other side, Bitta nudged up to be noticed as well.

Harous turned to Gaurin. "I have searched out the mountain pass," he said, "and I will lead our forces the best way to go."

Gaurin raised his eyebrows slightly. He had not personally explored this part of the area as Harous claimed to have done, but he knew mountains. Harous, however, was the ranking officer and Gaurin could tell that the marshal, for all his length of experience in arms, could scarcely hold himself back, driven by his eagerness to engage the enemy.

Leaving behind the noncombatants—the cooks, the physicians, the laundresses and a few other women who had trailed along behind their men—the Four Armies of Rendel marched out, each under its own flag. Someone had put together a guidon of sorts for the Bog-men, brownish-green with a device of a lupper daubed on it, and one of the warriors carried it proudly. Though they had come with wardrums, as had the other armies, these had been left behind on the generals' express orders. Stealth was the order for the day.

The vanguard, composed of the generals and officers, expected to take the brunt of the attack. Eight war-kats deigned to accompany them and paced alongside with enormous dignity—Gaurin's two, Rajesh and Finola, and those in the charge of Hynnel, Cebastian, and Steuart. Just behind the vanguard came the Nordor armsmen, and behind them, the Rendelians.

Tusser, of all the officers, had been assigned to go with his men, at Harous's express command. They straggled along behind the Rendelians, lacking any sort of military order.

Harous himself proceeded to outdistance the vanguard. Too far ahead, Gaurin thought.

Snow and wind make a capricious combination, particularly in mountain country. By a stroke of good fortune, the howling gale had been funneled into the narrow valley and had swept away most of the new snow through which they must make their way; consequently, the advance on ground level was much easier than it might have been. Rocks and other obstacles were clearly discernable under their fresh white blanket, and so were easy to avoid. Above, on top of the mountains, the winds had not been so fierce, allowing snowfall to accumulate to steep and dangerous depths. Gaurin kept a wary eye on that possible peril. He recognized this as avalanche country. If it had not been for the prospect of taking the enemy by surprise, he would have protested this present plan of attack even more vigorously than he had already done.

"We lose nothing by waiting a day or two, and have much to gain by sending out scouts to learn just what may face us," he had urged repeatedly in the counsel tent. "Particularly since the storm has struck so heavily. Otherwise we march into a situation where we are as blind men."

"Perhaps. But I for one cannot sit idle in camp in this fashion," Harous retorted. Around him most of the officers nodded agreement.

He had the young nobles thoroughly in his hand, Gaurin noted. Rash, foolhardy, inexperienced in anything other than set-piece battles, they were fairly itching to get into the fight. Well, he thought, many of them would get their first scars today and thereby learn a more mature caution.

The advance along the valley floor presented so few obstacles that the soldiers moved four abreast, thereby making much better time than if they had had to keep single file. At the muster of troops, each company commander had impressed on them the need for quiet. Nevertheless, they still made more noise than Gaurin could accept. He was constantly wary of the heavy snow piled overhead. He motioned to Cebastian, who was also glancing upward with a worried look.

"Drop back and tell the men they must be as quiet as possible," he ordered in a low tone. "No talking, no jangle of weapons."

"I know, sir. I will see to it."

With Cebastian to remind them, the noise level among the armsmen dropped appreciably, though still not as much as Gaurin wished.

Every stride took the corps deeper into the mountain pass. As they rounded a spur of rock and entered well into the valley, Gaurin noted a second road dug into the mountain flank to his left. Then, to the right, he glimpsed a flash of something high above, almost at the peak of the heights. Stopping short, he shielded his eyes with his hand. A momentary increase in the snowfall curtained the uppermost slopes. Rajesh and Finola had flanked him and now paused beside him. Above, springy, fragrant evergreen trees covered much of the mountainside except where a clean-scrubbed swath marked a path of one of the frequent avalanches. In a notch in line with this spot, the brightness of the morning, combined with the blue glitter of the snow—

Not snow! Ice!

Gaurin held up his hand, gesturing a halt to those behind him while he strove to find an answer. Rajesh lifted his lips in a silent snarl and Finola growled deep in her throat. The men in the front ranks, still obediently silent under Cebastian's insistence, clustered at the head of the valley, effectively blocking entry for those behind them.

Gaurin had seen situations such as this before. As with all ice rivers, whether atop a mountain or crawling on the ground, this one lay in a small rift it had carved between two higher peaks. These heights, he recognized to his dismay, were thick with new fallen snow. If the crust of old snow had melted, even a little, it would then certainly have refrozen during the last few days into a surface of pure ice. This promised marked danger. The slightest mischance would send the new snow plummeting down the mountainside in the chute where such disasters had obviously occurred many times before. If that happened now, and they were in the way, they would all be destroyed at once. Fortunately, it was easy, especially for a Nordor, to predict the limits of where the avalanche could be expected to fall.

Harous, unknowing that Gaurin had halted the advance, was still forging ahead. Gaurin risked the noise he would make, running to catch up, as the war-kats bounded soundlessly beside him.

"Look up there," he said softly. "We must turn back."

Harous surveyed the danger area Gaurin pointed out. "Yes, I see," he said. To Gaurin's dismay, he spoke in a normal tone that carried in the still air. "But I do not agree to any retreat. Rather, the order will be to advance so that we will win through before the snow or the ice gives way." He raised his arm to give a forward signal.

"Retreat, *now!*" Gaurin countered. "Believe me, I know this country! We proceed to great danger."

Harous shook his head. Then suddenly both men realized that the time for argument had run out. An Ice Dragon poked its head over the edge of the frozen river. Its rider was well established to see all happening below. A second Dragon appeared higher up on the slope, on the other side. The translucent blue and white ice began to crack and shift, and the booming sound echoed off the opposite canyon walls. Both war-kats went tense and lifted their lips to snarl aloud.

Harous simply stood, staring, perhaps in shock. Gaurin grabbed the High Marshal's arm and with sheer bodily force strove to drag him back the way they had come. Then, at the far end of the valley they had entered, Gaurin saw oncoming enemy soldiers along the narrow road cut high along the mountainside directly opposite the ice river. He knew the worst at once. The path of advance by the Four Armies had been turned into an ambush to trap them.

"Cebastian!" he shouted. "Now!"

Cebastian, knowing what to do, immediately set up a clamor, setting sword against shield and making as much noise as he could. Those men gathered at the head of the valley began to follow his example. However, many behind them, unable to assess the situation and confused by what seemed to be conflicting orders, hesitated.

A huge crystal of ice leaned out and broke off the lip of the frozen river. With deceptive slowness it dropped, bouncing off the slopes, shattering as it fell. The Dragon stationed high up on the mountain spread its wings and lifted into the air.

At that Rendelian soldiers found their voices. Their shouts and the din they made clashing weapons against shields filled the valley to drown out the sound of the fracturing ice above them. Even the war-kats sent up a howl. The heavy snow trembled, and with a kind of terrible inevitability, began to slip from the heights. Eerily, its descent at first was not a roar, but rather a whisper. The Ice Dragon that had been perched on the river attempted to take flight, too late. Finding its voice at last, the bellowing snow slide overwhelmed it. As the men below watched in awe, the awesome force of falling tons of heavy snow tumbled the huge beast as easily as if it had been a child's toy. In a matter of moments, its limp and broken body was completely buried. The avalanche poured into the valley floor, effectively blocking all passage save retreat along the way the armies had come. The high path carved into the opposite mountainside now swarmed with Frydian warriors.

Some of the destruction would have caught the vanguard had Gaurin not forced them back. The enemy soldiers, safe enough on their narrow road, sped to the attack. In the sky, four Dragons were a-wing. It could only be a moment, Gaurin knew, until those would alight on the mass of fallen snow, even before it had time to settle.

❦

Rohan, at the head of his troop, watched until the Rendelian soldiers were well on the march, the Army of the Bog-men trailing after. As best he could judge, the moment had come for him to take the sea-road, there to engage the enemy and keep them occupied until Harous arrived to fall on their flank and destroy them. With one such master stroke could the war be won. The leader might remain, but he would be helpless with no one to command.

They had easy going—a far easier route, Rohan suspected, than the floor of the valley pass. Therefore, he did not push the men, but rather tried to gauge as best he could what progress the others were making. If he attacked too soon, he ran the risk of losing too many of his men to superior numbers. If he attacked too late, the element of surprise would be gone and he would be left on the Frydians' flank, with too few men.

He could, he realized with calm fatalism, only do what he could, and hope for the best. The back of his neck tingled unnaturally, as always when he faced danger. He touched the little spray of herbs and grasses Granddam Zaz had given him, for luck.

When, according to the lay of the land as he remembered having seen it from the deck of *Spume-Maiden*, he estimated they were almost within sight of the Frydian camp, Rohan indicated a halt. His war-kats, almost invisible against the snow, crouched nearly within touch.

"Close ranks," he ordered. Dordan and Kather, each in charge of a squad of marines, grinned.

"We know what to do," Iaobim retorted irritably. He was another of the seasoned veterans who had once served with Obern, and who now served with Obern's son.

Rohan did not allow himself to take offense. "That you stand here now," he said agreeably, "proves it." He gave them what he hoped was a disarming grin. It would not do to have the Sea-Rovers begin to hold him, a newly armed youngling, in contempt, and they were all fully independent enough to do so. If they believed him arrogant, they would unceremoniously strip him of his rank and choose another leader, regardless of what the other commanders of the Four Armies might think or of his kinship with Snolli. In fact, he thought glumly, Snolli would approve of such removal and be not in the least sympathetic toward his grandson for what Snolli would consider stupidity. "Put it down to a case of nerves on my part."

"You'll get over that soon enough once the fighting starts," Kather said. He hefted his axe, his lips lifted in a crooked and somewhat cruel, anticipatory smile. He eschewed the protection of the fingerless gloves some of the others wore. His hand must have been cold, but his grip was firm.

"No time like the present to start," said Iaobim gruffly. "Give the signal."

"We'll reach the outskirts of their camp and take on whoever we find, and then charge for the center, making as much noise as we can." Rohan drew his sword and likewise decided to do without his glove. In a moment, he was bound to be quite warm enough. "Let's go," he said.

Only one Ice Dragon of the four settled onto the mass of snow that had fallen from the crest of the mountain. The footing was still unstable, but the Dragon's bulk crushed and made firm any shifting of the surface beneath it. The creature raised its great wings. Snow fell from under them. Then it opened its mouth, uttering a sound like a raging storm. More snow and ice belched forth from that awesome cavity in a great gout.

That, Gaurin thought, was only one of the perils they faced that day. With no large weapons, no catapults—at Harous's orders, he realized—they were at the Dragons' mercy. They would just have to take what came, and do the best they could. Suddenly, an idea, engendered by Rohan's report, produced another possibility for killing these creatures besides hurling stones at them. A spear, perhaps an arrow— The battle loomed and he forgot the ghost of the idea in the urgency closing in on them.

Rajesh and Finola, looking very small against the Dragon's bulk, bounded forward before Gaurin could stop them. Though the huge creature could have crushed them with one clawed foot, still they did not hesitate to attack.

One—Gaurin could no longer tell which at this distance—crouched fearlessly in front of the Dragon, making itself a temptation. The beast's great tail switched whiplike as the reptile screeched. The war-kats' tails lashed likewise, as they snarled their defiance. Dragon and rider's attention centered on the war-kat facing it. The other circled around beyond range of the Dragon's tail and launched itself in a prodigious leap. Claws and teeth cut at the Dragon's side, where it could not reach. The Dragon flailed in frustrated fury, and the shrill cries it uttered were not borne on a spray of ice. Now that it centered attention on one, the other war-kats attacked in the same fashion, sinking claws and fangs everywhere they could reach Dragon flesh. The beast went screaming mad, thrashing about and unable to dislodge its tormenters.

"Now!" Gaurin shouted. Behind him, his standard bearer

waved his flag and his Nordors rushed forward, swords and spears at the ready. Lathrom matched the others stride for stride.

Facing such an onslaught, the Dragon faltered and stepped back. Perhaps, as with the one Rohan had slain, it was not used to determined opposition. Nevertheless, it fought on, far from being vanquished. Its mighty limbs flashed up, and men began to fall. The rider pointed a slender metal rod that erupted bluish mist from one end. Where the mist enveloped the attackers, more men went down, coughing as if to tear their lungs open. And yet they pressed forward.

A brave armsman, close to strangling from the effects of the poisonous mist, ducked between and under the Dragon's forelegs. There, it might be possible to find a vulnerable spot.

The rider shouted a command, and the Dragon shook itself. The great wings stretched to their fullest height and it began to lift from where it had alighted. Men scattered. The war-kats leaped to safety and came bounding down the hillock of snow, their tails battle-fluffed. Once they were out of range of the creature's claws and icy breath, they stopped, crouching, and all joined in a yowl of defiance that echoed from the snowy slopes on either side.

While the Nordors and Rendelians had been engaged with the Dragon, enemy soldiers had made great advance along the pathway cut into the side of the opposite mountain.

"Go and see to the injured," Gaurin said to Cebastian. He turned to Hynnel. "It is plain that we have been ambushed. Now I fear for Rohan."

Hynnel's hand tightened on the hilt of his sword. "It is

possible to go around the Frydians on the mountain path. I've been in this valley before but from the north. Now I have my bearings. The Frydians are on a newly made road. However, there is an older one, higher on the slope. If we can gain that one, and if fortune favors us, we can reach Rohan's detachment."

"I will keep them engaged so they do not deter you. May fortune indeed be with you, cousin."

"And with you as well."

They clasped hands. Then, with nearly half of the Nordors behind him, Hynnel raced toward the left face of the valley, war-kats bounding ahead of him. In moments, Gaurin could see some of the Frydian soldiers at the head of the column hurrying to clamber upward, obviously aiming at Hynnel's detachment. Most, however, did not understand and kept to their path. Once past those at the forefront, Gaurin knew that Hynnel had a good chance. It all depended on whether his own remaining command could keep this first wave of invaders busy enough so that Hynnel could get through.

"Attack!" Gaurin shouted the order, heading toward the spot where the press of battle would be greatest, only to have Lathrom catch his arm.

"You are needed elsewhere," Lathrom said. "Please, sir, go back and arouse Harous. Something seems to be the matter with him. He seems dazed. In any case, the Nordors can't hold these Frydians forever, by themselves, and the Rendelians are in disarray. Grant me the boon of leading our men, until you can return with a larger force."

Gaurin gazed at him intently for an instant before nodding assent. "In the Oakenkeep you are my second in command," he said. "Let the lead be yours here and now."

"Depend on me," Lathrom said. Uttering his own deep, booming war-cry, he broke into a run, followed by his personal detachment of men close on his heels. Gaurin waved Rajesh and Finola after him.

In moments Lathrom's men had engaged the invaders, now defenders, in battle. Hynnel and his company were able to fight their way through scant opposition, so gaining the high road. The war-kats, on the hunt, snarled full-throated challenges into the cold air. Here and there, above the din created by the clash of weapons, an enemy armsmen screamed, to be suddenly stilled.

Despite the chill, Gaurin wiped sweat from his forehead as he considered Lathrom's comment about Harous's strange action—or rather, lack of it. With long strides, he hurried toward the High Marshal, meeting Harous's lieutenant, Chevin, bound in his direction. Gaurin paused to give Chevin terse orders. The younger man sprang to action, rounding up a handful of men and heading down the road to join Lathrom and the Nordors, already in the thick of the fight. Then Gaurin made his way toward Harous only to discover that instead of marking the battle order with the attention such a tense situation required, the Lord High Marshal and Tusser were in the midst of a dispute.

"Dragon flying," Tusser said, obviously not for the first time. "Not hurt bad. Goes toward Bog. I go, too."

"You'll stay here, to provide reserve support, as I commanded."

"Reserve support now must come from the Army of Rendel, which so far has seen little fighting," Gaurin interrupted. He kept sharpness out of his tone only by an effort. "You might notice that over half of my Nordors are currently holding the pass against the invaders. The other half of my army is going to Rohan's relief."

Harous blinked. "Then we must send men to help. Where is Chevin?"

"I met Chevin on my way here, and he is already taking care of it." Gaurin let the rest of his thought—*no thanks to you*—hang unspoken between them.

The High Marshal shrugged. "We seem to have the matter well in hand, then."

Gaurin had to bite back his words before he said something that would have called for blood between the two of them. This matter was far from well in hand, he thought, and it seems you have done little enough about it. Two Ice Dragons had been destroyed and one slightly wounded, but three more remained ready to attack at any moment. Rendelian and Nordor wounded—and some dead—were being carried off the field even now, from the skirmish. The Dragon that had brought them down was already dwindling to a mere speck in the sky, winging its way southward. Soon, Gaurin knew, it would drop to earth and walk. At that point, perhaps it could be outflanked and overtaken.

Lathrom's report had been accurate. Harous did not look well. Two spots of color high in his cheeks made him appear feverish.

"Why," Gaurin asked carefully, "do you think the Dragon is not headed toward the Bog?"

"It is flying in that direction only to throw us off," Harous said with more than a trace of scorn. "It must be going back to some other encampment unknown to us, to have its scratches healed."

"Yet it did not waver or veer in flight," Gaurin pointed out. "Its path lies straight south. Therefore, I believe that General Tusser is correct. Its hurts may be minor, but its rider knows that it cannot hold its own in another fight such as we just had. So, instead, the rider picks what he thinks is the weakest target in the land they seek to conquer, and that is the Bog."

"I go," Tusser said. "Defend Bog."

"No," Harous repeated flatly. "You will stay here."

By this time several of the young officers, some bleeding from wounds, paused nearby, certainly overhearing their commanders' argument in the midst of a fierce, pitched battle. Such a scene was hard to overlook.

"Tusser has as much right to defend his own homeland from those who would conquer it as any of the rest of us," Gaurin pointed out. "If I thought the Dragon were threatening Rendelsham or the Oakenkeep, and it were in my power, I would make sure that this pass and the coast road were defended properly and then go to their relief, orders or no."

Several of the young officers were nodding agreement, a fact that Gaurin could tell was not lost on Harous. He expected an answering outburst from the High Marshal. Instead, he looked away, feigning a strange and uncharacteristic indifference.

"Tusser go *now*," the Bog general said, "kill Dragon. Then Tusser come back—with army."

Gaurin waited in vain for an answer from Harous. "I will take that as a pledge of honor," he said.

Then Tusser did something that, as far as Gaurin knew, was unprecedented. He held out his horny hand for Gaurin to clasp. Gaurin took it. "Yes," the Bog-man replied sternly. "Pledge of honor."

Then he turned and, at the head of his war party, set off at a steady, distance-eating trot back toward the road they had come up just a few days before.

Harous watched him go, a pinched expression around his mouth. "Good riddance," he said, almost spitting the words. "I never expected anything from him and that ridiculous 'army' of his. I don't know what fool had that notion, to drag the Bog-men along. One can never trust those mud dwellers."

"The fool who 'dragged them along,' as you put it, was my kinsman, Rohan," Gaurin said. This time he didn't even try to keep the anger and exasperation out of his voice. "And I do not propose to leave him to die by Frydian hands this day!"

Paying no more attention to the High Marshal of Rendel, he rallied a hundred Rendelian soldiers. Uttering a shout that relieved at least some of his frustration, Gaurin threw them into the struggle at the snow mound. There the battle had widened as it spilled over from the road itself. Even though it was not the best footing for a battle, still it gave the Four Armies—two, actually, since Rohan's men were still presumably fighting on the other side of the mountain pass, and the Army of the Bog had departed—more room in which to maneuver.

Then Gaurin turned to those remaining. "We came too close to being trapped here. Somehow, our plans became known to the enemy. The Sea-Rovers must be in terrible straits, waiting for our successful attack on the enemy's flank, an attack never to come now. We must go to their aid. Who is with me?"

Ten

In the Frydian camp, the northerners were waiting for the Sea-Rovers. All their plans at naught, the marines found themselves in a desperate situation as Frydians enveloped them from three sides. The Sea-Rovers, almost as one, uttered fierce battle cries joined by war-kat screams. Then they took a stand, sometimes with a battle comrade if possible, alone when they had to, and steadied themselves to meet the first wave of attack.

Rohan had no time to marshal his thoughts before he found he was defending himself against two of the stocky, flat-faced invaders. He slapped aside a spear-thrust with the flat of his blade, and in almost the same motion drove it through the body of his second opponent. When he swung around to cut down the remaining foe, he found two more again facing him. He had no idea where Keltin or Bitta could be, though he could hear their snarls and screams echoing in the distance. He judged that they had slipped to the rear, to cut down any laggards.

Gripped by the rhythm of battle, he somehow found his thoughts clearing. This is not right, he said to himself. We were stealthy enough, our scouts out. How had the Frydians known, been so organized? The Sea-Rovers should have taken them by surprise. Also, once the first staggering shock was past and his men had begun to settle down into the discipline of fighting, he could see there were not as many of the enemy in the camp as there should have been.

Therefore, not only were the northern invaders waiting for the Sea-Rovers, but they also must have sent a larger portion of their forces against the army toiling its way through the mountain pass.

With his heart in his throat and the back of his neck tingling fiercely Rohan realized that those in the mountain pass had marched straight into an ambush, even as had the Sea-Rovers.

"Pull back!" he cried, and heard his order repeated by those who heard it over the din. "Find a defensible spot!" They would stand fast as was their nature, selling each life as dearly as possible.

The marines were quick to obey. They knew what they now faced. All were more seasoned than he. Though they preferred to be on the attack, they practiced also the discipline of defense. Someone had firmly planted Rohan's battle flag and the Sea-Rovers rallied to it. Here the battle swirled, weapons clashing in a clamor full of danger and death.

Incongruously, as if he had stepped out of time, Rohan remembered a long ago day in the Great Fane of Rendel, a conversation with the good priest Esander, and a book. Most of all he remembered the words, which he had sworn would be his guide as the way he would live his life. They sang in his head in rhythm to his sword strokes.

Though caution and common sense are certainly important, sometimes a risk is called for.

If you laugh, you risk appearing a fool.

If you weep, you risk appearing sentimental.

Reaching out for another is risking involvement.

Exposing feelings is risking revealing your true self.

Placing your ideas, your dreams, before a crowd is risking rejection.

Loving is risking not being loved in return.

Living itself carries with it the risk of dying.

Hoping is risking disappointment.

Trying is risking failure.

Nevertheless, risks must be taken, because the greatest hazard, pitfall, and danger in life is to risk nothing. If a person risks nothing, does nothing, has nothing, that person becomes nothing. He may avoid present suffering and sorrow, but he will not learn, feel, change, grow, love, or live. Chained by his fear, he is a slave who has forfeited his freedom.

Only that person who dares, who risks, is free.

Today Rohan was indeed daring to the utmost degree, accepting the ultimate risk. He believed with cold certainty that he and his friends and kinsmen could, perhaps *would* die where they stood. He hoped that those left on the ships, his grandfather in particular, would come to know that they died well.

Because he must, he hoped that Anamara would not grieve overlong.

Gaurin led the detachment of Rendelian soldiers at a double-time trot back through the mountain pass, up the coast road. This was not the sort of rushed pace war-kats liked, so he left them behind. Rohan had his two. That was good, though more would have been useful in the battle he knew must lie ahead. To their credit, the men did not seem inclined to want much rest but instead were eager to go to the aid of the brave marines on whom such a large portion of the fighting was now falling.

Pushing the men as hard as he dared, Gaurin kept them moving. He could well guess what the Sea-Rovers must face. Frydians were fierce fighters, never more so than when they felt they had the advantage.

The Rendelians were panting by the time the sounds of battle began to reach their ears. Nonetheless they redoubled their efforts. They were practically at a dead run by the time they rounded a pile of rocks that marked some kind of boundary. Spreading out quickly, they joined the fight. Gaurin found himself beside a tough Sea-Rover fighting gamely despite the blood running down his brawny weapons-arm. Had he been but a few minutes more on the road, the man would likely have been cut down.

"Just in time!" the man gasped. "We thought we were done for!"

Gaurin dispatched the Frydian before him and slipped an

arm around the Sea-Rover's shoulders, as he was obviously too far gone to walk unaided. "We have been busy over on the other side as well," he said. "We came as quickly as we could."

"We know," the Sea-Rover said.

When Gaurin had settled the wounded man in a spot out of the worst of the danger, he himself plunged immediately back into the fray.

With the unexpected—and extremely welcome—arrival of reinforcements, the balance began to shift in the battle in the Frydian camp. By ones and then twos, and then in groups, the northerners began to break and run. Gaurin became aware of an increase in the din coming from the right, and realized that the survivors of those Frydians who had started down the hidden mountain road into the death valley must be in full retreat and what they found before them now could not be a welcome sight. Soon their pursuers, Nordors and Rendelians with war-kats bounding ahead of them, came pouring after them, into the camp area. In the middle of the battleground, Lathrom and Gaurin met. Wearily, they leaned on their swords and clasped hands.

"Well done," Gaurin said.

"Better done," Lathrom said.

Rohan joined them. He had a cut on his forehead but otherwise he seemed all right. Keltin and Bitta were by his side; Bitta limped, shaking her paw now and then. "Better done indeed," he said, indicating the Sea-Rovers who had lived through the fighting. "If you had not arrived when you did, I doubt that we could have lasted much longer."

Cebastian and Chevin likewise joined the small knot of officers. Both had wounds that needed treatment. However, they could wait as men with worse injuries got the physicians' first attention back at their camp.

"Yes, my thanks as well," Chevin said. "We have won a good victory this day."

Gaurin nodded. He knew that by rights, he should have been congratulating Harous instead. Harous, however, had been conspicuously absent from the fray both in spirit and in body. Perhaps, Gaurin hoped, after he had taken the detachment of men up the shore road, Harous had roused himself from that strange torpor. "Another such victory could finish us," he said. "Where is the High Marshal?"

"He is seeing to the cleanup of the battle site at the mountain pass. He has ordered me to ask you to do the same here."

"Of course," Gaurin said.

Working with quick efficiency, both Nordors and Rendelians dragged the stocky bodies of the Frydian dead into a pile for burning. Others put together makeshift litters for the worst wounded and started them on the trek back to their camp. Then they too retreated southward from the enemy site, carefully setting the haphazard groupings of tents and shelters on fire as they went. Within moments the entire area was ablaze.

Rohan arranged a litter for Bitta as well, for her paw was now obviously unable to bear her weight. It seemed only fitting to honor his gallant companion in such manner.

✿

Harous felt as if he were burning with fever. Where was Flavielle? She had promised to oversee the battle, to drop the ice river on the heads of their enemy. The plan had been so perfect. Could she have been riding the Ice Dragon that his men had wounded? He could not make himself even contemplate that hers could have been the one caught in the deadly avalanche, and that she may now be dead.

No. It was impossible. Later, he thought, clinging to a hope beyond all hope, he would see her again, hold her in his arms.

In the meantime, he busied himself with ordering the clearing of the battlefield. His head pounded with every heartbeat and despite the frigid day, he was sweating. He found that he did not regret the numbers of Rendelian or Nordor soldiers who had fallen, or been wounded. Instead, he resented the fact that the Bog-men had deserted the battlefield on the flimsy pretext of defending their portion of Rendel. If they had been where he had ordered them to be, perhaps the odious Tusser would have been found among the dead.

Or, perhaps he was correct and the Ice Dragon really was headed for the Bog. In that case, given the poor weapons the Bog-men carried, and their equally weak attempts at armor, the odds were definitely with the Dragon, no matter how many minor wounds it had sustained. The result would be the same—Tusser would be dead, along with the rest of his contemptible excuse for an army.

He hoped, then, that Flavielle had ridden that beast. She would return to him in triumph.

"We won, sir." It was Reges. He was favoring one leg, and Harous realized that the young noble had suffered a sword slash to the back of his calf. A little better aimed, and he would have been hamstrung. As it was, he would probably recover.

"So we did," Harous said. "So we did. Where is Chevin?"

"Still on the battlefield."

"Tell him to report to me."

Reges saluted and hobbled off to do as he was bid. Presently, Chevin, battle-smudged but without apparent hurt, appeared. "Sir?"

"How does the enemy?"

"They have broken, sir, and are on the run."

"Pursue them back to their camp," Harous said. "If the fight has gone out of them, then let them go. Only be sure that they have truly fled, and then, if you can find Gaurin, tell him to see to the ordering of that battlefield even as we are clearing this one. Do you understand?"

"Of course, sir."

Chevin saluted again and turned to do Harous's bidding. The Lord High Marshal returned to his thoughts. Perhaps Gaurin had perished, not that it would matter if Ashen were widowed once more. Harous knew that he belonged, heart, soul, and body, to the Sorceress Flavielle, and even the slight impediment of his false wife was of little concern to him now.

Strange. He had not thought of Marcala but for that once, when he had encountered Flavielle not far from this very spot, and that was to remember how she had made an attempt on his life.

His heart cramped again. Flavielle. She was the true mate for a man such as himself.

His thoughts began to race madly, driven by his fever. Where were the remaining Ice Dragons? Why had the Rendelians faced only one of the five remaining after Rohan had so treacherously slain the sixth? With a Dragon buried in the snow and the wounded one fled south, why had the other three riders not come to its aid?

No, she could not have deserted him. The odds of her being among those now curiously absent from the field of battle had shortened dramatically.

If she had perished in the avalanche . . .

"Did you bring medicines?" Gaurin asked, as he escorted Ashen, Royance, and their followers through the camp. Here and there faint moans of wounded men came from tents and shelters.

"No," Ashen said. "I had hoped to arrive before—" She clutched at his sleeve, suddenly alarmed. "Who is hurt? Rohan?"

"He has a few scratches, but is unharmed. I was able to send a detachment of our forces to his relief. A few of the young Rendelian nobles were too rash and got their first scars today, but most of the wounded are our foot-soldiers."

"Is there an infirmary?"

"Yes. However, their supplies are already running low."

"I will go there at once, and see what I can do."

"As for me," Royance said, "if you will find me a tent somewhere, and a bed, I find that I need a little rest before I can make myself useful. Driving a dog-sled at my age—"

Gaurin smiled, despite the gravity of the situation. "Sir, your staunchness shames the rest of us lesser men. I doubt that any of us could have accomplished what you have."

"With enough need pushing you, you could. But now that I am here, I am weary the way I was not, on the journey."

Reges of Lerkland limped past. He had a fresh bandage around the lower part of one leg. Gaurin called to him. "Would you please see to Lord Royance? He needs a place to rest himself."

"It would be my privilege. If you don't mind sharing a tent, sir," Reges said.

"I've slept on the ground, in the open, often enough on campaign, though not in the snow if I could help it," Royance answered stoutly.

"Well, here you'll at least have shelter, and some warm food. Please follow me, sir."

Royance waved at Gaurin and Ashen, starting off with Reges. Jervin, close as a shadow, trailed behind his master.

"When you have rested a little, we shall speak about this, er, business you mentioned, sir," Gaurin said.

"Yes. In the meantime, Ashen can give you the tale, but keep in mind that hers is evidence from the heart, and not what can be seen or touched."

"I will, sir."

Then Royance and the young man disappeared from view down one of the makeshift streets of the camp.

Gaurin turned to Ashen. "Before you go to the wounded, we must talk. In private."

He led her to his own tent, giving orders to a passing soldier that a jug of hot soup be brought at once. Inside the shelter, a war-kat reclined comfortably on Gaurin's camp bed fastidiously cleaning its fur and another dozed in the folding chair. "Rajesh, Finola, please get down. This is my lady, Ashen. Make your manners."

The two beautiful creatures roused themselves and

stalked over to her. She had the impression that they did so not out of obedience, but rather from curiosity. "May I touch them?" she asked.

"Yes. They will not hurt you."

She stroked their heads, cautiously at first, and then with growing confidence as the war-kats rubbed against her. "I didn't see any of these except at a distance, before you marched off from Rendelsham. They are quite splendid. Are they really as fierce in battle as people say?"

"Later I will tell you about how they teased an Ice Dragon that was attacking us. But now, I want to hear what you have come such a long and dangerous way to tell me."

They sat, Gaurin on the side of his bed and Ashen in the chair, with the war-kats close by, their heads conveniently placed so the humans could scratch them behind their ears. She accepted the cup of hot soup gratefully, and then as she sipped it she outlined for her husband the terrible thing that had happened to Lady Marcala, and the even more dreadful accusations she had made.

"The Dowager was inclined to put it down to Marcala's illness," Ashen finished.

"But you believe her," Gaurin said. It was not a question.

"Yes, I do. Her evidence was enough for me, given what I have seen with my own eyes. Not to mention the matter of my necklace."

"Then it surely is enough to warrant some close questioning of the gentleman in question. But Lady Marcala—how is she?"

"She still lived, when Lord Royance and I left Rendelsham, but was very ill. After so many days—I don't know."

"I will send word that all the officers are to meet in the

counsel tent," Gaurin said. His eyebrows were drawn together in a stern line. "Stay here."

"No, I will go to the infirmary tents instead."

"Very well. Just be where I can find you, in case you are needed." His expression softened slightly. "Royance must have his rest disturbed, I fear."

"He will not mind," Ashen said. "He knows the necessity."

"Hynnel's tent is nearby. We will meet there. I must discuss this matter with Royance before we give the others this dismal news, and I want my kinsman with me for his good counsel."

He arose from where he had been sitting on the camp bed, and Ashen likewise stood. He embraced her and, for a moment, she allowed herself to luxuriate in his presence. "How I have missed you," she said.

"We are together now. After we have settled this vexed question, I will consider whether I can bear to send you back or not."

Ashen's heart beat a little faster at his words. "I will go now and start helping with the wounded."

He kissed her lightly before they left the tent. The warkats had to be left behind against their wishes. They wanted to follow Ashen, and they were dissuaded only when she reassured them that she would see them later.

Harous made his way through the camp, glad of the hubbub that allowed him to pass almost unmarked. He barely acknowledged the salutes of his guards outside the command tent, his goal his private quarters beyond.

"There is water heated. Shall we bring it, sir?" one of the guards asked.

"Yes. Set it on the table in the main room, and I will manage for myself. If anyone wants to see me, say that I am not to be disturbed."

All he wanted was to strip off his sweat-soaked garments, to be dry and cool once more. He could not bear the thought of laving his body in hot water. Nor did he wish anyone's company just now. He felt he could not even endure the light of a candle.

As he hauled a sodden mass of layered tunics over his head, he caught a familiar scent. A delicate touch on his back made his skin tingle from head to foot. Was he dreaming? Was his imagination, fired by the fever that wracked him, now going to torment him with ghosts?

"You are not dreaming." Flavielle spoke hardly above a whisper.

The fragrance of her perfume enveloped him. She pointed one finger and lighted a candle without touching it. Then she helped him off with the soiled clothing, handing him a soft woolen robe. The bell outside his private doorway sounded, indicating that the guard had brought the water as instructed. She waited long enough to give the man time to leave. Then, cautiously making certain that the main room of the tent was deserted, she brought the steaming basin into the inner chamber.

Flavielle made him lie down on the camp bed. She sprinkled a few drops of an elixir into the water and crystals of ice formed around the edges. Soaking a cloth in the mixture, she loosened the robe, and began, patiently, to wash his body. The icy water felt wonderfully refreshing.

"You are ill, my own," she said. "More than you should be. What is the matter?"

"I feared that you were dead. There were two Dragons, and you said you would be overseeing the battle, the ambush, and one Dragon died in an avalanche and the other was wounded—"

"Sssssh." She touched her fragrant fingertips to his lips. "The Dragon caught by the snow was, indeed, mine."

"But you live!"

"Do you think so little of me? Did you believe my Power so slight that I could not escape that or even greater danger?"

"I am never afraid, but I was, this time, for your sake."

Having finished washing the sweat from his body, she drew the robe around him again. "There. You will feel better soon," she said.

"I am better already, but whether it is the potion you used on me or merely your presence, I do not know."

The Sorceress arose and began searching his clothes chest for fresh garments. The soiled ones still lay in a heap, and she kicked them into a corner. "When you dress again, you must wear lighter clothing," she said.

For the first time it registered on him that she wore only a thin tunic, belted at the waist. Even when she was outside, this was covered by an equally light cloak. "And yet you are warm, in the snow," he marveled.

"Yes. Here, drink this—all of it."

She held another vial, similar to the one from which he had drunk before, to his lips. Again he swallowed the contents without question. She put her hand on his forehead for a moment.

"Your fever is gone now," she said. "When it comes upon

you again, do not worry. Know that it is only your former life burning itself away, making you worthy of acceptance by the Great One Whom All Serve, and who is my special master. Before long I shall take you to him myself, let him know of your great deeds, how valuable an ally you are and how dear to me. Perhaps he will even bless our union. But that will come later. Tomorrow you must confer with your generals."

"Don't leave me."

"It is only for a little while. I must find my lieutenant, Farod, and the other riders. Also Chaggi, the leader of our Frydian allies. We have some rallying of our own to do, you know, for while there was no clear victory on either side, still there were losses. I will take one of the remaining Dragons. I was not expecting to be tumbled head over heels and nearly buried beneath a mountain of snow." She smiled a little ruefully. "I did not think your warriors would be so resourceful."

"That was Gaurin's doing. He is a Nordor, and he could recognize that the snow was ripe to fall."

"Gaurin. I will mark the name."

She kissed him. With a gesture, she dimmed the candle until it gave off no light though it continued to burn. In the gloom he could sense that she had left. Then the light flared up again.

In command of himself once more, he arose from the camp bed and began to dress in the fresh, lighter-weight tunic she had laid out for him. The sweaty garments still lay in the floor. He called one of the guards, instructing that the sodden mess be taken to the laundresses.

On the morrow, he would confer with his officers after

he had gone over the reports that would be coming to him shortly. It would be interesting to see what new plan of battle they would devise, and even more interesting to think of ways to turn it against them.

Eleven

"*Lord Royance,*" *Gaurin said,* "Harous will not be expecting you. Should we not inform him that you are here?"

"In due time. For the moment, I would rather let my presence be a surprise."

With a little rest and warm food, the old gentleman had regained much of his strength and all of his aura of command. He sat on the camp bed in Hynnel's tent, a war-kat dozing beside him, its head pillowed on his knee. It was not one that Gaurin recognized, but this independent breed often napped where it pleased.

Gaurin, Hynnel, and Lathrom found places for themselves as they awaited Rohan's arrival. Only Gaurin and Royance knew the particulars, but the others were well aware there were grave matters to be discussed. Their demeanor reflected curiosity and concern. In a few moments the young Sea-Rover ducked through the opening. A fresh bandage was wrapped around his forehead.

"Please pardon my tardiness. I wanted to see how Bitta was faring after we got her back to camp."

"Is she badly hurt?" Hynnel asked.

"Her paw is swollen and bruised, and the physician thinks one of the small bones is broken. Someone must have managed to strike a blow with a mace or a club." Rohan stopped abruptly and rubbed the back of his neck, frowning a little.

"She is young yet, and has learned a valuable lesson at a relatively small cost," Gaurin said. "Now we come to the reason why we have gathered. Lord Royance, please tell our trusted companions of what you have learned. There is no time to lose; we must confer quickly."

In quick, terse terms, the old nobleman outlined the accusations against Harous, not failing to include such extenuating evidence as he could muster. For a moment, there was complete silence in the tent. The drowsy war-kat shifted, making itself even more comfortable against Royance's leg.

Lathrom was the first to speak. "I am the only native Rendelian here," he said, gazing at Royance, "saving your lordship. If there has ever been treachery like this before in this country, I have not heard of it. Or elsewhere."

"Not in the Land of Ever Snow," Hynnel said.

"Nor with the Sea-Rovers," Rohan said. He rubbed the back of his neck. "It is unthinkable—if it is true."

"Therein lies the problem," Royance said. "How do we prove this?"

"Ashen sets great store by that necklace," said Gaurin,

"and the evidence of her own eyes is compelling."

"And yet it is tainted by magic," Royance pointed out. "On both sides."

"I have heard a description of something similar if not identical. It sounds like a Diadem of Concealment," Hynnel said slowly. "It is a headband," he explained when the others looked at him inquiringly. "In it is set a gem with which the Diadem creates the fog. This fog is, naturally, most dense around the wearer's head."

"But wouldn't the wearer be blinded?" Lathrom asked.

"No, for he is inside the enchantment," Hynnel replied. "It does not affect him personally."

"It is unfortunate that no one thought to search Cragden Keep for this Diadem," Royance said.

Gaurin raised his eyebrows. "Perhaps Harous has it with him."

"Probably. Such an item could be very valuable to anyone, particularly to someone who wanted to conceal his identity." Lathrom laughed. "An excellent tool for a spy."

"Supposedly, during the storm, we sent out spies to nearly freeze themselves. They came back with very little information judging from the way the battle went. I did not notice that our Lord High Marshal offered his magical protection to any of them," Hynnel stated dryly. "If, indeed, there were any. However, spies or no spies, I have a problem picturing Count Harous as a traitor."

"We all have problems picturing him as a traitor," Lathrom said flatly. "Nonetheless, the evidence against him seems strong."

Rohan appeared to be lost in thought. "The rod," he said.

The others in the tent turned to stare at him questioningly. He frowned and rubbed the back of his neck again, as if something there was fretting him.

"You remember. Well, Lord Royance, you wouldn't, but the rest would. The rod with the handle that I brought back from when the Sea-Rovers killed the first Dragon."

"Yes?" prompted Gaurin.

"Well, when we gave it to Harous for safekeeping, he put it in a chest in the command tent. I remember noticing that there was a lock on the chest, but didn't think anything of it at the time. I also remember noticing that when he put the thing inside, it clanked as if striking another piece of metal."

"Perhaps that was the Diadem," Lathrom observed.

"And perhaps not," Gaurin said. "We cannot speculate on what we do not know for certain."

"Then I will go and ask our Lord High Marshal to show me the chest, and its contents," Lord Royance stated firmly. "It is entirely within my right to do so, being as this is one of our enemy's deadly weapons."

"And then, when the chest is opened—"

"I will see what else lies inside." Royance carefully slipped the war-kat's head from its pillow on his knee and arose from the camp bed. Roused, the war-kat shook its head and ears. Then it leapt up and bounded through the tent opening.

"Let us now hope that the other contents of Harous's chest are innocent," Royance continued. "In spite of everything, I am not eager to discover that he has turned against us. If that is the case, I fear that all is lost."

"Go and tell my lady of what was decided here," Gaurin said to Lathrom, "and then join us at the command tent."

Lathrom saluted and turned to do his lord's bidding. The others followed Gaurin in the direction in which the war-kat had already disappeared.

❦

Harous, having finished a light meal, was busy at a small table in his private quarters going over the first of the reports from his officers following the battle. He sensed a presence and looked up, frowning, having given strict orders he was not to be disturbed—

"Flavielle!" he exclaimed in pleasure as he jumped to his feet. "Oh, how glad I am to see you returned so soon! Come to me, dear one."

She allowed only a brief embrace. Again the scent of her perfume enveloped him. "We have no time for dalliance, my Harous," she said. "I fear that we have been discovered."

She did not smile and Harous grew alert immediately, aware that the situation must be grave indeed. Until this moment she had never before come to him other than in the dark of night.

"What shall we do?" he asked.

"I had hoped that you would be able to lead the armies into another disaster, but this is not to be. Lord Royance is in the camp and even now approaches with some of the nobles at his heels. I was—let's say I was nearby, though they did not recognize me."

He accepted her words as truth. Royance's presence could mean only one thing. All his suspicions were confirmed. Marcala had indeed tried to poison him, and must have drunk the dose meant for him. Then she had decided to tell her false tales while she still could. Hatred flashed through him; he hoped she had died, and in great pain.

"What shall we do?" he asked again.

"We must flee, for in a few moments the entire camp will be aware, and then nothing I can do will keep them from killing you. Come. Together we will ride Ice Dragons, and *you* will lead the Army of the Great One against what remains of those you once commanded. Victory will be ours!"

"We cannot risk going out the entrance, past the sentries, where we could be seen. Nor can I chance going out into the main enclosure and retrieving my Diadem of Concealment." Harous managed to smile, even at this tense moment. "I kept it in a chest out there, almost in plain view."

"You are ever the audacious and daring one," Flavielle said. Her mouth softened, but only for a moment. "Leave it. I will cover us with shadow for as long as it takes for us to make our escape."

She gestured with both hands, and, as the room darkened slightly in Harous's sight, she almost vanished in the gloom. He took up a dagger and cut a slit in the back wall of his tent big enough that both could duck through. Then they ran, two shadowy crouching figures, through the camp.

The Lady Marcala lay abed in the quarters that had been assigned to her next to the Dowager's apartment. True to her word, Ysa had been a frequent visitor, coaxing Marcala to sip a little broth, or try to eat a crust of bread. Also, Master Lorgan had proven himself to be a skilled physician. Because of his treatment she was almost without pain and, indeed, felt stronger than she had when she had come to Rendelsham Castle three days ago with her tale of treachery and murder.

It was, she knew, only temporary. Beneath the gentle masking of Lorgan's strengthening tonics, the poison continued its deadly work.

She needed to know what was happening outside the room in which she lay. Touching a bell beside her bed, Marcala summoned her maid, Reuta. The girl, encouraged at her mistress's apparent improvement, happily babbled all the gossip she knew.

Marcala listened without comment, but was pleased to learn that the Bog-princess, Ashen, had done precisely as Marcala had wished her to do. That the fool had managed to summon the wit to drag old Royance along on her errand pleased Marcala immensely. Harous would surely have no chance to defend himself, not with the Head of the Council dispensing the stern justice he was famous for.

Nevertheless, Marcala wanted to witness the outcome for herself. Only then would death grant her peace. She continued to listen until the maid had finished. "That is very interesting and amusing, Reuta," she said. "You have made my heart merry as it has not been in too long. In fact, I think I will get out of bed for a while today."

"Yes, Lady," Reuta said. "But remember that you are still weak. You have been so ill."

"I will sit in a chair with my feet up. To achieve this much will hearten me."

"Master Lorgan and Her Highness might not approve."

"Is the Dowager in her apartment?"

"No, Lady. She has gone down to the Hall for the midday meal. Shall I take word that you wish to see her?"

"No, I would not disturb her."

"I will go and fetch soup made with lentils. That is strengthening."

Marcala allowed the maid to help her into a dressing gown and help her as far as the chair. Though she desired no food, she needed to get Reuta out of the way for a while. This small burst of strength coupled with Ysa's absence might not come again before it was too late.

"Thank you. The lentil soup sounds good. Bring me also new cheese and bread. I believe I may have a little appetite today."

"I will be back before I've left!" The maid, obviously delighted, scurried through the door.

Marcala waited a moment, and then pulled herself to her feet. Clutching at whatever came to hand for support, she made her way out into the corridor, and thence into Ysa's apartment. It was deserted, as Marcala had hoped, all of her ladies having accompanied their mistress to dinner. Without hesitation, Marcala entered Ysa's bedchamber and looked around.

Ah. There, on a table, that must be a jewel chest. If Ysa was as predictable as Marcala had always found her to be—

She opened the chest and lifted out a tray filled with costly baubles—brooches and rings for fingers and ears, most set with rubies or emeralds, the gems of Oak and of Yew. In the space beneath lay necklaces of all kinds, from heavy and ornate to simple ones suitable for everyday wear. She lifted one of the most elaborate of the necklaces and discovered under it, just as she had hoped, the little amulet she had taken from the chest in Harous's secret room. It still lay safe in the dark gray velvet pouch.

Slipping the strings of the pouch over her finger for security, Marcala put all to rights in the jewel chest, exactly as she had found it. Then she returned to her rooms as quickly as she could. She tucked the pouch under her pillow and had time to settle herself in the chair and even to catch her breath a little before Reuta appeared, bearing a tray with the soup, bread, and cheese she had requested.

Then Marcala suffered the maid to watch her while she ate. To her surprise, now that she had accomplished this small feat of stealing back the amulet, she really did have a touch of appetite. She finished everything on the tray and let Reuta help her back to bed.

"Now it's time for a nap, my Lady," the maid said. "You deserve it. Master Lorgan will be so pleased to learn of your progress!"

"A little sleep sounds very good," Marcala said. "Please do not disturb me for at least an hour."

The maid tucked her in, made certain that the curtains were drawn so that no untoward brightness of day would disturb her mistress's rest, and then closed the door behind her.

Immediately, Marcala took the velvet pouch out of its place of concealment and shook the amulet into her hand. She had no idea what sort of creature it depicted—winged and furred rather than feathered. The tiny yellow gems glittered as if its eyes could see even in the dim light. She rubbed it, while calling the spell of activation back into clear memory.

As the Bog-men had expected, the Ice Dragon came to ground and began to walk toward the Bog, keeping as close to the sea as possible using the coast road. Tusser and his followers had no trouble in cutting inland just enough to stay out of sight and pass the dangerous beast. He knew of a good spot for the Bog-men to attack, well short of the boundaries of their homeland.

The Bog general had the luxury of a little time in which to make his preparations. He motioned to Sumase, his second in command, to sit by him and the two conferred in relative privacy.

"Now I sorry I go to fight with Rendel," Tusser said. "Outlanders always trouble. Rohan friend maybe, Gaurin also, but Harous no friend."

Sumase spat onto the frozen ground. "Never friend to Bog, Harous. So now we get whole Ice Dragon to fight, just us," he said, grinning. "How you think we do this?"

"I have idea," Tusser said. "We still ahead of Dragon."

The other man lifted his head, as if searching with both eyes and ears. "Yes. I hear it walk, walk, heavy. Still far away, though."

"Find man who runs fastest. Something I want, something I take long ago when there is other big fight in Bog. Your man goes, we keep Dragon busy here until he gets back, brings bags I keep hidden."

Sumase grinned wider. "Bags not made of lupper-hide?"

"Yes, you know ones I mean, with royal mark on. Your man may have to make Vanka give."

"Everybody know what bad temper Tusser's wife has. I get Lorko. He strong. He run fast, and can sit on Vanka also."

"Good. Now, you know how to stir up big flyers? They hate us, but hate Dragon more maybe."

"They nest in cliffs around here, and south, too. While we wait for Dragon to get here, maybe we push eggs out of nest or kill fledglings. It be just like old times, you and me, eh?"

"Yes, good times. Harder now, though. If we get birds on our side, and maybe Gulpers, too, we can kill Dragon and rider, both." Tusser's lips lifted in a mirthless smile. "Then Outlanders see how well Bog-men fight!"

Sumase drew back and stared at his leader. "You go back to Harous when Dragon is dead?"

"Tusser give word. We go back. But not Harous. Rohan and maybe Gaurin."

Sumase stared off into the distance, plainly disapproving. "Maybe. I send Lorko anyway." Then he hauled himself to his feet and went in search of the Bog warrior, to tell him of the thankless errand he would be sent on.

❧

Marcala, too keyed up to lie in bed, moved to the little table in her bedchamber. Twice she assayed the spell of animation, and twice she failed. Something she was doing, or not doing, was keeping her from success. She closed her eyes, picturing the spell book as it had been in the secret room off hers and Harous's apartment. In memory, she opened the cover and turned pages until she came to the right one.

The writing was beautiful, picked out in gold and red on the capital letters. Her hand moved as once again she seemed to touch the page, hastily memorizing the spell. Then she realized what she had done wrong. The incantation was "flyer live" and not "flyer fly."

She took the amulet in her hand. With newfound confidence, she began to murmur aloud.

Flyer live, by night and by day,
Harken to these words that I say.
Flyer live, by day and by night,
And bring to me the gift of thy sight!

For a long moment nothing happened. Then the amulet stirred in her grasp and began to grow. The golden gems of its eyes became real, came into focus still glittering, and the little creature unfolded and stretched its wings.

It was not something to be petted or stroked. Its glare could only be described as malevolent. Perhaps it was resentful of having been called into being.

Marcala did not care. She held it out on the palm of her hand. "Go," she told it. "You know the one I seek. Go and seek likewise."

It lifted rather than flew from her hand, and made a circle of the room. Marcala remembered, belatedly, that she had not opened a window for it. Such proved unnecessary, however, for the creature faded into nothing even as she watched. A dizzying moment as it passed through a wall, and then she was with it as it soared upward, seeing through its eyes.

Having accomplished this much, she could do the rest in bed, and indeed, she was exhausted as she had never been before. She crept back awkwardly, stumbling over the furnishings of her room, unable to see them clearly, and climbed in. Gratefully, she lay back on her pillow and pulled the covers over her thin, wasted body, smoothing them so that

Reuta would not suspect that her mistress had been about, unsupervised.

Up, up she went, one with the newly born creature. Below, everything was cold and white, dotted with the near black of evergreen trees. Above, the sun was almost unnaturally bright. Snow sparkled in the air, as if suspended in a clear blue sky.

She turned north. Time's outlines became blurry; now she fancied she could detect the twin tracks of sled runners in the snow, and then it seemed she saw the sleds themselves—two of them, hurrying northward even as she did, only slowly by comparison. She left them far behind.

There, ahead, was what could only be the camp where the armies commanded by Harous were bivouacked. She circled it, noting the areas where the Rendelians were quartered, set aside from the place for the Nordors. Virtually isolated from the rest was another set of shelters and for the first time she got a glimpse of one who could only be a man of the BaleBog. Next to that was the Sea-Rover encampment.

Having gotten her bearings, she found a place to perch and watch, invisible, from the top of a tent pole. She recognized the pennon flying over this large and imposing shelter and knew it had to be Harous's quarters. Inside she heard male voices but could not make out clear words though she sensed they were making plans for an impending battle. She discovered that she did not want to enter, and knew this was the flyer's preference rather than hers.

Then Gaurin left the tent with Rohan. A little later, the other Nordorn nobleman—Hynnel, she remembered—left with another Bog-man. She thought about following them, but decided against it. She—the flyer—closed their eyes, and in that strange time compression, night fell and then it became day again.

Harous left the camp. She launched herself skyward and, from a great height, observed as he made his way alone down a valley carved between two towering mountain ridges.

She was watching when he hid behind a rock for a moment and then emerged to embrace a woman who was waiting for him.

"So I thought," Marcala murmured to herself. But her voice had the effect of disturbing the flyer. Their vision shifted, and she knew they had become, if only briefly, visible. She resolved not to speak again, if she could help it.

Their vision shifted again, and she was once more one with the being she had conjured from a stone amulet.

Her husband and the woman mounted the back of a huge white beast waiting nearby. An Ice Dragon. It lifted into the air.

Marcala and the flyer soared even higher, mindful to keep their quarry in sight. As they flew, Marcala wondered. Where had she seen this woman before?

Then she remembered. At the Grand Tourney, when young Rohan had done something incomprehensible and the Magician stood revealed as the Sorceress, Flavielle. Everyone in the viewing stand, where Marcala had been given the favorable seat close to the Dowager Ysa, had been petrified. Then, in a burst of thunder and snow, Flavielle had disappeared. Ysa had been left to defend her very life for having brought such a being into the Court.

The Ice Dragon alighted once more and Flavielle and Harous entwined in a passionate embrace. Marcala forbore to follow the guilty pair into the shelter made of tree branches, and this time it was by her inclination as well as that of the flyer.

She flew in restless circles around the shelter, thinking to wait and follow one or the other when they finally emerged. It would, she surmised, be a while. She knew all too well what was transpiring inside.

"Harous," she murmured. "I have no interest in where his doxy goes."

Again the flyer lurched in its course, disturbed, and their vision shifted.

Too late, Marcala realized how close they had come to the Ice Dragon. Its snaky neck lashed out. It opened its mouth, and the last thing she and the flyer heard was the sound of its teeth crunching into the tiny morsel of flesh and sinew. A loud noise in her ears, pain, the echo of a woman's laughter—

With a shock that made her entire body spasm, Marcala returned to herself. Terrified, she thrashed for a moment in the restricting bedcovers. Instinctively she clutched at her limbs, certain to find them broken and mangled. The Dragon's teeth had been so huge on her, its breath so cold and foul—

Then she began to come back to herself. She was intact, unharmed, or would have been except for the fact that she was dying from her own poison. Only the flyer had been destroyed.

Marcala's lips lifted in a small, bitter smile. Ysa would never have any benefit at all from the bauble she had ordered her loyal friend, the Countess Marcala, to go and steal for her. Marcala didn't even know if what was left had become stone again and now rested in the belly of the Dragon, or if it had spat the fragments out into the snow.

All Marcala was certain of was that she had now been supplanted in Harous's uncertain and fickle affections. She was glad anew that she had managed to convince Ashen, if not her erstwhile friend the Dowager Queen Ysa, of Harous's treachery. The sleds Marcala had marked traveling northward at such a feverish pace could only have been carrying Ashen and whomever she could persuade to accompany her.

The strain of her foray into magic was taking its toll, she realized. Then, Marcala knew it was more than that. The small store of artificial strength she had been granted from the tonics and potions had come to an end. She was dying. A moment of panic seized her, as quickly stilled.

"Let it happen," she whispered. "I have done what was needed and now I know the truth. Let Harous wallow with his new light o' love as he would. Very soon he will be exposed for what he is, and I will be avenged."

She strove to straighten the bedclothes again, aware of her growing weakness. Then she composed her limbs, folded her hands across her bosom, and closed her eyes. More gently than she dreamed possible, she drifted off into a sleep from which she knew she would never awaken.

"We must give her as fine a funeral as we can arrange," Ysa said to Lady Ingrid, who had brought the news of Marcala's death. "The Cragden tomb will now hold the most beautiful and accomplished countess that line has ever known. Please notify Lord Royance."

"Lord Royance is not in Rendelsham, Madame," Lady Ingrid replied. She looked down, as if fearing Ysa's wrath. "Nor is he in the city, as far as anyone knows."

"Not here—" Ysa stared at her lady-in-waiting, frowning. Where could he be? Then, all at once, she knew. That cursed Ash wench! She must have gone directly to Royance with Marcala's mad tale of disloyalty and treason, and the old fool had been taken in by it. They were probably halfway there by now.

She made sure her face was composed and showed no distress beyond what the death of her great favorite would be expected to cause. "Notify Lord Wittern," she said to Ingrid. "He is, after all, the King's great-grandfather. He will send word to all the nobility still in Rendelsham so that they may gather and pay proper respects to the wife of our Lord High Marshal in his absence. I will prepare the list of whom to summon."

"Yes, Madame," the lady-in-waiting said. She hurried off to do Ysa's bidding, obviously relieved at not having been required to bear the brunt of the Dowager's displeasure.

Ysa's mind was already busy with details of the near-royal funeral to come. Rannore would have to be present, even in her increasingly obvious condition. *Lady* Rannore, she thought with some contempt, and not Her Highness, the Young Dowager Rannore of Rowan, Yew, and Oak. That title had always rankled Ysa. It came much too close to proclaiming her aged. . . .

Gattor of Bilth, who had removed to his town house in Rendelsham when he learned that the great encampment of the Four Armies would be placed almost at his doorstep. He must attend as well. Who else? Lady Anamara, she supposed. She went to her writing desk, took a piece of paper, dipped a pen in the inkwell, and began to make notes. If she tried hard enough to keep herself busy at this task, she could ignore the truth that Marcala's death had been, in some respects, a relief to her. The Countess had, right from the start, been entirely too clever for Ysa to trust her as much as she would have liked. Marcala had served her purpose, even as Harous had served his.

It occurred to her to wonder if Harous really had turned traitor or if it was only a figment of Marcala's poisoned imagination. Well, either way, it would all be resolved. Now Ysa could afford to be grateful to Ashen for having dragged Royance out on what she hoped was a fool's errand. Royance would not preside over a solemn moment here in the city where his presence was virtually required, but he would, in a just and equitable manner, ascertain Harous's loyalty.

Even if the remote possibility that Harous was toying with the idea of betraying his country proved true, she trusted Royance to deal with the upstart count and put him back firmly in the ranks of its unswerving, staunch nobility.

She still had the black dress and jet jewelry from the funeral of her son, King Florian, and that Sea-Rover Obern. They might be slightly out of fashion by now, but they would do. After all, Rendel was at war and some sacrifices must be made.

The scratch of her pen filled the room as the Dowager went on with her plans and list-making.

Twelve

Joining the handful of other women who had been pressed into service as nurses, Ashen found herself almost submerged in the needs of the wounded. The worst off were those who had encountered the blast of mist from the rodlike weapon the Dragon rider had carried.

"It was like breathing in fire," a Rendelian soldier told her, gasping for breath. "And it still burns—"

"Hush," she said soothingly. "Don't try to talk. I will bring you cool water to drink."

"Make it more than cool. Ice itself wouldn't put out the fire. And an ice pack for my chest, please! It still burns."

Around her, others who had been involved with the fight with the Dragon clamored for the same. She busied herself with tending to their requests until the pitcher she carried was empty and all the ice used. And still they begged for more. She emerged from the infirmary tent where she was working, to take a short rest before returning to her labors. A short distance away, she spotted Rohan and waved to him. He hurried over to join her.

"It's good to see you, Ashen," he said. "But what brings you here, of all places? I just got a summons to go to Hynnel's tent, and I think Lord Royance is there with Gaurin and some others as well. Is there something amiss? The back of my neck is tingling, the way it does when there is danger around."

"I fear we are all in danger," Ashen said. "You are hurt!" She gently touched the fresh bandage on his head.

"Just a scratch. But my war-kat, Bitta, has an injured paw. You have a way with animals you learned from Granddam Zaz."

"Yes," she said in answer to his unspoken question. "I will look in on—Bitta, is it?"

"Thank you. Now, I have to hurry."

Then he was gone. Ashen was glad he had not had time to press her for an explanation of why she was here. He would find out soon enough, from Gaurin and from Royance. Far better than they be the ones to tell him and those few others they were prepared to take into their confidence.

She dipped water into a pitcher, adding fresh, clean snow from the interior of the nearest drift to cool it. She couldn't carry enough snow to make into ice packs and still take water to the injured. Someone else must do it. Bracing herself, she returned to her task of trying to save the lives of those who, Ashen feared, were beyond saving.

She wished Zazar were with her. But she saw no way to send word to the Wysen-wyf that her services were most sorely needed.

❦

Tusser carefully stationed his men where the terrain would be to their advantage, be it ever so slight. Here, a low cliff surmounted by trees flanked the coast road on one side so closely that the Ice Dragon's flanks would scrape the stones, and on the other, a steeper cliff dropped almost straight down into the sea. The big problem lay in making sure the Dragon kept to the road and did not take flight. However, with Bog-men to battle, Tusser felt confident it and its rider would not attempt to flee.

Also, he believed, there was a certain other advantage, one that would even the odds. He watched down the road, hoping that the man Sumase had sent would return in time. Things would go poorly for them all, if he did not.

To his relief, he caught sight of Lorko, pushing through the brush to the side of the road. The Bog-man waved triumphantly, showing the three sacks of flammable powder he carried, the ones Tusser had filched during the fight with the Dowager's men. That weapon of Outlander force was one all his plans depended upon.

"Vanka not want to give," Lorko declared, dropping his burden before the headman, "but I make her anyway."

Tusser turned to Sumase. "Who is best thrower?"

Sumase frowned a little. "Hili," he said after a moment. "He hit mark very often."

"Then send Hili up in a tree at top of cliff," Tusser instructed. "When Dragon comes by, Hili throws powder in sacks on Dragon. You understand?"

"No. But I tell him."

Tusser grinned. "You'll see, later. Now get everybody in place. Dragon near."

Sumase went off to do the headman's bidding. The timing was good, Tusser believed. Judging by the way the ground underfoot trembled slightly with the beast's footfalls, it must be just around a bend in the coast road. Then Sumase returned to Tusser's side.

"I send somebody to stir up birds also," Sumase reported. "Maybe even Gulper or two, if we lucky."

"My plan works out, nothing be left for Gulpers or birds either," Tusser returned grimly. He hefted a couple of shortened spears, the shafts behind the points oddly wrapped in greasy rags. "But good thought, though. You got fire in pot?"

"Just like you tell me. But I not see—"

The Dragon came into sight. Its rider drew back on the reins, obviously assessing the narrowness of the pathway and whether it would be to his advantage to urge the beast aloft. At that moment, several of the giant birds inhabiting the cliff beneath the battleground flapped into sight from the seaward cliff edge as if to cut off the Dragon's escape. Tusser whistled through his fingers and the Bog-men jumped up from their hiding places, shouting and brandishing their weapons.

"Run, run," some of them chanted.

Others named the rider coward, and not a few added coarse and unflattering comments as to the man's ancestry.

The rider urged his mount forward. Now the Dragon could not spread its wings to drop snow upon them, but a gout of ice issued from its maw as it roared defiance. A few Bog-men, mad for battle and heedless of Tusser's orders to await the signal to attack, rushed forward, jabbing with shell-tipped spears. The rider pointed a metal rod at them but his mount's wild twisting movements made a good shot impossible.

"Back!" Tusser shouted. "Get back!"

He couldn't wait to see whether they obeyed or not. The plan must be carried out, for this would be the only chance he got. The headman looked up toward the top of the low landward cliff and waved. Hili waved back. Tusser saw him draw back his arm, aim, and throw.

One sack hit squarely on the Dragon's back and powder scattered down one side, with some spilling over the ridges on its back to the other side as well. Neither the Dragon nor its rider appeared to notice. The second sack, not as well aimed, hit lower on the Dragon's flank. However, the third struck the rider as well as engulfing the Dragon's head with the deadly powder.

Some of the giant birds were now in action against the great reptile. Others swooped toward the men from the Bog. Tusser could delay no longer.

He stuck the point of one of his shortened spears into the fire pot. The rags caught fire immediately. He launched the spear. It caught the Dragon in the chest, at a spot where only a small amount of powder coated its scales. The second fire-tipped spear lodged in the beast's neck. With a roar that stopped even the most battle-crazed of his men in their tracks, the Ice Dragon was instantly engulfed in flames.

"Back, back!" Tusser shouted again. "Everybody, get back!"

He did not have to repeat that order. The Bog-men scrambled away from the writhing horror the Dragon and its rider had become. Mad with pain and fear, the beast roared, trying to stretch its wings. It succeeded only in losing its footing on the narrow road. Two of the giant birds were struck by the flailing Dragon and, in turn, caught fire. The rest of the flock scattered, flying for their lives, all appetite for battle gone. Three Bog-men went over the edge of the cliff, and their screams blended with those of the giant birds and the flaming Ice Dragon.

A thick stench of burning Dragon-flesh and scorched feathers filled the air. With a second roar the enormous beast shivered all along its spiny back. It shook its head and, as Tusser watched, something flew off and dropped to the ground—the rider. His body still blazed, and Tusser knew it would do so until the powder had burned itself out.

Again, the Dragon stumbled, coming too close to the seaward cliff edge. It scrabbled frantically at the rocks, finding no secure hold. Then it fell, and as it dropped it stretched its wings in a last vain effort to fly.

A spiraling trail of smoke and sparks arose in its wake as it followed the Bog-men it had, perhaps inadvertently, slain. In the shocked silence that ensued, those atop the cliff on the shore road clearly heard the dull crunch as it smashed into the waiting rocks out of sight below. Then the silence was broken by the sucking sounds of splayed feet pulling huge misshapen bodies from the waters, and familiar deep grunts. The Bog-men knew the Gulpers were about to feast.

Tusser drew a deep breath. Now was the moment, he knew, when he would prove himself even better than his father Joal had ever been. Joal would never have known even how to attack such a danger, let alone destroy it. He turned to his companions, grinning.

"*That* how we kill Dragons," he said with an air of careless confidence, as if this feat were one that the Bog-men accomplished every day.

Sumase whooped, and within a moment the remainder of his men were bellowing with the kind of laughter that only comes after escape from a moment of great peril. Even Hili, still up on the cliff above and relatively safe, shouted along with them. From his vantage point he began pelting them with small stones until Lorko and Kipu climbed up and threatened to throw him off.

"What about this?" Sumase said, when the commotion had begun to die down. He indicated the body of the Dragon rider, still burning in the middle of the coast road.

"Leave," Tusser said. "If birds want, let them have."

Sumase grunted.

Lorko came up to them. "We go back to village?" he said. "Vanka say she have something to talk to Tusser about."

It was Tusser's turn to grunt. Lorko was not the most diplomatic of men and he had said Vanka had not wanted to give up the sacks. He could well imagine Vanka's displeasure, and he saw no reason to endure it sooner than he had to. "Go get rod from rider. Proof we kill. Push over for Gulpers if you want. Then we go back to where we fight," he said, fingering the badge he wore as General of the Bog Army. "Tusser promise. Give pledge of honor."

❦

Royance, Gaurin, Hynnel, and Rohan made their way through the camp, the command tent their objective. Snow was beginning to fall again, Royance observed wearily—big, heavy flakes. In a matter of moments it was snowing heavily enough to make visibility uncertain at a distance of more than a few feet.

"I will speak to Harous first," Royance said, "and see if this matter can be settled without quarreling. That is my duty, as Head of the Council."

"Of course," Gaurin said. "Your head is cooler and much wiser than ours."

Hynnel and Rohan also nodded assent, though Royance could tell that they were inclined to proceed with more directness and less diplomacy than he exhibited. If only they knew, he thought. He would gladly take Harous by the throat and shake the truth out of him, if the Lord High Marshal by so much as a breath indicated that the charges against him held even a fraction of truth.

Nevertheless, he smiled, mustering all his diplomatic skills. "Time enough for hostilities, if it comes to that, young men," he said. "Ah, we have arrived."

"Is Lord Harous within?" Gaurin asked the guards outside the door.

"Yes, sir. He had his breakfast some time ago, received preliminary reports of the battle, and has not left his tent," one guard replied. He shivered a little.

"You must be cold, standing here in the open. Go and get some hot food," Royance said kindly. "I do not think anybody is going to attack our headquarters, not while we are inside. And surely not in the heavy snow." Then, when the grateful men had gone out of earshot, he added to his companions, "The fewer ears to overhear what will be said in the next little while, the better."

Gaurin and the others nodded and followed Lord Royance inside, where it was markedly warmer because of the brazier that always burned. The main room of the tent was empty.

"He has his private quarters beyond," Hynnel said. He led the way and touched a small bell hanging beside the entrance. There was no stir from inside and Hynnel made bold to open the flap.

The chamber beyond was empty, yet there was an indefinable sense that it had been vacated recently. A trace of something like perfume lingered on a breeze wafting through a rent in the far wall, bringing flakes of snow with it.

"Did something creep into the camp and attack Harous from behind?" Rohan cried, alarmed. "Some fell northern beast?"

"I think not," Gaurin replied. He examined the edges of the slash in the tent wall. "This has not been torn but cut, as with a dagger."

"But who—" Rohan scowled, his hand on the hilt of his sword. "Lord Harous was taking no chances on meeting with us," he said, answering his own question.

"We must go after him," Gaurin said. "Or them. I see two sets of footprints leading from the tent. Human footprints."

"We must go quickly," Hynnel added, "or risk losing them altogether."

"Yes." Gaurin looked from Hynnel to Rohan, both his kinsmen, one by blood and one by marriage. "Are you with me?"

"Of course," Rohan replied, and Hynnel also nodded assent.

Gaurin turned to Royance. "Sir, diplomacy is no longer an option and this is a matter for younger men, as you yourself put it. Please remain behind in safety while we three go and bring our errant Lord High Marshal back to you."

"I would almost argue with you for the privilege," Royance returned, "but I see the sense in it. Go quickly, while you can."

Without another word, the three slipped through the hole in the tent wall. Royance retreated into the main chamber, closing the flap firmly behind him. Stirring up the brazier for more warmth, he settled down to wait for their return.

Ashen stepped outside the infirmary tent again to replenish the supply of snow needed to cool the water. No need to worry that the white drifts would run out, she thought wryly. Already the fresh snowfall was accumulating on every surface and had reached almost knee depth in the paths. Those would have to be cleared soon for passage among the blocks of tents.

She discovered it was easier, somehow, to deal with the ones who had suffered wounds in the fighting with the Frydians. Their injuries were straightforward, and when their hurts were cleaned and bandaged, they began to heal.

Not so with the men who had breathed in what they were now calling the Dragon's Breath. Everything she tried to do for them, it seemed, simply made matters worse. She wiped her forehead with the back of her hand and straightened up, easing a kink in her back, to see Lathrom approaching.

"Greetings," she said. "And how does my Lord Gaurin? And my Lord Royance?"

"Well enough, Lady Ashen," he replied. "We conferred and now they have gone, with Lord Hynnel and young Rohan, to pay a call on Harous. Lord Gaurin sent me to inform you."

For no reason she could think of, Ashen caught her breath sharply. She twisted the opalescent bracelet she still wore on her arm, and realized that it had grown extremely warm—almost hot. "Gaurin is in danger," she murmured aloud.

"What say you, Lady?" Lathrom said. "No, no danger, surely. You are tired—"

"Gaurin is in danger," she repeated stubbornly. "Or will be, soon. Where did you say he has gone?"

"To the command tent," he said. "Lady—"

She had already left him behind. The command tent could barely be detected. The fluttering russet-colored pennon bearing the device of a tower showed in spite of the thickening snowfall, however, and Ashen floundered toward it.

At the doorway of the tent she nearly ran into Lord Royance. She stumbled and he caught her by the arms before she fell.

"How now, Ashen," the old lord said. "What is your hurry? Has something happened?"

He brushed snow from her shoulders, and belatedly she realized that she had forgotten her cloak in her haste to find her husband.

"Gaurin," she gasped, searching for air. A knot of panic gathered in her throat, making breathing difficult. "Where is he?"

Royance's snowy brows drew together in a frown. "I suppose I must tell you. He and Hynnel and Rohan have gone after Harous," he said. "I stayed behind."

"Which way did they go?"

"Come inside. You must be half frozen."

"Please, my lord. Where did they go?"

"I will show you."

Half frantic at what she considered the old gentleman's waste of time, Ashen allowed him to draw her inside the command tent, where the brazier took the chill off the air. Royance opened a flap in the wall toward the back, revealing the private quarters. A small pile of snow was building ever higher on the wooden planking of the floor.

"It seems our bird has flown the nest," Royance commented. "And so Gaurin, Rohan, and Hynnel have gone after him."

"They are in danger," Ashen said hoarsely. "Great danger. I must find them!"

"Ashen, my dear, please calm yourself—"

"No!" she cried passionately. She shook from head to foot, not entirely from the cold. "I cannot! They—he is in danger, and I can help. Please do not hinder me."

Royance looked into her eyes for a long moment. Then he nodded. "You are not to be gainsaid now any more than when you came to me determined to come to the Camp of the Four Armies. Very well, at least take my cloak. I will be warm enough here."

"Thank you, sir!" she said. She fastened the fur-lined garment around her shoulders. As Royance was considerably taller than she, she had to be careful not to step on the hem and trip herself. "Let us hope that I am mistaken, but I cannot rest until I go to him."

With that, she ducked through the opening in the tent wall. It took her a moment or two to get her bearings. Looking at the ground, she knew she had no time to waste. The footprints of those the three men followed had long been swallowed up in the fresh snowfall, but she could still see traces of those left by their pursuers. Unless she hurried, those, too, would vanish.

She pulled the warm cloak closer around her and started off through the drifts, not knowing which direction to take if she should lose the trail or, for that matter, if she would become so lost that nobody could find her in the storm and she would perish.

In her hut in the Bog, Zazar stirred her kettle and droned a tuneless song. All of her varied sources of Power had told her much the same thing: Some great event was approaching. She knew not whence, or what this would be, though she did suspect. She was glad to be back in her home, if only temporarily, for this was where she could best perform the ritual she was now attempting. If she had remained in the Oakenkeep, she would have had to return for the proper materials anyway, so what was the sense in it? The Oakenkeep was not home at present, not with Ashen, Gaurin, Rohan, Anamara, and the other young people whose strength and energy brightened the very air around them being away in Rendelsham. She felt something very like affection for them, a feeling that annoyed her very much. A Wysen-wyf had no time for such frivolities.

"Change wrought by a Changer," she crooned as she stirred.

The concoction in the kettle displayed streaks of many colors never blending, only swirling endlessly under the strokes of her wooden paddle. Red, green, blue, gold, purple, they spiraled in the wake of the blade the Wysen-wyf wielded. She added a few bits of thread from a ball she had taken earlier from a secure hiding place. The mixture foamed and gave birth to a cloud of smoke. When that cloud cleared, the contents of the kettle had formed a definite pattern. Zazar set the paddle aside and began another song.

"A Changer I brought into this world, and nurtured. A Changer who knew not what she was. A Changer who has read, and learned, yet done naught until—"

Was it to be now? No, the Wysen-wyf thought as she stared into the kettle. But soon. Very soon. Would it be in time? Experimentally she picked up the paddle again and gave the mixture another stir only to watch it settle into the pattern that it had shown after the addition of the threads. She knew she could stir until the dawning of another day, and this design would not alter. It was as unchanging as the Web of the Weavers.

Which, Zazar thought with a trace of humor, was only to be expected, since the fibers she had cast into it were said to be trimmings from that same Web.

She sobered again immediately, concentrating on what lay at hand. One at such labor must be ready for whatever came. At present she knew not what would be required of her, but it would surely be what she had always provided. Zazar turned aside from the kettle to begin opening jars and boxes, laying out various herbs, spices, dried grasses, and other items of her craft. From behind her came a sound as of a muffled explosion and, briefly, an orange glow lit up the interior of the hut. She didn't glance back; she knew that the colorful contents of the kettle had disappeared.

The Wysen-wyf continued her preparations, knowing it was very necessary to be ready when the summons came. Another sound came from behind her, a softer and more reassuring one. Then something soft and furry rubbed against her legs.

"Hello, Weyse," Zazar greeted the newcomer. "You understand, don't you. I had hoped you would come."

For answer, Weyse leapt up onto the table where Zazar was working and hunkered down on her hindquarters, her clever little paws crossed over her plump belly. She began uttering a series of squeaks interspersed with chirps and an occasional purr. Her head was cocked to one side, as if she knew she was being understood.

"No, I don't know exactly when we will be summoned," Zazar said. "We shall simply have to wait until then." She stroked Weyse and listened to her burbling purr. Then she returned to her preparations.

Weyse continued to watch Zazar for a while and then, growing bored, wandered off to another part of the hut where she poked inquiringly into a small bag left untied on the floor.

"Yes, it's a bit of the mixture of dried berries and grain you love. I put it down for you to find. Don't eat it all at once."

Despite herself, the Wysen-wyf smiled fondly on the unearthly little being who was her frequent companion, and on whom she relied more than she knew it was good for Weyse to know.

Then she returned to her tasks. By the time she was ready

to go to bed, she had a large pack filled with various supplies, good for healing or—she hoped it would not come to that—more deadly purposes.

Weyse found her own sleeping place, as was her habit. Sometime during the night, a steady, cold rain began to fall and despite her fur coat that usually kept her comfortable, she snuggled her way onto Zazar's bed and curled up beside her. The Wysen-wyf, grateful for the extra warmth, tucked Weyse under the coverlet where they slept undisturbed until morning.

Thirteen

Gaurin set a brisk pace, Hynnel and Rohan following in his wake. The snow was not as heavy as it had been, though flakes continued to fall. It would not do for them to slow down, however, for those whom they pursued could still escape. Gaurin was still in the lead as they topped a small rise, from where they could get as good a look at the surrounding countryside as was possible through the snowfall. They were, Gaurin realized, close to the road to the valley of death. The snow had laid a kindly veil over the land and for a while at least, no visible traces of that terrible battle remained.

With a motion of his hand he stopped his companions. "Look. But be careful. We must go with great caution now," he said softly.

Hynnel and Rohan crouched so they could not be seen,

and each peered cautiously over the edge of the ridge. They saw what Gaurin had glimpsed—a shadow, or rather two shadows close together, stopped for the moment at least, in a small clearing. *And these shadows had left footprints!* Hynnel pursed his lips as if he might whistle, but made no sound.

"The snow was our friend this time. I don't think they know we are here. I believe they are headed for the valley where the battle took place," Gaurin murmured. "Perhaps they have allies waiting for them there."

"With Ice Dragons?" Hynnel whispered. He shaded his eyes with his hand, trying to see through the falling snow-flakes. Unexpectedly, the snowfall abated.

"Perhaps." Gaurin also shaded his eyes, to no avail. "There are three Dragons left that we know of unless more await in reserve to the far north. We must take even more care now that the weather has cleared."

"Three Dragons. That's one apiece," Rohan said.

Gaurin and Hynnel turned to him in disbelief, but he grinned to show that he was only joking.

"Brave words," Hynnel said. "Let us hope you do not have to eat them."

"They would not be very tasty," Rohan admitted.

Gaurin shook his head sadly. "Alas for all of Lord Royance's obvious hopes that Harous would not be found traitor, I am now convinced that is exactly what is happening."

"He must be stopped," Hynnel said with equal softness, but his tone was grim.

"Aye, and his companion with him," Rohan added. He took a grip on the hilt of his sword. "Shall we go at them in united charge?"

"It may come to that," Gaurin replied. "But for now, I

think they have not yet realized that they are being followed. Let us take what cover we may. There are trees and rocks off to the right. Thus, we may work to get ahead of them. Then when we have cut off their escape, let us take them captive. We will return them to the camp and the justice that awaits there."

"If they do spot us beforetimes, then we can charge them, young Rohan," Hynnel said. He smiled indulgently.

"We shouldn't split up," Gaurin cautioned. "Follow me, and from now on, no talking. Hand signals instead."

Rohan nodded, and Gaurin knew that he remembered what he had been taught from the times they had gone out hunting at the Oakenkeep. Hynnel needed no reminder, having grown up with these same signals. Gaurin led them off the trail to the right and up a slight slope, where a stand of deep green trees promised a shelter from which to maneuver themselves into a good position.

Carefully, with his two companions only a step or two behind, Gaurin searched for spots to tread where no snap of twig or squeak of packed snow would betray their presence. The ground was very stony in this area, and even on the floor of the valley entrance he could make out hillocks that could be hidden rocks.

They could do no better than draw even with the ones they pursued, for more outcrops of rock barred their way. Crouching down to survey the land, it was clear to him that their present position was better than hoped for, however. Because of the trees' location they had managed to come very close to their quarry. All three realized their advantage; now the question was how to exploit it in the best way possible.

Those two shadows had halted now, apparently believing

they were free of pursuit. Voices drifting up to the hunters confirmed this.

"I think that we are safe enough away to dissolve the shadow," a woman's voice said clearly.

Behind him, Gaurin heard the stifled hiss of Rohan's indrawn breath and his hand snapped up in warning.

"No one is even aware that we have gone," answered another voice, a man's. Gaurin recognized Harous. "Let that old fool Royance come knocking. Nobody is home!"

One of the shadows moved, and then both people stood revealed. Gaurin frowned. Neither was clad in the kind of garments needed for frigid weather. Indeed, the woman—an astonishingly beautiful creature—wore only a thin dress that hid none of her charms, with a light cloak tossed over her shoulders. Harous was also lightly attired, though not as scantily as the woman.

Gaurin turned to Rohan. Without a sound, he mouthed the word "Who?"

With exaggerated movements of his lips, Rohan replied silently, "Flavielle."

The Sorceress! A number of pieces of a puzzle abruptly fell into place for Gaurin. This could not be a new thing, this treason of Harous's. He must have been held in thrall by the Sorceress, Gaurin realized, well before the poorly planned battle that had almost cost them all too dearly to continue. But how had such a betrayal come about?

His years of training at the hands of Cyornas NordornKing's military tutor took over. One of many things the retired warrior had drummed into him was to look at a situation from the enemy's point of view as well as his own. Therefore, the battle had not been poorly planned at all, from the viewpoint of the Dragon riders and their Frydian allies. That the Four Armies had managed to rally and then had come out of it as well as they had, killing a Dragon in the bargain, was remarkable.

Gaurin decided to risk a whisper to his companions, hopeful that the conversation the two below were having would cover any sound that might carry to them. They were now discussing Dragons, and observing that the Sorceress's lieutenant, someone named Farod, was late arriving.

"We must move to take them before the Dragon comes," he said softly. "The one representing the greater danger, I think, is Harous. He is mine."

"I'll take the woman," Rohan murmured. "I know her."

"I will help whoever needs it," Hynnel said. "But I think they will not go easily. We really can't be sure which of them is the more dangerous."

"We will find that out speedily enough."

With that observation, Gaurin arose from his hiding place. "Count Harous of Cragden, Sorceress Flavielle, surrender yourselves at once! I command it by authority of King Peres, Lord Royance of Grattenbor, and all of the land of Rendel!" His words echoed, booming from the rocky heights all around them.

Then he charged down the slope toward the two who now turned to stare at him, as thunderstruck as if he had erupted out of the ground itself.

Harous recovered quickly. He drew his sword and put the Sorceress behind him. "You will have to take me, Gaurin!" he shouted in turn. "I won't come tamely, at your call!" Then, at the sight of the others, "Three to one, eh? Those are a coward's odds."

"You are my captive," Gaurin said, grating out the words. "There will be no unfair fight here."

"Give over, and there will be no fight at all. I will take custody of the woman," Rohan said. Both he and Hynnel flanked Gaurin now, with drawn weapons.

"Gaurin, is it? I have marked you as a special enemy." Flavielle gave a sneering laugh. She took a step to stand firmly beside Harous. "How highly you rate yourselves, you poor fools, to think three of you can stand against those who are your betters in every way!"

A three-forked lightning-bolt of power flashed from her hand to send Rohan stumbling back. He lost his footing and fell, his body slamming heavily onto one of the snow-covered hillocks. A cry of pain almost drowned the sick sound of a bone in his arm snapping. A second fork of the power-bolt branched toward Hynnel, halting the action just begun, while the third arced around Gaurin. With a metallic crack, his sword shattered, the shards glittering as they dropped to sink at once into the snow. He hurled the hilt at his enemy and reached for the dagger in the top of his boot.

The Sorceress threw back her head and uttered another taunting laugh. "So much for our enemies. Now, do with them as you will, my Harous!"

Sword at the ready, Harous took a step forward.

The Bog-men under Tusser's command decided, after their first flush of victory, that they did not want to rejoin the fighting forces they had left to do battle with the Ice Dragon. Tusser found an open spot of ground where, according to their custom, they could sit and discuss the matter. As headman, he alone was privileged to stand.

"We not need Outlanders anymore," Lorko said sullenly. "Stay here, go back to huts, get warm."

"Too warm for Tusser, maybe," Sumase said with a wide grin.

He waggled his eyebrows knowingly and several other Bog-men sniggered. Lorko's story of how Vanka had vigorously objected to giving up the sacks of powder, and her threats of what she would do to Tusser the next time she saw him, had gained wide circulation among the surviving members of the Army of the Bog.

"Tusser not happy to go back either, but give word," the Bog General repeated stubbornly.

"Maybe we go by big city of Rendel," Kipu said. "I hear Outlander talk in camp, they say headman over all of us live there. Maybe we go see him. Maybe him and Tusser fight."

That drew a more open laugh and even Tusser had to smile at the thought of a hand-to-hand battle for the position of headman over the entire land. His perspective had broadened considerably as a result of their foray out of the Bog, even if that of most of his companions hadn't. He recognized that there was much, much more to their world than the Bog, or even the occasional Outlander who blundered into it, risking being flung to the Gulpers in their deep, dark pools.

"Tusser not fight with child, and headman King still child without many hairs on his chin," he said. "But I fight anybody here who decide they not want go back to battle camp with me." He hefted a shell-tipped spear and assumed a belligerent stance.

Lorko looked up but, at the prospect of facing his headman in combat, thought better of it and turned away.

"Well?" Tusser challenged. "Nobody fight me?"

Silence, and, following Lorko's example, nobody except Hili, the smallest of them, was bold enough to meet his gaze.

"I fight you," he said, grinning, "if we throw rocks. I beat you then!"

The tension that had gripped the circle of Bog-men dissolved abruptly as the men erupted into shouts of laughter.

"That good one!" Lorko said, wiping tears of mirth from his eyes. "Nobody beat you throwing rocks. Or bags of powder that burn."

"Yes!" yelled Sumase. "How the great high and mighty Outsiders know how Bog-men kill Dragon all by their selves, if we don't go back and tell them? Answer me that!"

Within moments the same men who had been on the point of mutiny were nodding in agreement and nudging each other over the prospect of lording it over the Outsiders who had treated them like hut-guests who had overstayed their welcome.

Sumase got to his feet, hefting his shell-tipped spear. "You and me," he said to Tusser, "we go tell. Rest can stay behind and burn backsides in hut fires if they want. We laugh at them for cowards."

"Lorko no coward," the warrior grunted. He, too, lumbered to his feet. "And no friend of Lorko coward, either." He glared around the circle, and one by one the Bog-men followed his example and stood up.

When the last one was standing, Lorko nodded at Tusser. "We go now," he said.

Ashen found her path a little easier once the snowfall lessened. She still had no idea of where she was going, but surmised that it was in the direction of the battle fought by the wounded men she had lately been tending.

Why would anybody choose to return to that site, she wondered. Then she remembered the tale of the two Ice Dragons, and how one had been buried in an avalanche and the other had flown off in the direction of the Bog.

Perhaps Harous, in his treachery, hoped to fly away as well, to his new allies. She frowned, in spite of everything still unwilling to assign such depths of wickedness to the man who had brought her out of the Bog and set her feet on the path that Zazar had foretold her. And, she reminded herself, killed Kazi in a wanton act of cruelty. A complicated man, Lord Harous, never more so than as at this moment. Surely he must think himself well justified in his action, however mysterious.

Ashen toiled on. Ahead lay a small rise from the top of which she could see better what lay ahead. The sound of voices raised in dispute floated toward her on the still, cold air, and she redoubled her efforts.

She achieved the crest of the rise just in time to see the terrifying scene unfolding below her. Gaurin, Hynnel, and Rohan stood to her right, swords drawn, and opposing them, Harous—and the woman Ashen had briefly seen revealed as the Sorceress! Lightning crackled from the woman's hands.

"No—" she cried, and knew that her protest was in vain.

She stepped into a strange kind of time, where everything seemed to move slowly. The Power from the Sorceress's hand split into three arcs. Rohan went down, clutching at his arm, and Hynnel stood frozen in midstep, unable to move. The shards of Gaurin's sword glittered in the air as they fell. The Sorceress laughed, and Harous, his weapon intact, took a step toward Gaurin, who did not flinch as he reached for his dagger.

At that moment, Ashen realized what he had truly meant when he had pledged his life's blood for her protection. Incongruously, in this leisurely, delayed time, she remembered his exact words, spoken to the shade of his father in the catacombs of the ruined Bog city of Galinth, words meant to be conveyed to the ghost of her first husband, Obern. "It is thanks to Obern that you may now go in peace, and in honor," Gaurin had said. "When you see him, tell him that his lady is well, for I have her in my care. Assure him that nothing will happen to her while I live."

And here he was, unhesitatingly ready to offer himself even unto death if it would delay for a moment the approach of danger to her, or to any of those he led.

A fierce wave of the same spirit engulfed her. "Never! This shall not be!" Ashen cried aloud, her words unnaturally drawn out. "He will *not* die, if I can prevent it!"

With a fury she had never known herself capable of, she drew herself to her full height. Arms upraised, she found a ball of pure Power gathering in her hands. Scarcely knowing what she did, she hurled it down at the tableau before her with every ounce of strength in her.

Below, several things were happening, all almost at the same time.

"Here," Rohan shouted, his words slow and hollow sounding. "My Rinbell sword will fight for you!" He managed to grasp the hilt of the weapon with his good hand and toss it to Gaurin, who caught it neatly.

Another lightninglike blast gathered in the Sorceress's hand but before she could launch it properly, the scintillating ball of Power Ashen had hurled went thundering into the little clearing.

The Sorceress staggered back. Her bolt of Power, misaimed, smashed into Harous from behind. He took a staggering step forward, only to spit himself on the sword Gaurin had just brought to bear. Hynnel, released from his paralysis, rushed toward Flavielle with weapon upraised. She had barely time enough to grab a slender rod from her belt before he was upon her. A cloud of mist gushed from one end of the rod, taking Hynnel squarely in the face. With a superhuman effort, he managed to take another step and cut her down where she stood before he dropped.

Time abruptly snapped into its accustomed pace again. Ashen, released, fairly flew down the slope toward the scene of carnage. "Gaurin!" she screamed. "Oh, Gaurin!"

He didn't turn, though she knew he had heard her. Instead, he was easing Harous to the ground. She reached them in time to hear Harous tell Gaurin not to try to pull out the sword.

"It would do no good, only cause me more pain. Let me die as I deserve, with the blade of justice piercing my body." He shuddered. A trickle of blood escaped his lips. "Flavielle—"

Gaurin glanced toward where the woman's body lay. "She is dead," he told Harous.

"And with her the spell she laid upon me. Did I really turn traitor?" His gasping voice held a plaintive note.

Ashen knelt beside him. "It was not your doing," she said, seeing no need to torment a dying man with the tale of his many misdeeds.

"Aye, but it was, and more—" His eyes seemed to clear, to come into focus. "Is that you, Ashen? I'm not just dreaming?"

"I am here."

"How does my Lady Marcala in Rendelsham?"

"Ill, but well enough when I left her."

He smiled grimly. "Not for long, I'll warrant." The effort of speaking was almost too much for him. He coughed. "I'll see her soon." He grasped at Ashen's hand, and looked from her to Gaurin. "Tell them I'm sorry," he said. "Tell them—"

"We will," Gaurin replied.

But the dying man could not hear him. With the lightest of sighs, the spirit of Count Harous of Cragden, Lord High Marshal of Rendel and Commander of the Four Armies, slipped from his body and was gone on a faint breath of wind.

Then both Ashen and Gaurin turned to the others. It was obvious to Ashen that Hynnel was wounded even worse than Rohan. Both men lay in the snow where they had fallen, moaning in pain. "See to Rohan," she said as she turned her attention to Hynnel.

"It was the burning mist," Hynnel managed to croak. "I tried not to breathe it in, but it entered my lungs anyway. It burns, it burns—"

"Don't try to talk," Ashen said. She looked at Gaurin. "How does Rohan?"

"He is lucky he came out of this with nothing worse than a broken bone," Gaurin said, sparing a glance at her from where he was carefully examining Rohan's injury. "Don't move your arm before I splint it, unless you want to lose the limb. The break seems clean, with no splinters coming through the skin, and that is good. Can you walk?"

"Yes, and I can talk, too," Rohan answered, somewhat irritably. He tried without success to stifle a groan. His face was very pale. "Why do you ask?"

"Well, Hynnel can't move, and I will not leave him alone, nor will I leave Ashen unguarded. Therefore, you are going to have to be the one to get back to the camp and bring back warriors and a litter for Hynnel. Can you manage it?"

Rohan looked up as the gravity of the situation sank in. "Of course," he replied stoutly. "It's my arm that was broken, not my legs."

"I wish I had one of those silly silk roses you used to conjure out of nothing, so that I could make you a temporary sling," Ashen said.

"That was all my tiny gift of Power was ever good for," Rohan said. "That, and lighting candles without touching them. I doubt that I could do even that, now. All that's left is that tingling on the back of my neck when danger is nearby." He blinked in sudden comprehension. "The war-kat in the tent!" he exclaimed. "No wonder my neck was killing me. They always go in pairs, but that one was alone. Now it is clear! That must have been Flavielle, disguised. And to think Lord Royance actually petted her!"

With the stoic practicality of a seasoned warrior, Gaurin removed the cloak from Flavielle's body and began tearing it into strips. "Ashen, please see if you can find some small, straight pieces of wood so I might bind Rohan's arm in a temporary splint."

"Of course." Ashen knew what was required; she had splinted broken limbs before. She got up immediately and hurried to the little copse of woods where Gaurin and his companions had hidden. When she returned, she discovered that her husband had dragged the bodies of Harous and Flavielle off to the other side of the valley entrance and placed them in the shelter of yet another upthrust of the rocks that made footing so treacherous in this area. Hynnel was sitting up after a fashion and Gaurin was just finishing raking fresh snow over the bloodstains.

"Will these do?" she asked.

"Admirably, my Ashen."

"A tree had fallen, and there's quite a lot of dry wood at that spot."

"Good," he said. "That means we can take shelter there and perhaps even have a small fire to keep us warm while we wait for Rohan to return."

"I don't need a fire," Hynnel said. "I'm burning."

Indeed, Ashen thought, he did look more than a little feverish.

"Nevertheless, a fire we shall have, if we need it," Gaurin said. With swift efficiency he was already busy fashioning a makeshift split and sling for Rohan's arm out of the strips of cloth he had torn from Flavielle's cloak. "Rohan, if you think you are ready, please be on your way."

"I'll be back before you fairly know I've gone."

"Don't forget to tell them that we may be expecting the arrival of an Ice Dragon, so they should come quickly, and prepared."

"I will." The young warrior saluted awkwardly with his

left hand and immediately took off at a ragged jog along the path so many feet had made in the snow, his balance uncertain but his resolve firm.

"Now, my Ashen," Gaurin said, turning to her. "While we wait you can explain to me whence came that great ball of Power that did so much damage, and at such a timely moment."

Fourteen

*I*n *a short time* Gaurin had found shelter for them in the stand of trees and had built a small fire of dry wood that gave off very little smoke. Hynnel lay nearby on a bed of dry needles and fresh boughs, his cloak wrapped around him only because of Ashen's insistence. He had sunk into something like a coma. From time to time she left the circle of warmth and checked on him anxiously when his moans grew audible.

"I truly do not comprehend where that burst of Power came from," Ashen said when she returned from one of these visits. "All I know is that Harous was on the verge of killing you, and everything in me said *no*. I raised my arms, there was something between them, and then I was—well, I suppose you could call it 'pushing' and you know the rest."

"I think the Rinbell sword really did fight for me," Gaurin said in his turn. "I had not consciously raised it, and yet it was ready when Harous stumbled against it." He unsheathed the weapon and examined it curiously. "Very fine work," he said.

"I think I was responsible for both Harous's and Flavielle's deaths," Ashen said in a small voice. "If I hadn't thrown that ball of Power—"

"If you hadn't done it, Rohan, Hynnel and I would be dead now and you as well when the fugitives discovered your presence, as they were bound to do. If anyone is responsible for their deaths, it is they themselves."

Ashen could not dispute these blunt facts. Nevertheless, she was sorely troubled by the events in which she had played such a pivotal part.

"Come and rest, my Ashen," Gaurin said. He leaned against the trunk of the tree under which they sheltered and opened his cloak for her.

Gratefully, she crept into the warm, safe haven of his arms and nestled against him, mindful not to hamper him in case danger approached and he needed to be free to defend them all. With another glance at Hynnel, who seemed to be resting as quietly as possible under the circumstances, she drifted off into a light sleep.

🌢

She awoke to the unmistakable sounds of a pitched battle. Gaurin was not at her side but the spot he had occupied was still warm. She turned to Hynnel who was valiantly trying to struggle to his feet.

"Don't do that!" she said. She moved over beside him. "I think we're safe enough in the shelter of these trees, at least for the time being."

"But my kinsmen are fighting—"

"And you are wounded," she said sternly. "Let them defend you. And if all else fails, let me defend you."

He smiled at that. "Gaurin has told me what a fierce woman he married. I believe him. I saw the Power, you know."

She smiled in return, but inside her heart was sinking. He was obviously fretful at being excluded from where his duty lay. "Would you like me to go peer out and report to you what is happening?" she said.

"I would appreciate it." He coughed so violently she was fearful he would start hemorrhaging.

She gave him ice to suck, and the coughing fit eased. Then she made her way cautiously toward the edge of the little copse of woods. Pushing a springy branch out of the way, she gained an unobstructed view of the spirited skirmish out on the rock-strewn plain leading to the valley.

Rohan had sent a considerable force to their aid. She recognized Cebastian's guidon, and was glad that Rohan had had the wit to go to the Nordors. Gaurin had foreseen accurately; perhaps at the same time the rescue party had arrived, an Ice Dragon had appeared. Now the warriors were intently engaged with it, trying to damage it without being harmed themselves. A pair of war-kats circled the Dragon, tenseness apparent in their every move.

It was Ashen's first sight of an Ice Dragon. She found herself holding her breath as she watched. The terrible, unnatural beast was so *big*! If it craned its neck it might be able to peek over the walls of Cragden Keep. Certainly several of them would make short work of the walls surrounding Rendelsham Castle for, unlike Cragden, they were meant for show only and not for real defense.

The war-kats, one on either side, fearlessly hurled themselves onto the beast's flanks and fastened themselves with teeth and claws. Its skin shivered as the Dragon shook itself, but the war-kats were not dislodged. The Dragon rider pulled vigorously on the reins. With a roar that gusted ice crystals into the air the huge beast did not exactly take flight; rather, it flapped its wings and bounced, barely aloft, apparently hoping to catch some of the warriors in its talons. The war-kats leapt to safety as men scattered, depriving the enemy of any easy target. By mere happenstance the Dragon veered toward the copse of woods where Ashen crouched, watching, and the tip of one of the great wings buffeted the trees above her. The trunks, almost as springy as the low branches, were knocked violently askew, rebounding in such a way as to spray the entire area with the snow that had coated their limbs.

Ashen retreated at once in the unexpected shower to see if her patient had been harmed. Hynnel had barely been touched, and only a few chunks of the heavy, packed snow had fallen on him.

"I think they are trying to tire the Dragon," she told him.

"How many men?"

"I didn't count them. Perhaps fifty."

"Go back again and see what's happening."

She nodded. She had not sighted Gaurin when she had been watching before, and could not rest until she knew his whereabouts. By the time she had found another good vantage point, however, the battle was over. As she watched, the

Ice Dragon lifted into the air, tucking its feet against its belly. Then it flew back in the direction from which it, presumably, had come. The war-kats squalled a last challenge and then sat down and began to wash.

Presently she spotted Gaurin leading a squad of men toward the copse and she emerged from that shelter to go to him.

"Are you all right?" she asked anxiously.

"Unharmed. The heavy spears our men were armed with were more than the Dragon or its rider wanted to contend with."

"Do you plan to go after it?"

"No. It is imperative that we leave here immediately before the rider returns with reinforcements. Cebastian and some of our most trusted men are packing Harous's body in ice for transport with us, thence to be sent to Rendelsham."

"Where it will be given honorable burial," Ashen said bitterly. "Does he deserve it after what he has done?"

"We cannot do otherwise."

"And Flavielle?"

"There is no reason to do any more than pile a cairn of stones over her. We must get Hynnel back to camp where he can be cared for, and this episode has shown me that I cannot tolerate the thought of you in danger. I am of a mind to send you, with the honor guard for Harous, back to Rendelsham."

"And I am of a mind not to go."

He smiled then, the creases at the sides of his mouth meeting the crinkles at the corners of his eyes in the way that always made her heart turn over. "Of course you wouldn't. I will think on the matter. But in the meantime you will stay in camp where you are relatively safe and not set foot outside the walls."

"That I will agree to."

❦

Once returned to camp, Gaurin and Ashen settled Hynnel in the physicians' tent. Then they, with Rohan, whose broken right arm had been properly set and splinted, consulted privately with Lord Royance in Gaurin's quarters before joining the remaining officers in the command tent. There they told him the true circumstances of Harous's ending, sparing nothing.

"You have done well," Royance told them. "Better that Harous die swiftly and cleanly than face a traitor's trial either here or in Rendelsham. He will return and be laid to rest a hero. It is pretense, yes, but pretense for the ultimate good of the country. Much better that, than his treachery be known to cause dismay throughout the land. Dynasties have fallen for less cause."

He brushed his hand across his eyes and Gaurin knew the old gentleman, despite his resolute words, had been profoundly shaken by what had happened. Royance must have harbored a hope, however faint, that Harous's loyalties had remained true.

Then Royance took a deep breath and squared his shoulders, putting all his private feelings aside. "Rohan, do any of the men you sent to Gaurin's aid know aught of what he has just told me?"

"No, sir. Gaurin gave me no instruction on the matter but I knew that telling them would not be wise. On the way back to camp I had time to construct a plausible story. Actually, I embellished the truth just a little."

"Tell us these embellishments so that we will not destroy the pretense unawares."

Gaurin also was interested, for he had relied on Rohan's good sense and discretion out of instinct, not by plan. Cebastian had not volunteered any details of the story Rohan had taken back with him and Gaurin had not asked. It was, however, obvious to him that the brave young knight had no idea of the true state of affairs.

"As far as Cebastian knows," Rohan related, "the marshal ventured out alone, as he had done before, to survey the battleground, perhaps to learn where we had made mistakes so we would not repeat them. Knowing his danger, we went after him, to escort him back safely. We found him in combat with Flavielle, and her lieutenant, Farod. She distracted him, and Farod, the one the Nordors fought later, bested Harous. Then Hynnel was injured, striking her down in turn. We were nearly killed ourselves. The lieutenant fled to retrieve his mount. Hynnel, Gaurin, and Ashen would surely have perished when Farod returned, had they not sent me back for aid." He smiled. "When you think about it, this tale is not that far off the mark."

"If you wanted to develop it, you have some natural talent as a liar, you scamp," Royance said wryly. "Very clever. The tale will hold up if there is not too close scrutiny of it."

Rohan had the grace to blush. "All I did, really, was bring Flavielle's lieutenant into it earlier than he actually was."

Despite the gravity of the situation, Gaurin was amused. He had not thought Rohan to have had such a quick wit.

Ashen spoke up. "You are without question the ranking noble here, Lord Royance. As such, I have something to ask of you."

He turned to her courteously. "It is granted, of course, but first I must tell you this. You are in a unique position, my dear. You are not a ruler, as the Dowager Ysa continues to be, but you were the one with the wit and courage to act on vital information on a matter that affected the country's safety where she did not. I perceive you may well have a great deal more to offer us."

"Not I so much as my Protector, Zazar," Ashen replied. "We need her here. *I* need her here. And I petition that I be allowed to send Rohan in one of his swiftest ships to fetch her."

"How say you?" Royance asked the young knight.

Rohan glanced down at his arm ruefully. "I'm out of the fight for good this time," he said. "Even with Granddam Zaz's potions this won't heal by the time the war's over, I warrant. So I am available to run messenger service. I will go, and gladly."

"Good," Royance said. He arose from Gaurin's camp chair and the others likewise stood. "Now let us join the other officers before they begin to wonder what we are doing in secret. That is how rumors are born and rumors are the last thing we need to contend with just now."

"I will leave you to it, for my responsibility calls me to the infirmary tent," Ashen said.

"Go with our gratitude," Royance replied. He took her hand and kissed her fingers. "I take this liberty with your permission, of course, Gaurin."

"I, too, am very proud of my lady," he said.

Then they left his cramped quarters and each went to his or her duties.

When Royance, Gaurin, and Rohan arrived at the command tent, Royance took Harous's former place at the head of the table while the other men found their own seats. Royance wasted no time in trivialities.

"We need to settle several matters, all pressing," he said without preamble. "First is selecting an honor guard for Count Harous's body to escort him back to Rendelsham. Though we can ill afford to have any of our officers or men absent, nevertheless we must send a full complement. Chevin, as Harous's lieutenant, will lead them."

The young noble bowed his head in assent.

"Pick whom you will to accompany you, but not more than a dozen. Rohan will not be among them, for I have assigned him another errand. There must be a military funeral with full honors. Let the Dowager make the preparations, only impress upon her that your swift return here is vital for everyone's safety." Then Royance looked at each of the men in the tent, piercing them with his hawklike gaze. "The next matter. Who will be our new Lord High Marshal?"

Steuart glanced up from the dagger he had been toying with. "I propose that you assume this office, sir," he said. "Who else but Royance of Grattenbor is as well qualified?"

Royance shook his snowy head. "Alas, I fear that what so many have told me is correct. My fighting days are over."

Lathrom spoke up. "There would be no need for you to take the field, sir. Leave that to younger warriors. You carry with you a lifetime of experience. Please, sir. Guide us now."

"It is well thought on," Gaurin said, pleased to know that his private preferences were those of his fellow officers as well.

"I will speak for Admiral-General Snolli and add my voice to that of the others in voting aye," Rohan announced. "I have no doubt that when General Tusser returns he will also agree."

Around the table, the junior officers nodded. Cebastian, Steuart, Reges of Lerkland, Jabez of Mimon, Gidon of Bilth, Vinod of Vacaster, and Nikolos of Grattenbor, who was Lord Royance's deputy, all thumped the table with the flat of their hands in approval.

Chevin, Harous's lieutenant, was the last. Harous's death had hit him hard, more so than the other officers. He arose from his chair. "Sir, with the death of my lord, I have lost my will for command. When I return from the sad errand you have assigned me, I ask leave to be excused from my duties as an officer and be allowed to join the common soldiers, there to fight in the front ranks and perhaps to die."

"Denied," Royance said. "You will remain a part of the staff of officers, and do your duty as you have been trained."

Chevin sat down again, but he did not raise his head.

"Lord Royance, you must have Lord Harous's badge of office," Gaurin said. "He left it behind when he—when he departed the camp. I will get it."

He entered the living-quarters area of the command tent, gratified that the meeting, so far, had gone exactly as he wished. It was only natural that Royance would become their new marshal. In anticipation, he had found a moment to give private orders to Jervin, Royance's steward, to see that the rent in the far wall be repaired and the room made habitable once more.

Jervin waited within. "All is ready, sir," he said.

"This will suit Lord Royance well," Gaurin said, looking around. Everything was, indeed, neat and tidy. Royance was well served. "Where have you put Harous's personal belongings? We will send them back to Rendelsham, of course, but there is something I need for Royance, a badge of office. It is a medallion on a chain."

"Here, sir." Jervin indicated a small chest on a table nearby. Gaurin recognized it as the one that had originally been kept in the main section of the tent. "I gathered everything of that sort, put it inside, and brought it here."

Gaurin lifted the lid, not surprised to discover several items including what had to be the Diadem of Concealment and the rod that emitted Dragon's Breath in the chest. He laid the rod aside, picked up the medallion, and returned to where the officers were waiting.

"Sir, please allow me the honor," he said.

Royance nodded, and Gaurin ceremoniously put the chain over the old noble's head, arranging it on his shoulders.

"I have something else for Lord Royance," Rohan said.

Royance raised one snowy eyebrow. "And what would that be?"

"Sir, I was granted a pair of war-kats. Like me, one of them has an injured paw. She is out of the action, and her mate will not fight without her. Please, allow me to place them in your care at least while I am gone on my errand. I can think of no one I would rather have in charge of them."

The old gentleman smiled. "It's been a long time since I

have had the privilege of having the company of war-kats," he said. "I will be honored."

"Thank you."

"There is another pair of war-kats to be reassigned," Gaurin said. "Hynnel lies in the infirmary and until he can fight again I propose that they go to you as well."

Royance quirked one snowy eyebrow. "I am like to be covered with war-kats at this rate," he said. The officers seated around the table laughed, not entirely out of politeness. "Perhaps Lathrom deserves them more. But, as with all war-kats, they will go where they will and not always where we would have them."

Rohan turned to Gaurin. "Now that that's settled, I also have a boon to ask of you."

"If it is in my power to grant, I will do so."

"Please do me the honor of keeping my sword and using it in place of the one that was broken. It is said of a Rinbell sword that it will fight for its wielder, if the cause be just. It was my father's."

"The honor is mine," Gaurin said. "I think it fought for me once, and will again. I thank you."

Rohan turned to Royance. "Now, with your permission, sir, I will depart on the errand you have assigned me, but before I leave, I will bring Keltin and Bitta to you. Bitta's the one with the injured paw."

He arose, bowed, and left the tent. Gaurin judged that the time was right to bring his special project before the officers.

"I have been thinking," he said, and recounted the tale of how the trees had flexed and bent under the buffeting of the wings of the Ice Dragon. "When we were fighting the beast it reminded me of an idea I had earlier for a weapon to use against them. Now that we know what we are facing we need to build catapults, of course." He hoped no one would remember that Harous had opposed this project. "What I am proposing now is something new. If we could set two of these young and springy trees in a stationary platform, like the arms of a bow, we might bend them back with a windlass. Then we could set another tree, its branches trimmed and the point sharpened—"

He saw looks of interest and comprehension dawning on the faces of some of the young warriors. Even Chevin came out of his despondency and Royance nodded thoughtfully.

"With this machine," the new Lord High Marshal said, "you could pierce a Dragon from a good, safe distance."

"That would be my hope," Gaurin replied. "And we could always fall back on catapults to throw great stones at them."

A few others had not received this idea positively. Steuart arose to speak for them. "It seems to me," he said, "that this might be beyond the customs of war. Would not this weapon be entirely too powerful?"

"Perhaps," Royance answered, "in another sort of warfare. But look you, young Steuart. The Ice Dragons are an unprecedented weapon of war in and of themselves. This—this giant bow that Gaurin is proposing is but a counter to what we face, not an escalation of weaponry."

Steuart considered the High Marshal's words. "There is merit to what you say. I will lodge no further objection."

The Lord High Marshal nodded, his authority and leadership almost palpable. "Then set the men to finding trees suitable to the task and build as many of both of these machines, as possible." Royance glanced around the table. "It will serve to keep the men's minds off our recent near disaster in battle. It is always well to keep them busy, and ourselves as well."

❦

Snolli merely shrugged at the news that Lord Royance was now High Marshal of Rendel. "Makes no difference to me," he said. "Go, be an errand boy. Take *Spume-Maiden.* I'll stay here and fight from my deck on *Gorgull,* the way a Sea-Rover should."

Gratefully, Rohan accepted and set sail before his grandfather could change his mind. A few days later, he arrived at the Sea-Rover stronghold. With a good wind behind them they had sailed past the cliffs at a brisk pace, but not so swift that he had not been able to make out the remains of what had once been an Ice Dragon at the bottom of a precipice. It was rapidly being reduced to bones by predators.

"Wonder how Tusser did it," he said to himself, and made a mental note to ask later. His vote for Royance as High Marshal in Tusser's name had been but wishful thinking. When he had heard how the Bog-men had gone immediately to defend their own piece of Rendel, he had had no doubt but that the Dragon would prevail and kill them all. He found himself unexpectedly hopeful that his somewhat capricious ally was still among the living.

Even if there had been an anchorage anywhere on the rocky rim of the Bog, he would have dared go no other route than the familiar one he had known since childhood, full of good hiding places in case Bog-men less friendly than Tusser were about. That meant anchoring *Spume-Maiden* in the harbor at New Vold.

Harvas, her captain, offered to accompany Rohan into the Bog, but he declined the company. "Trust me, I will be quicker gone and returned if I go alone," he said.

"It goes hard with me to let the Chieftain's grandson venture into that dark and dismal place," Harvas replied. "I got my first look when we sailed along the cliffs and had to fight great birds and nasty swimming horrors. You were just a mewling brat at the time."

"Well, Snolli isn't here and I'm all grown up now," Rohan said. "Believe me, I am. I'll be all right. When I was a youngster I spent almost as much time there as I did at New Vold or the Oakenkeep. But if it will make you feel better, go with me to the Barrier River and post guards until I come back."

The captain had to grudgingly settle for this concession. He selected half a dozen of his burliest sailors in addition to himself and then, with Rohan safely placed in the middle, they journeyed cross-country, thence along the river to the familiar ford.

There Rohan left them, despite renewed protests from Harvas. Almost gratefully, he plunged into the dank gloom of the Bog and, alone and without any untoward incident except nearly slipping on a patch of ice, arrived at Zazar's hut. To his surprise, he found the hearth cold and the Wysen-wyf sitting on a large pack half asleep, her fur-lined traveling cloak about her shoulders. Weyse was curled beside her, napping.

"Looks like you were expecting me," he said.

"Of course I was," Zazar said, unsuccessfully stifling a yawn. "And you're late. Sit down, sit down. Supper grew cold a long time ago, but I can strike the fire again and warm it up if I have to. What happened to your arm? And your hard head?"

"It's a long tale, and I'll entertain you with it on the ship."

"Ship? What ship?"

"The *Spume-Maiden*, Granddam. She's mine now—or, at least, close enough to claim her for my own."

"No need for a ship just to go to the Oakenkeep."

"What?"

"Did that knock on your head make you deaf? I said we didn't need a ship just to go to the Oakenkeep. Maybe you've gone daft instead."

Rohan felt the conversation slipping rapidly from his grasp. "Let's start over. My ship, the *Spume-Maiden*, is waiting for us. The Oakenkeep is not our destination."

"Oh," Zazar said.

"I thought you knew—"

"Well, maybe I don't always know everything," the Wysen-wyf admitted grudgingly. "There are some details I might be a little vague on. I expected Ashen might have returned from Rendelsham to the Oakenkeep, and we were going to be with her. That's why I was all packed and ready. You had me thinking we'd be sailing down the Great Barrier River like a flock of loons."

Rohan held onto his reason with both hands. "No, Granddam," he told her, "we're going north, close to where the battleground is. Ashen is there and she sent me. There have been many terrible things happening. You're needed."

"Then why didn't you say so? Here you are, dawdling about wasting time with story-telling and asking for supper with the fire out and the ashes swept. That doesn't make any sense. We have to get going! You take the pack, and I'll look after Weyse. Don't keep babbling at me. You can just wait awhile and give me the whole story once we're on the ship and on our way."

She set off at a brisk pace, leaving Rohan to shoulder the pack lopsidedly, and wonder at why he was so fond of Zazar when she had to be the most difficult, exasperating woman he knew.

Fifteen

🌿

A cloud of almost palpable gloom hung over all of the city of Rendelsham and, in those parts of the country where the heralds had taken the news, over Rendel itself. With the death of Count Harous, Lord High Marshal of Rendel and leader of the Four Armies, the spirits of the people dropped sharply. No matter that he had died a hero; his absence was sorely felt.

Harous's body was already in the family crypt of the vault at Cragden Keep, kept packed in ice, awaiting the final, private rites. An effigy lay in the Great Fane of the Glowing, resting upon Harous's shield and covered with the Marshal's banner showing the badges of the Four Houses—Oak, Yew, Ash, and Rowan. As much of the populace as could make their way into the Fane filed past in respectful mourning until the day of the funeral, when the nobility occupied the choice spots in the Fane and only the luckiest ones of the commoners would be able to crowd in to watch.

The Dowager Ysa, First Priestess of Santize, the premier lady of Rendel, stood beside her grandson, King Peres, as the service for Count Harous droned on. There were no fireplaces in the Fane, of course, and no braziers either. It would have been unendurable had it not been warmed a little by so many bodies packed in it. Her hands, bare of gloves so that the Four Rings could clearly be seen, were stiff and blue and she wished for boots such as the men wore. The floor was so cold that her feet were numb. Though she kept her demeanor grave, giving the proper responses at the proper times, her thoughts were busy, occupied with other matters.

Two state funerals within such a brief time, and an entire House, a staunch ally of both Oak and Yew, now vanished as if it had never been. What a pity, Ysa thought, the late Countess Marcala had not fulfilled her dynastic duty and produced an heir. Now, however, when the Cragden vault was closed, it would never be breached again, for Harous was the last of his line. Ysa made a note to order a magnificent monument be erected over the entrance to the vault and seal it permanently, with appropriate sentiments carved into the stone attesting to the bravery and valor of all the Cragdens, the last count the most staunch of all, falling in defense of Rendel.

Poor Marcala, so ill that she had been out of her mind at the last. Ysa didn't believe a word of the nonsense she had babbled. Poison indeed. A strange malady, yes, but natural. Ysa hoped it would not bring more cases in its wake. She made a note to consult Master Lorgan and have herself examined thoroughly, in case she had contracted something.

After all, she had been most assiduous in nursing her poor, doomed friend.

Vaguely, she hoped that the exiled king of the Nordors, Hynnel, would recover from the injury suffered when he had gone to Harous's aid. That wretched Sorceress and the weapon that burned out men's lungs! Ysa rued the day she had ever trusted the woman. But then, she had not known she dealt with any but a Magician, a man, being totally unaware that the woman was going in disguise. All of the Dowager's innate distrust of her own gender came back upon her full force. Better, far better, she thought, to rely on those she knew from long acquaintance that she could trust such as the unfortunate Marcala. Or unearthly servants, such as the flyer Visp.

She glanced past the King to Lady Rannore, his mother. Her shameful condition was very apparent, and in Ysa's opinion, to the point of dictating that she retire from public view. Ysa knew that Rannore had been questioning members of the military escort for news of her baseborn husband's wellbeing even as Ysa had questioned them for news of how the war was going now that the Lord High Marshal had fallen.

Perhaps it was all to the good that Royance had gone haring off into the snowy wilderness with the Bog Princess Ashen on that fool's errand. Royance was, Ysa had to admit, the best qualified of all Rendelian senior nobles to take up Harous's duties. Despite his silver hair and the age that would have bowed his shoulders had he not fiercely resisted all such signs, it had been little over a score of years since he had defended his property, or what he deemed his, in full siege from neighbors too ambitious. He knew full well what he was about, even if he did not take the field personally.

The ceremony was drawing to a close. Harous's effigy, still resting upon his shield, would now be shouldered by his military honor guards. Then the funeral procession would wend its way out of the Fane, through the streets of Rendelsham, and along the well-worn road to Cragden Keep and the vault that awaited. Ysa and King Peres, of course, would form the head of the cortege which would also include those senior nobles still in the city for the Countess's recent funeral. Out of the corner of her eye, Ysa glimpsed Wittern of Rowan, the King's grandfather. Just behind him would come Gattor of Bilth, as lazily sleepy-eyed as ever. He had come in for his share of criticism, Ysa knew, because the war was being fought practically in his back yard, with Bilth Keep close by. Surely he should have been in residence but Gattor had never been a warrior. His conflicts had ever been conducted in the shadows and few were the times men could more than speculate on his part in the sudden collapse of an ally of a House rumored to be encroaching upon his own holdings. It was no surprise to Ysa that he preferred to stay in Rendelsham now, where he was relatively safe.

Valk of Mimon, Jakar of Vacaster, and Liffen of Lerkland ranged themselves behind Gattor. It remained only for her and the King to assume their positions and then the final portion of this sad occasion would begin.

Despite the solemnity of the moment, she was glad that only her feet would suffer. Her black mourning dress was heavy and warm, and she would not be required to go without a cloak. It was enough that she, the Dowager Queen, wearer of the Four Rings, holder and guardian of the true power in Rendel, would be forced to go on foot, to honor the dead.

King Peres turned to Lady Rannore. "Madame my mother, you are excused from this last sad journey," he told her. "Please, return to Rendelsham Castle where you will be warm." He gave her one of his rare smiles. "And also for the sake of my brother, or sister, who waits to be born."

"Thank you," Rannore said. "I will obey."

Then Peres addressed Ysa. "And you also, Madame Granddam. This is no matter for women. Let the men take up what is rightfully their duty."

"I would gladly go, to honor Harous, but will stay behind, at your request," Ysa told him.

"When we have come back from Cragden, we will send for our fair cousin Hegrin," Peres continued. "She dwells, we are told, in Rydale, for the safety it affords. But since there is no longer any safe place in this land, we would have her by us and to that end have already written out a letter to this effect. To lend a kind note to our request, we have bethought ourselves of a certain strand of pearls, strung with sapphires, in the royal treasury. Please have it ready when we return, for we would send it to her, in loving friendship."

Ysa opened her mouth, and then closed it again. There was that in her grandson's face that told her protest would be futile. Instead, she dropped a small, stiff curtsey. "Yes, Your Majesty," she said.

Inwardly, she was furious, warning bells clanging a far from melodious din in her mind. She knew full well what this might entail, with the King now of marriageable age, if barely. Now, while Ysa searched out the pearl and sapphire necklace, she would have to begin thinking of a way to thwart what was surely to become a dangerous situation, with the daughter of the Ash heiress and the King of Rendel in such close proximity to one another.

Dalliance was one thing, but marriage another and, unlike either his father or grandfather, Peres was not one likely to be given to trifling with a woman's affections. When he wed, she, Ysa, would choose the girl and the daughter of the Bog-Princess Ashen was, without a doubt, the last one Ysa would ever consider.

"Come in, young Chevin," Lady Rannore said. She showed Chevin to a seat by the fireplace where spiced wine was being heated by her maid. "I am told that you will be leaving Rendelsham now that the funeral is over."

"At first light tomorrow." Gratefully, the young knight pulled the chair closer to the warmth and accepted a goblet of the steaming mixture. He drank deep and then set the goblet aside, rubbing his hands to get some circulation back into the fingers. "Thank you, Lady Rannore," he said. "It was brutally cold, on the way to Cragden and back, in formal clothing. Now I fully understand the wisdom of the many layers of tunics and other garments that Lord Gaurin and Lord Hynnel bade us wear. We would not have survived our first week in the encampment without them."

"It was a sad journey, bringing Lord Harous back for burial."

"Sad and more than sad. But we are most grateful that Lord Royance was there, to step into the breach. He is a brave old gentleman, and I doubt not that he will lead us well."

"Please forgive me for asking again. Blame it on my condition. You are certain that my lord Lathrom is well?" Rannore asked.

"For a few moments by your fire and the pleasure of your company, I would answer the same question a dozen times over," Chevin replied gallantly. "Yes, he was as well as any of us when we saw him last."

"Almost I would not ask for tales of his exploits, but I find that I must."

"He fought valiantly at the battle of the valley. If it had not been for him leading our men against the Frydians who hoped to fall upon us when we were in disorder after the avalanche, I daresay that the war would be over by now and ourselves not the victors."

Rannore shook her head in wonderment. "Would that I could be there, with my kinswoman Ashen. Tell me of her as well."

Chevin smiled; obviously this was a pleasant topic for him. "She is the very embodiment of what we fight for," he said. "Without a thought for her high station, she tends the wounded from daylight to dusk. She always has a word for everyone she meets, and just to see her lifts all our spirits."

"Keep her safe, when you return." Rannore sighed. She took a packet, wrapped in waterproof covering and tied with yellow ribbon, from the table nearby. "Please take this to her. In it are letters for her and for my husband as well. Tell her— tell her that we who wait behind are concerned for her."

"She will be safe, as long as any of us have breath in our bodies," Chevin promised. "Oh—I almost forgot, in the press of other matters. I do know something that might lift your spirits a little. You know that Rohan suffered a broken arm and is out of the fight."

"Yes, I had heard. It must go hard with him."

Chevin smiled. "We might tease him about making a capital errand-boy, but we know he chafes at it. Anyway, there was a story in camp, before the honor guard left, that Rohan had been sent off on another mission, to bring the Wysenwyf of the Bog with him when he returned."

"That is news indeed!" Rannore exclaimed. "For what purpose?"

"That I do not know, Lady."

"It is one more mystery among so many. Perhaps Rohan can report to Rendelsham Castle now and then, as part of his duties, and bring us news."

"I will suggest it to Lord Royance," Chevin promised. "And now, Lady, I must regretfully say my goodbyes. My thanks for your hospitality, and know that I will deliver your messages to Lady Ashen personally."

He rose from his chair and Rannore attempted to do likewise. Her bulk made the task difficult. Chevin offered assistance.

Rannore put her hands on his shoulders. "I will give you three kisses to take with you," she said. She touched her lips to his right cheek. "This is for Ashen, who is my dearest friend." She kissed his left cheek. "This is for Lord Royance, whose bravery and valor is an inspiration to us all." Then she kissed Chevin lightly on the lips. "And this is for my sweet husband, whom I would fain have by my side, were all well with the world."

"I will convey these dear messages as faithfully as I will

your letters," Chevin said, "and count myself fortunate to be your messenger. Farewell, Lady, until I see you again."

Ashen settled once more into the routine of the camp as she awaited Zazar's arrival—always supposing that Rohan would be able to persuade her to leave the Bog and journey northward.

Boredom always being a soldier's worst enemy, it became a great diversion to the warriors to occupy themselves, when they were not constructing catapults or working on the windlass that would propel the giant crossbow, to make bricks of snow and construct walls around every tent and shelter, replacing the casual piles and drifts.

Some of the men, stationed to the north side of the encampment where the winds were strongest, had discovered that such a snow wall, instead of making them colder, had the opposite effect. Consumption of wood for fires and braziers went down sharply, and warmth was conserved. Soon, little could be seen of individual dwellings as snow walls arose everywhere. The command tent, the infirmary, and the tents occupied by the officers were enclosed first and then the men worked on other areas. Ashen was amused to see signs appearing on the walls to aid the men in finding their way, now that other landmarks had quite disappeared inside what was becoming known as the Snow Fortress.

To her further surprise and sometime amusement, every war-kat in the Fortress, once it had come into her presence and sniffed her and, presumably, found her acceptable, became her friend. If she ate with the officers in the command tent, Bitta would try to climb up into her lap and, if rebuffed, would hold up her injured paw for Ashen to massage gently while Keltin blatantly stole tidbits from her platter. Pyegan and Rosela, Hynnel's war-kats presently under Lord Royance's care, sat by, patiently waiting their turn for Ashen's attentions. If she took an hour to go back to the tent she now shared with Gaurin to lie down and rest from her nursing duties, either Rajesh or Finola would come and stretch out close beside her. More than once she awoke to discover one on either side, keeping her warm, as now. She sat up, yawning.

"You are very good, faithful creatures, and very big nuisances," she said affectionately, giving them kisses on the tops of their heads. "I would stay, but there is much work to do."

She eased the stiffness out of her back. Warm she might be, but two war-kats took up a lot of room on the narrow camp bed.

She put on her cloak and stepped outside, grateful for the snug, fur-lined boots she wore. It was snowing again. It seemed to her that it was always snowing here. The best thing one could say was that the falling snow made battle impossible, and also provided the cooling packs and chilled water for the men suffering from the effects of Dragon's Breath. As she made her way down a passageway of snow-brick walls toward the infirmary tent, the war-kats pacing beside her, she passed one of the laundresses who carried a stack of clean clothing that steamed slightly in the cold air.

"Is that for Lord Gaurin?" Ashen asked.

"Aye, marm, and a bit for you as well," the woman replied. She eyed Rajesh and Finola warily and gave them a wide berth. "Now that yon beasties not be within his tent, I will go in and leave all upon the bed, if it please you."

"The—the beasties won't harm you," Ashen said. "Only our enemies."

"They be in residence, I dasn't go in," the woman said stubbornly, "but leave all outside."

"Very well," Ashen said. "I thank you for your good service."

The woman bobbed her head, blushing, and slogged on through the deepening snow, leaving a faint sulphur smell in her wake. Ashen wondered idly how the laundresses managed to find water for washing and air hot enough to dry the garments that they were still steaming later. She promptly forgot about the matter as she entered the infirmary tent.

Dragon's Breath victims, segregated from the others in a curtained-off area to make caring for them more efficient, had not improved since last she checked on their condition. However, Ashen thought as she made her rounds, they were not much worse and the rest were healing rapidly enough that several could be discharged on the morrow. Hynnel seemed the most ill, but then, she thought, that must have been because he had taken the mist from the hollow rod Flavielle had wielded full in the face whereas the others had encountered such only in passing. The armsman, she learned, who had charged full at the Dragon atop the mound of snow after the avalanche had been afflicted as badly as had Hynnel, and he had since died. Only one of the warriors, Norras, seemed close to being as ill as her kinsman.

"Water," Hynnel whispered when she came to his bedside. "Please, water with ice in it. The jug is empty."

He lay drenched in sweat. Ashen peered around the curtain and called to two of the other women busy at the other end of the tent to help her change his bed and the clothing he wore.

"Let me sponge you off as well," she said. "Would that make you feel better?"

"Whatever you do, you make me feel better, dear cousin," Hynnel said. He made a gallant effort to smile, and Ashen's heart cramped with pity for him.

In a few moments, she and the other women had stripped the soiled garments from him and had efficiently made up the bed with fresh linen from the pile the laundresses had brought. It, too, was still warm and also smelled faintly of sulphur. Ashen sat down on a stool beside the bed and began to wash Hynnel's face and limbs with cool water as he drank thirstily from the newly filled goblet she gave him.

"I wish I could do more for you," she said. "And those others who are suffering from the same malady. Would you like something to eat?"

"Just water for now," Hynnel answered. "Please, be sure the jug is filled to the brim. Perhaps you could leave a second one as well."

She shook her head. Since he had been brought back he had refused everything but a few bites of bread, and now she could count his ribs. "You must eat something. You are wasting away."

"Perhaps a little cold meat, later."

"I must go and tend others now," she said, "but I will be back." On impulse, she dared to tease, to threaten him playfully. "With a dish of cold roast fallowbeeste if I have to go and hunt it myself."

To her pleasure, he smiled again and it reached his eyes.

"I said you were a fierce woman," he said. "And now you prove it again."

"Sleep if you want to," Ashen told him. "I will be nearby."

Then she arose and went back to her duties.

Far to the north, the Dragon-rider Farod waited outside the curtain of ice that shielded the Great One Whom All Served from the blasphemy of being viewed by unworthy eyes. Soon enough he would speak, and Farod was in no hurry to learn what the Great One would say. The fact that he had been sent for boded ill for him, and he cringed at the thought of taking full blame for the disastrous loss they had suffered.

The hood on Farod's light cloak was thrown back and, had he wished, he could have looked at his reflection in the ice curtain that would have shown him what service to the Great One had wrought upon his features. Once golden of hair with skin that turned dark brown in the summer months, Farod now was bleached from the cold, his hair and skin as white as if frost-bitten. This frosty skin was stretched taut over sharp bones and his eyes, the only color to be seen in his face, were sunk into the sockets and covered by lashless lids.

Flavielle's body lay on the bier carved of ice that occupied the center of the chamber where Farod waited. With his own hands he had washed her clean of the blood of her death-wound, a wound that she would not have suffered had he been nearby, and caressed her covertly as he had done on too few occasions while she was living. Then he had composed her limbs, dressed her in transparent white and laid her here, to wait.

He stared at her, full of longing, fingering the hollow metal rod he had taken from her body. "From this day forward I vow I will use no other weapon in battle," he murmured. "Ah, my Flavielle, most brave, if only—"

An answering whisper came from behind the curtain. "She is dead. She cannot hear you."

Soft as it was, the sound filled the chamber and echoed from the icy walls.

"You loved her." The Great One had not posed a question.

"She was my commander. My superior. I gave her my love, yes, and my respect."

"You gave her more. You loved her and still do, the way a man loves a woman."

It was true. He had loved her more than his life—more than anything, even the Great One, so much that he was happy even for the few crumbs of her affection she tossed him now and then, when she was not otherwise occupied. He begrudged every moment she spent with someone else, but to no avail. She ruled this aspect of her life completely, as she did in every other matter.

He had never known such rage as when he returned for her and discovered her dead, with her latest lover with her, and a force of the hated Nordors ranged against him, bearing long and heavy spears that presented even him with a threat. He had had to retreat, for a time, until they had departed and he could gather the lifeless form of his beloved and bring her back to the icy palace wherein dwelt the Great One. If her lover's body had still been with her, he would have worked great mischief upon it, but it was gone. He could only surmise that the Nordors, for reasons of their own, had made off with it.

The voice behind the ice curtain whispered on. "And why should you not be in thrall to her? I desired and loved her as well—yes, even I. She would have been the greatest of consorts, by my side, after she conquered the world for me. She was perfect except for—shall we say, certain weaknesses of her flesh. She was indiscreet. She wanted Power for her lover, equal to her own. I found it hard to overlook."

Farod's limbs would not support him and he went down to his knees. Thus had Flavielle whispered in his ear, on occasion, of Power that they two could share. This was worse than being blamed for her death. The Great One knew all! "Forgive me, my lord."

"Oh, it is not you to whom I refer." The voice, still a whisper, filled his head. "I was willing to let her have some indulgences. You are forgiven, for you are among those who are in my trust. But she went outside our circle, searching for other pleasures. That was her undoing, I fear."

Farod bowed his head in silence, hoping that the Great One was truly as indifferent as he seemed to be, and would not order his death with his next words. Then a tendril of thought, as fragile as mist, wafted through the ice curtain and insinuated itself into Farod's head.

Instinctively he fought against this invasion as he realized what memories were being sought. "No—" The cry was as suddenly stilled as more tendrils emerged and wrapped him in a cocoon from which there was no escape.

—the first time, long ago, when he had dared touch her, and first her denial and then her eager response—her summons that brought him and the Ice Dragon to Rendel and their flight with

the half-conscious girl they had abandoned in the Bog—Flavielle locked in an embrace with him as they flew back north—another embrace as they waited atop the mountain before the avalanche—

Farod writhed, as much as his bonds would allow. Surely this—this probing that uncovered every secret would bring him to painful death. He could only hope that it would be swift coming.

"There, there," the Great One whispered soothingly inside his head. "This is good. Very good. Your remembrances will give me much pleasure. I am grateful for them. So much so that I will award you her position. You, Farod, are now the leader of the Ice Dragon Riders."

Abruptly the tendrils withdrew. Farod discovered that he was lying on the floor of the ice chamber, on his face.

"I must not drain you of all your memories at once. I will savor them instead, one by one. It may take years."

"My lord." Farod could only mouth the words, but he knew that the Great One heard.

"Arise. You must now advise me. The war has not gone well. What shall we do now?"

Shakily, Farod pulled himself to his feet by holding onto the ice bier. He did not dare risk a glance toward the occupant. "Our Frydian allies are no match for any but the Bog army. Chaggi, their commander, agrees. Three of our Ice Dragons have been destroyed. Snow now falls where our enemies are encamped and there will be no fighting until it ceases. My lord, we need more allies—strong, able men."

"We have them," came the whisper from the Great One behind the ice curtain. "I have already sent for the Baron Damacro and his human army. When the snowfall stops, you will lead them, the remaining Frydians, and the three Ice Dragons in an all-out attack." Then the Great One seemed to change the subject. "Do you know a man called Piaul? Or one called Duig?"

"No, my lord."

"Duig is true, but Piaul and his followers were in her thrall as well. They came to me, following after her when she left Rendel. They did not know they were going to war. Yes, she convinced them to turn to our cause, and I think it takes no imagination to know how she did it. Piaul and his soft-handed friends have had some interesting times, being trained by Duig. They will fare worse than you. Much worse. You will put them in the vanguard, where they will be destroyed in the next battle."

Relief that he was still in the Great One's uncertain favor made him bold. "Our enemies will be demoralized with this bold action and we will surely triumph!" Farod said, louder than he intended. The echoes boomed from the chamber walls, nearly deafening him.

"I will personally see that you do."

Farod remained there, unmoving, for a moment, uncertain as to whether or not he had been dismissed. Then, to his amazement and alarm, the floor around the column of ice began to shift, to change, and walls sprang up with great swiftness. In moments Flavielle's body and the bier on which it lay were encased in a shimmering, crystal dome. If he had not leaped back quickly into the only obvious entrance into the chamber and pressed himself against the icy wall of the corridor outside, he would have been enclosed with her.

As he watched, the transparent tomb floated toward the ice curtain that did not part but yet allowed it passage through. In another moment, all had disappeared.

Farod discovered that he was shaking, as if from an ague, and all his limbs were weakened. The Great One Whom All Served had granted him a reprieve, that much was certain, but he had no illusions that this was anything but temporary. He lived only because he was still useful. He had detected, through the pain and fear of the tendrils that had penetrated his skull, an even greater depth of malice than he had ever observed the Great One display. When the war was over, whatever the outcome and supposing that he survived it, and his memories had been thoroughly wrenched from him, he could look forward to nothing but the most painful, agonizing death that the Great One could devise.

Any direction he looked, he found nothing but death staring back. If he had been free, he would have fled to the other side, even as Harous had turned traitor, but he knew that even that avenue of escape was blocked for him. The Great One would smite him down before the thought was half-formed.

Perhaps, if these new allies could bring the swift victory he had promised, and the world was the Great One's to savor, he could crave the boon of a swift death. That wan hope was all that was left to him.

Sixteen

he return of Tusser with his little army bearing their trophy of war, the mysterious hollow cylinder that spat Dragon's Breath, was almost completely eclipsed a few days later by the arrival of the Wysen-wyf of the Bog. Men crowded the walls of the Snow Fortress, eager to get a glimpse of this famous and mysterious being, and were rewarded by the sight of a stocky figure stumping doggedly through the snow as if she hurried toward a welcome shelter.

"Zazar!" With a cry of pleasure and relief, Ashen hurried toward the stockade gate and the Wysen-wyf. At the last moment, she restrained herself from embracing the older woman, knowing that Zazar had never encouraged or even allowed such open gestures of affection. Nevertheless, Ashen was glad to see her Protector and not only because Zazar's skills were so sorely needed.

"It's cold out here. Where am I to live?" Zazar asked by way of greeting. She stared at the walls of snow-bricks. "You can't expect me to dig a hole in this miserable mess." She was dressed in many layers of oddly assorted clothing and in addition had slung a shawl over her heavy cloak, which gave her a very peculiar appearance.

"There is a snug tent already prepared for you," Ashen said, "close by my own." She glanced beyond Zazar. "Where is— Oh. I see him." Rohan came staggering up the path, lugging a large pack with his good hand, followed by others of the Sea-Rover crew of his little ship, *Spume-Maiden*. "Give you good greetings, Rohan," she said. "Well met after a successful journey. Set the pack down. Someone else will carry it for you."

"Not likely, Ashen," Rohan said. "Granddam Zaz has been most particular about who touches it. Seems that only I will do." He glanced around. "A lot has changed since I went away, it would seem. How d'you find your way around? Oh, I see. Signposts. That's clever. Hope there's one saying 'This way to the Sea-Rovers' place.' "

Something wriggled and chattered under the shawl around Zazar's shoulders, and a furry nose poked out, sniffing the cold air.

"Weyse!" Ashen exclaimed. "You—you brought her with you!"

"Of course I did. I couldn't leave her behind, not when she offered to go," Zazar said.

Delight and concern warred within Ashen as she stroked Weyse's head. How would this little creature fare with the war-kats stalking through the encampment?

She would find out soon enough, for Rajesh and Finola

appeared as if out of nowhere, to station themselves by her side. Weyse stared at the war-kats and, as if nonplussed, the war-kats stared back. Then they turned away and Finola began to wash. Ashen breathed once again, relieved that a catastrophe had been averted. It would have brought an ill omen to Zazar's arrival had they decided that Weyse was prey, a suitable mouthful for any who chose to chase her down and trap her, and there was none who could say them nay, not even Zazar herself.

The Wysen-wyf had been watching the interplay between the furred ones as if she knew the outcome beforehand. "Well, that's settled," she said. "Show me to this tent and let me catch my breath. Then we will go and see the men Rohan tells me are suffering from something called Dragon's Breath."

"How was your journey?" Ashen asked as the three of them made their way down one of the snow-packed streets. Already the newfallen flakes were ankle deep, and the passageway would need to be swept again.

"The water was choppy and the ship tossed more than I was comfortable with, but we survived. The coastline is still marked with fire-mountains, though they are not as active as they were at first. Daresay they'll start up again if the Great Foulness decides to come down from the north."

"You can't think such a thing is possible!" Ashen protested.

"I can't think it isn't. His Putrescence must think by now that the war needs his personal rotten touch, what with his pet Sorceress dead and all. Very brave of Harous to have fought her. She was a danger to all she came in contact with."

Ashen exchanged glances with Rohan and bit her lip. Obviously he had told her the story he had concocted for the benefit of those who had not encountered Harous and Flavielle and suffered for it. She nodded; she was not yet prepared to tell Zazar the truth about Harous's association with that evil woman, though that time must come. "Even braver," Ashen said, "for Hynnel to have killed her. He was grievously harmed in that encounter and it was for that, as well as many other things, that I have begged you to come."

Zazar shrugged. "I knew I would be sent for, sooner or later. Is this the tent you spoke of?"

"Yes. Come inside. I gave orders that you should have hot soup waiting for you. And for Weyse," she added.

Zazar, Ashen, and Rohan entered the shelter and at Zazar's direction the young Sea-Rover put the bulky pack on the camp bed. Zazar took off her shawl and cloak, laid them aside, and looked around with a skeptical expression on her face. "I suppose this will do," she admitted grudgingly.

"It's as good as any accommodations we have," Rohan said. "You even have a small brazier, to keep you warm once it's lighted. Now, if you don't need me for anything else at the moment, I must report in."

He gave them both a salute and ducked back out through the tent opening.

Ashen also removed her cloak and sat down on the bed. She uncovered a tray that had been left on the little table beside Zazar's bed. The soup was still hot enough to steam in the chilly air. She offered it to Zazar. "Here, please. The soup will warm you up and make you feel better."

Zazar, unaware that the chair she now occupied was considered a luxury, accepted the cup of warm liquid and drank half of it. Then she set the rest down for Weyse and turned to Ashen. "Very well, let me take out a few things from my pack and then I'm ready to go see the people you are so concerned about that you dragged me halfway across the world. Weyse, you stay here."

The little furred creature seemed perfectly content to obey, snuffling greedily over the cup Zazar had given her. Zazar retrieved the shawl from where she had dropped it and arranged it on the camp bed for Weyse to snuggle into later, if she wished. Then the Wysen-wyf opened her pack, took out a few items, and tucked them into a smaller pouch. She drew the strings tight and slipped them over her wrist, and donned the cloak again.

Ashen fastened her own cloak and then the two of them left the shelter.

"As you'll see, the infirmary tent is close by. The one Gaurin and I share is just a few steps farther on." Ashen indicated a place where Gaurin's spring-green ensign flew, indicating that the General of the Nordorn Army was in the camp. "You'll soon learn your way around."

"Bet it takes a large brazier to heat that place. I wonder why he has to have such a bigger tent than mine," Zazar commented, peering through the doorway left in the snow wall.

"Of course it's bigger," Ashen snapped. "It has to be! He's the commander of the Nordors and second only to Lord Royance himself!" She bit her lip but couldn't call back her sharp words.

Unexpectedly, Zazar grinned. "For a while there, I thought you'd lost all your spirit. Good to see you haven't.

Yonder's a banner with a pestle and mortar. Is this the infirmary?"

"Y-yes, it is," Ashen stammered. It was the first time, to her recollection, that Zazar had ever teased her. She had been known, many times, to torment those she was fond of, particularly Rohan and sometimes even Gaurin. In a flash of insight she realized that this marked some kind of turning point in their relationship, but what this actually meant, she could not tell. At the least, Ashen felt an unusual trace of affection radiating from the old woman.

They entered the tent, into the familiar, to Ashen, smells and sights of the sickroom. Efficiently, Zazar examined the few men still present with battle wounds. Most had been discharged and only the worst hurt still remained. The other patients were, expectably, accident cases or, more numerous, frostbite victims.

"And how are you treated?" Zazar asked one.

"Snow packs, marm," the soldier told her. "Then, when we're thawed out a bit, warm compresses."

"That's good. Very good."

"Mostly, we gets our ears or noses frozen when our hoods fall back and we don't notice. Sometimes toes or fingers gets it, too. Don't take long, not in this weather, y'see."

"Yes," the Wysen-wyf said, nodding. "I do see."

Then she turned to Ashen. "Show me the others."

The two women moved toward the curtained-off area. Inside, the women Ashen had trained had just finished changing the beds and helping the disabled men into fresh clothing. The laundresses had not yet come to gather the soiled linen to be washed.

"Greetings, Hynnel," Zazar said. She pulled up a stool by his bedside.

"Well come indeed, Madame Zazar!" Hynnel exclaimed. He immediately began coughing. "Forgive me. Sometimes, when I speak too loudly or enthusiastically, this happens." He wiped his lips on a scrap of linen he grabbed from a nearby stack of similar pieces of cloth, clean and neatly folded.

"Do you often bring up anything when you cough?" Zazar asked.

"Not often, though it seems I should. Mostly, I am just exhausted by it."

Zazar opened her pouch, selected a small packet, and shook the contents into the cup that was always nearby Hynnel's bed. She poured water into the cup, stirred the mixture, and gave it to him. "Here," she instructed. "Drink it all down, no matter how bad it might taste."

Obediently, Hynnel put the cup to his lips and swallowed. Then he handed the cup back to Zazar and smiled. "It isn't nearly as nasty as I thought it would be, and I can feel the heaviness in my throat and chest loosening a little."

"Good," Zazar said. "That's its purpose. This is no remedy, understand, but if it eases your symptoms, that cannot be a bad thing."

"Most gratefully accepted, great Wysen-wyf."

"You may have to cough again, and if you feel the need, do it. It will be to your benefit to bring up what's troubling you."

"I will." Then Hynnel lay back upon his pillow, pulled the bedcovers up, and fell into a light sleep.

"I have never before seen him do that—pull the sheet

and blanket over him, I mean," Ashen whispered, not wanting to disturb Hynnel's slumber. "He is always complaining of being too hot."

"Yes," Zazar mumbled absently. With a touch so gentle it did not disturb the sleeping man, she took his wrist and counted the heartbeat. Then she felt his forehead, pulled up one of his eyelids, and sniffed at his breath. When she had finished, she beckoned Ashen to follow her outside the curtained-off area.

"You say he complains of being too hot?" she said.

"Yes. And the other men as well. We can scarcely keep up with their demands for cool water and ice packs to put on their chests. They say they are burning up."

"Hmmm." The Wysen-wyf absently tapped her fingernail against her teeth, thinking. "There is no fever. I would have felt it on his skin, or smelled it on his breath. There was something, though, something else—"

At that moment, three laundresses came in to gather up the soiled clothing, bearing fresh garments to replace the used ones. They brought the usual whiff of sulphur with them as they entered.

Zazar reached out her hand and caught one of the women by the arm. "You, there," she said imperiously.

"I's done nothing wrong!" the woman exclaimed. Fear reflected in her face and her eyes opened so widely the whites showed all around the irises. "I's no thief, marm, never stole nothing!"

"Nobody is accusing you." Zazar leaned forward and took a deep breath, smelling the stack of clean clothes. "Where d'you go to do your washing?"

The woman relaxed just a little. "Why, to th' hot pools, marm."

"Hot pools. And the water smells like this?"

"Yes, marm. Fearful stink it is some days, but you gets used to it." The woman laughed suddenly. "You thinks we heats our water over cookfires? Couldn't keep up with th' demand, if you takes my meaning!"

Ashen frowned, puzzled. One small mystery solved, but another revealed. "I've never heard of any hot pools," she said. "Where are they?"

"Why Powers love you, marm, they's just a bit off to th' east, they is, and around a bend. Some of us can drive, so we takes the dog sleds there and back. With enough willin' to go, light enough work. Better'n back home in Rendel where we has to scratch for what we gets and keep fires under kettles at that."

"Put away your clean linen inside, and gather up the soiled clothes. Then show me the pools," Zazar ordered. She turned to Ashen. "I want to try something. Look you, ever since the stirrings from the north began, we have been troubled by unrelenting snow and cold and ice."

"That is true, if you leave out the fire-mountains."

Zazar made an impatient, dismissive gesture. "That's nothing but the Great Foulness creating deep stirrings that make the earth crack. Perfectly natural, if you can call such disturbances things of nature. No, snow and cold and ice are his, and precede him like an army of heralds."

"Then," Ashen said slowly, "the men suffering from Dragon's Breath are not hot—"

"—but cold!" Zazar finished for her. "Here, let me show you. Is there water heated?"

"Yes, we always keep some at simmer for emergencies, to wash away the matter that comes out sometimes when their cuts are nearly mended, and for the frostbite victims as well."

"Show it to me."

Puzzled, Ashen directed Zazar to the place at the far corner of the tent where their tiny remaining stock of medicines was kept. A small kettle sat to the rear of the brazier, and nearby stood a larger vessel full of water with which to replenish it.

"Close your eyes," Zazar ordered.

Ashen obeyed. She felt a draft as if of the tent flap opening and then shutting again, and heard some soft splashing.

"Give me your hand."

Ashen held out her hand, felt Zazar's strong old fingers on it, and then it was plunged into liquid. She cried out and struggled against that implacable grasp but to no avail. Without willing it her eyes jerked open. "Why would you scald me, Protector?" she protested. "I have done nothing—"

"Look, Ashen." Zazar released her hand and gave her a scrap of linen on which to dry it. "This water is not hot. It is near freezing. See the bits of ice still floating in it."

Ashen rubbed her hand, trying to understand.

"It is in how the mind perceives what has happened. You were expecting hot water, and so your mind told you that was what it was. You know better now, don't you."

"Y-yes," Ashen said.

"As with you, so with the men beyond yon curtain. When they are in the process of thawing, frostbitten fingers, toes, noses, ears feel as if they are afire. The Dragon's Breath froze the lungs of any who breathed it in, and it registered with them as burning instead."

"Then what we—what I have been doing has only made them worse!" Ashen exclaimed, appalled.

"No, you did the right thing and for the same reason that you do not plunge frozen fingers into hot water to thaw them, not if you want to keep them intact. Now the time has come to introduce these poor frozen bodies to warmth. I was thinking of a hot bath and wondering how I could arrange it under these conditions. Now the way is made plain to me."

"We will need the sleds for the men, and litters as well. I'll go and get Rohan to arrange for them."

"Yes, do," said Zazar, already lost in her own thoughts. "I have something else in mind for him to do as well, and the sooner he starts, the better."

While waiting for Rohan to organize a stretcher party, Ashen and Zazar returned to the Wysen-wyf's tent. There, Zazar said, she wanted to inventory the stores of medicines she had brought with her, and Ashen could help.

"I've got something that, when taken over time, will help boost men's resistance to the cold," Zazar said. "We'll have to measure doses carefully. Supplies are limited until I can go back to the Bog and bring more, now that I know what's needed."

"Anything, at this point, will help," Ashen said somberly.

"And," Zazar added with a mysterious tone, "I have a little something else in mind as well."

It was on Ashen's lips to ask what that might be when they ducked through the opening to Zazar's new living quarters and she caught sight of a tableau that almost stopped her heart.

Rajesh and Finola had returned to the tent, nudged their way inside, and made themselves at home. Rajesh occupied the chair, and Finola reclined at her ease on the bed, with Weyse clutched in her paws. To Ashen, it appeared, at first glance, that she had Weyse's head in her mouth. Ashen took a step forward, a cry of protest on her lips, but Zazar stopped her.

"Look again," the Wysen-wyf advised.

A rumbling purr, interspersed with contented trills, filled the air. So far from harming Weyse, Finola was industriously washing the odd little creature with her rough, pink tongue, and both the war-kat and Weyse were enjoying the experience immensely.

"I don't believe you need be concerned about Weyse's safety in camp," Zazar said. She laughed aloud, a sound that Ashen had heard but seldom, and never, in her recollection, in amusement. Derision, yes, and even disbelief, but never delight, such as now.

Someone outside the tent cleared his throat, signaling for attention. "Come in, Rohan," Zazar said, still chuckling.

"I have four sleds ready and enough litters for the rest," he reported. "What is *that*?"

He was staring, unbelievingly, at the scene on the camp bed.

"One of Gaurin's war-kats—"

"Finola," Ashen supplied.

"Yes, Finola. Well, she seems to have adopted Weyse."

Rohan began to laugh in turn. "And just look at Rajesh!"

he exclaimed. "He looks every inch the proud papa!"

"Well, it's plain to see that it's safe to leave Weyse alone while we go to find these hot pools," Ashen said. "What of Gaurin? Did you tell him what you were about?"

"Of course I did. He's going with us. There have been rumors of fresh stirrings to the north, and he would guard you and your charges. Also," he added, nodding at Zazar, "he sends his kindest regards which he will convey in person within a very short time. Also, Lord Royance wishes to pay his respects."

"I always said Ashen did herself more than proud when she married Gaurin," Zazar remarked. She rummaged in her pack again and added a few more items to the pouch fastened to her wrist. "Well, let's be off. This Royance fellow can wait. I'm as eager to see the pools as any."

To Ashen's dismay, the war-kats insisted on coming with them to the pools. With both her and Gaurin leaving the camp, there was no denying them, and Finola carried Weyse in her mouth, as gently as she would have carried a kitten. Weyse made no objection, but Zazar rescued her neverthe- less, preferring to settle her on the sled that would carry Hyn- nel.

If the war-kats accepted Weyse, the same could not be said of the sled dogs. They bristled, lifting their lips in deep, scarcely heard growls, and in spite of the harnesses they wore, began to stalk stiff-legged toward the small furred one. Im- mediately, the war-kats took up vigilant positions flanking the sled and issued answering growls as their tails lashed from side to side. The men assigned to driving the sleds waded in fearlessly, slapping dogs aside and establishing discipline in a no-nonsense manner, thus avoiding an unpleasant incident. Reluctantly, the dogs assumed their positions at the fronts of the sleds and dropped to the ground, elaborately ignoring what they were forbidden to touch.

Eight men touched by the Dragon's Breath were brought out of the infirmary tent; the four who were the most ill rode the sleds where beds had been prepared for them, and the others, despite protests, were conveyed in litters gladly carried by their companions.

Gaurin, swathed from head to foot in his wulvine-lined cloak, found a moment to greet the women. "Your presence is most welcome, Madame Zazar," he said. He lifted her hand to his lips, and in spite of the heavy mittens she wore, kissed it. "And you, my Ashen? Are you well?"

"Always, when I catch sight of you."

He smiled, and Ashen's heart cramped at how tired and worn he looked. With the worries and responsibilities of war to burden him, there were more lines in his face than before. In an effort to lighten his day, she told him of the dogs, the war-kats, and Weyse, and was rewarded by seeing him throw his head back and laugh out loud.

"How wonderful!" he exclaimed. "We must be sure the story spreads. It is just the thing to lift soldiers' spirits. Building snow-brick walls has lost its appeal, and the war engines are almost completed."

"Boredom is one of our worst enemies, I have learned," Ashen explained to Zazar. She gazed at the guardsmen lined up, waiting for Gaurin's command to march. "I believe the drama of the war-kats and Weyse, plus the discovery of the hot pools the laundresses have kept secret, will provide conversation material for quite a while."

The laundresses, as if hearing themselves mentioned, came into view, loaded down with the bundles they had been accustomed to conveying by sled. Soldiers stepped forward to help.

"Good enough," said the woman to whom Zazar and Ashen had spoken earlier. She loaded an enormous pack into a soldier's waiting arms. "You gets 'em dirty, so you might as well lend a hand when it comes to taking 'em where we gets 'em clean again."

The soldiers laughed, and then Gaurin gave the signal to move.

The place of the hot pools could be sensed long before the caravan arrived. Steam rose well above the ridge of snow-covered rock that surrounded the place on three sides. Inside this little pocket in the mountains, Ashen discovered humid warmth that prompted her to remove her heavy, fur-lined cloak. The laundresses were already taking the bundles of soiled clothing from the soldiers carrying them and making for their favorite spots in the series of sulphurous pools that dotted the landscape. The sled-drivers placed the conveyances in an area that looked to have been used for the purpose many times before, and unhitched the dogs. They trooped, as if by habit, to a particular place and lay down to sleep.

The war-kats likewise found locations from which they could observe all that was going on and, if necessary, sound a warning. Finola settled Weyse between her paws, and there the little creature from the Bog stayed.

"Come, Ashen," Zazar said. "We must locate a pool that the laundresses do not use. It must be very warm without being boiling hot. It might be necessary to bring snow in to cool it, at least for the first bath."

Obediently, Ashen followed the Wysen-wyf as she tested the temperature of one pool and then another. At length, after rejecting several, Zazar found a pond, somewhat distant from the rest, that seemed suitable. It was not fed directly from the ground, as the others were, but was the result of runoff from a small one that the laundresses did not use. With the help of the guards, the women brought their patients to the pool and saw to it that they immersed themselves in the warm water. With this accomplished, Ashen found a few moments to look around at this strange place.

Though snow still fell, even here, it sizzled as it struck the water. The ground around the pools, though devoid of vegetation, still was warm enough that snow did not collect. The air seemed too moist to allow for the drying of the clothes after they had been washed, but on a higher elevation some distance away Ashen discovered the ingenious solution the women had devised.

Perhaps with the aid of some of the men who, on occasion, drove the dog-sleds, they had erected a drying shed and filled it with racks. Here the rocky ground was heated, perhaps from the underground passage of the water, and the air was dryer. All that was necessary was the flow of air, and someone had rigged a panel woven of twigs and branches that served as a fan to move the air through the shed when the natural breeze did not suffice.

There was a definite routine to the laundresses' activity. Certain pools were used for the actual cleansing; other pools were reserved for rinsing. As the now-clean articles soaked, the women entered the shed and took down the clean, dry, warm garments, folded them neatly and wrapped them to keep the snow off. Then the women returned to the rinse pools, wrung out the clothing, carried it to the shed, and laid it over the racks. One woman untied the ropes on the fan blade and started its motion while all waited for Zazar to judge that the sufferers from Dragon's Breath had completed their initial treatment.

"A very neat arrangement," Gaurin commented with some amusement. "It is one that, I confess, I had not even questioned until now. I was just grateful that we could all stay clean and dry."

Ashen was not allowed the luxury of remaining long in her husband's company undisturbed. Zazar called to her.

"Come and help me mix a certain potion," the Wysen-wyf said. "It must be drunk soon after being stirred and I only have two hands."

Whatever taste the mixture had was disguised by the sulphuric tang of the hot water. Zazar would not allow snow to be melted for the brew.

"No time," she said. "We must get this into them while they are still warmed from the bath. And anyway, this water must contain healing properties as well."

When Hynnel had been given his dose, he had scarcely swallowed it before he began coughing. "Madame Zazar!" he said, breathless, "this is even worse than before!"

Zazar crouched down beside him where he still lay in the pool. "Yes," she said, touching his shoulder with unaccustomed gentleness, "and will be for a while. I will be frank with you. The Dragon's Breath froze your lungs where it entered them."

He stared at her, comprehension growing on his face. "And now it is like the situation when a wound mortifies, is it not?"

"Yes. The tissue that was frozen is dead, and must be removed before you can hope to get better. That means you must cough." She handed him a clean scrap of linen.

The other men were likewise beginning to cough, deep and racking, and they reached eagerly for other scraps of linen that Ashen and a couple of the laundresses gave them.

"You won't bring up much, the first time," Zazar said, dusting her hands and getting to her feet. "But once begun, it will continue. Now, your lungs are loosened by the beneficial heat and my herbal drink. Later, back at the infirmary, we will wrap you in blankets and heat stones to place beside you to help the process."

Then the men were helped from the pool, covered warmly, and settled in litters or sleds. The company of laundresses, invalids, healers, and guards started back for the camp.

"One moment," Gaurin said to Ashen and Zazar. "When we get back, your presence is required in the command tent."

"What for?" Zazar demanded.

"I believe that Rohan mentioned earlier that we had had word of some stirring among our enemies to the north. If we are to fight again, you and Ashen must be informed of our plans, so that you can make preparations of your own."

"In anticipation of what we and the physicians will be facing later," Ashen finished for him, through numb lips.

"Yes, I fear so."

"Gaurin, I want to go with you, when you march out," Ashen said, an edge of urgency in her voice.

"Never!" he shouted. And then, more softly, "Never. No, my Ashen, I would never put you into such danger, or allow you to put yourself in peril—not while there's a breath left in my body."

"I realize that there is some risk involved, but hear me out." Ashen tried to sound as calm and reasonable as possible. "We will set up various areas so that we can work more efficiently, treat the most serious cases first while the ones less severely hurt can wait. If I am there, I can make judgments on the spot as to where to send the wounded so that we don't waste time."

Gaurin frowned, a single line cutting deeply between his brows. "It is unprecedented, entirely contrary to all the customs of war. Nevertheless, I will think about it," he finally said grudgingly.

As they once more came in sight of the encampment, Ashen determined to bring it before the meeting to which she and Zazar had been invited. Gaurin would be expected to try to discourage her, and she should have known better than to approach him privately. But the other officers might see the sense in her suggestion.

And anyway, it wasn't as if she was anticipating taking up a sword and plunging into the thick of combat. She would stay well back from the fray—though, she knew with a sinking feeling that thoughts of Gaurin's safety would be uppermost in her mind.

Also, she had to admit if only to herself, if Gaurin were

wounded, she would be in a position to tend his hurts immediately.

Something bitter rose in the back of her throat. No! she cried silently. He must not be hurt. She would die before she let anything happen to him.

Seventeen

_Of *course I know* who Lord Royance is," Zazar said impatiently. "I've just never met the man, that's all."

"If you had, you would never have referred to him as 'that Royance fellow,' " Ashen said. "It sounded disrespectful."

"I think that Madame Zazar is having some amusement at your expense, my Ashen," Gaurin murmured in her ear.

Ashen stared first at her husband and then at the woman who had nurtured her from the moment of her birth. Zazar quickly glanced away but not before Ashen caught a definite twinkle in the Wysen-wyf's eye.

"What has gotten into you?" she demanded. "We face a horrible enemy, whose weapons do such terrible damage, and I see you more merry than ever I have known you to be in all my life."

Zazar sobered. "A fair question, deserving of an honest answer," she replied. "Perhaps it is because I sense that all is now drawing to a conclusion. Whether for good or for ill, I cannot tell."

"Would that you could, Madame Zazar," Gaurin said somberly.

"We should be tending the wounded," Zazar said, "instead of wasting time in meetings."

"Our patients are so tired from their excursion that all they want to do now is sleep," Ashen pointed out. "It will do no harm to meet with our brave officers before they march off to battle."

Zazar shifted Weyse on her arm; beside her, Finola nudged against her anxiously. "Oh, don't worry so much," she told the war-kat. I won't let anything happen to your 'baby.' "

They reached the command tent and Gaurin ushered the women inside. Lord Royance looked up from his place at the head of the table and rose to his feet. The younger officers, including Harous's newly returned honor guard, hastily followed his example.

"Great Wysen-wyf of the Bog!" Royance exclaimed. "Your presence is most heartily welcome to us!" He bowed to her. "Ashen, my dear, it is good to see you again as well. Come, gentlemen, make a place for our honored guests."

Chevin came forward to escort both Ashen and Zazar to seats at the far end of the table; Gaurin took his chair next to Royance as his second in command.

"I have a message for you, Lady Ashen," the young knight said. "There were three messages in all, and I have delivered the first two." He glanced at Gaurin, who nodded. Then he kissed Ashen on her right cheek. "This is from Lady Rannore, who is proud to call you her dearest friend."

"As she is mine. Thank you, Chevin."

Then Ashen gave her attention to the discussion as it resumed. Snolli nodded at the women and then took up his tale.

"We must've put a good fear in 'em," he said complacently. "They won't send another of those Dragons after us soon, that's for sure, not after we killed one and left it to wash up on their shore. We sail as we please, up and down the coast, far enough out that they think we can't see what's going on."

Seated beside him, Kasai, the Spirit Drummer, looked up from the small drum he had been stroking, and spoke. "They don't have our secret," he said, grinning. "Chieftain's got a far-see glass and all they've got is those flying monsters that won't come close."

"I have heard of viewing instruments such as this," Royance said, "and think that one would be useful on land as well. If you ever come across another, please keep me in mind."

"I will. Anyway, what we've seen is companies of men, marching from the north. Sometimes there's a Dragon with 'em, sometimes not. They don't seem to be in any great hurry. We lose sight of 'em somewhat to the north of the burnt Frydian camp. I think they turn inland."

"This has been confirmed by our scouts and hunters," Gaurin put in. "Also, that they are not all Frydians. Our enemy has found better allies."

"Indeed," Royance said heavily, "I recognized some of the descriptions of cognizances. Some of us remember certain nobles who departed Rendelsham in the wake of the revelation of the viper our Dowager Queen had, unwittingly, harbored."

Steuart spoke up. "Piaul and his followers. At the time we thought ourselves the better for their absence."

"Just so. It is a terrible day when those on whom we should rely turn traitor."

Ashen glanced at Royance but his countenance showed nothing beyond his statement. He is a better master over his feelings than I, she thought. I could not keep it to myself that the biggest traitor of all is the man whose position he now occupies.

A sudden commotion between her chair and Zazar's attracted everyone's attention. Bitta had nudged up to Ashen, as was her wont, to have her hurt paw massaged. In so doing, she had apparently come too close to Weyse, dozing comfortably on Zazar's lap, and Finola objected strenuously. Both war-kats were now fizzing at each other, fur bristling. Pyegan and Rosela, Hynnel's war-kats now in Royance's care, stalked forward, possibly to join in. Rajesh was on his feet, alert and protective, but not yet menacing. In seconds the command tent could have been filled with snarling, battling war-kats had not Royance intervened.

"Stop that at once!" he shouted sternly. "Both of you. Bitta, go to your bed. You, the other one—"

"Finola," Gaurin supplied. "Her mate is Rajesh."

"Yes. Well, you, Finola, sit. And be quiet. Rajesh, Pyegan, Rosela, leave be. Leave be, I say!"

There was no gainsaying Royance's authority, not even by independent-minded war-kats. The animals obeyed, if reluctantly.

"Now," Royance said, looking around the table at the officers who were a little more interested in the diversion than was seemly. "We know of the enemy's approach. It is up to us to choose the battlefield. Gaurin?"

Gaurin arose, placed an upright support on the table, and unrolled a map on it for the others to see. "Here is our camp," he said, pointing to a drawing of a stockade battlement. "Here, the sea, the ruined Frydian camp, and here the valley where our first battle was fought. It was no good battleground to begin with, and has been rendered even less so by the avalanche that still blocks the valley floor."

"Not to mention the frozen river above, dropping ice spears on any who pass," Lathrom said, his deep voice rumbling in his chest.

"Farther north, and to the east, there is a wide valley where, unless my guess is wrong, the enemy is gathering," Gaurin went on. "There are ways in and out from several directions, including from the south. I think that they plan to rush down upon us, when their numbers are complete, and take us by surprise. I propose that we turn the surprise on them instead. Let us secretly take our engines of war— the catapult, the giant bow—through one of these paths and, when we have gathered, fall upon them in a battle that will finally decide the war."

"They have eyes just as we do, and scouts," Reges said. "What is to keep them from sending those flying horrors and discovering our plans?

"I think they will not be expecting any such move on our part," Gaurin answered. "Further, we will travel at night, and hide ourselves during the day. Our white outer garments will help with this disguise and we will conceal our engines with tree branches. Remember, we have not seen a Dragon aloft for many days now. I think they are reserving them for later, when they attack in force."

Ashen had been studying the map from her place at the foot of the table. It was boldly drawn and, if accurate, showed a spot that might be used for the immediate treatment of the wounded. She arose. "May I have permission to speak?"

"Granted, of course," Royance said.

Quickly, she outlined what she had broached to Gaurin, omitting the fact that his reaction had not been favorable. This battlefield he had chosen, however, was so far from the encampment of the Four Armies that even he must see the wisdom in her proposal.

"We can expect casualties. What will you need, in setting up this new thing—I suppose you'd call it a field infirmary?" Royance asked, interested.

"A few women, some men to act as litter-bearers, bandages and salves."

"And me, probably," Zazar said grumpily. "Leave it to you to make me freeze out in the open instead of tending to the badly hurt, the way I should."

Ashen turned to the older woman. "I will not ask you to go with me," she said, "for I know where you would be the most valuable."

Zazar was not mollified. "You would put yourself in more danger than you should. It's a good enough plan—more men will live, and the lightly hurt can go back to the fight sooner—but there are others who can do this just as well or better than you. Let one of the physicians from the infirmary take this post."

"I will agree to have a physician there with me. But I must be—" Ashen bit her lips before she could finish her statement: *I must be near Gaurin, lest he be hurt and I am not there.*

"Well, I suppose that will have to do." Zazar turned to Rohan. "Do you still make those silly silk roses out of thin air?"

Startled, Rohan nodded. "Yes, but not very often these days."

"Make me one now."

"I really need two good hands—Wait, here it is."

A pink silk rose appeared and dropped on the table in front of the Wysen-wyf. She picked it up and promptly shook it out into a length of thin, almost transparent fabric. "Do you have to color it?" she asked her foster grandson.

"Why, no, it takes more effort only I thought you might like a pink one—"

"And do they always have to be all folded up like this?"

"No, Granddam. But there's not much to delight ladies in simple strips of uncolored silk."

"I'm not thinking about ladies," Zazar snapped. She handed the silk to Chevin, who happened to be sitting next to her. "Here," she instructed. "Wrap this around your nose and mouth. Tell me what you think."

Obediently, Chevin wound the strip of silk around his head. "I can breathe through it, if that's what interests you," he reported.

"Of course you can breathe through it. The air's chilly in here, despite everything. Do you feel a difference?"

"Yes, Madame Zazar. Breathing is much warmer, for some reason."

Zazar snorted. "The reason's simple. Your own breath is warm, coming out, so it softens the cold when it comes in again." She turned to Rohan. "D'you think you can make enough of these—just strips of cloth, mind, and white, not colored—so that every soldier can have one before they go marching off again?"

Comprehension dawned on Rohan's face. "I can certainly try, Granddam," he said. He glanced around the table. "And it will give me something more important to do than just run errands. Not that I minded," he added hastily.

"Good enough for you, if you were silly enough to get your arm broken," Snolli muttered, and beside him the Spirit Drummer sniggered behind his hand.

"Well, get to it," Zazar instructed. She turned to Gaurin. "When d'you plan to move out?"

"Not for a few days yet," he said. "Thanks to our great Admiral-General Snolli's information, we will know when our enemies have gathered enough that they may begin their assault. My Lord Royance will give the orders for us to go."

"Then you'd better keep in close touch with me, Royance," Zazar said. "I'll be brewing up something I've been thinking about for a while, that will help the men's resistance to the cold. Should come in handy if you're going to march 'em through the snow."

Far from being incensed at the untoward familiarity Zazar displayed by omitting his title, Royance, Lord of Grattenbor, Lord High Marshal and Head of the Council of Rendel, ally and kinsman of the House of Oak and as mighty as a king in his own right, arose from the table and bowed once more to the Wysen-wyf. "It was a fortunate day that brought you to us," he said. "And we thank you for all your efforts."

Rohan soon found that manufacturing strips of white silk out of nowhere was very tiring when it was done in such large numbers. Zazar, however, was relentless.

"Our men may be subject to Dragon's Breath when they get where they're going. No sense in having them half dead before they even get there," she said sternly, and Rohan went back to his chore.

Ashen kept Rohan's energy up by seeing to it that he had plenty to eat. She gave him a table in the infirmary tent close by where Zazar set up her store of medicinal herbs. There the Wysen-wyf brewed small amounts of first one and then another potion until she got the formula right.

"We're going to need more than I brought. The herbs are potent and we don't need as much as we might with another mixture," she muttered, almost to herself, "so they will last a little while. But I will have to send you—no, I will have to make you take me back to get more before we're done."

"Will I still have to make white silk wrappings while we're gone?" Rohan asked hopefully.

"Of course!" Zazar snapped. "Now stop being so lazy and get back to it."

Ashen watched the two with a mixture of affection and exasperation. Affection won, not only for Rohan, but, somewhat to her surprise, toward Zazar as well. It was an emotion she was not accustomed to associating with the Wysen-wyf. With every minute that passed, she was more and more grateful for Zazar's presence and the miracles she had already accomplished.

Most of the men who suffered from the effects of

Dragon's Breath seemed to be greatly improved. Only Hynnel and Norras showed slow progress. That, Ashen thought, was because these two were the worst afflicted and so would be the slowest to recover.

Prudently, Ashen waited until Rohan was absent before voicing these thoughts about Hynnel and Norras. No sense in worrying the young knight unduly.

"Those two will never recover fully," Zazar told her bluntly. "When so much of the lung has been destroyed, there is no restoring what is gone. It is good that they still live and that must be laid to your good nursing. And my potions and the hot baths, of course. But they will be invalids for the remainder of their lives, and the slightest ailment might carry them off. Same with the other six, only not in such a measure."

Ashen's first impulse was to reject Zazar's words, but in her heart she knew them to be true. She would, she decided, think about it later, when she had more time. Instead, she asked, "And the white silk coverings? Will they help our brave warriors resist the Dragon's Breath in the coming battle?"

"They will, with my strengthening potion to help." Suddenly, and uncharacteristically, Zazar reached out and took Ashen's hand in a gentle grasp. "Do not fear for Gaurin," she said. "He has devised a way to destroy these horrible Dragons at a distance, and he has come through other battles with nothing worse than scratches."

Tears welled in Ashen's eyes. "It's just that— Well, I am sick with worry about him, and I haven't heard from Hegrin nor she from me since I've been here, and it is all becoming more than I can bear."

"You can bear it, Ashen Deathdaughter. You have no other choice."

Ashen was forced to smile through her tears; the rough edge was back in full measure in Zazar's voice, and this somehow served to comfort her more than the Wysen-wyf's unaccustomed gentleness. "Thank you," she said simply.

"It's no more than you should have thought of yourself." Then Zazar changed the subject abruptly. "Have you done much reading, and you know the kind I mean, lately?"

"Well, not since I've been here, of course," Ashen said.

"It might be important. Tell me what you've learned."

Obediently, she related to Zazar the arrangement she had had with Esander, the kindly priest at the Great Fane of the Glowing, but it was when she mentioned the book Esander had given her that Zazar's interest and attention sharpened.

"Describe this book," she ordered.

"Well, it is both very old and extremely valuable. It is bound in blue velvet and the hinges and locks are of gold set with precious gems. The title is embroidered in pure gold as well, and there are many gemstone beads in the stitching. It is called *Powyr*. The word is spelled oddly. There is a second title, also embroidered in the velvet, and this is *Ye Boke of Ye Fayne*, also spelled oddly. The paper is cream-colored and not at all affected by the years. The writing on it is beautiful, with the capitals all picked out in red and gold, and there are colorful illustrations on the title pages of each section. When I am not reading it, I keep it locked away in a cabinet that only one other person has a key to."

"And that would be—who was it? Ayfare, your maid. She was with you when you visited me, and you were so sick."

"Yes." Ashen stared off at nothing, remembering Obern's child she had miscarried, almost at the cost of her life, and how Zazar had saved her.

"I would like to see that book."

"I brought hardly anything with me from Rendelsham, and in any event, when we journeyed to the capital, I left it behind at the Oakenkeep," Ashen replied, puzzled. It was the first time she could recall Zazar showing any interest in any book or tablet that she did not already have access to.

"You don't understand, Ashen. I need to see that book."

Ashen gazed into Zazar's eyes, and the old woman stared back implacably.

"Very well, then. I will have it brought here. I don't know how, exactly, but I will arrange it."

Zazar shrugged. "Oh, that's easy," she said airily. "When Rohan and I return to the Bog, I'll drop him off close by the city. There he'll pick up Ayfare, check on his lady, see how Rannore is faring—Lathrom will want to know—and bring Ayfare to the Oakenkeep. I'll meet them there, we'll find the book, send Ayfare back to take care of Rannore, and then I'll return here before you'll know I'm gone."

"You do seem to have it all worked out," Ashen said.

"Of course."

A burst of lightning briefly brightened the interior of the infirmary tent, closely followed by a clap of thunder. Zazar went to the entrance and peered out. "Storm," she commented briefly. "There'll be no movement of soldiers, enemy or otherwise, until it dies down. But that doesn't mean a ship can't sail. Snolli told me that the sea is not nearly as disturbed as we might think, what with all the commotion on shore.

All is relatively quiet here for the moment. You know the routine of caring for the injured. So, I think Rohan and I will leave at once."

❦

A week later, Rohan, accompanied by Ayfare and four of his marines as guard, rode through the gate at the Oakenkeep. There was no sign of Zazar, nor of Harvas, whom Rohan had assigned to help the Wysen-wyf accumulate the herbs and other items she would need and then transport the bags and bundles to *Spume-Maiden*. According to plan, the *Spume-Maiden* should now be lying at anchor in the sheltered harbor at New Vold.

He left his horse in the charge of one of the grooms and made his way, despite the blowing sleet mixed with snow, immediately to one of the lookout towers. He gazed west, and then realized that Zazar would be coming from the south instead. She would not dream of entrusting her precious goods to anyone she had not trained from infancy, and Rohan knew she would have insisted on stowing them herself in a place that suited her.

He could just make out a solitary figure on the road, approaching the Oakenkeep. He wished for a far-see glass of his own, but knew this could be none other than Zazar. Who else would willingly be abroad on such a blustery day?

He descended the stairs from the tower and hurried toward the residence. There, inside the Hall, Ayfare had already seen to it that a small fire burned in the familiar shelter of the screens. Rohan smelled food being heated and his stomach growled. He had not had hot victuals since leaving Rendelsham.

Within an hour, Zazar was sitting comfortably at the little table inside the screened-off area, noisily slurping a bowl of thick soup that steamed in the chilly air. "All's taken care of with the herbs," she reported. "We'll have plenty, if the war doesn't last too much longer. I added some salves and materials for making poultices as well."

"I'm sure that everything you chose will be put to good use," Rohan told her.

"Yes, well, did you remember to take the mixture I gave you, that helps you withstand the cold? I wasn't there to remind you, and you probably forgot."

"No, Granddam, I did not forget. And you are right. It does seem to make the effects of this beastly cold weather easier to endure."

"Good. You may be growing up a little. And how was everyone in Rendelsham? Your wife?"

Rohan felt his face grow warm. Their reunion had been wonderful, so much so that he felt he could not stand to tear himself from her arms. But in the end he had kissed her lips, her eyes, and her forehead, and bade her good-bye. To her credit, she stood staunchly and watched him ride away without weeping.

"My wife is well, as is Lady Rannore. If we win the war speedily enough, her babe may be born into warmth and light."

"Lathrom will be glad to hear it," Zazar said around another mouthful. "And Her Highness?"

"I caught only a fleeting glimpse of the Dowager for I reported directly to King Peres. I daresay she isn't much interested in me these days. The King appreciated my report, though, and is pleased that the war still seems to go well. He expressly asked me to send runners with news of the anticipated battle." Rohan reached for the pitcher of mulled wine and poured a goblet for himself and, at her nod, for Zazar. "I did learn one interesting thing. My sweet sis, Hegrin, must be quite a young lady. She is due to arrive at Court any day now. The King's sent for her. She'll be staying in Gaurin's and Ashen's apartment, where Anamara and Rannore and Ayfare will all look after her."

"Hmmm." Zazar's eyebrows rose, but she made no other comment.

"It's only natural," Rohan went on, "that the King would want people near his own age around him. He's surrounded by old men, long in the tooth, who are unable to go out and fight. They're turning him into one of them, or at least trying to. Hegrin will be like a blooming rose in that decrepit company."

"Some might say old Royance is a bit long in the tooth for what he is currently doing," Zazar commented with a trace of acid in her voice.

"Well, there's old, and there's old, if you take my meaning," Rohan said. "If everyone there had even a trace of Lord Royance's spirit, the King might not be longing for younger companionship."

"He may have an eye toward something more than that," Zazar said. "Something more important. More permanent."

Rohan turned and stared at her. She stared back, the corners of her mouth turned down. "No," he said finally. "He's too young, not to mention Hegrin. They're still just children! Impossible."

"As you say," Zazar retorted. "But children grow."

"Impossible," Rohan repeated, but he had to admit that

Zazar had given him something to think about. He pondered whether to relay this information to Gaurin or Ashen.

Before he could make up his mind, Zazar put her empty goblet on the table with a thump and arose from the bench where she had been sitting. "Ayfare!" she called.

A moment later, the Oakenkeep's head housekeeper appeared. "Yes, Madame Zazar?"

"If Rohan did as I instructed, he told you I've spoken to Ashen about a particular item she keeps locked away in a cabinet."

"He did, Madame. I have the key right here." Ayfare indicated a bundle of keys dangling from the chatelaine around her waist. "Please follow me."

Ayfare led them up the stairs to the private apartment Ashen and Gaurin shared. Without hesitation, she crossed the living quarters to a large upright armoire. At the base of the armoire was a set of drawers that could be locked—the cabinet of which Ashen had spoken. Ayfare inserted a small key into the lock on one of these drawers and turned it. Then she opened the drawer and stood back so that Zazar could examine the contents.

Rohan peered over her shoulder. Whatever it was that was so important, it was wrapped in what looked like waterproof leather and tied with a silver ribbon. Disappointed, he said, "Is that it? Perhaps you'd better open it just to make sure."

Zazar hefted the package, feeling the outlines of the contents with her strong old fingers. She pulled one end of the wrapping loose just enough that Rohan caught a glimpse of blue.

"No, this is it," she said. "But I will open it. In private, if you please." She glared at him.

Accept defeat, Rohan bowed and left the room with Ayfare close behind him. She pulled the door shut.

"Do you know what's in that package?" Rohan asked her.

"I think it's a book," Ayfare replied, "but why she set such store by it I don't know. We have other books."

Indeed, the Oakenkeep boasted an extensive library for a private residence. Upwards of a dozen volumes on various subjects graced the shelf behind the table where Gaurin was accustomed to working, and that was besides the books of accounting he meticulously maintained. Only Rendelsham Castle could claim more, and except for the Dowager's notorious appetite for reading, those books went mostly untouched.

"I suppose we might as well go back down where it's warm, and wait for Granddam Zaz to get through with whatever she's looking at," Rohan said, a little glumly. It was bad enough that his broken arm—mending, according to the physicians, but still keeping him on the sidelines—rendered him fit for nothing more than being a messenger. Worse, he now felt he was not trusted.

He and Ayfare descended the stairs and re-entered the warm area behind the screens. Disconsolately, he reached for the pitcher only to have Ayfare grab it first and place it on the hearth to warm again.

Just as he was pouring the mulled wine into his goblet, Zazar hurried around the screen and sat down. He stared across the table at her. She was obviously more than a little agitated and out of breath.

"What is it, Granddam?" he asked. He reached for Zazar's goblet to refill it as well.

"I've been glancing through the book—yes, you might as well know what it was, even if it's far beyond you. What I've learned will come as a surprise to several people, though I anticipated it. Did Ashen ever tell you about the time when she was tending to your father, and tried to use magic for the first time?"

"No!" Rohan exclaimed. "What happened?"

"Well, she had just found him. He had been knocked off the cliff and fallen into some ferns. He was hurt and lucky to be alive. Anyway, I wasn't there and she tried to contact me."

She had brought Obern to the room Rohan was familiar with, in the ruined city of Galinth. Despairing of his life, Ashen had stirred together a mixture such as she had seen Zazar use on rare occasions and dissolved it in water from the pipe. Then, hoping she had done it right, she drank off the potion.

"She wound up in—well, I suppose you could call it an underground chamber. I knew she needed me, but I was caught in a pillar of fire, which is why I hadn't gone to her by then."

"You were caught, you say?"

"Yes," Zazar snapped in some annoyance. "Even with me, sometimes experiments don't go exactly the way I'd like."

There had been another woman in the room when Ashen arrived. It was the Dowager, then Queen Ysa of Rendel. Both women had stared at each other, astonished, until Zazar made them concentrate on the issue at hand.

"I should have known it would take both of you," Zazar had said. "Well, come on then."

She held out one hand to Ashen, and the other to Queen Ysa. Ashen took her hand at once, but Ysa hesitated a moment. Still, she did what was required, and then Zazar stepped out of the fire and it died behind her.

Then Zazar had introduced the two, telling them that they would meet in the outside world sooner or later.

"Ashen went back to Galinth and tending your father, Ysa returned to whatever she was doing in Rendelsham, and nobody was the wiser," Zazar finished.

"What a tale!" Rohan exclaimed. "But what has this got to do with this mysterious book you spoke of?"

"You are a dunce," Zazar said flatly. "We three were tied at that moment, and now the time has come to use that bond in defeating our common enemy."

"B-but how?"

The Wysen-wyf averted her head, unable to meet his eyes. "I do not know," she said. "I only know that this is what will be required of us." Then after a long moment she turned and looked him squarely in the face. "I know one thing more. You now have another errand to perform, perhaps the most important you have ever embarked upon. When we leave the Oakenkeep, I will go to New Vold, and thence sail north with the supplies I gathered. Harvas will not like learning that you will be left behind, but I will deal with him. You will return to Rendelsham, and persuade the Dowager Ysa to come to the encampment of the Four Armies as quickly as she can."

Rohan just stared at her, mouth agape while a hundred conflicting thoughts chased themselves through his mind. Finally he found his voice. "This is no trifling task you have set me to," he said.

"I know. Do you still have that brush of herbs and grasses that I bade you wear in your helm?"

"Yes, I keep it ever close by me though my helm is useless in such cold as we endure. It is stored here, in an armoire in my rooms, along with my other gear."

"Go and get it," Zazar instructed. "Wear it and your mail coat when you go into the Dowager's presence."

"Do you think it will help?" Rohan asked.

"Again, I don't know. But there were forces beyond either of us at work when I devised it for you. Now such forces may themselves prompt you what to say, what to do, to get this pampered lady to follow my command."

"May it be so," Rohan responded somberly. "I will be frank with you. There have been times when I doubted your wisdom and your foresight. Not so now. I will go to Rendelsham and do my best to do your bidding."

"Good. What Ysa will think of this, nobody can tell, but I can guess she will be reluctant."

Rohan grimaced. "Reluctant" was a very mild way to put it, if he knew anything about the Dowager and, having been in her company for many nights during his training in the Queen's Levy, he was certain that he did.

"I say this also to you," Zazar continued. "Persuasion is preferable, but if all else fails, take her by force, bound and gagged, and drag her behind you."

Rohan was shocked. "It is that important."

"It is."

Then Zazar did something very uncharacteristic. She

arose from the bench where she had been sitting, took Rohan's face between her old, brown hands, and kissed him on the forehead. "You will not fail," she told him. "For all our sakes, you cannot."

Eighteen

The Dowager Ysa stared at Rohan, standing before her as a supplicant in the room she had set aside for such matters. Here at specified hours she allowed those to come who would plea for her to intervene with King Peres, or for the favors that only she could bestow. These occasions pleased her greatly, for there were always large numbers of people waiting in the antechamber. Further, because so many of these petitions concerned private matters, she received them alone and their attention centered entirely on her. Guards stood outside the doors, of course, but none dared disturb what went on within, not even one of the Dowager's ladies.

Out of curiosity, she allowed Rohan to enter ahead of the rest. At his greeting given with less than the deference she felt she deserved, she decided she should have left him cooling his heels instead. It would have done him some good, surely. Taken down his arrogance, if only a little.

The young knight had definitely matured since she had first seen him, a stripling youth come in answer to the summons of the Queen's Levy. Now he stood before her clad in deep blue, the Court color, over chain mail and with his helm tucked under his arm. The stains on his mail sleeve from the fire powder still showed. The mail was obviously freshly polished, so the marks had not been left as a form of boasting. Yet, despite his martial appearance, he was still far from being a presence to be reckoned with.

Nor had the Dowager forgiven him for what had happened to Anamara. She blamed him entirely for the fog that had fallen over Anamara's mind, that had led the girl to the brink of death. A fragment of a plan flitted across Ysa's thoughts. Perhaps that marriage could be set aside. Ysa could think of more valuable dispositions of what amounted to her royal ward, than bestowing her upon someone little better than a hedge knight for all his connections with the Sea-Rover leadership.

Rohan's words penetrated the indifference with which the Dowager was regarding him, and her attention suddenly came into focus. "You—you want me to *what?*" she demanded incredulously. "To journey north, into the army encampment? To subject myself to the harshness of the clime, the discomfort not to mention the dangers, and for what purpose?"

"My granddam, Zazar, the great Wysen-wyf of the Bog, has decreed it," Rohan replied. "She says—"

"Oh, I know what she says," Ysa said irritably. "You needn't repeat it." Indeed, Zazar's bizarre request—an order, actually; Ysa knew one when she encountered it—was one of the few things Rohan had told her since this interview began that had engaged her attention. To be sure, Zazar had a fearsome reputation—as formidable as Ysa's own—but that was no reason for her to leave the comfort and relative warmth of her private chambers in Rendelsham Castle to put herself into peril just on Zazar's say-so. "It is a ridiculous demand. I will not do it."

"Granddam Zazar says you must," Rohan replied.

"And if I refuse?"

The young knight had the grace to blush and look down. "Then I am commanded to take you unwillingly, if need be."

Ysa arose. From the height of the dais on which her chair stood she could glare down at Rohan with the full force of her displeasure.

"Never!" she cried. "It is impossible! All I have to do is cry out and you would die before you laid a hand on me. I will not be dictated to in this fashion!" She gestured toward the door. "Now, get out before I summon the guard and have you removed—willingly or unwillingly," she added with more than a trace of spite.

"Please, Your Highness," Rohan said. "I merely follow the orders of those more versed in certain *arts*—" He put a slight but definite emphasis on the word. "—than I."

He moved his good hand and an emerald-green silk rose, Yew's color, appeared in it. He offered it to the Dowager. Without her consciously willing it, she stepped down from the dais and took the rose from him.

"Yew's color," Ysa murmured.

Despite its being made of silk, she lifted it to her nose. At that moment, the ridiculous tuft of dried herbs and grasses in the crest of Rohan's helm began to give off a slight but unmistakable vapor that rose in the air and enveloped both the Dowager and Rohan. The odor was fresh and clean, despite the desiccated appearance of the sprigs, and Ysa breathed it in deeply.

She stared at the young knight. "Thank you for your gift," she said, vaguely surprised at the gentleness of her own words. "Know that your demand is both insolent and insulting, but for that very reason I must give it due consideration because of your bravery in speaking so to me. You would not have dared voice such, had it not been important."

Rohan bowed. "Thank you, Your Highness," he said. "Let us hope—for both our sakes—that you grant me my plea."

"Go now," Ysa said. "You will have my answer tomorrow."

"I will return at this hour." Rohan bowed again, and left the room.

As if in a dream, Ysa noticed that sometime during the interview the tuft of grasses and herbs had disappeared from Rohan's helm, no doubt falling to dust at last. Now, perhaps he would wear a proper ornament in his helm. A plume, perhaps, in Sea-Rover colors.

When Rohan had bowed his way out of Ysa's audience chamber, she sat long, thinking, wondering why she had not had the young man arrested. She stared at the green silk rose she still held and sniffed at it again. The fresh scent had all but disappeared. On impulse, she arose and called one of the guards.

"Please tell the ones waiting to see me that I have an

important matter to attend to," she instructed him, "and I will grant them interviews at another time."

"Yes, Your Highness," the guard replied. "But some will be very disappointed."

"Of course. They always are. Nevertheless, I must be about the matter of which I spoke, and so tell them."

The guard bowed and turned to do Ysa's bidding. Ysa left the audience chamber by another door and returned to her apartment. There she selected a plain cloak and put it about her shoulders, pulling the hood up over her head so that, she hoped, nobody would recognize her.

She made her way out of Rendelsham Castle and across the courtyard to the Great Fane of the Glowing. There was that within that she must see.

She glanced up as she approached. The Fane boasted windows both great and small decorated with pictures made of pieces of colored glass, set into the openings with great skill and artisanship. None, however, was as beautiful or as elaborate as the circular one surmounting the main doors. Designed for no purpose other than sheer decoration, this window glowed as if it created its own light even on a dreary day such as this one was. The flowers and leaves, picked out in jewel tones—ruby and garnet and rose quartz; sapphire and spinel and lapis; golden topaz and yellow quartz and citrine; emerald and chrysophase and jade—represented the Four Houses. Her own father had contributed many of the green elements, even as Boroth's father had supplied red ones. She could remember the day, fraught with tension, when the completed window had been lifted and cemented in place. Who had given the yellow ones? She remembered—

Erft of the House of Rowan, elder brother of Wittern, the current head. The late Aldren of the House of Ash had contributed the blue so that all Four Great Houses were well represented. All great nobles. All departed.

But it was three of the smallest windows that were the focus of Ysa's quest this day. These particular ones were located on an upper balcony, virtually hidden from all but the most inquisitive, and few of those, after discovering them, would return more than once. Exquisite as the windows were, nonetheless they inspired vague feelings of dread. For these windows changed with time, and no artisan's touch could account for the shifting. One of these windows depicted the hands and Web of the Weavers. When the land awakened as the Great Foulness stirred, this picture, which had changed only a little from the oldest man's memory, began to shift. Now if someone watched patiently, he could see the dark hands of the Weavers moving. Since the last time Ysa had beheld it, the Web had taken on a different appearance. Now it showed a dreadful tangle, a snarl of white, where the Web of Time accepted no thread of color except for the occasional strand of red—the color of blood—and where fell shapes moved obscurely on hidden business of their own.

The second window, the one showing a Bog-lupper, was no less alarming. The small lupper that had once sat beside a pool had now vanished into the underbrush and a huge lupper with a mouth full of sharp teeth had emerged onto the land.

It was, however, in the third window that the most frightening phenomena had once been seen, before Ysa had ordered a curtain nailed into place to cover it and hide it from unwary eyes.

This mysterious window had ever shown a blank face, white and barely translucent. Its very lack of design made it uninteresting. Then something began stirring in its depths as if a creature more deadly, more horrifying even than the one making its way out of the Bog-pool were emerging from a heavy snowstorm.

Ysa stood before this window for a moment, gathering her resolve, before reaching out and pulling the dusty curtain loose from the nails holding it in place.

She had thought herself prepared, but she wasn't. There, in the whiteness, distorted through a cold, icy veil but nonetheless discernible, she saw the face of Rendel's greatest enemy. Sickened, she felt as if the breath had been knocked out of her. Inadvertently she touched the window. She recoiled, taking a step back and wringing her hands, as if they were covered with cold slime from this briefest of contacts. And this horror was what Rohan and Zazar were summoning her, a woman, to face?

"No," she murmured aloud into the chill air of the upper balcony. "I cannot. I will not."

At that moment she felt a stirring of the Four Great Rings on her forefingers and thumbs. Horrified, she stared down at them. They had begun to move, to slide from the places they had occupied for so many years. She clenched her fists so hard her joints cracked, but the Rings continued their slow, inexorable passage. Her heart pounded in her throat. They were departing from her and there seemed to be nothing she could do to stop it. How could they betray her so, when she had been so faithful, had toiled for so many years in Rendel's service?

Or, she thought suddenly, was she the one betraying the Rings? Could it be that they had joined with the Wysen-wyf in their insistence that she engage in what must be the greatest folly of all?

Well, if so, if it would take her own life's blood to save Rendel from the putrid presence in the window—a putrescence that, she knew, was only a pale shadow of the reality—then so be it. A measure of calm descended upon her.

"I spoke from emotion. Now I speak from responsibility and duty. I will journey north," she said to the presence in the window, "and if the Powers decide that I must give up my life to destroy yours, then I am ready."

The Four Great Rings snugged themselves into place on her fingers again. She stroked their familiar presence gratefully and her heartbeat slowed. She felt, somehow, that had she persisted in her denial of Zazar's summons, not only would the Rings have gone she knew not where—certainly not to the wispy young King Peres—but Rendel itself would have been doomed. It had been a near thing.

She could no longer bear to gaze at the creature depicted in the third window. Not even a curtain newly nailed in place would keep the evil from radiating out and defiling the Fane. She turned, searching, and found a small piece of ornamental statuary. It depicted the Four Trees and was made of porcelain, not stone, but it would do. Shielding her face, she swung it and both the ornament and the window dissolved into tiny bits that no one could ever reassemble. Cold wind, mixed with snow, began to blow through the open hole where the window had been. She could not bear to touch this space, even in an attempt to fit the curtain back over the nails that had once held it.

She descended the stairs, throwing back the hood on her cloak so that all who saw her could recognize her. The Chief Priest of the Fane hurried toward her, apologetic.

"If only you had told us you were coming, Your Highness," he said, clasping his hands unctuously, "we would have given you the proper welcome befitting one of your exalted rank."

"A window has broken up there," Ysa said, pointing in the direction from which she had just come. "The upper balcony."

"We will have it replaced at once—"

"Do not bother," the Dowager ordered imperiously. "There are two more that should be taken out as well."

"But—but, Your Highness, the balcony will be dark—"

"Then light candles." A sudden suspicion caused Ysa to peer at the priest more closely. "You've never even seen those three windows, have you?"

The priest flushed. "No, Your Highness. There are rumors, but one does not pay attention to such things."

"You should have," she said bleakly. "The windows are unnatural. Take them out, and then close up the holes with brick and mortar. I want it to seem as if they never existed."

"It will be done." The priest bowed.

Then Ysa swept out of the Great Fane and back toward Rendelsham Castle. With her decision, she now felt much more like herself—strong and in charge of most of what went on in Rendelsham. Between now and the time when she must depart on this fool's errand—this brave act, she corrected herself silently—there was the little matter of Hegrin's imminent arrival at the city. Surely there would be time to arrange for an interview with this child.

Yes, Ysa definitely felt better now that a decision had been reached. She regretted only the timing. She might have to be more blunt than her usual wont as she put an end to any fantasies the girl might be entertaining about a relationship between her and King Peres.

"How very pretty you are!" Ysa exclaimed. "That sapphire and pearl necklace is very becoming and goes well with your lovely blue dress. Come here, and let me look at you."

Hegrin curtsied. "Thank you, Your Highness," she said. Obediently, she approached the Dowager.

"You look very much like your father," Ysa said. "Same shade of hair and eyes. You're thin, though, like your mother, even though you have more color to you. Haven't they been feeding you, tucked away as you have been, off in Rydale? If you don't finish your lessons, do they make you go to bed without any supper?"

Hegrin's golden giggle seemed to light up even the corners of the room. There was a dimple at the corner of her mouth. "Oh, I have a very good appetite!" she exclaimed. "My nurse, Beatha, says I should be very fat indeed, considering how much I like sweets."

"Here," Ysa said, amused. She offered the platter of spice cakes the girl had been eyeing. "Now let us sit down and become friends. You must tell me all about yourself. I am very interested, you see."

Ysa took her accustomed chair by the fire and Hegrin

perched on one of the low seats where she could easily reach the cakes.

"There really isn't much to tell," the girl said, her voice muffled. She swallowed, and then took another bite. "They took me to a nice apartment where I'm staying with Lady Rannore and Lady Anamara. I call both of them 'aunt' but it's very complicated. Lady Rannore is my aunt by marriage, and Lady Anamara is Rohan's wife and he is almost my older brother. My mother and father are both away fighting in the North, and King Peres sent for me to come here. Beatha says the King is a kind of cousin."

"Yes, I suppose he is. His father and your mother were half-siblings."

"Beatha says that isn't too close a kinship—" Hegrin clamped her lips together, as if she knew she had said too much.

"Any kinship at all with the King is something to be cherished but not abused," Ysa said, helping herself to a spice cake before the child devoured them all. "Do you understand what I am telling you?"

Hegrin's brow wrinkled as she thought, and Ysa was struck once more by how young and innocent she was. Perhaps there was nothing to worry about after all, but she had not remained in command of the land of Rendel through Boroth's reign and then Florian's and now Peres's by relaxing her vigilance.

"No, Your Highness, I don't understand. Not really." Hegrin helped herself to the last spice cake.

"Well, never you mind," Ysa said. She allowed herself to pat the girl's hand. "It's just grown-up matters. Worries and fears. Nothing to bother yourself about."

Hegrin's face cleared and she smiled again. "I'm glad. The King wants me to come and play a game of cards with him later. If I win, does that mean I am abusing my kinship with him?"

Ysa smiled in return. "Of course not!" she exclaimed. "He would be in danger of becoming a little spoiled, if everyone let him triumph—not that there are that many young people in Rendelsham Castle, at least none of high enough rank to invite to play games. Go ahead and win, if you can."

"Oh, I will, Your Highness," Hegrin said, laughing. "Rohan taught me that game a long time ago, and I know all the tricks!"

Then Ysa dismissed her, but kindly. Hegrin smiled when she curtsied, and pulled the door closed after her when she left.

The girl could be dissembling, Ysa thought as she stared into the fire. Still, she was a cheerful, pleasant presence in these dark days. Perhaps *too* cheerful. Giddy, Ysa decided.

What wretched timing that she, the Dowager Queen and true ruler of Rendel, had been—*summoned* was the only word for it—summoned to go on some fool's errand north, out of her warm and comfortable apartment. She could still refuse to go, but she didn't allow the thought expression, even to flutter in privacy at the edge of her mind. She could still feel the movement as the Great Rings had shifted on her fingers. No, not again would she risk such a thing.

Young Hegrin was, Ysa thought, ill enough chaperoned by her Aunt Anamara, but added to that the protection of Ysa's former daughter-in-law Rannore, who had proved herself a slut twice over, and the potential for mischief between Hegrin and King Peres became intolerable. The girl needed another guardian, that was plain enough, but who? Of her personal ladies, Ysa intended to take her favorites, Ladies Grisella, Gertrude, and Ingrid, so that she might be looked after properly. None of the other ladies were as steady, or as trustworthy as these three, and certainly not ones to whom the guardianship of such an important person as the daughter of Ashen and Gaurin could be entrusted.

Then Ysa smiled. When he died, the former king, Florian, Ysa's son, had been embroiled with a woman at Court. She had, of course, been no better than she should have been to form a liaison with Florian, but when she had been found out openly after having been duped by Florian to add poison to Ashen's medicine, she had undergone quite a remarkable transformation. Ysa had seen this sort of thing before, when someone's transgressions, upon being brought to light, then wrought a complete change of character. So it had been with Florian's wench—now what was her name? Ysa searched her memory. Ah, yes, that was it. Jacyne, wife of a minor court official. She had become the very model of propriety and moral rectitude. She could be trusted to see to it that nothing questionable went on between Hegrin and Peres while Ysa was unable to oversee the situation personally. Also, Jacyne was bound to be grateful to know that her former transgressions had now officially been forgiven and her status at Court not only restored, but also actually enhanced. She would teach giddy little Hegrin to be sober and decorous, and would even be grateful for the opportunity. Ysa liked having people feel deep gratitude to her. It made them reliable, knowing as they did that what the Dowager had bestowed, she could also take away.

Hegrin pulled the door shut behind her and leaned on it, her eyes closed.

"Did your interview with Ysa go badly?" Aunt Rannore asked.

"Would you like something to drink?" asked Aunt Anamara.

"No to the first question," Hegrin answered, "and yes to the second. You were right, Aunt Rannore. That lady is one who seems to see right through you." She accepted a steaming cup of fruit juice, such as she was accustomed to at home, and sipped from it. "She gave me cakes, but nothing else, not even water with a drop of wine in it. I suppose she thought me still a baby."

Her two aunts bade her sit and tell them all that had transpired between her and Her Gracious Highness, the Dowager Queen Ysa.

"I tried to be myself, as you instructed, Aunt Anamara, and yet appear a bit simple and young for my years."

"That quality was, I think, what the Dowager found attractive about me. She thought I could be useful to her, and so I would have been, to my detriment, had not good fortune intervened," Anamara said soberly.

"I was in a different situation, of course, when I first came to Rendelsham," Aunt Rannore commented. "My one-time mother-in-law is very fond of having more power over people than even her exalted station entitles her to. But come, tell us. How did she appear? What did she say?"

"Actually," Hegrin said as she drained her cup, "she

seemed a little distracted as if something more important was on her mind."

At that, Aunt Anamara's face clouded. "I know," she said. "Rohan has told me of his errand. His Granddam Zazar has given orders that Her Highness accompany him to the encampment of the Four Armies, to what purpose the Wysenwyf will not say."

"She is my granddam also," Hegrin said thoughtfully. "And if she has decreed that the Dowager go northward, then go she shall. I wish I were going."

"As do we," Aunt Rannore said with a sigh. She put her hand on her abdomen. "If only my child were born—"

"And if only I had the least skill in arms," Aunt Anamara added. "The Army of Rendel would be greater by two. But you, dear niece—"

"I know, I know," Hegrin said. "I'm too young. I've been told that all my life. Too young to go hunting with Father, too old to cry about it, too small to climb the high towers at the Oakenkeep, too big to act like a boy in skirts." She smiled, knowing that a mischievous dimple danced at the corner of her mouth. "But I'm not so young that I don't know about the plans to marry me to King Peres, if he decides he likes me well enough."

"Hegrin!" both ladies exclaimed in unison.

"I've heard that most of my life also. My nurse, Beatha, was always going on about it. My mother tried to make her hush, but she'd just talk behind Mother's back."

"Well, then," Aunt Rannore said. "And what do you think of such a thing?"

"I think it's silly." Hegrin offered the pitcher of juice to both her aunts and then poured more for herself. "All the King wants is a companion close to him in years. No need to make such a fuss about it."

The two ladies exchanged glances.

"Well, it remains to be seen what, if anything, will come of it," Aunt Anamara said firmly. "Probably nothing at all, as you said. But still, it pays to stay on the good side of the Dowager, if ever you can find it."

Rohan stared at the assembly before him, trying not to show his dismay. The Dowager Queen Ysa had, in a very short time, put together an astonishing assortment of boxes and bundles and her three ladies likewise each had a similar accumulation. They wore traveling garments made of impractical dark silk velvet, with equally impractical embroidered cloaks over them.

"—and, of course, my personal chef and his staff," Ysa was saying. "Please notify them to make the proper arrangements."

"I am sorry, Madame," Rohan protested, appalled, "but this will not do. There is no way we can transport so many people and goods. We are limited to the two dog-sleds I was able to engage, and accommodations at the Snow Fortress are much less than Your Highness is accustomed to."

"You cannot expect me to go into this primitive place alone, with nothing of what I am accustomed to, for my good comfort," the Dowager retorted haughtily.

"The soldiers in the field find warmth and comfort in many layers of fine wool," Rohan pointed out. "The women, too. Also, our food may be plain, but nourishing."

"Perhaps Ashen stoops to such indignities as eating common soldiers' provisions and wearing their clothing, but for me, it is quite impossible. I do have my station to maintain." Ysa sniffed audibly.

Rohan knew he must devise an acceptable compromise, or the Dowager might refuse to go altogether. She had come close enough to it when he had told her of Zazar's instructions and then had changed her mind on what seemed to him to be a caprice. A pampered woman, Granddam Zaz had called her, and a better description Rohan could not devise. He felt like picking her up bodily, velvet and all, lashing her to one of the sleds, and setting forth at once, leaving boxes, bundles, ladies, and chefs in the swirl of snow left by his passage. But that would have been, at best, unadvisable. He had to find a compromise that the Dowager would accept.

He softened his voice and manner. "Your Highness, I beseech—yea, I implore you to show our dear nation your great mettle, how well and nobly you can endure the conditions under which your brave soldiers fight for us all. Think on it, Madame. By so doing, you will likewise inspire them to even greater efforts, and thanks to you the enemy will know utter and lasting defeat. Only you, as their warrior-queen, can accomplish this."

To Rohan's relief, Ysa actually pondered his words. "What you say may well be true, young Rohan, but still you cannot expect me to forego so many comforts that I should perish," the Dowager said at last. She seemed to Rohan to be somewhat mollified, but not yet ready to capitulate.

"Please trust my experience, Madame. Take only one lady, no chefs, no staff, and leave three-fourths of your goods behind. Believe me, you will not need silks and velvets at the Snow Fortress. They will only be a hindrance and a burden, and the shapeless woolen garments you despise are the best things to keep you from freezing. Here in the city I will find you warm, fur-lined boots and a good cloak likewise lined with fur. Know that our soldiers will be heartened more by your presence in good, practical garments such as these than in all the elaborate Court garments your seamstresses can devise."

The Dowager shook her head. Then she grew pale and clenched her fists—convulsively, Rohan thought. An odd gesture on her part. Her entire manner changed. She smiled, though to Rohan it seemed more than a little strained.

"Wait, perhaps you are right," Ysa said, her voice eerily gay in stark contrast to her imperious manner of a moment earlier. "But on my own terms, as I may. A warrior-queen. That suits me. I will take a diadem with me." She turned to her ladies. "Very well, it is decided. Of you all, Lady Ingrid is the youngest and, therefore, best likely to endure the hardships of both the journey and the sojourn in—what interesting name did you call it, Sir Rohan? The Snow Fortress. Therefore, you, Lady Gertrude, and you, Lady Grisella, will stay behind."

The two thus singled out began to protest, but privately Rohan thought the one chosen to accompany the Dowager looked the most dismayed. To give them as little time as possible for lamentations, he set them to work. "Please have the baggage returned to Her Highness's apartment and unpack it all. While you are doing this, I will see to acquiring boots and the fur-lined cloaks I spoke of. Then I will help

Lady Ingrid pick out the best and most practical garments for our royal lady to take with her." He turned to the Dowager. "I realize that, in my zeal to keep you warm and comfortable, I came too close to forgetting that great ladies must be beautiful as well as valiant. I apologize. Believe me, Madame, between us, we will have you turned out in such a fashion as to dazzle our warriors and daunt our enemies."

Then he bowed himself out of her presence, grateful to have avoided yet another crisis involving Her Gracious Highness, the Dowager Ysa.

Both Anamara and Rannore were openly amused at the task Rohan proposed for them though they strove to be serious.

"I know who sewed the best woolen garments, here in the castle," Rannore said helpfully, "and I think there is still a small store of them. I will take care of that part of the errand."

"And I will find the boot maker who served us so well, and the man who made your cloak," Anamara said. She was biting her lip to keep from laughing out loud.

"Please don't tell anybody who these things are intended for, lest the tale get about," Rohan pleaded. "I don't know why, but I feel it would be far better if Her Highness did not leave Rendelsham with any great pomp or display. She might be annoyed at this, but that is the way it must be."

"Annoyed? She will be furious. No doubt you will have to promise her a grand triumphal parade upon her return," Rannore said, "complete with a victor's crown and rose petals strewn in her path."

Their sobriety stretched until it broke and both ladies dissolved into mirth. Even Rohan had to smile at the picture his kinswoman's words had painted.

"Dear husband," Anamara said, struggling to regain her composure, "I know that you have given us the lighter tasks here. How much more difficult it has been for you, first to persuade the Dowager to go with you, and then to impose on her the conditions under which she must live. I do not envy you."

"I don't envy me either," Rohan replied, "especially not when she might break her promise at any moment, and never give it a second thought."

"Then we must work quickly, before she changes her mind," Rannore said decisively. She turned to Anamara. "Come, sweet coz, and let us to our tasks. Painful though it is—and none knows it better than I—the quickest gone is the soonest returned. Let us hope that this scheme of Zazar's has the desired effect and brings a quick end to this dreadful war. And our loved ones will then come home to us again."

"Let it be so," Anamara said somberly.

Rohan took her hand and held it against his heart. "Aye, in truth, let it be so."

Nineteen

With the Dowager Ysa and her lady-in-waiting, Ingrid, hastily outfitted for their sojourn in the bitter northern cold, Rohan could no longer delay his departure.

"Would that I could stay with you, my Anamara," he said, "but duty calls me."

"I know." Anamara's wonderful deep blue eyes filled with unshed tears. She touched the sling that still held his injured arm. "Only this keeps you from being in the thick of the fighting that is yet to come, and for that I am thankful."

Rohan knew that if the Four Armies were not successful in the coming battle that he, and even Lord Royance for all his years, would be called upon to try to delay the onslaught that would carry the enemy even to the gates of Rendelsham. Then such laggards as Gattor of Bilth, Valk of Mimon, Jakar of Vacastar, and Liffen of Lerkland would have to take up arms. But, he reminded himself, wars were fought by men in their prime, and these lords of Rendel were long past their fighting years. Also, they had not stinted when it came to rallying men loyal to them, and maintaining supply lines. All had done their part, as it was given to them to do.

He kissed Anamara's eyelids and the tears spilled down her cheeks. "Do not worry, my dear," he told her. "I am certain that Granddam Zaz has something very special and surprising in mind, with her insistence on the Dowager's journey to the Snow Fortress."

Anamara tried to smile, though her lips were trembling. "Maybe she wants Ysa to lead the next charge," she said. "That would undoubtedly frighten them all away."

Rohan laughed aloud. "That's my brave girl!" he exclaimed. "Now, give me a kiss to remember in the days to come."

"I will," she said, "and more than that." Suddenly she lowered her head, and her cheeks blazed red. "I—I thought I could tell you straight out, but I cannot."

Rohan tilted her head up again, studying her features. Then it came to him, what she was trying to say. "Is it true? Are you with child?"

"I think so, though it is still too early to be sure."

"Now, more than ever," he told her solemnly, "will I endeavor to return to you quickly, and in one piece. You, and our child—"

She nodded. He pulled her into an awkward one-armed embrace.

"Now go," she said with as much bravery as she could muster. "Do not worry about me. After all, Rannore is here, not to mention young Hegrin, and I will be looked after with great care."

It took all of Rohan's resolve to bid her farewell, but somehow he managed it. The Dowager would be waiting, and, as he had told Anamara, his duty bade him go when he would much rather have stayed.

In the short space of time when Rohan had been gathering what he considered the proper gear for Her Gracious Highness, the Dowager Queen, Ysa had found a moment to send for a certain other lady and give her instructions.

Lady Jacyne was, to Ysa's amusement, very uncomfortable at being summoned into the Dowager's presence. And well she might be, Ysa thought. After all, as the last of a long string of the late King Florian's mistresses, she had been deeply involved in Florian's scheme to poison his half-sister, Ashen. That Jacyne had been duped by Florian was of small concern; what did matter was that she was the only survivor of the plot, other than Ashen, of course. Florian was dead; Obern of the Sea-Rovers, Ashen's former husband, was dead; his replacement Gaurin, cemented a better alliance than the Sea-Rovers had ever offered; and Ashen had ceased to be a constant irritation. Ysa smiled to herself. No doubt Jacyne hoped that she had been forgotten, now that she had discovered honesty and faithfulness to her husband.

"You sent for me, Madame?" the woman said nervously.

"I did, indeed. Come here."

The stale smell of the woman's flesh reached the Dowager long before Jacyne approached. Ysa could see the grime in the lines of her throat, and the grubby, untended hands. Her clothes were none too clean, either, even though they were a rusty black that might have hidden some of the soil. Apparently the Lady Jacyne now believed in the mortification of the flesh.

Ysa folded her own clean, well-manicured hands so that the Four Great Rings were clearly visible. "I have decided to go to the encampment of the Four Armies, and hearten our brave men by my presence. One of my wards, the Lady Hegrin, needs a reliable guardian in my absence. You seem to me to be suitable. A purse goes with it, of course."

"But Madame," Jacyne said, "is not the Lady Hegrin already well looked after by her kinswomen? Even your own former daughter-in-law—"

Despite her overall contentment at Jacyne's appearance and apparent great change of character, Ysa straightened and turned the full force of her displeasure on the lady. "You dare to question me? Lady Hegrin needs a change of guardians. That is all you need to know!"

Jacyne wilted at once, and Ysa had to struggle to hide her smile.

"Beg pardon, Madame, it is just that I never dreamed—"

"Well, your rediscovered virtue is something that I felt deserved a reward," Ysa told her, softening. "I expect you to keep a close and strict eye on Hegrin and not allow her to fall into wanton ways because of—well, call it unfortunate associations." She named the figure she had decided to award Jacyne. "Will that amount be satisfactory, for you to maintain the girl in comfort, if not luxury, and still keep some for yourself?"

"Oh, more than satisfactory, Madame!" Jacyne cried.

"Please, know that you can count on me to oversee your ward very carefully indeed!"

Ysa could fairly see the woman calculating sums, and knew that Hegrin would probably not get the benefit of any of the money that Jacyne would receive. No new dresses every week for Hegrin. That did not entirely displease the Dowager. After all, Hegrin probably had funds of her own to maintain herself, and in any event, she was the Bog-Princess's daughter.

She dismissed Jacyne. "Now go," she said, handing the woman a folded paper. "This is your warrant both for the custody of the girl, and to call on my privy purse."

Lady Jacyne bowed herself out and when she was gone, Ysa allowed herself to smile openly. So much for that stupid little snip Anamara, who had slipped from the Dowager's control, and so much also for that slut who had trapped Florian into marriage and now was on the verge of bearing a child of someone little better than the lowest rank of noble.

Ysa could not prevent Hegrin from associating with King Peres, for it was by his command that she now lived in Rendelsham, inside the very castle. But with Jacyne now playing watchdog, the chances of an unfortunate alliance were lessened. She could now go off with a clear conscience on that fool's errand the Wysen-wyf of the Bog was insisting upon.

A week later, Hegrin and Peres sat at a table facing each other, with a game board set up between them. Hegrin leaned her head on her hand, her mind obviously not on the game. Peres glanced at her keenly. The placement of the pieces, determined by a roll of the dice, seemed certain to give Hegrin an early, easy win. She had not, however, taken her opening advantage, and Peres knew this was unlike her.

"Is anything wrong, sweet coz?" he asked.

She looked up, startled, opened her mouth as if to speak, and shook her head instead.

"Be frank with me, my dear cousin. I feel there is something amiss. How can I help if I don't know about it?"

"Please, Your Majesty, I don't think there's anything you can do."

Peres turned over a game piece, ending the contest. "I am the King," he said, smiling. "What is there I can't do?"

"But it's your granddam's order—" Hegrin clapped her hand over her mouth.

"Aha," Peres said, keeping his tone neutral. *Her* again, he thought. "It is my orders that count, coz. Remember that. Now, what has Granddam Ysa done this time? Let us see what we can do to make you smile again."

The urge to confide in him overrode any instructions Hegrin might have been given to hold her tongue. "I am no longer in the care of my Aunt Anamara and my Aunt Rannore!" she said hotly. "Instead, I am given into the keeping of Lady Jacyne!" The way she spoke her name told Peres plainly how odious Hegrin considered the lady to be.

Despite his best intentions, Peres raised his brows in some surprise. Naturally, he had heard all the rumors and knew that his late father had been involved with Jacyne in a sordid relationship just before his death, and before he, Peres, had been born. Now why would his granddam replace Lady Anamara and his mother with this one-time trollop as her guardian?

The answer lay in thinking the way Granddam Ysa did.

Peres was schooled enough in this, having observed it all his life and, on occasion, had used his granddam's scheming ways to outmaneuver her. He knew his granddam was very vexed with his mother, Rannore, even though she now strove to hide it. She must be vexed with Anamara, too, though there had been nothing even remotely like the row that had occurred between the two women when his mother had returned to Court, married to someone she loved, but whom Granddam thought beneath her. He smiled at the thought that even while this row was going on, he was knighting Lathrom a second time and granting him lands and manors enough to make him rich. Granddam had been very wroth indeed, when she learned of it.

Therefore, the Lady Jacyne must serve some other purpose. Then he understood. Jacyne owed the Dowager much, while the other two ladies—his mother especially—did not. Granddam was using Hegrin to punish Anamara and his mother. And Peres knew this to be grossly unfair.

"Whom do you wish to have as your guardian?" he asked Hegrin. "There must be someone, while your mother and father are away."

"Of course," Hegrin replied. "I was most happy with my aunts. There was no cause to tear me from what family I have close at hand during these perilous days."

"And you aren't happy with Lady Jacyne?"

Hegrin made a face. "She tries to be very holy. She is always reading to me from some book on how to behave, and she makes me go to the Fane twice a day, morning and evening, and she never laughs or even smiles. I must embroider—not clothes for Aunt Rannore's new baby, but silly little mottos instead that are supposed to 'improve my mind.'

She makes me eat gruel for my supper because she thinks I am too fond of sweets—well, I suppose I am, but eating gruel won't cure me of that. But the worst is—" She leaned closer and her voice assumed a confidential tone. "She doesn't wash and she *smells*!"

"Smells."

"Yes. And won't even use any perfume to try to cover it up. Neither Aunt Rannore nor Aunt Anamara smell, but that's because they wash every day." Hegrin looked down again, and her cheeks grew pink. "Lady Jacyne even disapproves when I wash." Then she gazed at Peres, a plea in her green-blue eyes. "She's trying to make me over to be just like her! And I hate it, coz, I simply hate it!" She bit her lip. "Your Majesty, I mean."

"When we are alone, you may call me 'coz,' or even by my name," Peres said. "I am your friend, just as you are mine. We two are like bits of sea-wrack, washed up on shore just now. And I will not have any sweet coz of mine so ill-treated."

He got to his feet and went to a desk in this room he had designated as his own, where he could play games or read or talk, or otherwise behave as one his age and not necessarily as the King of Rendel. Rummaging through the mess he had allowed to accumulate atop the surface, he found a piece of paper and then, eventually, a quill and inkwell. With a sure hand he wrote a few words, sanded the writing, folded the paper and dropped wax from the nearest candle, sealing it with his own signet. Then he tugged on a bell pull and a few moments later his personal body servant, a youth named Tamkin who was a few years older than he, appeared.

"Please find the Lady Jacyne and inform her that I will

see her in the Council chamber within the hour," he told Tamkin.

"Yes, sire," Tamkin said, and hurried off to do the King's bidding.

"Here, coz," Peres said, handing Hegrin the paper. "This officially rescinds Granddam Ysa's orders, just as I will inform your former guardian. You are now returned to the care of your aunts, just as before."

He was rewarded by seeing a veritable sunrise of a smile break over Hegrin's features. "Oh, thank you, Your Majesty!" she cried.

"Then I take it you are pleased."

"I am happier than I can tell you."

"Good. I don't have to see the Lady Jacyne for an hour, and if it's a little longer than that, the wait will do her good. We still have time to play that game, and do it properly this time, if you like."

The dimple at the corner of her mouth danced mischievously. "Oh, I do like, coz, and this time I'll beat you fair and proper, too!"

He laughed aloud, pleased anew that he had thought to have his fair cousin brought to Court. Sometimes he felt that the weight of the entire world was on his shoulders, and she provided exactly the kind of gay diversion he needed. He was growing very fond of her.

And also, he admitted to himself, thwarting one of Granddam Ysa's mean little actions was quite pleasant as well.

"Oh, no, this won't do," Ysa said, looking around the dwelling place that had been set aside for her and Lady Ingrid. "This won't do at all."

Plainly, two tents had been combined with the snow-wall separating them removed, and a doorway of sorts cut to join them. In the second "room" thus created, Ysa could see a jumble of boxes and bundles, but Lady Ingrid was nowhere in sight. There was a bed in each room, and a chair in the one that was, presumably, hers. A small brazier took the worst of the chill off the air.

"It is the most spacious we have to offer," Jabez told her deferentially. "The only lodgings that are larger are those of the High Marshal."

"Oh, yes. Royance. Well, he will simply have to give way to me," Ysa said imperiously.

"I am sure that the High Marshal would have done so already, but refrained because his living quarters are in the command tent, and there is much commotion there, with messengers coming and going, and the officers planning the next assault. I think the Lord Marshal thinks you would not find it restful."

Ysa frowned and turned her back. "I'll be the judge of that, later," she said. "I will see Zazar now."

"Yes, Madame."

She sensed rather than saw him bow, and a gust of chilly air told her that he had left the tent. Glancing around, she realized with a certain distaste the conditions under which Rendel's armies lived in the field. And where had these two tents come from? She had a sudden suspicion that the former owners didn't need them anymore.

She went into the second room. There was barely space

enough for the second narrow bed that had been hastily moved in for Lady Ingrid's use, and not even a chair. She quickly determined that some of the boxes of clothing were missing, and then found that they had had to be stacked outside, between the side of the tent and the wall of snow. Shivering, she returned to the relative warmth of the part of the tent that was hers. What had she gotten herself into? Not for the first time, she wondered why she was here.

The command tent young Jabez had spoken of was undoubtedly much better than this. Well, if need be, she thought sulkily, it would have to be turned over entirely to her. Surely Royance and his officers could make their plans somewhere else.

"You wanted to see me?"

Ysa turned to see Zazar standing in the doorway. She had a basket in one hand, an odd little furred creature in the crook of her other arm, and she was scowling.

"I did. I wanted to know the meaning of why you had me dragged all this way, through the snow, out of my—"

"I will tell you when I'm ready, and not a moment before," Zazar said. The scowl turned to a look of amusement. "Your business now is to wait. Oh—and you might lend a hand in the infirmary. We could always use another nurse. Lady Ingrid is already making herself useful, unlike you."

It was the Dowager's turn to frown. "How dare you address me in that fashion!"

"Oh, drop your airs, Ysa," Zazar snapped. "In case you don't, I remember when you came to me in the dark of night seeking a potion that would keep Boroth in your bed. You were much more polite then. I sent you away if you recall, telling you that if he would not stay for regard of you, no magic of mine would keep him there." The Wysen-wyf looked at Ysa keenly. "It was about that time that you began to read and to dabble in Power yourself, wasn't it? Tell me. Were you successful in your endeavors?"

Ysa felt her cheeks grow hot. "That is none of your—" She looked away, unable to meet the implacable gaze that cut through her to where the truth lay. "No. I was not." Then, with a remnant of her accustomed hauteur, "No one knows it better than you. After all, you fostered my late husband's bastard."

"Aye, Ashen Deathdaughter, whose birth killed the king's true love and who is proven to be far better than the seed from which she sprang. For all that you have put her through and the grace with which she endured it, you should respect Ashen."

"Respect?" Ysa echoed. "I can barely tolerate her presence."

"Even after all these years."

"Even so."

"Well, it's time you put the past behind you, and more. She will rise to be more than either of us, though as yet she knows it not."

Ysa had no answer to that. She sniffed and turned away.

"You are living among soldiers now," Zazar told her brusquely. "We all work here, even you. As I said, drop your airs and stop acting like someone whose every whim must be catered to. Follow me now. Learn of the real world."

Reluctantly, the Dowager Ysa found herself trailing after the Wysen-wyf. Studiously, she ignored the war-kats stalking through the camp and the odd little furred creature that Zazar carried. With Zazar, she ducked into a tent full of steam from vessels of simmering water and the smell of medicines and sick men. Zazar directed her to one of the beds, and with a shock, Ysa realized that the occupant was Hynnel, the son of the late Cyornas NordornKing, only so wasted and thin she scarcely recognized him.

She sat down on a stool beside the cot. "Do you remember me?" she asked with unaccustomed gentleness. "We met but briefly, when you were on your way to the Oakenkeep and your kinsman Gaurin."

"Yes, I remember," Hynnel said. He endeavored to smile. "I was seeking directions only and you were gracious enough to come outside the city and greet me."

"It was no burden. Your father—"

A cloud passed over his face and Ysa immediately realized her blunder.

"He is no more, and I fear that I will soon follow him."

"Not if I can help it," Ysa said brusquely. "Now, you must tell me. What is your treatment, and how can I best carry it onward? After all, I can't just sit around and wait to be catered to. I am here to help."

Far away to the north, the being known to his enemies as the Great Foulness and to his thralls as the Great One Whom All Served was in conference with his most trusted officers, if indeed, there was anybody he truly did trust.

Farod, leader of the Dragon-riders, was speaking. "I have set the order of attack," he said. "You, Baron Damacro, will engage the main army. Our Frydian allies will destroy the remains of the Bog-men, and my Ice Dragons will lend assistance wherever they are needed. Agreed?"

"Agreed," replied Damacro, a dour-faced man clad in black fur.

"And my place?" asked Duig.

Farod bared his teeth in a kind of smile, watching Duig. He did not cower, the way most men did at such a grimace laid over his pale and frosty skin stretched taut over sharp bones. "Second only to the Baron in command of our ground forces. You have another task, however. You will send a picked body of men and undertake to destroy the ships of the Sea-Rovers. We have suffered enough from them, both from their audacity in striking down one of our Dragons, and from the way they seem to be able to spy out our movements even when they sail at a great distance from land. However, if their ships should happen to sink under them . . ."

"I understand," Duig said, grinning. "A few small boats, quiet in the night, and an augur to bore holes in the hulls—yes, we can manage the Sea-Rovers, me and my men."

"This means that you will not have the honor of being in the van of our all-out attack against the Four Armies. I suggest that honor should go to our former Rendelians, Piaul and the men he leads."

"Thus can their loyalty to the Great One be proved," Duig said. "Excellent."

"And you, Great One?" Farod asked, turning to the ice curtain behind which his overlord sat. "Do these plans suit you?"

The familiar whisper came from behind the icy curtain, filling the chamber. "Anything that will remove this obstacle from my path suits me. But I warn you, do not fail me."

"We swore fealty, Great One," Baron Damacro said. "We will not fail, for we know our reward—either way."

The Baron, Farod knew, had been promised the governorship of Rendelsham.

"Just so," the Great One whispered. "The Four Armies are almost ready to march into our trap. Are all our forces ready?"

"Awaiting only the final placement to close all avenues of retreat behind them," Farod said.

"And is there no word of any special plans they have been making, even as we have been preparing?"

"As I told you earlier, our spies have brought back reports of some kind of construction they have been doing—machines on great wheels. But further than that, we know not. They leave the machines outside their walls. I do not think it a matter of great importance."

"How many machines?"

"The reports vary. They are nowhere near completion. One looked like a siege engine, and the other—no one knows. The enemy is most likely engaged in an enterprise without any thought to guide it."

"Beware," the whisper came. "Beware. Do not make the mistake of thinking our foes are weak or simple-minded. I fear these unknown machines, finished or not. We must destroy them before they can get them in place. Our enemies are to be crushed. To make sure, I have decided to come and see the battle for myself, once it has begun."

It was an unprecedented statement. Never before had the Great One Whom All Served ventured beyond the ice curtain that sheltered him from unworthy eyes. Farod bowed. "I and the Dragon I ride will personally look to your safety," he said.

"My Power is such that you will not be needed," the

Great One retorted, "but your presence will be welcome nonetheless." The entity behind the curtain shifted, and the curtain grew more opaque. "Now go. I feel that the final battle grows nigh, perhaps even tomorrow. Make your final preparations to meet the foe, even as I make mine."

"Tonight, late, in the dark of the moon, we march," Royance said. He looked around the table where his officers were gathered. "We should arrive just before dawn. Is everything in readiness?"

"It is, sir," Gaurin reported.

"Show me your proposed order of battle," Royance commanded.

Gaurin approached, unrolling a map that the officers around the table had not as yet seen. There was a soft intake of breath as all but Royance viewed it for the first time.

"Here is the valley I spoke of earlier. Our spies have brought back sufficient information that we could draw out the terrain as you see it. My guess, based on their reports, was that this is the place where the enemy was gathering. Our scouts have confirmed that my guess is correct. More are moving into the area daily, both the Frydian remnants and men as well. They appear ready to move. We must thwart this advance. While their numbers are large, they are not more than our warriors can deal with." He took up a piece of chalk and marked a route on the map. "This is the road I propose to take, and have already ordered the catapult and giant bow to be carried to this place, where the road bends about a minor valley where the machines can be concealed. They should already be there, hidden under white cloth and tree branches."

"But sir," Steuart protested. "We cannot use the engines! They are not even completed! They lie half-built just outside our walls!"

Gaurin smiled. Around the table, the other junior officers were looking bewildered as well. "I see that my plan was successful, and the secret kept even in the privacy of our own company. It was a ruse. While there were engines left lying unbuilt outside, elsewhere the real ones were being completed by a squad of Nordorn engineers who were sworn to silence."

"You could have told us," Steuart said, an edge of reproof in his voice. "Our labor was for naught."

"Far from it. My hopes were that with this diversion, I could give you young men training in how these engines of war work, and at the same time convince our enemies that our labors were fruitless."

"I see, sir," Steuart said. "But I still wish you had let us know of your plans."

"The very hair on my own head does not know my plans," Gaurin replied. "Not all of them. You are hearing of them now, only because we march tonight. I am putting you, Steuart, in command of the giant bow, and Cebastian in command of the catapult."

The two young knights brightened. "Thank you, sir," they responded. They arose, bowed, and resumed their seats.

"I assume that you have crews already trained, and I will assign some of my Nordorn engineers to you as well," Gaurin said. "When you bring those engines onto the field of battle, only at the first shot will we know how successful we were at concealing our readiness."

Snolli stirred in his chair at the conference table. "And what about the Sea-Rovers' part in all this?"

"We ask for the aid of two-thirds of your marines on land, and that your ships with the rest in reserve stand ready offshore, Admiral-General," Gaurin said. "We do not know if the enemy plans to make a flanking attack from that direction. If they do, then it will fall on you to prevent it."

"Agreed. Also, if any of 'em try to escape by taking to boats and heading back north with their tails between their legs, we can squash 'em like fleas." Snolli laughed.

"We will count on you," Royance commented soberly. "Now. What about this scheme of Ashen's to set up a field infirmary just behind our battle lines?"

Gaurin grimaced. "I could not talk her out of it, sir, and I dared not order her to stay behind. Every man with a wife will understand this."

There was a ripple of laughter around the table, even from those who were not wed.

Gaurin acknowledged their understanding, and then continued. "Ashen has been gathering bandages and medicines the past two days and has already gone ahead. But at least she will not be alone. Madame Zazar has decided to be with her after all."

"Staunch Ashen. She puts the bravery of our warriors to shame. Staunch Zazar as well."

Just at that moment, the Wysen-wyf appeared in the doorway of the command tent.

"Zazar who but for misfortune should be at home tending to her business instead of here, freezing, in the middle of a war," she snorted. "Royance, that person I spoke to you about has arrived."

Royance started to his feet. "Then I should go and greet her!" he exclaimed.

"No hurry. She's busy at the moment." Unexpectedly, Zazar grinned. "You'll never believe what she's doing."

Twenty

"M adame," Lord Royance said, bowing low to the Dowager. "How noble of you to come. Your presence here will gladden the hearts of our men as they march out to do battle."

It was on Ysa's tongue to tell him that it was not her idea to come to this forsaken spot and that if she had her way, she would still be in her warm apartment in Rendelsham. Then it occurred to her to wonder why, exactly, she had *not* had her way in this, a relatively trifling matter. Royance was still waiting for her response. She held out her hand for him to kiss.

"Could I have done any less?" she said.

"Will you say a few words to the company, as they prepare to march away? General Gaurin is even now setting the order."

"Of course," Ysa said. Privately, she wanted nothing more than to lie down and have Lady Ingrid rub her back and her feet, and to get several more braziers in to make her truly warm and comfortable. However, she stifled these feelings. After all, she had seen with her own eyes some of the effects of battles she had only heard about previously. Poor Hynnel.

She put her fur-lined cloak around her shoulders, and, grateful for the fur-lined boots she had scorned when she first saw them, followed Royance out to the makeshift platform that had been hastily erected so that she could be seen by as many of the armsmen as possible. He helped her up, where she stood revealed in the flickering torchlight.

Ah, the young faces—and so many of them fledgling knights who had dined at her table. Ysa felt her eyes fill with tears. She spoke with unfeigned emotion.

"All of Rendel knows and honors your efforts on our behalf. Let no man here, however humble, think himself anything but a hero. The lives and fate of those you left behind now lie in your hands. We are proud of you."

A murmur of approval rose, growing in volume. Royance held up his hands. "No cheering," he reminded the men. He turned to Ysa. "The officers have impressed on the soldiers that no untoward noise must be allowed, no sound of movement, lest the cold, still air carry the news to enemy ears."

"I see," Ysa said. She nodded and waved to the men as they passed the place where she stood.

But as the Bog-men came near, one of them, a kind of chieftain by the medallion he wore around his neck, paused.

"You are mother of headman over all of us?" he asked.

Ysa regarded him for a long moment before she answered. "The King, Peres. I am his granddam."

The man shrugged. "So he send old lady in his place. Still just little boy." Then he marched on, oblivious of the scowl that Ysa sent after him.

When the last of the warriors had departed from the camp and Royance had helped Ysa down from the platform, he escorted her to her tent. Then he bade her farewell for a time and disappeared back in the direction of the command tent for the nervous wait he must endure until they returned.

"Lady Ingrid!" Ysa called.

"She isn't here."

With a start, Ysa realized that Zazar was waiting for her in the shadows, where the dim light from the brazier did not reveal her at first. She carried a wrapped package under one arm.

"What do you want now?" Ysa asked. "It's late. I'm tired. Surely the wounded men can wait until tomorrow before I must go back to the infirmary."

"Oh, that tent is in good hands," the Wysen-wyf replied. "I've put Ingrid in charge. You're going to be needed elsewhere, though, and me with you."

"No!" Ysa protested. "How dare you take my only lady-in-waiting from me! I told you, I'm tired. I want to lie down and go to sleep."

"Well, you can't. Come with me."

With that, Zazar grabbed Ysa's soft, white hand in her brown, wrinkled one, and began dragging her through the night.

❧

Gaurin, in the van of the Four Armies, led the way cautiously. Because there was no moon, the going was particularly hazardous, a condition that he felt was more than compensated for by the covering darkness. All the war-kats, except for Bitta, and Keltin who would not leave her, ranged alongside the men, passing completely silent on their padded, lethal paws. Even Finola's instincts to fight at men's sides and perhaps engage Ice Dragons had overcome her desire to mother Weyse, the odd little creature from the Bog, and she paced beside Gaurin, almost near enough to touch.

His second in command, Lathrom, was close by his right side. Cebastian and Steuart, each with their picked company to operate the catapult and giant bow, trailed not far to his left, ready to peel off into the little closed valley where the great machines waited. Behind them came what had once been the Four Armies, almost melded into a single fighting force with divisions under the command of the junior officers. All—Nordors, Rendelians, Sea-Rovers—now marched as one. Only the Bog-men kept their separate identity. As many men as Rohan could create lengths of silk for wore these scarves over their faces.

They came to that slight break in the canyon walls where Ashen had proposed setting up her front-line infirmary. Though a slight glow was beginning in the eastern sky, there was no gleam of light from the black shadows and Gaurin didn't know whether she could even see him as the army passed by. He was tense with the gnawing desire to see Ashen at that moment, hold her in his arms, but instead he forced himself to march on.

Behind him he heard a faint sound as if of a sigh, and knew that Cebastian and Steuart had discovered the spot where the two engines lay hidden. The young officers knew that when the sounds of battle began, their crews should pull the catapult and the bow out and, if possible, bring them to bear.

Ahead, Gaurin sighted the first faint flicker of lights inside tents. He could not tell where the Ice Dragons were picketed, if indeed they had been brought down from where they usually stayed hidden. A glance to either side assured him that his men were edging forward, eager for the battle to begin. Gaurin shared their excitement, their fear, their tension. This fight would end it all, one way or another. They must triumph or the unlucky survivors would live only to see their world end.

Drawing the Rinbell sword, cognizant of the telltale sound it made, the ring of steel cutting through the cold dawn air, he gave the signal.

With a cry that seemed to come from a thousand throats simultaneously, the Rendelian army broke into a dead run and poured through the gap in the canyon walls. Many of the enemy, not yet awakened for the invasion they thought they would initiate, died before they could kick free of their blankets.

Around the advance rose the sound of clashing steel, of the screeching and yowls of the war-kats. The shouts of men added to the din. It was nearly impossible to hear any orders. Yet, from the rear of the enemy camp, a sound erupted that overrode all others.

Gaurin looked up. Two Ice Dragons had appeared. One roared again, and a gout of ice and snow erupted from its maw. The distance was too great for this to have any effect. The Dragons began to stump forward. The enemy forces scattered before the monsters as they spread great wings, threatening to knock men to the ground, as Gaurin had seen them do before. Snow swirled from the flashing of these wings. He glanced behind him. By the growing morning light he could see that Steuart and Cebastian and their crews had, indeed, dragged their engines of war out where those could be brought to bear.

He shouted a warning. The missiles would probably fly over his men's heads, but there was no sense in taking unnecessary risks. Gaurin hoped those manning the great projectiles could get their shots off before the war-kats, giving in to their instinctive hatred of Dragons, dashed ahead, putting themselves in peril.

The sharp twang of a slashed rope cut through the air as the "arrow" from the giant bow—an entire tree-trunk, carefully trimmed and sharpened—whistled overhead, flying at the target. With a jarring thump, the projectile hit true. Fatally skewered, the Dragon faltered, crashing with a thud that shook the ground. Its rider attempted to jump clear, only to be crushed under the weight of the Dragon's great head.

Despite the fate of its companion, the second Dragon couldn't halt its ponderous progress. The rider, unable to turn his mount, hampered by the necessity of going forward without trampling those of his own army, tried to guide it over the body of the downed beast instead. At that moment, Cebastian let go the catapult. The cradle hurled a rock the size of a plow horse. Its flight was slower and more awkward than that of the arrow, but its effect would be no less devastating if it hit the target.

A heartbeat earlier and the monster would have met the fate of the first, being crushed rather than taken down by a giant arrow. However, the second missile only slammed into one of the creature's forelimbs. It was not for naught; the cracking sound that echoed through the vale could be nothing but that of a gigantic bone, breaking.

"Forward!" Gaurin cried. "Finish it off!"

A man, a human warrior, was in his way, and he paused long enough to strike him down. The man's face, vaguely familiar, was so pale and frightened that Gaurin almost regretted that blow. A thought which passed before it was fully formed. The incident slowed him enough, however, that he was not first to engage the wounded Dragon.

Someone—Gidon, he thought—had grabbed the odd weapon used by the Dragon-riders from the one who had fallen, and was now turning it on the one still atop the wounded animal. A gout of freezing mist shot out of the end of the rod. The Rider snatched at his cloak, seeking to cover and protect his face. Not for the first time, Gaurin wished for bowmen, but they were useful only from ships where the air was not as cold as it was on land. Here, in this extreme cold, strings would break and the bows themselves would crack.

Now war-kats swarmed over the wounded Dragon, ignoring the downed one. With them, Lathrom led a detachment of men armed with heavy spears, men and beasts attacking with single-minded ferocity. The Rider strove to pull his mount up, to fly, but the Rendelians quickly crippled the beast's wings. War-kats squalled, clawing their way up the Dragon's flanks, and one of them pulled the Rider from his perch.

That fight was as good as over. Gaurin took a moment to look around, to see how the rest of the battle was going. Some Rendelians were down, more wounded than slain. He could see others beginning to carry the injured from the field of battle, back to where Ashen and her physician helpers were waiting.

As far as he could tell at this point, the surprise had met with great success. The enemy apparently had no idea that they were going to be attacked, rather than be the attackers. In the distance, he could see the Bog-men engaging such Frydian allies the invaders could persuade to return to the battle, driving them from the field.

His warrior's instincts were humming. This victory was too easy, bringing no satisfaction. Gaurin knew he must keep himself and his men vigilant, lest they be taken from the rear or the flank by reserves hidden and waiting for their own moment for surprise.

He paused to wipe battle-sweat from his forehead, and then ran to help wherever he could, in the areas where there was still resistance. A large pocket of the enemy had rallied around someone who was obviously a leader, and this would have to be dealt with.

🌹

"Zazar!" Ashen exclaimed in surprise. "I thought you said you had no intention of coming—" She stared at the woman accompanying the Wysen-wyf, unable to believe her eyes. She dipped a deep curtsey. "Your Highness."

"We don't have time for all these nice manners," Zazar said brusquely. "The wounded will begin coming in any time now." She thrust a package at Ashen. "Here. Read this, where I've got a passage marked."

"But—"

"Don't argue with me! Fetch a candle and start reading." Obediently, Ashen led the two women into the tent where she had placed her stockpile of bandages and medicines, placed the book on the table, lighted a candle and opened the book.

"This is something I had not yet come to," she murmured as she read. She looked up into Zazar's knowing eyes and then into Ysa's uncomprehending ones. "I can scarcely believe it—"

"Nevertheless, it is true. The day has arrived when the change foretold shall at last be wrought by a Changer. That's you, girl. And Ysa and I are destined to play our parts in it."

"Me?" exclaimed the Dowager. "No! I won't—"

Zazar turned on her. "Shut your mouth!" she said.

Her voice was not much above a whisper, but it carried such force that Ysa's cheeks turned pale and she swayed back a step as if she had been struck. "You will do your part, even as I, because you must. Even if you have to be tied and dragged to the spot, when the time comes. *You have no choice.*"

Ashen expected another outburst from the Dowager, but she was silent—not acquiescing, but no longer making protest. She might have been in shock.

"When?" Ashen asked.

Zazar shrugged and looked away. "That I don't know. I know only that the time is upon us but the very moment is still a mystery. We will know it when it happens."

"In the meantime," Ashen said, her lips numb, "we must do our duty. Your Highness, will you help with the wounded, or shall you stay here in the tent?"

"I—" Ysa began, her voice a croak. She glanced sideways at Zazar, and continued. "I will help."

Unconsciously, Ashen twisted the iridescent stone bracelet she wore. It was very warm under her fingers. Let me not think of him, she thought, and prompt him to desert his own duty and come to me instead. "The battle has begun," she said aloud. "I can hear it. We do not have long to wait."

A slight commotion outside made all three women turn, alert. Ashen opened the tent flap to discover Hynnel outside. He clutched at the tent pole to keep from falling.

"What are you doing here?" Zazar cried. "You'll kill yourself, man! And however did you get here?"

He coughed, trying to smile. "I climbed onto one of the dog-sleds when they left the Snow Fortress. I couldn't stay behind, not when the final battle was about to begin."

"Then you shall watch, but from a distance," Ashen said soberly. She turned to Zazar. "I understand. If it were Gaurin, there would be nothing that could keep him from his companions at such a time and I can expect nothing less from his valiant kinsman."

"I—I'll get you something hot to drink," Ysa offered. She looked at Ashen. "You have had the wit to order broth or soup prepared, don't you?"

"Yes, a good pot of it has been heating ever since I arrived," Ashen said.

"Then you must get back into the sled, where you can be covered and warm, and I'll bring it to you," Ysa told Hynnel. She regarded him with what Ashen could only think of as a proprietary air. "Then we'll take you to a spot where you can see what is happening. You're still in my care, you know."

"He's her special project," Zazar muttered in Ashen's ear as Ysa helped Hynnel limp back to the conveyance. "She won't be any good with somebody who's bleeding, so let her keep busy with him. She'll stay out of our way at least, until we need her."

"Here come the first litter-bearers," Ashen noted somberly. She moved toward the larger, open tent where the physicians waited. They were already lighting lanterns and making everything ready. There, they would treat the lighter hurts and apply immediate aid to those more gravely injured before sending them back to the Snow Fortress on one of the waiting dog-sleds. Ysa would have to find Hynnel another place to wait.

The sound of great wings flapping overhead made both women look up, but whatever creature was causing the sound was hidden by clouds.

Out in the water offshore, Snolli Sea-Rover had taken up command of his fleet of ships again, listening to the familiar sounds he had known for many years—the creaking and groaning of the reliable old *Gorgull*, the quiet splash of water against the sides, the occasional cough or clearing of the throat by one of the waiting men. Overhead, the stars blazed down almost as bright as moonlight. No one would sneak up on them unawares.

His grandson Rohan had done well enough, he had to admit—grudgingly. But when it came down to the real business of fighting, it took somebody like himself—old enough for caution, still hale enough to look forward to a battle. He wished that a couple of those flying nastinesses, the Ice Dragons, would come and try to attack *him* the way one had young Rohan. He didn't care for the upstart brat's having bagged one and the Chieftain of the Sea-Rovers not.

Oh, well, he thought philosophically. If all we get to do is pick off stragglers trying to get away, that might be good enough in a war such as this one. If only that miserable Great Foulness, or whatever they called him, had had ships!

He felt edgy and restless, wishing that he could be more heavily involved in the fight. He tapped his fingers nervously on the rail and realized that he was unconsciously following the rhythm of Kasai's Spirit Drum. The small man who had been his companion and chief adviser for many years was sitting on the deck next to him, eyes closed, stroking his drum, but so softly that the sound was almost inaudible.

"If you're going to do a reading for me, then do it. Don't just dab at it and say that you're doing something important," Snolli said irritably.

Kasai's eyes opened. "But I am reading for you, Chieftain," he said in a remote voice. "Listen and take heed. Fighting enough for all and everybody plays a part. This night, all things end and all things begin. Day will bring us a new world. Change, change, all is changed."

Snolli stared at him, the gray hair lifting on the back of his head. Fighting, eh. For an instant he wished for his Rinbell sword back in his hand, the one he had awarded to Obern, which had then gone to his grandson. General Gaurin carried it now, as a loan from Rohan. It could be in worse hands, he grudgingly admitted to himself. Anyway, he had his axe. His hand tightened on the handle. The axe was a proper weapon for a Sea-Rover.

Kasai's voice continued to whisper, nearly lost in the wind. "Change, change, change . . ."

Twenty-one

arod could not remember ever having been as cold as he was now. The Great One Whom All Served rode the Ice Dragon with him, soaring high above the battlefield, and watching what went on there. Farod had thought he knew cold, was inured to it, but he had never before experienced such a dead, desolate pit of utter frigidity before. Compared to this, ice was warm. With an effort, he kept himself from shivering.

The Great One observed the destruction of two of the three remaining Dragons impassively. "It doesn't matter. They are good for very few things, such as observing from a distance. They frighten the ignorant, and are useful for pulling down walls. If we encounter resistance when we reach Rendel and the cities therein, I may have to bring more of them out of the egg."

"Shall we fly back north, then, to the hatchery, O Great One?" Farod asked.

"Of course not. I wish to see the outcome of this battle. And there is something else—a pulsing of Power such as I have seldom felt before. Go *there*." The Great One pointed an icy finger toward a spot they had flown over a few minutes earlier, just as the Rendelians were well enmeshed in the valley trap that had been laid for them.

Obediently, Farod tugged the Dragon's reins and the great beast turned in its flight. Off to the right, he could see the Sea-Rovers' ships through a momentary gap in the high clouds. Even now, men armed with augurs should be making their way toward them, in boats with muffled oars.

"We may have to set down upon the ground," the Great One whispered. "This Power is very troubling to me. It will have to be eliminated before we can count our victory here complete. Not only is it unprecedented in its strength, it is also a kind of Power I have never encountered before. It is as if strands were, somehow, braided. . . ."

Farod made no comment, but urged the Dragon higher, where it could continue circling without being in imminent danger of either the giant bow or the engine that hurled boulders as big as draft animals. Perhaps they could not be aimed upward; Farod did not want to take the chance.

❧

The knot of warriors in the thick of the battle were, as far as Gaurin could ascertain, in command of the immediate situation and there was no need for him to intervene, just yet. The Army of the Bog-men was likewise well occupied, containing the remnants of the Frydians. Here and there, both

Frydians and the men newly arrived from the north were beginning to surrender.

He glanced at the ring of low mountains surrounding the valley they were in. It looked to be a prime spot in which to hide reserves, supposing the enemy had guessed they would be attacked—

—which they had!

In the light of full dawn, he could make out the movements of men hastening down from their places of concealment. In a moment, they would fall on the ones too occupied to look up.

No wonder the resistance to the Rendelians' first assault had been so feeble! Gaurin's gorge rose at the thought of those men who had been sacrificed, not informed of the possibility of attack, just to make sure the enemy trap succeeded.

"Lathrom!" Gaurin shouted.

"Here, sir!"

"Look you to yonder hills, and rally your men!"

Lathrom needed but a glance and the situation became clear to him. Immediately he began issuing orders. A detachment of spearmen ran toward his banner and by the time the enemy reinforcements had reached the campsite, they found themselves facing a barricade of determined Rendelian opposition. More than a few of the enemy fell, forced onto spear points by the impetus of those behind them.

Quickly, Gaurin ascertained that there seemed to be no more of the enemy than their scouts had reported. Now his task was to order the battle and maintain his warriors' discipline while at the same time protecting those who had given up. Not that any of his men wavered or showed any signs of hesitation at the sight of fresh armsmen bearing down on them. His heart swelled with pride at the valor and courage of his adopted countrymen.

Still, there was that third Ice Dragon. He looked in all directions, including up, but could see nothing through the thin cloud cover. Then an unmistakable call surged through his consciousness, a beloved voice speaking his name.

Ashen! She needed him. He could no more resist that signal than his heart could resist pounding at the thought of her being in danger. He called to Lathrom again.

"The battlefield is yours to direct," he said. "Ashen is in danger and I must go to her. I—I have no choice."

"You should not go alone, sir," Lathrom said. "Let me send someone with you, to bring help if you should need it."

Gaurin favored him with a wry smile. "If there is something that my lady, Madame Zazar, and I cannot deal with among us, then sending men after me would be useless."

Lathrom gazed at him for a moment, and then nodded. "Good chance to you, sir," he said, and then returned to the battle.

Snolli Sea-Rover watched, amused, as three little boats approached the waiting ships. The men in the boats had done all the obvious things—worn dark clothing, muffled their oars—but it was plain they were no real seamen. The faint phosphorescence of their wake was plain as daylight to eyes trained to see, and despite their attempts at silence, enough of their clumsy noise drifted through the still, frigid air that even a novice could detect someone approaching. Obviously they didn't realize that not only did sound carry with eerie clarity across water, but also that the least whisper was magnified in this cold to the point that the speaker might as well have been standing at Snolli's elbow.

"D'you think we ought to get the biggest ship first?" one of the men in the boats asked.

"Aye, that'll be the one with their leader on it, or I miss my guess."

"Ssssh. We're getting close."

Snolli grinned and stepped away from the rail lest gleam of teeth betray that the men on board the ships were thoroughly aware of the approach of the would-be attackers. He gestured to Kather, who grinned in return.

Kather then coughed loudly. Answering coughs from *Wave-Ruler* and *Stormbracer* acknowledged *Gorgull*'s signal. Presently, Kather and two more of the Sea-Rovers who were not assigned to the land forces slithered down ropes to wait, near to the water line, for the approaching boats to come close enough. Snolli knew that on the other two ships, still more Sea-Rovers were doing the same thing.

He felt a slight bump as the small boat collided with *Gorgull*'s hull and shook his head, scowling, at such ineptitude. Then he heard the subdued sounds of a scuffle. Presently, Kather reappeared on deck.

"We needn't have sent three men to meet them," he reported, obviously pleased with himself. "Wasn't but two of them in their little cockleshell. And their augur."

Snolli didn't need to be told that all were now residing at the bottom of the frigid sea on which the unharmed ships floated. He nodded. "Good work," he said.

"Duty," Kather said with a shrug. "And a pleasant break in the monotony."

He walked away, and Snolli found that he agreed with

Kather. It *was* monotonous, waiting for the outcome of a war fought mainly on land, while they waited out of the thick of the action.

Again he longed for one of the Ice Dragons to fight. At least that would break the tedium, as disposing of would-be scuttlers of ships had not. For a moment he toyed with the idea of leaving only a skeleton crew with the ships, now that any danger to them had been disposed of, rowing back to shore, and joining the battle.

He had given his word, though, that he would station himself here, and so here he would remain.

But he still wished for an Ice Dragon to fight. That, at least, would give him something to do.

Ashen stepped outside the tent to oversee the loading of the last of the wounded onto dog-sleds for transport back to the Snow Fortress. She was gratified to observe that even those whose injuries needed more care than they could give were not gravely hurt. Gaurin must have been very successful in the surprise attack he had planned so carefully. A few prisoners, under guard, were beginning to trickle back as well, and this Ashen took as a good sign.

Zazar joined her, for once looking a bit weary. "We are not out of danger yet," she warned Ashen. "My bones are trembling and my teeth chatter and it isn't strictly from the cold."

"What else could it be?" Ashen said.

She examined the Wysen-wyf with a critical eye. Yes, there were definite signs of fatigue there, and Zazar's eyes looked as if she hadn't slept in a week. "You could go and lie down for a while, during this lull," she told her Protector. "There are enough people that we can spare you for an hour."

"Not yet. Come. We must get Ysa, and go someplace apart from here."

It was on Ashen's tongue to ask why, but she forbore to question Zazar. Though this weariness was new, the look in the Wysen-wyf's eye was not, and Ashen knew better than to try to gainsay her when she was in such a mood.

She found Ysa in the supply tent, still hovering over Hynnel, whom she had coaxed into the shelter. She had a cup of broth in her hands, which she was trying vainly to get Hynnel to swallow.

"No more, dear lady, I beg of you," Hynnel said. He turned his head away and caught sight of Ashen. His face lit up with pleasure. "Ashen, sweet coz! Tell me—how goes it with the battle?"

Ashen couldn't completely suppress a smile, knowing that Hynnel might be even gladder of her presence as a shield between him and Ysa's determined nursing than for what knowledge of the war she could bring him.

"I think it goes well," she said. "Our casualties are lighter than expected, and only a few men are gravely enough injured that we need transport them by sled to the camp. Also, our men are taking prisoners."

"That is good news all around," Hynnel replied, sounding very pleased. "If only I—"

"Yes, I know. I'm sure Gaurin misses you sorely."

Hynnel began to cough, so hard that Ashen gazed at him with alarm. He hadn't done this in several days. Could the journey from the Snow Fortress have overtaxed his meager resources?

"If you feel well enough, I must ask the Dowager to leave you for a little while."

Ysa started to protest but stopped when Ashen looked at her calmly. "Zazar bids us both come with her."

"I am quite well enough to be left alone as long as Madame Zazar requires," Hynnel said. He turned to Ysa. "Not that I do not welcome your so tender care of me, dear lady. No one could be more attentive. But other needs must take precedence, at least for a short time."

"Well, if you're sure—" Ysa said.

"I'm sure," Hynnel responded. "When you do return, you can bring me more broth. It has a special healing property, when you hold the cup for me with your own white hands."

Mollified, Ysa left the supply tent. Ashen turned to look at Hynnel once more before following, and was rewarded with a wink. She nodded, trying to hide her smile as she ducked through the tent flap.

Outside, Zazar was waiting. "Come on, come on," she said impatiently.

"Where are we going?" Ashen asked.

"I don't think it's fair, to be dragged out here in the middle of nowhere, in the cold and the snow, and then, just as I was really learning how to take care of an injured warrior—"

Zazar rounded on Ysa. "Stop your whining, woman!" she ordered. "Better that you should say nothing, when the time comes, than to keep up that incessant complaining!" Then she turned to Ashen. "I am looking for a place set apart. I want a high spot, well beyond the infirmary camp, or even the battlefield. Not too high, not a mountainside, but enough that we are breathing cleaner air than the smell of fighting or wounded men. It must also be a place where there is room for us all to stand."

Ashen frowned, thinking. "There is a small promontory to the north, just past the opening to this niche in the mountains," she said at last. "It stands something like a sentinel, near the opening to the valley where the enemy was encamped. Will that do?"

"Perhaps."

Without looking to see that the other two women were following, Zazar set off in the direction Ashen had indicated. Ashen hurried after the Wysen-wyf, trying to keep up with the brisk pace the older woman had set, and Ysa had no choice but to flounder in their wake. By the time the promontory came into view, Zazar was halfway up to the top, a surface that stood perhaps the height of three men above the valley floor. As Ashen had said, there was a space at the apex where the three women could stand, but very little more than that.

"Read this again," Zazar ordered as soon as Ashen also reached the peak, handing her the blue velvet–covered book.

The jewel-studded embroidery on the words *Ye Boke of Ye Fayne* glittered in the wan sunlight that was beginning to show through the overcast sky, and the title, *Powyr*, was too bright to look at. Ashen took the volume from Zazar and opened it to the page Zazar had marked with leaves from an ash tree, a rowan, an oak, and a yew. Obediently, she read through the passage once more. She closed the book and laid it down, but kept the leaves in her hand. A fleeting thought crossed her mind to wonder whence such had come, and then she raised her head at a sight that was enough to make a sturdy warrior blanch.

An Ice Dragon was floating down on noiseless wings to settle on the floor of the valley and a kind of universal silence settled with it. Such was the length of the beast's neck that the Rider and his passenger, sitting just behind its head, were on an eye level with the women standing atop the rocky scarp.

The hooded Rider, the one who controlled the Dragon's movements, fell and dreadful though he might be, paled into insignificance beside the entity who accompanied him.

This is the Great Foulness, Ashen thought numbly, dazed by the reality of his presence. He was close enough almost to touch. She could not take her eyes away from him. Behind her, Ysa gasped as if in recognition and for no reason that she could think of, Ashen remembered the white window in the Fane.

If I were a man, she thought, here is the creature with the face I would most like to bury my fist in. I think it would simply pass through it, because his translucent, cave-salamander skin and cartilage in place of bones would offer little resistance.

The opalescent bracelet burned on her wrist. Oh, Gaurin—She stifled the thought before it could find further expression.

Instead, she found herself saying, "You have come, at our command." Her voice and those of the women with her echoed in her ears, and she realized they were all speaking the same words. Ysa's voice trembled a little, but she made no move to retreat.

He uttered an almost soundless laugh. "I came because I chose to, and because I was—curious about the Power I sensed. And to think, it was only three feeble women, think-ing they could summon me at their will."

"You scorned not to use a woman as your chief minion," the three women retorted, their voices mingling but not en-tirely in unison. "You fear to face us."

"I fear nothing!" The whisper coming from the lipless mouth filled the space around them.

"You should."

At that moment, the Dragon-rider turned, alert to a faint sound coming from behind him, a little to the south. His hood fell back and Ashen recognized the person she had glimpsed but once before, in the battle between his mount and the Nordorn soldiers, over Flavielle's and Harous's bod-ies: Flavielle's lieutenant, Farod. The marks of the war-kats' claws showed clearly on the Dragon's hide.

"Take care, O Great One," the lieutenant said.

With a shrug, the Great Foulness lifted one languid hand and a column of glittering ice arose beside the Dragon. He stepped off and onto the top of the column. "I am quite safe," he whispered, "but get you gone. There is need of you later."

Obediently, Farod pulled the reins controlling the Dragon's head, urging it to take flight. At that moment, the wheeled conveyance of the great bow trundled into view. The bow was armed and ready, and Ashen recognized Steuart at the forefront, urging his crew on to renewed effort.

"Just a little way further, men!" he cried, his voice cutting through the silence as if from a great, great distance.

Then, catching sight of their quarry, the crew manning the bow went to work, frantically adjusting their weapon and aiming it at their target. To Ashen, their movements seemed slow, so slow, as if they worked in frigid water. Nevertheless, before Farod could coax the Dragon to flight once more, Steuart slashed the rope that released the great arrow fashioned from the trunk of a tree.

At that range, the missile traveled slowly. There was time for Farod to jerk back sharply on the reins. The Dragon turned, rearing. The arrow merely grazed the beast's flanks and traveled on harmlessly. Farod, however, could not keep his seat and fell to the ground. The Great Foulness, with another wave of his hand, caused a wall of ice to spring up, blocking Steuart and his men from attacking. The Dragon, freed of its rider and smarting from its wound, soared upward. Its squalls of pain sent snow cascading not only from its mouth and from under its wings, but also caused banks of snow on the ridges above to tremble and threaten to fall. It flapped off toward the west.

"Ashen!"

She looked in the direction from which that cry had come, startled, and discovered Gaurin rushing toward the scene of the confrontation between the Great Foulness, and the three women. He was alone.

"Go back!" she cried in her own voice. "Please, please, go back—"

But it was too late. Farod leaped up, prepared to fight, but his only weapon, the metal rod from which erupted the mist that froze men's lungs, had been lost when he had been thrown from the natural saddle on the Dragon's neck. Without the slightest hesitation, he charged at Gaurin. The sheer force of his momentum knocked Gaurin off his feet. When Farod arose again, he had a sword in his hand—Gaurin's sword. Gaurin likewise leapt to his feet and drew the only weapon he had remaining, a long dagger. The two men began to prowl around one another, taking each other's measure.

With anguish that tore at the very core of her being, Ashen forced herself to look away. The Great Foulness was beginning to make more magical gestures with his translucent fingers, not toward the battling men, but toward the three women who faced him alone and sorely afraid.

Dordan the archer nudged Snolli and pointed upward. "Look," he said.

"Ah," Snolli breathed. A slow smile spread over his face.

The Ice Dragon flew awkwardly. A great gash marked one flank, and it dripped malevolent ichor as it approached. It had noticed the three Sea-Rover ships stationed offshore and, even without a Rider to guide it, it was obviously positioning itself for an attack.

"Tell me again how you did it before," he said, not taking his eyes off the Dragon.

"Well, first we peppered it with arrows, but it never noticed until someone hit the eye. It went down, trying to rake the arrow out, but until Kather blinded it on one side with his spear nobody dared get close. Then Rohan jumped on the neck and managed to stick his sword clean through the thing's neck, just under the skull. I imagine he severed the spine."

"A lucky stroke," Snolli said with a grunt. He hefted his axe, the preferred weapon of the Sea-Rovers. "I gave Obern my best sword as his man-gift, and he bequeathed it to Rohan when he died. Since then I have not replaced it. But an axe in the right hands—" He grinned, knowing whose hands were the right ones in this instance. "Yes, an axe is enough for me."

"Please don't be foolish," Dordan said. "You are our Chieftain. Let others take on this dangerous task."

Snolli regarded his chief archer with a sour eye. "And did you have the same soft advice for my grandson?" he demanded. "*Pfaugh!* You've forgotten that I am not only the Chieftain of the Sea-Rovers but also the Admiral-General of the Four Armies of Rendel! There are—well, there were four generals until Harous fell. He did not scorn to lead from the front instead of from the rear as you would have me do. Gaurin and that Bog-man, Tusser, are in the thick of things, and even Rohan would be if he hadn't stupidly broken his arm. And you would have me hang back and send another in my stead?"

"No, Chieftain."

Dordan bowed his head, but Snolli could tell that the archer remained opposed to what he was determined to do.

"Dordan is right," Kasai said. He spat over the side.

"Don't be so sure of that, Spirit-Drummer," Snolli retorted. He turned to his waiting men. "Prepare boats," he ordered. "And get the spearmen ready."

When the Dragon came close enough, it was met by a hail of arrows from bows kept warm and well greased until needed. As with the other the Sea-Rovers had engaged, this beast dropped to the surface of the water, trying to dislodge the arrows that had hit its eyes, like so many grains of sand irritating it. Snolli took the bow position in one of the boats filled with spearmen, ready to transfer himself onto the Dragon's neck.

With rough efficiency, Kather's spearmen finished their task of blinding the horrible creature. More experienced now, they cast ropes over the head to give Snolli a more secure handhold as he leapt onto the thing's neck.

With a loud, triumphant cry, he launched himself from the boat and, with the ropes to cling to, made his way up to the spot where a natural saddle formed just behind the Dragon's skull. His axe, secured by a thong to his wrist, was already in his hand. He lashed himself in place with one of the ropes and began to hew at the vulnerable spot.

One stroke, and then another, and another. Snolli looked up at the anxiously waiting men in the boats, who were trying simultaneously to avoid the thrashing of the Dragon's great wings and yet stay close enough to take their chieftain back to safety. He laughed. "He's a tough one, but I'm winning!" he shouted.

He was already wet to the skin, but the foul-smelling ichor that drenched his clothing carried with it something far worse. It was as if it destroyed skin where it touched, the way mere frigid water could not. However, the vulnerable spot now lay revealed. With both hands, he brought the axe down, hoping to end it. Uncharacteristically, he longed for clean, dry garments, and to be safe and warm where he could be cared for.

"I am *not* old," he muttered. "In my prime." He struck another two-handed blow. One more stroke—

The axe fractured on impact with the hard bone, but he had cut nearly through the thing's spine. With a great spasm, it flailed limbs and wings, and tossed its head violently. Snolli kept his seat only because of the rope with which he had fastened himself. He had a confused glimpse of boats being broken into kindling and men being hurled into the sea.

Plainly, the Dragon was in its death-throes. There would

be no dishonor in abandoning it before it was well and truly dead.

He had tied the rope in a sailor's knot that would come loose when necessary. But something had fouled the knot. The Dragon's struggles had lessened, and it was beginning to sink beneath the surface. Snolli fumbled at the rope, tugging vainly and trying to free himself. His axe broken, he couldn't even hack through the rope.

There wasn't time for any of his men to reach him, even if there was anybody left who was able to. He could see plainly, dispassionately, what the inevitable end would be. He uttered one last triumphal shout while he still could. "I die well!" he cried. "And I take a great enemy with me!"

Then the Dragon's body took its last plunge to the depths of the sea, carrying Snolli Sea-Rover with it.

Twenty-two

$\mathcal{A}$top the rock projection, Ashen reached back and felt Zazar take her right hand, and Ysa's soft fingers grasp the left. She knew without looking that the other two women had likewise clasped hands. Thus joined, the Three faced the Great Foulness as one.

"In the Palace of Fire and Ice, thou wert once contained by the Ice. Thy keepers were much too kind. Thou hast broken thy bonds and let thy evil loose upon the world once more, and so now thou must be consumed by the Fire!" the Three intoned.

They took a step forward, and tongues of flame leapt up at their feet. In an instant they were engulfed in a silent column of fire that pulsated with Power such as had never before been unleashed. The Great Foulness flinched.

"You do not frighten me," he whispered, but his voice

shook and he averted his gaze. He gestured and a wall of ice began to grow around him.

"Thou shouldst be afraid," the Three said. "We are Power in all its aspects."

Zazar spoke alone. "I am the Eldest. I am the Power of Earth Magic."

Ysa spoke. "I am the Middle. I represent the Power of Learned Magic."

It was Ashen's turn. "And I am the Youngest, the Distiller of both Fire and of Magic."

Again they spoke in unison. "Thou didst come to this world unwelcome, and would not depart. Now we have been called to subdue thee, and so we are here. Thy time is at an end."

"Never!" the Great Foulness said, for the first time above a whisper. He pointed upward.

Above them, the snow atop the ridge that had been loosened by the wounded Dragon's outcries began to slide down the slope. In a few moments, the women would be swept away to their destruction.

Gaurin went into a defensive stance, prepared to dodge whichever way Farod attacked. The unnatural man seemed to possess an equally unnatural strength. Gaurin knew he could not hope to come out of this fight alive by relying on anything but skill, for with the loss of his sword, he was now overmatched both physically and in weaponry.

His sword! This was the famed Rinbell sword that Rohan had presented to him as the best available, a loan to replace his own shattered blade. Rohan's voice echoed in his ears:

"My Rinbell sword will fight for you!" he had cried when he tossed it to Gaurin during the battle with Harous and the Sorceress. "They say Rinbell blades, if they choose, fight for those who wield them, if the cause be just," he had explained later.

Therefore, it stood to reason that if the cause be not just, the sword would refuse its wielder's hand. Gaurin could only hope that this was the case, as Farod rushed toward him. He ducked under the blade and caught Farod's wrist even as the Rider caught his. Farod's grip was both strong and icy, and Gaurin feared he would be forced to drop the long dagger from his paralyzed hand.

They struggled so for a moment, and then both sprang back.

"My Lady Flavielle marked you for destruction long ago," Farod said, panting. "I will finish what she began!"

"Your lady was evil, as evil as your master," Gaurin retorted. "You think me overmatched? Come ahead and learn to your dismay what it is like to fight man to man, instead of the cowardly way you once hid behind an Ice Dragon's wings!"

With a roar of fury Farod attacked again. Gaurin ducked under the blade but was unable to prevent Farod from bearing him to the ground once more. The lieutenant leapt to his feet and stood over him, holding the sword high with both hands, blade pointing downward.

"Die like the inconsequential insect you are!" he cried hoarsely.

Then he hesitated, and the sneer on his face was replaced by a look of sheer disbelief. His arms jerked back and to the side, and the Rinbell sword dislodged itself from his grip to go spinning off into the snow.

Energy and hope renewed, Gaurin clutched at his enemy and hurled him to the ground though he was unable to bring his dagger to bear. The two men rolled over and over, neither managing to get an advantage. Gaurin was nearly spent when, to his own disbelief, he felt the hilt of the sword in his hand. It had come to him of its own accord! He planted both boots on Farod's chest and, using the strength of his leg muscles, managed to shove him away. Farod staggered toward him again just as Gaurin pulled himself upright. A flicker of doubt crossed his mind as to whether he was too spent to be able to raise the heavy sword.

He need not have been concerned. As if it were a living thing, a fresh companion in arms come to his aid, the Rinbell sword lifted itself so lightly that it might not have had any weight at all. He took a step forward and let Farod run onto the blade.

The Rider fell, dead before he reached the snowy ground, and Gaurin, his strength gone, dropped to his knees. Only now was he dimly aware of the shouts of Steuart's men coming from behind a wall of ice, and the faraway sounds of the battlefield whence he had come. He looked up to see a fell creature standing atop a pinnacle of ice, facing a column of flame that was about to be overwhelmed by a small avalanche hurtling directly at it.

He knew instinctively who the creature was, and knew also that somehow, impossibly, Ashen was in the midst of that flame. The snow would quench the fire, she would be destroyed, and there was nothing he could do to help her.

The snow hurtled down the mountainside, carrying all in its path, but just as it reached the rock upon which the Three stood engulfed in flame, it sizzled and vanished harmlessly into steam that was immediately dissipated into the frigid air.

"This cannot be," the Foulness whispered. "But how?"

"Thou canst not harm us with thy Ice magic," the Three said calmly. "And thou hast not the ability to withstand the Fire. Would that thy captors had known this, for in the Palace of Fire and Ice, this knowledge didst reside, forgotten. When thou didst destroy it and the good old man that didst dwell within, thou didst seal thy own fate. There are places aplenty, on other planes, where thou couldst have reigned undisturbed. But when thou didst lift up thine eyes and encompass to subdue this world, thou wert doomed to failure before thou didst begin. Prepare thyself, for thy brief ascension is at an end."

"Never!" the Foulness said, sneering.

Spears of glittering ice appeared in his hands and he hurled them at the column of fire before him. The spears never even reached the flames but vanished with nothing to mark their disappearance.

The Three who were engulfed in flame unclasped their hands. The tongues of fire grew even brighter as they separated briefly and then braided themselves together again as the women's hands joined once more. The four leaves that one of them had held were incorporated into the joined strands of fire and glowed with a radiance the Foulness could not endure.

"No," he whispered. "Please . . ."

The braided fire rose high and then descended upon the entity cowering atop the pinnacle of ice.

With a roar that could be heard back in Rendelsham, an enormous gout of smoke rolled upward, leaving behind only a scorched spot and a hole in the ground where once the Great Foulness had stood. Answering rumbles from the earth bespoke new tremblings and upheavals. The ice wall separating Steuart and his men from the others shattered into splinters, making them scramble for their lives lest they be crushed. An outline of the four leaves hung sparkling in the air, then vanished. In a flash of flame, the velvet-bound book disappeared almost unnoticed.

The entire world shook. Then it *Changed*.

Still connected with the other two women through their clasped hands, Ashen's perceptions soared high above the land until she could see all that was happening.

Fire-mountains dotting the coast gave a last cough and then collapsed one by one, their eruptions stifled by the earth that caved in on them. Far to the south, the sunken land that had been the Bog began to rise even as the surrounding mountains sank. All along the seacoast, water both foul and comparatively fresh cascaded into the ocean as the BaleBog lifted and merged into the mountains that had once hidden it from intruders' eyes. Giant luppers were washed from their deep pools along with other creatures, shrinking even as she watched them drop down the gleaming cliffs. The huge, unnatural birds took on their proper size and form once more and the ruins of the lost city of Galinth lifted to shine in the pale sunlight.

Bells rang in every Fane in the land, and the loudest of these came from the Great Fane of the Glowing in Rendelsham. There, people of high and low rank alike knew that something unprecedented had happened. Because they still lived, they surmised that their enemy had fallen at last.

Ashen shifted her focus nearer. Lord Royance, his silver hair blowing in the breeze, took the banner of the Four Armies from in front of the command tent and hurried through the Snow Fortress, rallying whoever was still present, encouraging them to rejoice. He, better even than the people in Rendelsham, knew the scope of the victory that had been achieved this day.

Finally, she looked down at Gaurin where he still struggled valiantly to get to her side. She smiled at him with great tenderness. Then she slipped lifelessly to the rock surface on which she stood.

She opened her eyes what seemed but a moment later, but which must have been some hours. As she looked around, her eyes began to focus and she discovered that she was lying in the infirmary tent back at the Snow Fortress. How she had come to be there, she did not know. Gaurin knelt on one side of her, clasping her hand, and to her astonishment, the Dowager Ysa occupied a stool on the other side of her bed. Zazar stood at the foot, glaring at her, fists on hips.

"Hmmph," the Wysen-wyf commented. "Back, are you? Good. I have work to do and no time to watch you sleep."

Then, without ceremony, she disappeared. Gaurin squeezed Ashen's hand even tighter and held it to his cheek.

"I thought you were dead or dying," he said, his voice low and tremulous with emotion. "But Madame Zazar said no, that you had only fainted. Given what little I saw of what was happening, I am astonished that you were affected as lightly as you are."

"I have something to tell you," Ysa broke in. "It is very important."

"It would have to be, for you to interrupt this moment between my wife and myself," Gaurin said, his voice as cold as his blue-green eyes.

Ysa slipped to her knees beside the bed. "It was those moments when we all faced the Great Foulness together— you, me, Zazar. I—well, I find that I must beg your forgiveness for the way I have treated you all these years."

"That is not necessary," Ashen told her. "It is all in the past, and best forgotten." She turned to Gaurin. "Please, let me get up. I'm not at all ill—in fact, I feel remarkably well. I want to go back to our tent so you can tell me what has happened while I was unconscious. Can we do that?"

"We can, my Ashen, but it would be better to go to the command tent instead. Lord Royance is waiting there, and he has been very anxious about you."

"Yes," Ashen agreed. "That would be better."

She threw back the cover and found that she was still fully clad, save for her fur-lined boots and cloak. While she was slipping her feet into the boots, Zazar rejoined them.

"I think I'll just go have a word with Royance as well," she said. "He's been feeling left out, not getting to fight horrible little pieces of evil filth like His Putrescence. I had better tell him how lucky he is."

"How lucky we all are," Gaurin said soberly. He slipped his arm around Ashen's waist, lest she be weaker than she thought, and stumble.

Glad of his presence, though not needing his support,

Ashen walked firmly through the snowy streets of the Fortress. There was something lacking—Suddenly, she knew what it was.

"Where is Weyse?" she asked Zazar. "And where have all the war-kats gone? Surely they were not hurt or destroyed—"

"No, my Ashen," Gaurin told her.

"They've all gone back where they belong," Zazar said brusquely. "After all, the need has passed." She turned to Ysa. "Daresay your little flyer has disappeared, too."

"Oh—" Ysa said. "Yes. Daresay." She seemed downcast at the idea, but did not dispute it.

Ashen digested this in silence. At a crossing in the road, they encountered someone who looked familiar and different at the same time. Ashen stared at him, trying to remember where she had seen him. He wore a breastplate made of shell and carried a spear. Then, abruptly, it came to her. "Tusser!" she cried.

Indeed, it was the Bog General, but so changed that he was all but unrecognizable. In contrast to his former stooped posture, now he stood straight and as tall as his low stature would allow. Even his features seemed to have changed, becoming regular and almost attractive.

"Lady Ashen," he said. He bowed, and then, as Ysa had done, went down to his knees.

She tried to stop him, but he shook off her restraining hand.

"You do—have done great works today. Great work." His words came haltingly, as he searched for the correct manner of speaking. "Bog-people now—we are now out from under long shadow that has been plague to us many years. No more

Outlanders. All one. I come now tell you—to tell you all Bog-people swear allegiance to Rendel. And to you." He arose again, grinned, and ducked his head. "Tusser now your man forever. Anything you need, you call upon Tusser and he will do."

He bowed once more and disappeared back down the snowy street, toward the area where the Bog-men had been encamped.

Ashen was so astonished she almost lost the power of speech. "I—I never thought such a thing would ever happen. The swearing of allegiance, I mean. His appearance is another matter."

"Both the Bog-men and the Frydians were transformed with the, the—"

"The Changing," Zazar supplied. "That's what happened. All Changed, as was foretold."

"So many changes that I cannot encompass them all," Ashen murmured faintly.

"Oh, you'll get used to it," Zazar said with an airy wave of her hand. "We're here."

Royance was standing outside the entrance to the tent. He, too, bowed to Ashen. "Come inside, my dear. There is much you can tell us, and much that you do not yet know."

"One thing I do not know is why everyone is treating me like some kind of royalty!" Ashen exclaimed.

"Ah, but you are that, and more," Royance said genially. "All of you. Please come inside."

"Don't spoil her," Zazar muttered, as if to herself.

Royance took Ashen's hand and tucked it into the bend of his elbow as he showed her to the counsel table where she had so often sat before, only much, much farther down. "Here are even more to greet you as the heroine you have become."

Looking around, she saw all her friends and acquaintances as they arose and, as had Lord Royance, bowed. Rohan, Lathrom, Cebastian, Steuart, Jabez, Reges—all the splendid young knights were there, along with someone who had not been present in the Snow Fortress before, though his keep stood hard by. Gattor of Bilth bowed like the rest, his plump, sleepy face devoid of expression.

"Greetings, Lady Ashen of Ash," he said. "I am in your debt, as are all of us here. You saved my lands from the Great Foulness."

"You saved the entire country!" Steuart exclaimed, and the other young knights nodded vigorous agreement. "There is no honor too great for you."

"Gentlemen, please," she protested. "It is too much. I am like to perish with embarrassment!"

"Then sit you down and listen to the great things you have accomplished," Royance said.

With the Great Foulness and his lieutenant occupied, facing three women who, inexplicably, seemed to pose a greater threat than did the armed men opposing their forces, the two armies met in a battle for which there could be only one conclusion.

Whereas Gaurin, when he left the field, had turned over command to Lathrom who was not only able, but also prepared to delegate in turn, only a weak chain of command existed among the enemy once both Farod and the Great

Foulness were otherwise engaged. In the chaos that followed these two leaders disregarding the battle, Baron Damacro, leader of the human army, had fallen, and with him had gone all pretense to order and discipline. Likewise, when Chaggi, leader of the Frydians, surrendered, that fight ended.

Among the dead were discovered the bodies of Piaul and his traitorous followers. They had been stationed, perhaps deliberately, where the brunt of the assault would fall on them. It was thought that Gaurin had killed Piaul, not recognizing him in the press of battle. Duig also perished in that skirmish though who had killed him no one knew or ever would.

Not all the news was good. Admiral-General Snolli was no more. The wounded Ice Dragon had attacked the Sea-Rovers' ships, and Snolli bravely finished off the hideous beast single-handedly, only to be carried down to the ocean floor with its body.

Though the day belonged to the Rendelians as far as the actual battle went, victory could not be declared as long as the instigator of all this evil survived. And then the unhoped-for occurred. The Great Foulness himself, inexplicably, vanished in a cataclysm that literally changed the face of all the land.

Gaurin had found Ashen lying crumpled atop the rocky pinnacle where three women had stood, facing the unimaginable without flinching. She was so white and still he had thought she had perished, but Zazar told him she yet lived.

And so he had brought her back to the Snow Fortress, carrying her in his arms as one would the honored dead for he thought, despite Zazar's assurances, that she surely would never awaken.

With the rounding up of stragglers and taking them prisoner being accomplished, the Rendelian army returned as well, many of them casting sideways glances at the Bog-men and at the Frydians, wondering at the changes that had been wrought.

❀

"It is a remarkable tale," Ashen said. "I mourn for Snolli, though he and I were at odds most of the time. He never forgave me for Obern's death. Rohan." She held her hand out to her foster son.

"He died a proper Sea-Rover death," Rohan said. "There is nothing to be sorry for."

"And now in the midst of the wreckage of war we find that you are well, Lady Ashen, and unharmed by this most extraordinary event," Royance said, his eyes twinkling warmly. "I do not know how, but we rejoice nonetheless." He lifted her hand and kissed it.

"She is a repository of Power," Ysa said, and all eyes turned toward her. She arose from her chair. "Lady Ashen— Princess. Your strength and the Power you wield cannot be gainsaid. I see now that I made a mistake, those years past. Here before this company I declare it. I see that Rendel needs you and not my grandson to be its ruler, its sovereign Queen."

"No—" Ashen said, but Ysa continued as if she had not spoken.

"Yes, I once declared that you could not succeed, any more than could the King's mother, Rannore. But that is only a custom and custom bows to princes. Peres is a nice enough boy, but we can likely find a cloud on his legitimacy—"

"No!" Ashen repeated, this time so firmly that even Ysa

took heed. "Do not say it. I do not want the crown under any circumstances, and certainly not what you are proposing. I never wanted it."

Ysa just stared at her, as if thunderstruck that anyone could deny the gift she was offering. Lathrom, who had been scowling at Ysa, slowly relaxed and took his hand from the hilt of his sword. Gattor of Bilth gazed sleepily at the Dowager, and lifted his eyebrows.

"Believe me, Madame," Ashen said more gently. "Your grandson's legacy is safe from me. All I want now is to go home, and there live out my days with Gaurin, and my daughter."

"Well," Ysa commented, determined to have the last word, "that will be as it may."

In a remarkably short time, the Snow Fortress had been dismantled and the prisoners set to the task of conveying the wounded on both sides to Rendelsham, where the physicians could begin their work of repairing the ravages of war. Rendelian soldiers, however, saw to the transport of Hynnel, Norras, and the four others still suffering the effects of Dragon's Breath, not trusting this precious cargo to their recent enemies.

Surprisingly, Zazar accompanied Ashen and Gaurin to Rendelsham. "I'll be only a few days here," she said. "Then I'll be returning to the Bog—or rather, what's left of it—to start preparing for a new Wysen-wyf."

Both Ashen and Gaurin stared at her, as if thunderstruck.

"Oh, don't gape at me like idiots. Nothing lasts forever, not even me. I am feeling the weight of my years, particularly after all the business with the pillar of fire." Unexpectedly, Zazar grinned.

"Y-you are welcome to come and stay with us after you have made your, your preparations," Ashen managed to say.

"Oh, I know that. And I might just accept your offer." Zazar peered at Ashen keenly. "If only to get the new one a good start."

"What new one?"

Zazar just laughed. "You'll find out."

Abruptly, she returned to her original subject. "Good thing I had experimented with that fire pillar so long ago, eh? It worked much better this time, I must say. I didn't have to be hauled out bodily."

With the cessation of war and the return of the fighting men to Rendelsham, Lord Royance resigned his position as Lord High Marshal of Rendel in favor of Gaurin, a move that met with great approval and was ratified at once by the Council. With this change in his status, the apartment in Rendelsham Castle was now deemed too insignificant for a man of Gaurin's high birth and lofty position.

"That means, I suppose, that we must remove ourselves to Cragdengard," Gaurin told Ashen. "It is the home of whoever is the Lord High Marshal, after all. Artisans are already at work on my banner, with my snowcat badge as a crest atop the arms of Rendel."

He was not prepared for her vehement reaction, almost as strong as when she had refused and disowned Ysa's offer of the crown of Rendel.

"Never," she said, her voice low and her face very pale. "I would have you give up the title first!"

"That I cannot do, my Ashen," he replied. "Duty binds

me. And I suppose that our using Harous's old town house is out of the question as well."

"Yes," she snapped. "It is."

Gaurin sighed. "Very well. I will give Cragden to Lathrom. It is my right to do so. And I will begin construction on a fine new house here in Rendelsham for us to live in. But if I have to build a new keep close by Rendelsham's walls, it will be very awkward. I must maintain the custom. The Marshal guards the city and the country as well."

With that, Ashen had to be content, though she longed for the day when she could return to the Oakenkeep. Her solace lay in the golden presence of her daughter, Hegrin, who had moved out of the rooms occupied by Rannore and Anamara. She now had her own room in their apartment, to Ayfare's delight and that of Beatha, Hegrin's nurse who had been brought to the city. Now that Beatha was established again as part of the household, she was elevated in stature and given charge of the girl in the manner of all highborn young ladies who were not yet betrothed.

Rohan and Anamara came to pay a call on Ashen before they left for New Vold, where Rohan would take up his new duties as hereditary leader of the Sea-Rovers. Ashen noticed that he was once more wearing the Rinbell sword.

"I already have an idea about how I will approach what might be a problem," he said. He flexed his arm, newly released from the splint. "You see, I am, in a way, half Rendelian and half Sea-Rover. This is the direction the rest of the Sea-Rovers will have to go as well, if we are to be a part of this country they have chosen. I think it will work out."

"My good wishes go with you," Ashen said. She looked at Anamara with a critical eye. Her condition was beginning to make itself obvious. "Be sure that Rohan takes good care of you and doesn't let you fall into the hands of the Sea-Rover women. They have no sympathy with anyone who is not one of their own, and you would suffer at their hands when your time comes. You are taking your maid Nacynth when you go, aren't you?"

"Of course," Anamara replied. "She assures me that she has some training as a midwife. Between her and Madame Zazar, I can do naught but prosper."

"Good journey, then, and send word back to me frequently of how both of you fare."

They promised to do so, and so departed.

Lathrom and Rannore had scarcely settled into Cragdengard when she was delivered of a beautiful little girl. As soon as she was able, the parents brought the King's new sibling to the city to be named, and also so that all could admire her and shower presents upon her.

"It is a good day when babies are born," Gaurin said, "and especially after the miseries we have had to endure of late. Have you noticed that the dank chill that enveloped the land for so long has begun to lift?"

"Yes," Ashen said. "My garden back home must be blooming."

"Our lives have changed," he told her, "and so you must likewise change."

"Perhaps," Ashen said. "But does it all have to happen so suddenly?"

Gaurin laughed. "You are in danger of becoming a provincial, my Ashen!" he exclaimed. "Surely you deserve whatever you desire, after the great work you and Madame Zazar—aye, and even Her Highness—did in vanquishing a mortal foe who would have defeated even me, but you must also be aware that your desire might run squarely athwart what is required of you now. You are, after all, a national heroine."

"I don't feel like a heroine," Ashen muttered.

"Come with me. We are bid to attend a gathering in the Great Hall, to honor Lathrom and Rannore's child, and the King will be there."

And so Ashen dressed in her best, with Ayfare's help, surprised that her dress fit so snugly. She was, it would seem, too used to the many layers of thin tunics that had been required at the Snow Fortress. Nevertheless, she and Ayfare persevered until she was turned out to both their satisfactions. At the appointed time, she, Gaurin, and Hegrin, also sumptuously clad as befitted their stations, entered the Hall where a large number of people had already gathered.

Zazar stayed behind in the room that had been given to her in the physicians' quarters, claiming to have no interest at all in whatever was going to take place in the Hall. It was as if she knew all beforehand. And anyway, she told them, she was much too busy for such frivolities.

Twenty-three

"**G**reetings, good people," Peres said.

Ashen couldn't help noticing that he looked much more mature than the last time she had seen him, before she had departed so precipitously in a dog-sled driven by Lord Royance to the camp of the Rendelian warriors. Tunics had shortened again, and where once the King's hose had sported wrinkled, baggy knees, now he displayed a well-turned, if slender, leg.

"We are gathered to honor the brave man who is second in command to our Lord High Marshal, Gaurin." Peres inclined his head in Gaurin's direction, and he returned the gesture, bowing low from the waist. He beckoned toward his mother and her husband. "Come forward, please."

The Lady Rannore, carrying her new infant, and Sir Lathrom approached the dais, as bidden. Peres smiled on all three. Also on the dais, but standing well back, was Ysa. She smiled as well, though to Ashen it appeared that her pleasant expression had been achieved only with an effort.

"There is much to share with you, my good friends," Peres continued. "First, there is the naming of my new sister. My mother has informed me that she wishes to honor her late sister, who would have been my aunt. So, give greetings to the new Lady Laherne!"

A buzz of laughter and murmurs of approval swept through the people gathered. Someone began clapping his hands, and immediately everyone joined in. Only a few in the room cast longing eyes at the feast that stood waiting on nearby tables.

Peres held up his hands for silence. "Today is truly a day of beginnings," he said. "I have yet another announcement."

He held out his hand to Hegrin where she stood with her parents, and, her face glowing, she nodded.

"What does this mean?" Ashen demanded.

"You'll see," Hegrin answered, the mischievous dimple showing at the corner of her mouth.

Ashen would have hindered her, but Gaurin laid a hand on her arm. She could only watch as Hegrin made her way through the crowd and up onto the dais beside the King.

"Now I present to you the lady who has graciously consented to become my wife," Peres announced. "Give greetings to Lady Hegrin, soon to be Queen Hegrin."

"Q-queen," Ashen gasped, as others around her quickly regained their poise and applauded anew. "When did this happen?"

"I daresay while we were both away at the war," Gaurin answered wryly. "Smile, Ashen. In a moment everyone will stop looking at our daughter, to stare at you."

Stiffly, Ashen obeyed, feeling that she displayed a grimace even more artificial than the one on Ysa's face. She felt a little ill.

"We will hold the wedding two weeks from now," Peres said. "Now, let us feast and rejoice to my new sister, and also to my soon-to-be wife!"

With a shout of pleasure, the people gathered rushed to the prepared tables. There they filled plates and goblets, and drank many toasts to both happy events.

Ashen stayed only long enough to satisfy proprieties, keeping herself as distant as she could from Ysa without being openly rude, after she had offered and received entirely routine and conventional congratulations. Fortunately, the Dowager did not seem eager to engage Ashen in lengthy conversation either, despite the apology she had tendered for the way she had treated the one-time Bog-Princess.

She went at once to her apartment and lay down with a cool cloth on her head. That evening she refused her dinner, pleading illness, and the next morning, she was sick again in earnest.

Hegrin was so young, so very young. . . .

During the whirlwind preparations for a royal wedding, Zazar sent word to Ashen that Hynnel wanted to see her and Gaurin. She set aside the embroidered skirt she had been working on, and went to find Gaurin. He was already at his kinsman's side in the private room in the physicians' quarters, where Master Lorgan could give him his full attention.

To Ashen's shock, he seemed to have wasted away in the few days since she had seen him last. And to her surprise, Lorgan did not attend her kinsman; Zazar did. A lesser physician hovered nearby.

"He caught a chill," Gaurin told her.

"You shouldn't have left the infirmary tent at the Snow Fortress and come out to the battleground," Ashen said immediately. "I was very fearful—"

"It could have happened then, and it could have happened along the way back here," Zazar said. "There is no way to tell. It could have been foretold the day he was born. All I know is, despite my best efforts, he is dying. Norras is already gone," she added.

"No!" Ashen turned on her. She felt ill all over again. "Say it not! To say it is to make it so! Send for another physician, Master Lorgan—"

"Madame Zazar is right," Hynnel said weakly, "and Master Lorgan agrees. In fact, it was I who told them, when I asked that you be sent for. There is that I must settle before I breathe my last." He looked up at the physician. "Have you sent for a scribe?"

"He waits even now."

"Then bring him in." Hynnel struggled to move up on the pillows, and Gaurin helped him shift to a more comfortable position, tenderly holding him while he coughed.

The scribe entered the room, wide-eyed at the sight of the great folk therein about whom legends were already forming. He found a stool, got out paper and ink, and began to write as Hynnel spoke.

"Put this in the proper form," Hynnel instructed him, "for

I know it not. Just write as I speak. I would not claim the title of NordornKing while we were fighting against our common enemies. I lived as just Hynnel, a man of the Nordors, thinking there was time enough later, should we prevail, for kingship and all that goes with it. But time has run out and now I shall die as just Hynnel. It is enough. I leave the kingdom shattered, but in hands strong enough to rebuild it." He took Gaurin's hand in his.

Ashen just stared at first, as the implications sank in on her. "No," she murmured. She didn't know if it was a protest against what Hynnel was proposing, or against his dying.

Hynnel managed to smile. "While the scribe finishes writing it with all the terms and details plainly put forth and hands it to me to sign, tell your lady wife about our country," he said.

Gaurin turned to Ashen while he continued to hold his cousin's hands in his. "Ah, the NordornLand. It is a place of fierce beauty," he told her. "Beyond and north of the deep cleft in the coast where the Sea-Rovers once held sway, there is a range of mountains, atop which is a high country where in summer the air is mild and green grass covers the hillside. Overlooking all once stood the Palace of Fire and Ice, now in ruins, but I remember it as it was. Snow falls nearly year-round, yes, but it is a soft and gentle snow, not like what we have endured for so long. White it is, as white as the fleece of the sheep and lambs whose wool the women spin into cloth so fine an arm-span of it would go through one of your finger-rings. I remember how snow covered the rooftops and sparkled like sugar on a plum cake. We would go out then, and slide on the ice and race sleds. Horse-drawn sleighs were decorated with bells that rang clearly in the clean air and people would laugh for sheer joy. You would love it there, my Ashen, once you had seen it."

"And," Hynnel added with a trace of a smile, "it is a long distance away from the Dowager."

"Too far from Hegrin," Ashen pointed out through stiff lips.

"Hegrin is to be married. She will have her own life. She does not need us anymore," Gaurin said. "Come, my Ashen. I told you that duty binds me. That was in regard to my being High Marshal of Rendel. Now a higher duty calls. Royance will find another High Marshal, who will fill the office admirably." He let go his kinsman's hands, arose from the side of the bed where he had been sitting, and took Ashen in his arms. "Will you join me? Will you be my Queen, and sit beside me on the Nordorn throne? Will you come and let me show you the beauties of my homeland?"

"More to the point, will you honor the wishes of a dying man?" Hynnel said.

Ashen could not bear looking into Gaurin's beloved eyes at this moment, when he was asking such a heavy thing of her. She disengaged herself from his embrace and walked to the window of the sickroom, where she stared out at the budding trees, twisting the opalescent bracelet on her arm. At last she spoke. "I disowned the crown of Rendel. I cannot also refuse the crown of the Nordors, though I never sought either." She turned to face Hynnel. "Yes, my kinsman, I will accept what the Powers seem to have set aside as my portion. I will honor your wishes, and work with Gaurin as his queen, to rebuild the country that I will take as my own."

He smiled, and his face relaxed. "Thank you. Now I can die content."

"He will die in aggravation if you don't get out of the room now," Zazar snapped. "Well, scribe, have you got it finished yet?"

"Yes, Madame Zazar," the man said. With shaking hands he sanded the paper and then gave it to Hynnel.

Zazar shook her head in exasperation. "Don't just stand there gawping," she told him. "He can't sign without ink and quill and something to rest the paper on while he signs. Give me your lap desk. I'll heat the wax for the seal."

With Master Lorgan and other physicians brought in for additional witnesses, Hynnel managed to scrawl his name at the bottom of the document. Then both Lorgan and Zazar signed under his name, and the others added their marks as well. The writing on the paper covered it only halfway so Zazar drew several diagonal lines to fill the rest and also to keep someone from adding a clause that might have negated the whole. Such things had happened. She dripped wax across the names, and Hynnel pressed his signet bearing the royal arms of the NordornLand kingdom into a large blob next to his signature. Zazar held it up and looked it over thoroughly when they were finished.

"That should pass inspection from anybody," she said. "Now, all of you get out. I mean it this time."

Hynnel put the ring into Gaurin's hands. "Here. Would that I had a crown, but it was lost with Cyornas. This will have to do until you have another made. I give you greetings, fair cousin and now Gaurin NordornKing. Reign long and well."

"Farewell," Gaurin said. As he had when Hynnel had come to the Oakenkeep, he kissed his kinsman on the lips. "Fare you very well."

Ashen likewise kissed Hynnel's lips. Then, with dignity, they left the dying man's chamber. It was only after the door closed behind them that Ashen gave way to weeping.

*

Hynnel slipped away from life that night, gently, with no pain. Zazar brought the news the following morning.

"I'm going, too," she told Ashen and Gaurin. "I stayed only for Hynnel's sake. And now that reason is no more."

"You won't attend Hegrin's wedding and see her made a Queen?" Ashen asked.

"I saw you made one, and that's enough," Zazar retorted. She looked at Ashen keenly. "I will, though, give you a new name. You are Ashen Deathdaughter no more, but Ashen Lifebringer."

"Please," Ashen said. "Stay just a while longer. I feel that I am just now getting to know you."

"No, bid me farewell, at least for a time. I daresay I'll see you again before all is finished."

Ashen knew better than to try to argue with Zazar when she was settled on a course. A day later, the Wysen-wyf, scorning the offer of a fine riding palfrey, set off on foot for the land that had once been accursed with a sickly miasma. Now, under the care of the Bog-men, it was turning into a beautiful part of Rendel, in which all could take pleasure. Naturally, Ashen and Gaurin informed Lord Royance of this good news and also of Zazar's departure. As Head of the Council, this was news he needed to have.

"We will miss your brave kinsman, and also Madame Zazar," Royance said. "Her sharp tongue was ever a delight to me, if you can believe it. It was easy to grow complacent, and she brushed away many cobwebs I had let grow too long."

He had news of his own. When Gaurin had resigned his post, Lathrom, at Gaurin's suggestion, had been appointed the new Lord High Marshal of Rendel with Steuart as his second in command.

"Again, it was unanimous. It was helpful that Lathrom is already in residence in Cragden, but I think that was just a coincidence," Royance said, his eyes twinkling. "Also, there is talk of Rendelian stonemasons going into the former Bog and rebuilding Galinth, making it into a place of scholarly research and contemplation, such as it had been rumored to have been before blight struck the land. Perhaps there are records hidden there that will prove this disaster coincided with the first appearance of the Great Foulness, before his confinement so many years past in the Palace of Ice and Fire, by a long-ago NordornKing. We have the story in legend, but it would be good to have the legend confirmed as fact."

"Zazar will be interested in helping with such a project," Ashen told him. "She knew more about Galinth than she ever told me."

"She knows more about everything than she ever tells anybody," Royance observed.

Ashen forbore to inform him that Zazar had made mysterious reference to making preparations for a new Wysenwyf. Perhaps nothing would come of it, though she doubted her own thoughts.

When she left Royance's chamber, he bowed low and kissed her fingers. "Do not be a stranger to Rendelsham, Ashen," he said. "Queen though you are, to me you will always be the brave child brought from the Bog and thrust into a world for which she was ill prepared, but which she conquered nonetheless."

Ashen knew she would miss Royance more than anyone else in Rendelsham, save for her daughter.

She sent word to Rohan about the great changes being wrought, and he replied by swift courier. She couldn't help smiling when she read his chatty note, obviously written just as things occurred to him:

> Greetings, newly made NordornQueen, and to Gaurin NordornKing as well. Sorry Hynnel is dead. He was a good man. You will be as glad to shake the dust of that stifling city from your royal shoes as I was. Don't worry about your goods back at the Oakenkeep. I've set Nalren and his staff to sorting through and packing. You'll want him there in the NordornLand. He is sweet on Ayfare, incidentally, but don't tell her. When you're ready, I'll send the boxes on *Spume-Maiden* and it can collect you on the way to save a long ride. It's no trouble and Harvas would like to have a look at the old Sea-Rover ruins up there anyway to see if we might resettle at least a colony some day. Oh—Nalren found a vial of some stuff tucked away in a chest of Father's old clothes, wrapped in one of his shirts. It was sealed with wax. Kasai said it was sea-plant poison and probably harmless by now but when I poured it into the harbor, we had dead fish washing up on shore for two days. Anamara is well, and she sends you greetings. Tell

Gaurin I'm looking for a Rinbell sword for him as a coronation gift. Don't know what to give you, but Anamara will think of something.

The day arrived for the royal wedding. To Ashen's surprise and pleasure, Esander, the priest who had been her staunch friend for many years, presided at the uniting. The royal couple looked very young, but very happy, and every noble had his role in the ceremony and the procession to and from the Great Fane. Ashen could not help but think of other weddings in which she had played a part. She had never dreamed she would someday fill the role of the bride's mother, and that her son-in-law would be the King of Rendel.

"May I ask Esander to come with us to the Nordorn-Land?" she asked Gaurin, once they had left the Fane to return to Rendelsham Castle where the feasting had begun in the Great Hall.

"Of course," he replied. "I think that is an excellent idea. He has always been your friend, and I think he is wasted here in Rendelsham."

"Yes, I will come," Esander said, when she broached the subject to him. "I would be greatly honored, Ashen NordornQueen."

"That is the first time anybody has called me that," she said. "We have not put the news about except to a few close to us, lest it detract from the young couple's special day."

"You were always considerate of the feelings of others," he told her. "When you depart, I will be ready."

"Thank you."

Ashen, despite her relief at leaving the city she had little cause to love, felt oddly sad that so much of her old life was ending. To keep herself occupied, she turned to the task of packing their belongings for the journey north.

During an interlude of rare peace and quiet, Gaurin slipped into the room where she was and interrupted her as she was sorting through the contents of a clothes chest. Carefully, he closed the door behind him and locked it.

"I have something of grave import to tell you," he said.

"I've had about enough of 'grave import' to last me for a long, long time," she responded. "What is it?"

"It is a request, actually."

Ashen sighed. "I am busy, you know."

"Well, there is this. We're alone, in private, one of the few times we've had since we came back from the Snow Fortress, and we should make the most of it. I am now the NordornKing. And every King needs an heir." He had a very serious expression on his face, the kind he assumed when he was teasing her.

She stared at him. He could not maintain his grave demeanor for long, and both dissolved into laughter.

Then she put her hand to her belly. Suddenly, a number of clues fell into place for her. The Snow Fortress, the narrow camp bed that encouraged intimacy, the ever-present knowledge that each night together might be their last . . . How long had she been carrying, without realizing it? She smiled at her husband, happy for the first time in many days. "I think the matter is going to resolve itself," she said, "but perhaps we should make sure."

He gathered her into his arms.

❦

In her apartment, the Dowager Ysa paced back and forth. All her beautiful schemes, all her plans, gone for naught! Peres married to the Bog-Princess's daughter—no, she corrected herself. She must remember that with Hynnel's death, Gaurin was now the NordornKing, which made Ashen the NordornQueen. She stifled a hysterical giggle at the thought. Well, at any rate, with Boroth's bastard daughter's elevation, little Hegrin was now, beyond any doubt, a worthy match for the King of Rendel. The land of the Nordors would ever be a staunch ally, and best of all, Ashen would live far away. Perhaps she would visit only occasionally, after her grandchildren were born.

Yes, though it was lamentable that so many of her plans had crumbled to dust before they could be put into operation, it hadn't turned out so badly after all. Both branches of the Great Families who were claimants—or, in the case of Ashen, possible claimants—to the throne were now united, this unity to be further solidified with the birth of a new heir in time to come. She sat down in front of the fire that was scarcely needed these days, and by habit held her hands out. She could afford to relax, for the first time in many, many years. An unaccustomed feeling. Rendel, as far as she could foretell, was safe at last and true peace was on the land. Perhaps she would even retire from public life. "Now there's a thought," she said aloud, amused at the notion.

A sudden movement on her hands stifled any laugh she might have uttered. Before she could clench her fists in denial, the Four Great Rings fell off her fingers. Even as she watched, the strange multihued metal that composed them vanished, twinkling, into nothingness. The wooden inlays— oak, ash, yew, rowan—crumbled to dust. All that was left were the tiny golden leaves. A sudden wind swept through the chamber from nowhere, and the fire jumped and flared. A puff of smoke made her eyes water and when she could see again, the gold had turned into real leaves. She leapt up, feeling unaccustomed twinges in her joints, and attempted to catch them.

To no avail. One of the tall windows in the chamber opened of its own accord. The leaves blew through the window, to scatter wherever the wind sent them. Unbelievingly, she watched them go. Then, slowly, she closed the window again and returned to her chair. She looked at her hands, thin and wrinkled and covered with brown spots, and felt her face. Dreading what she would find, she moved to her inner chamber and her dressing table, where she could look into a mirror.

Gone was the artificial, magical beauty and semblance of youth she had given herself, with the help of her books and the Four Rings, and that had sustained her all these years. Though her visage was not as ravaged as it had once been when she had used Power unwisely and it had taken its toll on her appearance, she now undeniably looked her years. A woman in late middle age peered back from the mirror at her.

The last remnants of her pride rebelled. She put the mirror aside firmly. The Dowager Queen Ysa, First Priestess of Santize, the premier lady of Rendel save for the new queen, would not present herself like this before the Court. She would not become an object of curiosity and, perhaps, of scorn. She would not have whispers behind her back, speculating on her sudden change of appearance.

What can I do, she thought numbly. *Where can I go?*

Then she knew. The Yewkeep still stood vacant, and it was hers by right. Or, she amended, if the King claimed title to it, then she would request it from him. He was certain to grant it to her, if only to allow her to remove herself from Court in as much dignity as she could muster.

She returned to her chair and sat long, staring into the fire, trying to learn to accept the passing of her role as the most important lady in all of Rendel.

And outside the castle, the leaves that were all that was left of the Four Great Rings rode the wind to a destination unknown.

Epilogue

It is in the courtyard of the Fane of the Glowing that the Four Trees can be found. Oak, Ash, Yew, and Rowan, they, even more than the marble columns within, stand as tall symbols of the four ruling Houses of Rendel. Once Oak leaves carried blight; Ash drooped sadly, shedding leaves even during the period of growth; and even Rowan looked ill with some unknown disease, a few green leaves still valiantly struggling to keep the tree alive. Only Yew ever throve. For years no trace of the ills that afflicted the other three touched this one and people looked upon the Trees and wondered.

Now they wondered no more, for the Four Trees all stood straight and healthy, with fresh green buds replacing the blight and new growth extinguishing every other sign of ill health.

From its building there had been three small windows in

the Fane, virtually hidden from all but the most inquisitive, that inspired vague feelings of dread. For these windows changed with time, and no artisan's touch could account for the shifting. One of these windows depicted the hands and web of the Weavers. With the advent of the thunder-star and the impact when it hit the northern lands hard enough to make the entire earth quiver and certain fire-throated mountains to awaken, this picture that had changed only a little from the oldest man's memory began to shift. Then the dark hands of the Weavers moved more quickly, and the web upon which they worked began to take on a different appearance.

The second window, which showed a Bog-lupper, also began to change during this time. The surface of the pool became disturbed, and a dark and fell creature emerged onto land.

But it was the third window that created the most unease. This mysterious window had ever shown a blank face, white and barely translucent. Its very lack of design made it uninteresting. Then something began stirring in its depths and it showed a creature more deadly, more horrifying even than the one still dripping from the Bog-pool as it emerged from a heavy, glittering snowstorm.

The Dowager Queen of that time, a powerful woman named Ysa, had destroyed this last window, and given orders that the other two be removed and the wall plastered over as if they had never been.

Quietly, unmarked by any, for people seldom ventured up to the balcony where the windows had once been set, they reappeared, only changed from their former design. Where once the white, translucent one had shown such a horrifying image that Ysa had been moved to smash it to splinters, now it revealed a beautiful, mountainous land, with a tall and fair castle looking over all. The window that had displayed a monster from the depths of the Bog now depicted a new city rising from the ruins of the old. The third was, perhaps, the least changed of them all. Now in place of brown old hands toiling, it showed a web with four familiar designs woven into it, complete and at peace.

In the Cave of the Weavers, the Three worked contentedly on the Web Everlasting. All the former snarls and tangles that had caused such dismay to the Youngest had smoothed themselves as if of their own accord, and for time foreseeable, all was well in the world.

Past them was the section where the horror had dwelt. Today had gone, and tomorrow had come, bringing with it resolution and relief. No longer was the Youngest eager to rush ahead to learn what lay in store for the ones both great and small whose lives wove in and out of the Web of Time. "The affairs of mortals, frail and fleeting as they are, do not concern us," she murmured.

"It is good that you have learned that lesson," the Eldest said, and then the Youngest knew she had spoken loudly enough for her Sisters to hear.

"There was death and mourning, and life and rejoicing," the Middle Sister commented. "What more is there to know?"

The Youngest paused in her work and, as was her habit, glanced back along what had been completed in Time's Web.

Andre Norton & Sasha Miller

There, even in the place where once chaos ruled, all was now order, in recorded lives and death, Kingdoms' rise and passing and even their rebirth.

At last she had come to understand the wisdom of never giving in to pity for the ones whose destinies they wove. There was no mercy available for those who were doomed, and never could there be any meddling with the design. To do such would be to create a worse tangle than the one the Three had just spent so much effort in bringing into order.

As always, the living would continue to believe that they were free to make decisions, to act as they believed fit, even as their threads passed through the fingers of the Weavers.

A sudden draft at the entrance to the cave made all look up. In swept four golden leaves. They lodged in the Web Everlasting, and immediately sank into it.

The Youngest and the Middle Sister looked surprised, but the Eldest merely raised one eyebrow, as if she had been expecting them.

"So, you're back," she said.